'A powerful, original story showing how Ireland's changing fortunes and race politics affected a disillusioned generation.' —*Irish Examiner*

'An intriguing examination of twenty-something angst and a skilful, nuanced portrait of contemporary Dublin.' —*Hot Press*

'Brilliantly encapsulates the frustration felt by anyone who dreams of making art their livelihood. Racial strife, juvenile delinquency, recession, professional and personal disaffection and you have the ingredients for a simmering dramatic stew.' —*Irish Independent*

'An interesting take on *A Clockwork Orange*. It is rare to find an author ready to purloin Burgess's intuition that music and the future of the novel are linked, much less the talent to envisage how that may be done.' —*Irish Times*

'Modern Ireland is portrayed at times in ways that are uncomfortable to witness but with vigour and a rawness that captures the changed energy of our nation. *Beatsploitation* is a strong novel by an impressive new voice . . . what [it] clearly demonstrates is that despite the difficulties our society faces, we're still producing some top literary talent that we can be proud of.' —Bord Gáis Energy Book Club

'*Beatsploitation* shifts into exactly the kind of oblique mirror-holding that good writers are needed for – especially at times like these, when change can be too fast to process.' —*Sunday Independent*

First published in 2016 by
Liberties Press
140 Terenure Road North | Terenure | Dublin 6W
T: +353 (1) 405 5701 | W: libertiespress.com | E: info@libertiespress.com

Trade enquiries to Gill & Macmillan Distribution
Hume Avenue | Park West | Dublin 12
T: +353 (1) 500 9534 | F: +353 (1) 500 9595 | E: sales@gillmacmillan.ie

Distributed in the UK by
Turnaround Publisher Services
Unit 3 | Olympia Trading Estate | Coburg Road | London N22 6TZ
T: +44 (0) 20 8829 3000 | E: orders@turnaround-uk.com

Distributed in the United States by
Casemate-IPM | 1950 Lawrence Road | Havertown, PA 19083
T: +1 (610) 853-9131 | E: casemate@casematepublishers.com

ISBN: 978-1-910742-25-9
2 4 6 8 10 9 7 5 3 1

A CIP record for this title is available from the British Library.

Cover design by Liberties Press
Internal design by Liberties Press

CITIZENS

Kevin Curran

LIB
ERT
I ES

To Helena. Thank you.

Prisoner 1821
Harry Casey
Frongoch
Wednesday, 26 July 1916

My Dear Mother,

I got here on Tuesday about eleven o'clock. We left Kilmainham on Monday about 11.30 PM and we were travelling all night. I stuck the journey all right. None of us were seasick, but I had to walk from Kilmainham to the boat, and as I had not done any long walking since I got up, I am feeling very stiff in the legs and my back is paining somewhat again. But I am sure I will be quite all right again in a few days. This place is much better than any of the others. We have our own officers and practically run the whole camp ourselves. The military do not interfere as long as things go all right. We are well fed and are very comfortable. It is situated high up in the mountains in Wales and is fine and healthy. We have a field for football etc, and as we are in the open nearly all day, it should do my lung a great deal of good.

I know several of the fellows here and a lot more of them are gone home last week, I am told. Batches of them are going home every day. All of them now gone have been up to London for the Advisory Committee, and only the few of us who came over together remain, and we have first got word that we are going up tomorrow to go before them. We probably will not be back till Saturday evening. So I will have been before them in all probability by the time you get this letter. I am only allowed to write one sheet in each letter.

They allow the fellows here to keep some money and there is a canteen in which you can buy anything you want, if you have the wherewithal. Don't be worrying about me. I am all right and this place should improve me a lot. Tell Sis I send her my very best love kisses, and that I will write her the next time, in a few days that will be. Let her know I am getting on very well (perhaps you would show her this) and ask her to write a little letter to me, if she can.

Also, do not be alarmed if a gentleman by the name of Paddy Mac Tuile calls. Please, allow him access to my room. I have corresponded with him recently, and he has agreed to aid me in a matter. However, should Davy or any other fellows ask about my Pathé cinemachine or the film reels, inform them everything has been destroyed. Under no circumstances allow him to enter the house. It is not easy, nor prudent, to express my reasoning in writing. Please God, I will be home to you all before very long and be able to explain everything. It's usually about a week after they have been in London that they are released. Address any letter to me this way:

Harry Casey
Irish Prisoner of War
Frongoch Int. Camp – South
Bala, North Wales

Don't forget the number. I hope all of you are very well. Don't worry and pray for me.

I must now close. With very best love to all.

Your loving son,

Harry.

Xxx

P.S. Send me a few penny stamps.

Cave quid dicis, quando, et cui.

Eight Hours

Neil scrunches the old page up and holds it out the taxi window. It goes *phit, phit, phit* in the wind, unfurling and flapping helplessly in his pinch. He closes his eyes and it sounds like a flag: the plastic green, white and gold rippling out the back window of his grandfather's car, USA '94 and Ray Houghton's looper. The pleasant smell of booze from his grandad's breath as they weave through the streets. The joy. Doesn't mean anything. The page. Just some old, worn greaseproof paper, blotchy handwriting, ornate and stiff strokes like nothing he's seen before. Worthless. Not what he's been promised.

His eyes open into now – 2011– and he listens to the sound of the paper, the rumble of the wheels and the old country and western music polluting the speakers behind his head. The taxi driver's drone: 'Yer not getting sick there, are ye?' Peering into his rear-view mirror. The eyebrows dipped. Distaste? This is what you've signed up for. 'I know what yer all like. I seen the heads on some of yis comin' out of that party. If I was yer neighbour, I'd have the cops called long before now. This hour of the morning. It's a disgrace, so it is.'

'Having a session to say goodbye to a friend going to Oz for work, in the grand scheme of things, is far from a disgrace. So, if ye don't mind, pipe down.'

Neil's paying for the fare, for the silence to decompress from the chaos of the apartment, not to be lectured by some comedown parasite. The driver's necessity makes a mockery of his morals. Capitalism makes taxi drivers of us all.

Slumped, his head cooling against the touch of the drawn window, the wind filling his ears, Neil lets the images outside reel by. The darkened shops, littered streets, empty bus stops, closed shutters, campaign posters for presidential candidates shaking in the slipstreams of passing buses. The memory of his grandad, George Hamilton's voice, 'Raaay Houghton!', the stagger into the car, glass bottle of Coke and a straw, packet of Tayto. The blue-and-red packet of peanuts. The little tricolour. He is nine and he is happy.

The dull green of Fairview fades under the bridge and he spies the opulence of Clontarf after his turn for the Howth Road and the red digits pass '8.00'. Neil only has a tenner on him and he's nowhere near Raheny. If the driver wasn't desperate, he wouldn't have taken him. Neil's resourceful, he can improvise.

His phone vibrates through his pocket and he pulls the sheet in and brings up the window. A sulking silence insulates the car. 'Kathy New' is calling. He pictures Kathy in her bed, sitting up, unable to sleep without him by her side. It's dark in Vancouver, just gone twelve. She'll cough, clear her throat, whisper in her hoarse tone, be tired, say a long, 'Hiii,' and be glad he's answered. Her eyes will stay closed, a smile will lift her cheeks as she pictures Neil, probably thinking he's in bed too, and they'll talk – briefly because of her credit – about her day, how boring it was without Neil to come home to, terrible not to have him to meet for lunch. She'll say how much she misses him, needs him – how great it is to hear his voice. He needs her to say it too. To be reminded she loves him, she wants him to follow her over. Still.

'Neil . . .' a voice says.

It's not hers.

There are giggles in the background, forced, contained shushes, muted laughter. A café outside flickers a warm neon and is gone. He squints into the passing feeling.

'Hello,' he whispers, holds the phone out, blinking into the blurry white, making sure it's Kathy's number.

'Neil,' the voice says, a grin colouring his tone. 'What's the craic man? It's Kenny. Remember me? We worked together in the mortgage centre. Kenny O'Keefe. What's the story?'

A vague recollection of a lecherous smile. Laughter fills the silence, hands clapping and music starting up and distant mumbles, men, before she saves him. Kathy.

'Hey babe, sorry about that. It's just the lads messing. What time is it in Ireland?'

'Eight.'

'In the morning?'

'Yeah. Where are ye?' Her joviality falls flat on his cold, grey mood.

'Huh?' she answers. 'Oh, just a house party. I met some guys in a pub after work. Kenny – he said he knew you. We were talking. I mentioned you. Well, he asked,' she giggles, the music and laughter continuing in the background, 'where my boyfriend was, so I suppose he did ask for you.' She's drunk.

'It's twelve there,' he says, 'I thought you'd be in bed.'

'I know babe – it's mad. They're from Dublin. This guy – Kenny – he says he worked with you. It's twelve? Wow. I've been out since six. Do you know him?'

Deny him. He should deny him. Neil knows how these things go. But her face flashes, and in this cold, new morning, looking into the unknown houses, the empty trees, his head beginning to bang, denying him seems like a bad idea. He'd seem more aloof. Aloof is a bad idea. Neil's on a different continent, that's aloof enough. He's absent in body. He needs to be present in her mind, her heart. Assert himself. Be there in his memory – her memory – by knowing him. Being their point of reference – and remaining so.

'Yeah,' he says, tired now, though nearly managing a thin cheer, 'yeah I do. Kenny. Yeah, he was great craic.'

'He's so good,' she says and hiccups. 'It's just so great to meet some people from home. I miss you baby.' And music gets whipped up in the background – Damien Dempsey, the new voice of sentimentality – and there's cheers and she's laughing and people are whooping and a girl's voice calls, 'C'mon Kathy, c'mon,' and she whispers, her voice muffled and fuzzy, 'Miss you, gotta go, I'll call you in the morning.'

'I've made you another YouTube recording. I'll put it up . . . ' He'd been recording the party before the cops entered the communal courtyard and stuck their heads through the window and spooked everyone with their luminous yellow accents. A snippet of home for Kathy, as requested.

The line is dead. Neil asks the taxi driver to stop and, as he does, throws the tenner onto him and dives out. The driver spits in disgust, but doesn't give chase.

'Ye owe me six euro ye little shit,' he protests limply.

Neil jogs to a stroll around the corner. Magpies in the trees, one for sorrow, two for joy, the lights strobing yellow in the newsagent's beside the café, fresh roses wafting from plastic crates outside a shuttered florist, a car crunching over the stones inside the church gates, 'Raaay Houghton!' and his grandad lifting him up and hitting his head off a low-hanging *bodhrán* in time to 'You'll Never Beat the Irish'. A truck, Brennans Bread red-on-yellow, groaning away. The faint glow of orange on the skyline. But everything's grey for Neil. He sees her dancing under Kenny's leer. The lecherous bastard. He is sick. He should be there. He needs to be there. He will be there.

An Old House on a Leafy Street Once Called Home

The flowers on the hall table are drooping. He looks to the stairs, the stairlift rail, cocks his ear to the ceiling, holds his breath, listens for a creak of floorboard, a spring of bed. Nothing. He steps out of his runners, begins to relax, closes the front door and starts for the stairs to get to bed for a few hours' recuperation. Her small cough disturbs him; it's a clearing of the throat. His hand stays on the banister.

'Is that you, dear?' her voice from beyond the landing calls, hoarse, old, tracing-paper thin. How could she have heard?

'Yeah Gran, I'm just getting myself a drink. Was checking if the milk was delivered.'

'It's Saturday, dear.' The pause, the gathering of breath. 'Is there not some in the fridge?'

'No.'

'Oh. I'm sorry, dear.' She clears her throat again, gently, and the sound of her slippered feet shuffling from the bedroom tells him she's moving. The landing creaks. 'I was sure I asked Olga to get some.'

He waits at the foot of the stairs, eyes flashing, ears ringing, head sizzling. Going to the toilet or coming down? Please make it the toilet. He needs a kip. He's spent. The click and hum from the steel beams embracing the wall answers his question. He ducks into the front room cursing, throws off his jacket and jumper, leaves the runners under the piano, ruffles his hair, blinks to try and clean up his eyes, stretches his jaw before throwing the new bunch of flowers in the vase and returns to the bottom step. Her head and shoulders are visible above the banister; she stares blankly while she glides diagonally down. She is muted when she reaches the bottom of the stairs. Her mouth is down-turned, her eyes dull. She is not as she was. She is lost in her own home. She is lonely.

They ghost down the hall, into the breakfast room, and he pulls out a seat at the table for her and takes out Saturday morning's handful of pills and laughs to himself at the irony. He places the pill box back behind the picture frame: his grandparents and uncles and aunts; his mother, in happier times. But she ignores the chair, his chemist's palm, and shuffles into the kitchen. Her back is bent, her shoulders round and hunched, sloping to the right on her stick. Yoda. He opens the curtains by the television. The grass glistens. She ducks her head into the fridge, her afro of grey briefly becomes a halo, and then she emerges with a full litre of milk shaking in her hand.

'I thought I saw this last night,' she croaks. The carton levitates dangerously until she lets it drop, with a faint smack, onto the breakfast table. He pretends to be relieved.

She sits in her chair – the leather upholstery, the stiff hospital cushions – and peers at the clock hanging on the wall over the breakfast table.

'What time is it, dear?'

He returns the kettle to the kitchen and pops his head around the door and thinks of telling her it's time for bed. She wouldn't know the difference. 'It's eight.'

She presses her lips together and shakes her head.

'I don't know what's wrong with me lately. I just can't seem to sleep. I never had this problem when Tommy was here. He made me feel calm.'

Neil disappears back into the kitchen without a word and readies the teapot and cups and saucers. He scalds the pot as she likes it and brings everything in on a plastic tray, pale roses on a blue background. He clears away the empty can of Heineken from last night, and her glass too, with a trickle of whiskey and water still lining the bottom. When he sits, he pours the tea and adds the drop of milk and she asks if he slept well. He responds without hesitation: 'I did Gran. Like a log.' The synthetic heat and thumping music of his apartment are a distant memory. The bang of hash and back-of-the-throat gag of coke a faint trace. Her quiet room, her gentle snore when he left her alone last night, the same.

Her lips press. 'I couldn't.'

She leaves it at that.

They sip at their tea, the heater tinkling as the timer kicks in, the liquid rattling the pipes, the clock with the huge numbers making purposeful ticks. He is shattered. Running on empty. His jaw's beginning to tighten, shift a little. He speaks to stop it locking. No other reason.

'Jim's coming in for you today, Gran.'

She looks at him as if he has disturbed her. He points to the A3 whiteboard under the clock – all the days of the week in print, the names of the people minding her scribbled down with a marker.

'Jim's in with you tonight.' An impatient raising of his voice.

She lifts her chin as if she's trying to read the whiteboard. She narrows her eyes.

Home help for five nights. Family for two. Always him for one. For now. Before he blows this joint.

'And then Olga is in on Sunday, Monday and Tuesday, and Isabella is in Wednesday and Thursday and I'm back with you Friday night again. It all comes round so quick, doesn't it?'

If you ask a question instead of making a statement she realises more quickly that you are making conversation, looking for a response.

She mumbles and fiddles with her cup, turns it in the saucer. He wonders if she sees the next six days as hollow things that she will lose in a haze of television she can't see properly, radio she can't hear adequately, daydreams she won't remember fully and little naps that will never rest her sufficiently. He feels a vague sense of duty, responsibility, when such depressing thoughts flicker.

'Next Friday,' she says, clearing her throat. 'What date is that dear?'

'The tenth.'

'The tenth,' she repeats solemnly and looks to the press beside the television. His Mass card is out. Nearly a month since Neil has last seen Kathy. Since they said goodbye. Since his grandfather's burial, Kathy's flight. Neil's aborted departure.

Neil eases out of the chair, battling as he does with a long, deep, drawn-out yawn.

'I'm just going back to bed Gran – just for a few more hours. I'm knackered.'

'But, didn't you sleep well? Why don't you stay and we can have a chat? Did you read the letter I gave you?'

Another theatrical stretch, overblown yawn as the ebb of the night's high fizzes away.

'I did. Just before bed. It's deadly. Really interesting. We'll talk about it later, yeah? I'm still really tired.'

'Did I ever tell you about my father? Did your grandfather tell you about him? How we have more words, typed chapters from him?'

This is a new tactic.

He rubs her hand, kisses her cheek.

'No Gran. You never did. Grandad said your father never went out in the Rising. Remember? Are ye sure the letter's actually genuine?'

'Of course, dear. We've had it for some time. If you're interested, there's more like that. Other material. More detailed.'

Jesus Christ. More? Patience deserts him, but he smiles, plays along, his fingers drumming the table. He holds no interest in letters, writing, mouldy paper, pens. The only paper he's interested in is legal tender. Preferably blue or brown. Bridges and windows. And, of course – most importantly – what his grandad promised before he passed away. Something of value. An object of worth. It can't be the letter, surely.

She looks up, her eyes so weak, the colour almost gone from the irises.

'Wait a moment dear,' she says and her chair pushes back on the carpet and she leans on her walking stick but can't get up. He takes her under the arms like you would a child.

'One moment dear,' she says.

Against all his better judgment, losing the will to stay awake, knowing a 'moment' for his gran will be an Iarnród-Éireann-time eternity, he lets her go. For all she's done for him, she deserves it.

The sun creeps over the back garden wall and catches thousands of illuminated specks shivering by the breakfast window. The rose bush his grandfather kept at the bottom of the garden is decimated, almost erased from history by the smothering hills of browning grass his uncles have dumped there instead of putting in the brown bin. Nettles are crawling away from the mess and slithering up the wall, nearly spoiling the kitchen window.

Her cough, more a clearing of the throat, shifts his attention, and then the stairlift whirrs and clicks and beeps. Her walking stick sounds off the radiator and she calls, 'Neil, dear. Neil. Where did the roses come from?'

'The florist's.'

'But I thought you were asleep.'

He regrets his answer and laughs off her reasoning, his early morning shop-lifting, and moves into the hall to find her leaning against the table, holding a fresh rose, out of breath.

'Sorry dear. If you could just help me in.'

He takes her under the left arm, feels her weight shift, and slowly – her feet dragging – escorts her into the breakfast room. She knocks his grandad's Mass card over as she takes her seat. Her chest draws up discreetly and deflates steadily. Neil's ready to collapse. Bollixed. Absolutely bollixed. Her wedding ring with the piece of thread on it knocks gently off the surface as she pats the table.

'Now dear,' she whispers, composed, 'see what I have for you.'

She takes a folded handful of greaseproof paper from her cardigan and places it in his sweaty palm. The pages are different, the messy handwriting replaced by uneven type. The ink is weak and blotchy in parts: strong on certain letters, light on others. Pages creased, dog-eared, browning. The lines are jagged, rushed things. Font like nothing he's seen on Microsoft Word. The top says 'Harry Casey: F Company 2nd Battalion'.

'Since when have ye had this?' he says, sapped by the number of words, pages. The effort.

'Make another pot of tea and I might tell you,' she says, her eyes creased with pleasure, a crooked finger pointing vaguely at the teapot under the cosy on the table.

Nothing Overdone
Can't Be Undone

Compound joint movements are key to getting a good base for the shoulders and arms. A standing barbell overhead press combined with chin-ups. The chin-ups kill him, but focus his mind. When he started out, his wimpy little wrists – weak from tippy-tapping away all day on the DVD-store keyboard – would strain under the stress, and he'd be hard pressed to go three, four, five without getting a big red face. A mix of embarrassment and pressure. Exhaustion. Defeat. He'd keep his eyes clear of the action around him: the pressed lips, the closed faces, creased brows, the vein-pumping efforts of the others in the gym. If he couldn't see them, they couldn't see him. He didn't need offers of help from the butch bitch in the sports bra or the Polish lad in the wife-beater. He knew what he was doing. He'd googled the exercises.

In a few months the chin-ups have become less daunting, the power to pull up over the bar less of an effort, the control when lever-aging his body back down the few inches and then the power to pull up again, is no longer beyond him. He can do twenty now. Tank. Whereas once the pounding dance music and the manic colours of

Sky News made him feel nauseas, the smell of sweat and deodorant dizzy, he persevered – and in his own way achieved something. He lives for it now. The noise, the sweat, the intensity, the challenge. Clearing out the weekend's excess, sculpting what remains.

Believe in something. Achieve something. Be something.

There are levels, he supposes, of success. Finding success. His was once the BMW 5 series. The blue-and-white sign of wealth, stature, power. The idea of the propeller blades swirling around the blue sky like a boss. That was success. Spinning round the city centre, window down, music blaring, screeching to a stop at the traffic lights, revving it up and burning away. He believed in the mystique of the car. The image it represented. But when you sell the car for less than you bought it for after only paying off six months of the motor loan with another four years left to go, success in such objects seems kind of ridiculous. Success shouldn't cripple you financially. He will stop paying off the loan when he leaves for Canada. In the Irish altitude training of dishonesty, all you have to do is breathe and you're acclimatised.

Neil takes the dumb-bells, decides to do eighty single curls on each arm. More than he's done before. It was a heavy weekend. He can get out what he puts in, and then some. Success. Achievement. The first few – right arm, left arm – are easy. Almost propelled by each other. A piston engine. A water mill. Perpetual motion. White propellers on a blue sky. His reflection in the mirror draws his eyes to his right shoulder, left shoulder. He sees his tattoos flex under the strain. Bulge and contract. The word 'svelte' – seen on the workout websites - comes to mind. Sleek. Impressive. Expensive almost. Powerful. Not ripped totally – but a bit of solidity. No moobs. Beer belly. Flumpyness, flabbyness. Even the words sound weak. Cheap. Broke. Embarrassing. Sleek. Svelte. Solid. Strong.

He may not have a car to start off with in Canada, but at least he'll look good. Because over there, he'll throw off the feelings of unemployment-inadequacy or worse still, being a customer-service waster in a DVD store. He will start anew. Get around with a new-continent swagger.

Because how he lives now is no way to live now. No way to live now. No way to live now. The repetition streamlines his thoughts. Focuses the mind. Clears the mind. Burns off the narcotics and alcohol, clears up the bad buzz with his housemates. The landlord complaining about the rent.

His housemate Dee saying, 'Don't ye care what he said?' Anger charging the sentence.

'Not really, no.'

Neil doesn't care. Really. Doesn't. Care. He should be in Canada now. Canada. Canada. By now. Canada with Kathy. Away from here. Away from them. Friends he's lived with for seven years. Outgrown the last two. They are simply a reminder of his comedown embarrassments. Drunken secrets and high revelations. He has seen his future. They're not in it. It's about time they separated. He makes them see their lives as they don't want to. Objectively. His imminent escape is a UV light on the stained bed sheets of their foul surroundings.

'He doesn't mind the parties, but he's not our friend. He made that very clear.'

'He's our landlord,' his other housemate, Coly, is piping in. 'He made a point of that. He wants full rent. On time. Every month.'

'Relax, relax. I'm a bit broke. I'm under pressure with flights and stuff. I just forgot.'

'Ye didn't forget this though, did ye?'

The blue credit union book hitting Neil on the chest. Lodgement receipts splashing out on contact and fluttering like falling silk to the floor.

'Ye left it on the mantelpiece. It was open,' Coly's adding. 'Ye didn't forget to lodge your savings Friday, did ye?'

Savings. Savings. Savings. Neil's savings multiplied by three will be his departing loan. An unrequited present from an unsuspecting credit union. It will never be paid back. If everyone else's doing it, why can't I? Neil on his knees scooping up the incriminating evidence.

'And you've no problem paying for the gym membership. We're doin' you a favour, Neil. You should've been gone last month. You should be gone this month.' Dee's moaning.

'Relax. It's grand,' Neil's saying, closing the door on them, escaping to his room, knowing that every day that passes is another day eating into his savings after his dole is swallowed up by rent and food. He had a part-time job in Movie Mayhem until he quit a day before he was due to leave. Luckily, he never gave up the dole. He'll be in Canada a few weeks before they cut him off.

A lad passes by and tries not to, but right at the end, gives Neil a glance through the mirror. A look not seen since sitting at the traffic lights with the music banging. The acceptance. Reaching a goal. Not ripped totally – but a bit of solidity. Flumpyness, flabbyness. Sleek. Svelte. Solid. Strong. Sleek. Svelte. Solid. Strong.

The push and pull. Hint of a burn in the joints. Pull on the biceps. Strain on the shoulders.

Achieve. Believe. Repeat. Canada. Kathy. A new life. A new him.

Achieve. Believe. Repeat. Canada. Kathy. A new life. A new him. A promise?

In his bedroom, away from his housemates. The old paper his gran gave him. The delicate fabric, like cotton on the creases. The sheets on his lap because the type comes through if they're held up. As far as the first line without yawning. Should've gone back inside and caused a row. No. He needs their hospitality, their cooperation, for just a few more weeks. His phone, iPod, anything to distract. He doesn't want to see them. He is bored. Reading is a last resort. He doesn't have an interest in revolution, or war.

The gym mirror begins to taunt him. His face is pulling wide on itself. No teeth yet, just a thin white strain on the lips, creased eyes. Putting the whole upper body into each lift.

Left, right, left, right. The teeth biting down now on the bottom lip.

Wars are yellow ticker-tape-teasers on Sky News.

Revolutions are events on crowded Third World streets where men with moustaches cry. A Movember apocalypse. Irish men don't wail into cameras here. We don't cry either.

Keep going. On and on and on. Sixty-eight. The burn. The strain, pulling.

He got involved in war once. Because everyone else was. Marched like a dope down O'Connell Street. Chanting.

Seventy.

It had felt like he was going to a festival. The spirit, camaraderie. Shock and awe. Shock and awe. Marching. New start. New him. New life.

Seventy-four.

Like a dope. Actually believing for a moment that it was going to achieve something. Walking. If it was that easy, everyone would be getting in groups. Want to change the world? Let's go for a walk. But they did. Thousands of them. They really believed that walking would change the course of history. Give me a break. History happens despite us.

Seventy-five.

In fairness, he shares updates on Facebook. 'Stop the genocide!' 'Demand fair trade!'

He does his bit for world peace. You don't have to be active to be an activist.

Seventy-six.

The revolution will not be televised. It will be liked and shared.

Favourited and retweeted. A status update shows real commitment to the cause. Bravery.

One more pull. Purple face, closed eyes, drained body. Failed attempt. Silent defeat. Small victories.

Harry Casey - F Company,
2nd Battalion #1

In which I capture the opening events of 24 April 1916 – A giddy setting – My good friend Davy declines to aid my artistic endeavour.

Even though I had been informed we were in earnest back at Father Matthew Park, and I had seen the Volunteers smashing windows and erecting barricades in the GPO, it was with Pearse's emergence from behind the curtain of the post office's pillars, somewhat pale and haunted-looking, with the proclamation in hand, that I became fully aware of the enormity of our undertaking. There would be no turning back.

After regarding the thoroughfare, making sure no one else had arrived with another cinemachine, the excitement of the occasion intensified. The bright sunshine and pitch of the shadows were most favourable for shooting my opening scene; my stand was firmly planted, three legs wide and stuck resolutely in the dirt tracks between the cobbles and the tram lines, my film loaded and prepared for action. Everything was as I had hoped, and from this sprung the sense of excitement. However high my spirits, they were matched in equal measure by a stirring sense of pride. There was, in addition to these great manifestations, perversely, also an awful undercurrent of impending dread.

The excitement derived from years of preparation. Emmett, Tone, Cú Chulainn, O'Connell, had all stirred my imagination through the stories I had heard at my mentor Joe Deasy's pantry table, and in the books from Gaelic folklore my late aunt Bridey had let me read. I was never artistic enough to create myths myself like the ones I had encountered in literature, nor was I imaginative enough to put myself by the side of O'Grady's Cú Chulainn and go on wondrous journeys and adventures such as the ones he had undertaken for Ireland.

Over time, through good fortune and outright chancery and luck, I had somehow managed to master the art of capturing a scene: a simple encounter in a black-and-white still-moment that could last forever. As the present efforts unfortunately attest, I was unable to render moments magical through the written word. Nor was my voice capable of singing the most lamentable tale, nor had I the ability to capture the essence of a moment through brush strokes on a blank canvas. A camera now, was a different story, and that device I took to like a duck to water.

And so I found myself standing on Sackville Street, my Pathé Kok with its four hundred feet of 28mm newsreel film loaded and ready, positioned at a slight angle ten yards back from Pearse, to his left as he looked up, about to capture the opening moments of our latest heroic push for national glory. Never mind Yeats, or Moore, Lady Gregory or Synge, I was about to become our new republic's first chronicler of the truth!

If only a camera had been present when Cú Chulainn had tied himself to the rock, I used to think. If only a newsreel man had been there when Wolfe Tone had met his fate, our nation would have had the representations of their deeds to draw strength from forever. Such thoughts sustained me while I read my history, watched the new plays and heard the songs about past rebellions. I had promised myself that when such a moment arose again, I would be front and centre, camera loaded, cranking, capturing the undeniable reality of the affair, for now, for the future, forever!

This is where the powerful influence of pride also took hold. Pride at being the sole witness, via the mechanical wonder in my hands, to what was about to unfold over the coming days – weeks. I was about to capture it all on film! I was unaware of how the revolution would unfold, but I knew that if I got close enough, I could document it, and if at all possible, in documenting our proud struggle, create something never seen before. The pride, of course, also swelled my chest when I saw Pearse, although somewhat diminished by the imposing backdrop of the post office's pillars, in his smart green Volunteer uniform, approach the middle of the boulevard. With the paper in hand, the hat at an angle, the sword and the uniform, he looked like something you would read about in the great stories of yore, did Pearse.

My oldest and best friend, Davy, in the GPO already on account of his insatiable impatience for the fight and high rank in the Volunteers (first lieutenant), had promised to give me a hand should I need it. He arrived beside me moments before the others did, resplendent in his uniform. He had an unremarkable face, yet if I was pushed to describe it, I'd say it was amiable and elastic. A friendly demeanour bulged his cheeks (though he was not heavy-set) and a sagging at the creases of his eyes and mouth gave his face, when he smiled, this distinctive elastic, globular appearance. Which was most unfortunate, as when he wore the green Volunteers cap it looked tight and strict and almost comedic on his oversized head. His freshly polished leather bandolier and the gold buttons of his tunic managed to divert the eyes but bore all the signs of only having been recently scrubbed to a high sheen. He was some sight.

'Well, I made it,' said I, my eyes returning sheepishly to the exposure indicator, setting it to '18' on account of the sunshine. When I beheld Davy, I felt somewhat cowed and lacking in my usual cap and jacket.

'That you did,' he replied, a casualness levelling his voice. 'In the nick of time too, it seems.'

'Afraid I'd get here before you? Is that why you forgot to inform me of the order?'

'Don't be a blaggard,' said he. 'You have too much talk for someone readying themselves for war.'

My reply, on account of the events unfolding, had to wait.

When Pearse, flanked by Connolly and Clarke, stopped and squinted towards the river, I bid Davy to ensure that the crowd, if one could call it such a thing, would refrain from wandering into shot. You see, I had worked quickly once Pearse took up his stance, cleared his throat and held the proclamation at arm's length. I had ensured I was a sufficient distance away so as to get him from the waist up, and also, at such a sufficient angle, so as to be able to pan up (I know, up!) to the portico and to the corners where I had spotted, moments before Pearse emerged, silhouettes raising the vertical colours of green, white and gold, and an Irish Republic flag. I was desperate to ensure such potent symbols of our insurrection would be included in my opening.

Whilst I nodded to Davy, who had taken his station on my immediate right, to keep any onlookers out of my shot, the impending sensation of dread, like a thunderbolt from Jupiter, sliced through my excitement and pride to leave me somewhat shaken. It would be an untruth if I told you that I never once had doubts about what I was about to take part in. Just before Pearse spoke, when a silence fell over the whole street, maybe even the whole city – when no gulls squawked, or trams chimed, or carts clattered, or gunshots rang – I think everyone dreaded, secretly, what was to come. We all worried about what our gathering, what his words, what our unnecessary, but yet, incredibly necessary deeds were to bring upon the people we loved, our city, our country. What was about to be witnessed. Created.

As this brief silence took possession, I gathered a deep breath and began to crank the camera with a tremulous hand. Although I had done this on many occasions before, in practice and at lesser affairs, I still kept, for the first few moments until I found my rhythm, my eyes firmly on the speed indicator to ensure it showed both white and red. Pearse began. With my free hand I checked my watch for the exact time. It was 12.46 and ten seconds. Once into my rhythm, two cranks a second, a steady up and a steady down, I nodded once again to Davy to usher people away from the camera. The camera, would you believe, in some cases more so than the speech, was capturing the gathering crowd's attention!

Men inched into view, street urchins and corner boys, staring dumbly at the camera whilst I cranked. Some waved their caps, others, proud and upright, held on to their lapels with a nonchalance that belied their interest. I gave in to their posturing, and since the general theme of what Pearse seemed to be addressing had all the people of Ireland at its heart, I panned slowly to his right, to the gathering crowd. One by one, the moment they countenanced the camera spin their way, they stiffened up like the bronze O'Connell behind us and became dignified, almost like extras, minor actors providing the solemn faces of the actual republic Pearse spoke of. One of the assembled crowd however, Clancy, a small squat man in his fifties from Cow's Lane, a friend of Joe Deasy's no less, lost himself and raised his hat high into the sky and shouted, 'Gerrup the yard!' He was shushed strongly by Clarke, Connolly and others. To see Clancy catch himself and become serious, almost reverential, was something to behold.

I regret to say I did not pay much attention to the content of

Pearse's words. My concentration was taken up by the cranking and constant checking of my viewfinder to ensure no unnoticed, discreet movements knocked me off my subject. Some time into the speech, surrounded by encouraging cheers and a few too many catcalls, I checked my watch again. I had been cranking for just over a minute. Mindful that each reel would only give me approximately four and a half minutes, I pulled out the knob beside the handle. Oh, but the first act was far from over! In the midst of it all, I called over Davy and whispered, wary of the speech: 'Give me a hand and grab a hold of the leg there so I can point the camera up at the corner.'

The gold badge on the top of his cap caught the light as it shook with displeasure until I explained what corner of which building I meant.

He obliged begrudgingly and managed to lift the camera by leaning back on the tripod. I had ensured the two legs were horizontal with the angle I would take so this manoeuvre could be attempted and would only need one tripod leg to be moved. It was, stupidly (in hindsight) an attempt at a shot I had never undertaken before and one I wasn't sure I could pull off. War makes one do silly things! If I was unable to crank the camera at the required speed while Davy held it at the angle, and then as I panned, slowly in order to keep the picture from jumping, across from the corner flag on the south corner to the one over the portico, the picture would shake. If I cranked too slowly, the light would saturate the film and halation would ruin the shot!

Once I had panned across and taken in both flags, I asked Davy to ease the tripod leg back to the ground, and as luck would have it, Pearse was coming to the end of his speech so I was fortunate enough to catch him finishing his last words and looking up. He glanced furtively, eyes almost closed, into the sunshine and the assembled crowd. I was about to pull out the knob beside the hand crank, turn it in one complete revolution and then crank the main handle once to indicate the end of the scene when I noticed the three men – Pearse, Connolly and Clarke – come together.

Without a second's hesitation, I panned, slowly so as not to blur the picture, across to Connolly, who took Pearse by the hand and partook in a hearty looking handshake and pat on the shoulder. They both, Connolly and Pearse, were impressive in their solemnity. One could tell how proud they were to have partaken in the event. Clarke, his eyes hidden behind the glare on his glasses, approached and embraced Pearse and whispered something and the three men, together in the sunshine, my hand rotating steadily, turned their backs on us, paused to look upon the new flags for a moment, and then moved towards the shady curtain inside the post office. My watch showed a minute, and I ended the scene.

'Thank you kindly, Davy,' I said, my hand finding his back. 'This day will go down in history, and we witnessed it.'

I tapped the Pathé. 'Millions more will too, thanks to this.'

Davy smiled. 'No, Har. Thanks to you. This thing here will travel the world, show everyone what I got up to. We got up to.' He nodded to the GPO. 'What they got up to. This will change things.'

'Indeed it will,' said I, content with my opening shots.

Davy looked at me, his lips pressed together hard, his eyes cold like steel, as if he was almost willing something into being. He regarded the setting before us, breathed heavily through his nose and, after rubbing my shoulder in a show of brotherly union, said, 'How about it Har, get some of the boys in here, will you?'

My mind wandered away up past Parnell, swept up Great Britain Street, up Summerhill and left onto the Clonliffe Road, stopped at number sixty-one and opened the gate and went by mother at the door and up into my bedroom and saw the wooden crate under my bed holding the three spare reels. I sucked my teeth.

'Come on Har,' said Davy, rousing me, a smile of embarrassment flushing his face. 'The chaps were all asking about it. I promised them. They want to be on the moving camera. What about it?'

Had he not been such a help leading up to the event, pitching in when I needed the blazing tripod shifted, I would have turned him down without a moment's thought. The sacrifices we make for our childhood friends! One hundred and fifty feet was all that was left on the reel. Thirty seconds, I reasoned, could be afforded. A short scene to gauge the mood of the supporting cast was, in so many ways, a nice touch.

To be set up in front of the GPO on that sunny day, smiling and joking with Davy while he called in to the men behind the destroyed windows and angular barricades, felt strange. The lack of enemy engagement, the silent, untenanted trams, the reading of the procla-mation, they made me almost giddy.

'OK lads,' Davy called in through the broken windows. 'Here he is. Look sharp.'

No one stirred.

'Be part of the revolution,' I offered.

A young buck by the name of Henry, disguised by the strong shad-ows inside, shouted back, 'Would ye not call this being part of the revolution?'

'It is,' said I. 'But it won't be enough in a few years' time.'

The lad, Henry, filled out his silhouette and squinted, tilting his head like he was working me out, making his mind up.

'And why's that?' said he, defiant.

'If we win, everyone will say they were in there. And if we lose, you won't be getting a statue.'

'So?'

'This is the proof of your heroics. And this will outlast any blast-ed statue.'

Davy regarded me anew, as if my sentence, although said to him any number of times in the past, had revealed the possibilities of our actions in a fresh, heroic light.

The Citizen Army men were the only ones to lean out the windows; they were probably the only ones to have seen or heard of the picture houses. I got a steady footing and, cranking again, panned slowly from left to right. They waved their handkerchiefs when they saw the camera come in line, took their caps from their heads, squinted and smiled and cheered. The camera, I was to learn, made the unaccustomed unnatural in almost all situations. Unannounced, in their shawls and barefoot, women approached the men at the barricades, and Henry, the young bucko who was full of lip, leaned out to one of them and kissed her. The cheer he got from his comrades would have been a perfect denouement for the scene, were it not for the sudden scrape and clatter of hooves on tramlines and cobbles, which emanated from the top of the boulevard.

'I think we better be moving,' said Davy, tugging gently on the tail of my jacket, his hat tipping lightly over his brow.

The cheering levelled off and one could instantly feel the sense of hushed dread stifle the men's bonhomie. The shawlies scattered. Looking up past the pillar, towards the Parnell monument, one could see Lancers, high on horseback, preparing to charge.

'Move it!' bawled Davy.

I backed away towards the Imperial for a better angle from which to witness the affair. Taking a few purposeful strides before noticing I was absent, Davy looked over his shoulder and stopped in his tracks, incredulous. We regarded one another.

'I thought you meant to fight,' said he.

'I do.'

'Well then?'

His eyes implored me to follow him. I thought of the other eyes, twitching behind the barricades, shifting from me with my camera and stand held tightly against my chest, to the horses lined and snorting, and thence to Davy.

'Dammit man,' he hissed, conscious of the stillness in the street, 'let down that bloody camera and come fight for your country.'

'I am bloody well fighting for it,' said I, and I heaved the camera, cursing him and his lack of vision.

A Long-Distance, Time-Delayed, Skype Relationship

He tucks himself in under the loose elastic of his old Londsdale track-suit bottoms after soaking up the proof of his antics with a fistful of toilet paper. Kathy's breathing still throbs in the earphone in his right ear, and his left ear, free of any appliance, searches out the sounds of the TV next door and the lads' conversation – for signs that they might have heard the bed squeak, or Neil groan. Everything seems grand.

Kathy pulls on a T-shirt and the screen glitches for a second, freezing a screen grab of her raised arms, covered head and two deep-red nipples. He takes the piece of card away from the bottom of the screen where he would've, if he'd not covered it, been able to see what Kathy saw while they got carried away. He never wants to see his own sex grimace. A sex selfie. Shattering the illusion of intimacy.

The picture strobes for a second and then catches up with her voice as she goes, 'Phew. Wow. That was wild. Huh?'

They giggle together, almost like they're in bed, and he sits up in front of the camera again.

'Deadly,' Neil says, flaked now, a bit tired now, flinging the soggy tissue at the bin like a basketball player. No swish. Crack shot. He's had practice.

'I actually want you more now than I did before we did that. It's mad.'

'Me too,' she says and her bottom lip gets tucked in tight under her teeth.

He asks if she's OK. She doesn't respond and instead fixes her hair behind her ears. Does it up in a clip. The screen pauses, the earphones hiss.

There was a time when silence wasn't easy for them. She never let it happen in the early days. But silence, he supposes, comes naturally – as do all things, given time.

Skype, though, for some reason, doesn't allow easy silences. They used to laugh at the novelty of its unnatural silences in the early calls. He didn't know why. The technology? Their reflection? The unease of talking to a screen? Or talking to themselves? The unreality of it all was novel. Having a fake conversation, imagining the person they loved was really somehow behind the screen. Imagining he could put his hand through the screen and touch her. Put on 3-D glasses and experience her. An imagined experience. Like cracking one off. There is an end to the time they spend looking at one another now. It is the technology for the sake of the technology. Not each other.

Until recently, the technology has blinded him. The, 'Oh, we Skype all the time,' line and the fawning gratitude for the technology can't mask forever how it isn't the thing itself. And every time he goes onto Skype now, he starts to get the nagging feeling of unreality, and the unreality of their relationship hits him with every awkward silence. He worries she may be feeling the unreality of it all too. People don't insult each other with the word 'wanker' for no reason. It's an empty exercise in alternative reality. This is relationship wanking.

Kathy blows a breath, unfolds her arms and shifts back, away from her laptop, up the bed. 'Work is mental already. The office is full of dicks. I'm like . . . I think I'm the first Irish woman they've ever met. They tell me they didn't think we had colleges over there.'

'Really?'

'Yeah. There's one lad, Brad, state of him, keeps on coming over and looking at what I'm doing. He's like, foreman or something on site. Such a tool. And his breath stinks.'

Neil chuckles. Kathy is fighting the silence. Neil, after tugging away, is fighting sleep.

'I think it's the coffee. You know that real dank, rotten, stale-coffee smell? And he leans over, right into my screen, "Hey there, what ye doin?" Perv.'

They share a laugh.

'He just keeps on hassling me to go for drinks with them. Eh, a construction company night out? No thanks. I make up different excuses. But then, last Friday, I bumped into them with the guys from Dublin. It was so awkward.'

'Was that when I called you?'

'Yeah. I meant to tell you. I was celebrating.'

'Celebrating?'

'Well, kind of. I wasn't going to. I'm moving out of the hostel. Not moving out, 'cause I never moved in. Never unpacked. But, I've got a place. A proper place.'

She's settling. Without Neil. He sits up. Stretches his neck to the screen. Shit just got real.

'I thought we agreed you'd wait for me.'

Kathy speaks in an apologetic, low whisper. His heart's thumping. Is this the it's-not-you-it's-me line? One last fling and goodbye?

'The guy I met – you know – the guy you worked with, from Dublin.'

'Kenny.'

'Yeah, Kenny. He's living in this big house beside a lake. There's like, twelve people in it. Mostly Canadian. But he said there's a bed goin'.'

'I'm sure he did.' That lecherous smile.

She tuts. The top of her nose wrinkles. The angry giveaway.

'Don't be so cynical. He's being kind. It's cheaper – *and closer* – to work, *and* I'll meet people. I kind of didn't want to tell you 'cause I know you're having a rough time already. But it just came out.'

'But you have your cousins.'

'They live miles away. They have their own lives. These people are cool, Neil. They're my age. Our age.'

'They'll be cool all right with a single girl like you moving in.'

'They know I'm going out with someone.'

'Someone?'

'You.'

Her face approaches the screen; her eyes lean close to the camera like the faded Virgin Mary picture in his gran's bedroom.

'I love you. I miss you. There'll be space for you too. Kenny said people come and go all the time. You'll have your accommodation sorted. That was one of your worries, wasn't it?'

Neil looks out the window of his bedroom, the communal court-yard, the square of grey and white clouds hanging over the Dublin sky. The threat of rain. The gloom of entrapment. The dwindling excuses.

'Yeah, I suppose. That's one thing sorted. All I need now is cash.'

'You have cash,' she laughs.

'Well then, more cash. Enough cash.'

'Have you not found out yet what your grandad promised?'

'Haven't had a chance.'

'Maybe it's that old diary you've been reading for your gran. It could be worth something.'

36

'You haven't seen it. It's in bits.'

'Ye never know, Neil. My dad's friend's sister found an old Paul Henry painting in her attic, like, ten years ago. It was worth a fortune.'

An Ireland at the end of the rainbow. The old cottages, big bold sky, apocalyptic clouds. His grandad had a framed copy in the back room. A depressing, unreal depiction of an Irish village. True, it was about to lash, but it lacked a Londis.

'I doubt it. I just can't seem to get a chance to ask her about it 'cause she keeps on getting me to read these things.'

'Try and make a chance.'

'I'm going to. This Saturday. I'm staying Friday. I'll let her relax Friday night. I'm heading out with the lads after she goes asleep. So, I'll ask her Saturday.'

The screen glitches. Her hand moves to her hair as if caught in a strobe light. He'd do anything for her. That's why he needs the cash. He needs to start on the right track in Canada. Hit the ground running. Kathy doesn't suffer fools. Especially broke fools.

'It could be a Paul Henry.'

'Hardly. Anyway, I'm a new man, look at these . . . '

And he pulls up his sleeve to show her his improving biceps and they talk about the gym and he misses her more and promises her more. The world, or whatever part of it they can buy. Anything to keep her calling.

Another Close Call

He's at the top of the stairs, back tight to the banister from trying to avoid any creaks in the middle of the steps, when her voice comes from behind her door. It's half open. Not how he left it.

'Yes Gran,' he calls in, 'it's me. I'll be in to you now.'

His legs come together, and he creaks over the last steps. He rubs his face before going in, opens his mouth, stretches his jaw, opens his eyes wide to try and clear them, blinks a few times and knocks.

'Come in, dear,' she whispers, her voice blanketed as if she's smothered in a cold.

It takes a second for his eyes to adjust to the warm gloom of the room, the thin metal blinds, horizontally tight, blocking out the street-lights. Her silhouette sits on the edge of the bed. The hall light bleaches the darkness. Her fuzzy hair is a shock of grey and white. Her legs, with their veins and liver spots, are exposed below her nightdress. Her feet, the nails dark and uncut, barely touch the carpet. The intimacy of her image in the nightgown and her feet with the grotesque nails send a shiver of repulsion through him. Her dependency is a responsibility.

'I'm sorry, dear,' brings his eyes to her face, and out of the murky light he sees black, flaky patches of something smeared on her cheek, around her nose and her hands. She's gripping a darkened tissue, dabbing gently at her face. His heart drops into his empty gut, and in the lurch, makes him gag. Red Bull, Jägerbombs, pills.

'I had a bit of a nosebleed,' she whispers, almost apologetically.

The morning light filters in and dark, dried wine blotches on the once immaculate white pillowcases become clear.

'Ah Gran,' Neil says, and moves over to her, crouching down to look at her face. She shakes her head slowly.

'I called for you but . . . '

'I fell asleep downstairs in the big chair.'

'So you were here? I thought you might have been gone again. I didn't know you were here.'

'Of course, Gran, of course I was here. I'm always here.'

The lie so easily muttered. His conscience arrives. What a prick. You are a prick.

'Oh,' she says, and her face goes blank and looks to the ground. Neil feels shocking. Not just because the end of the party is draining away, but as a person, a grandson.

He touches her hand, feels the soft, loose skin, warm and coloured by the blemishes of decades. He points to the device around her neck.

'Why didn't you press the panic button, Gran?'

She frowns, brings the tissue to her nose. There's no blood, but still she sniffles.

'I didn't want to be a burden,' she says.

What might have happened if she had pressed the button and the call had been made to the security company? If his uncles and aunt had been called, had got here before the ambulance, had seen he wasn't there?

'You're not a burden.' He rubs her back, 'D'ye hear me? You're not a burden.'

She attempts a smile.

'I don't know, dear.'

'You're not a burden, Gran. Now, how long was it bleeding for?'

'I'm not sure.'

'Well, it's stopped now.'

'I'm not sure, dear,' she goes on, 'maybe I shouldn't be here. Maybe I should think of a home. This was always our home. It doesn't feel right anymore. I'm being selfish.'

'Don't be silly. This *is* your home.'

She shakes her head, her shoulders slumped, her hands twisting the stained tissues.

'No it's not, dear. It was our home. Tommy's and mine. We were the first on the avenue. Did you know that? Here since 1950. Sixty-one years. We never spent a night apart for decades. Until his fall. But I was younger then. I'm not able now. Perhaps it would be . . . I'd be better suited. Maybe the time's right.'

Her breathing rattles through to his hand as he rubs her back. He tells her not to worry herself about such things, and he goes to the hot press for fresh pillowcases, sheets, quilt cover. He's glad to get out of the room for a moment. Compose himself. Is this a trip? Pinch himself and he'll be scagging on the couch back in the apartment, the others giggling at his freaked moans.

He rubs her face gently with baby wipes in the gloom, her breathing deep and regular. The odd car passing outside is a gentle *shush*. Her eyes are closed as he cleans, but the many eyes from the hologram of the shroud of Turin, the Sacred Heart of Jesus picture with palms outstretched, Mary in her blue silk gown are silently observing, judging. This is not a trip. Images like that would never have crept in there. When he finishes, he suggests she'd be wise to get some sleep, and tells her he's going back to bed himself. The previous night's high has deserted him completely, and the initial adrenalin rush of dealing with the sight of so much blood has disappeared. He's barely able to function once the bed is made, her face is clean.

'Don't go,' she says, back in bed, the sheets pulled up to her chest.

'I'll be back in a few hours Gran,' he explains. 'It's half seven in the morning. I'll be right next door if ye need me. I'm just going for two hours more sleep.'

'Stay dear,' she says, patting the empty side of the bed. His eyelids twitch. 'We would chat about all sorts. He was some talker. He really was. Why don't you stay for a chat?'

'I will in two hours.'

'How's your friend?' she says.

'Which friend?'

'Your lovely girlfriend. She visited before.'

'She's in Canada. Remember I told you, Gran? She went about a month ago. I'm joining her soon. Remember? We'll chat about it later, but ye really should get some sleep. I'll be back into you in a few hours.'

'Don't go.' He doesn't know if she means out of the room – or to Canada. 'Wait a moment, please.' Her finger extends vaguely and points to the locker. 'Before you go, can you read something for me?' she says, a meek grin, a touch of pride on her lips.

'What is it?'

The fog of withdrawal is making him impatient, bored, guilty, confused. He wishes he was tripping. Click his fingers and he's scagging on the couch.

'More chapters.'

More? The word depresses him. There's more of this tale to be told. Of an idealistic fool changing the world with his poxy camera. Hopes and dreams of grandeur. Of a republic. This republic. What a joke.

He tries to lift his cheeks, raise a smile. Show appreciation. But his patience – and Kathy's, he's sure – is wearing thin.

Departures, Where Once We Loved to Be

People thought they were mad. They were mostly the soured older ones who didn't understand anymore what it was to give yourself over to something. An idea. Love. The pure blind innocence and foolishness of it all. They couldn't see the sense in leaving a good job to go on a year-long holiday. Especially in the rising climate of fear.

Their new 60-litre rucksacks checked in, carrier bags over shoulders – heavy with insurance forms, passports, Lonely Planet guides and cameras – they queued to go through departures while Kathy's ma and da held themselves together and sniffed and tried not to make a scene. They followed Neil and Kathy, separated only by the black seatbelt barrier, as they edged towards the security gate.

'Look after her, won't you now, son,' Kathy's da said, just before they had to take a turn away from them. Others behind tutted as the gap got bigger leading to the checkpoint.

'Of course I will, Bill,' Neil said, trying hard to maintain the blood-pressure-pump grip.

'She's my little girl. Remember that. You've not known her long, so remember that much. She's our little girl.'

He'd given Neil's hand a final squeeze, and let his stare linger ominously. As they came apart, Neil heard Kathy's mother whisper to her, 'There's no shame in coming home early if it doesn't work out, love.'

Kathy didn't reply. She pressed her lips and turned to Neil with a weak smile, a scared smile, and they waved to them and moved away. Neil nearly clicked his heels.

The moment they went through the security check he was already in another country, on another continent. Free. He kissed Kathy and hugged her and resolved there and then there'd be no shame, Kathy wouldn't be coming home early, it would work out. For the first time it was just the two of them. No sisters or others joining them for drinks, no trips – every weekend – to her parents' or the lads disturbing them in the apartment. They were alone – and free to be themselves, become themselves.

Some English lad in a hostel in Sydney, on one of their first nights, sucked his teeth and said, 'A couple backpacking? Not a good idea. It'll either make you or break you.' He took a slug from his VB and winked at Kathy and said, before laughing, 'My money's on break ye, darling.'

Neil jumped across the table and nailed him. They were kicked out that night and ended up staying in an expensive hotel. It was the first argument of their travels. He got used to the insinuating looks, the flirtatious lines, but never got used to the fights, and always losing to her.

From the living hell of strawberry picking south of Cairns, to the camping weekend on Fraiser Island, to the stoner week in Nimbin and the boredom of Brisbane, to the luxury of Noosa, the cosmopolitan cool of South Yarra and the Espy in St Kilda, to the never ending flatness on the road to Uluru and on to the empty boredom of Perth and the cosy comfort of a hammock in Geraldton, they stayed together, grew together and learned to take refuge in one another. They enjoyed new company, but insulated themselves from the quiet, lonely desperation of single backpackers looking for a two-day hostel buddy – or in Kathy's case – a quick ride.

They came back to Ireland darker, different and deeper in love. And even though they returned to their old jobs, they did so in precarious positions. Last one in, first one out. Their work colleagues, the ones who'd sat on their arses while Neil and Kathy had travelled the globe, would shake their heads in a few months' time when Neil and Kathy were let go and say, 'It's terrible. Just terrible. And to think if ye didn't do the year away.' Neil would see in these eyes the secret, ecstatic confirmation that they were justified in staying, their jealousy was unfounded; in the long run, the people who went around the world were the ones who would regret going away, not them.

But Neil regretted nothing. Regrets nothing. He just remembers the feeling before they came through arrivals, after collecting their rucksacks and seeing the *'failte'* disappear as the doors swooshed open. Kathy squeezed his hand and leaned in.

'I've never loved someone as much as I love you now,' she'd said. 'And even though I'm going back to my folks' and you're going to your mates', we'll be so much closer than when we left a year ago.'

Kathy's parents and sisters had a huge banner saying 'Welcome Home Kathy' waiting to meet them. One year later, they were at the airport again, with another banner, only it was at departures, and it said, 'Bon Voyage Kathy', and Neil was standing with them, waving her off, fresh mud still on his shoes from his grandfather's burial.

Harry Casey - F Company, 2nd Battalion #2

The opening salvos captured – Davy aims his anger
askew – We gather at GHQ

Lest I betray my agitation and anger Davy further, I delayed a few moments before setting up my camera. He had the temper of a fiend, and, having being on the receiving end of it many times before, I was loath to bring it out in this instance.

The Lancers had fanned out across the boulevard, but seemed to set their gazes, from what I could discern, on the GPO. Much to Davy's annoyance, we were not there, you see. We had tried to gain entry once the Lancers had appeared near the Parnell monument, but after my stalling and then laboured lifting of the stand, those inside the GPO, presumably on orders, had gone and barricaded themselves in. Regardless of how hard Davy knocked, or shook his hat about shouting, 'It's me for God's sake!' they didn't respond. 'Leave it be Davy,' I had called. 'We'll take cover at the Imperial.'

He had groaned, aware of the danger in procrastinating, and

looked to the Imperial, the lofty silver shopfront windows and the shadowed area under its awning.

'We can still be of help,' said I, 'should they need it.'

'They bloody well need it now,' he said, 'and where am I? Outside as usual. If this is all the action there is and I'm stuck with you looking on, Har, there'll be trouble.'

We had crossed the road in haste, much to the derision of the crowds gathered at the end of the street. They were hanging out of lamp posts and struggling for space on the parapet of the bridge, waiting. We were the late arrivals who block the view of the stage seconds before the show begins.

'They think we're retreating,' Davy had snapped.

'And what's it to you? Sure, look at them. They're the ones looking on. We're by no means in the stalls Davy. We're still on the stage.'

Davy's anger had seemed to subside when I said this, but the sucking of his gums and the long, frustrated breaths he emitted while peering up towards the line of impressive horses let me know it was far from assuaged altogether. Had it not been for the arrival of a ragged group of Volunteers smashing their way into the GPO, I believe Davy would have accepted his fate. However, the Volunteers' arrival and their messy entry into the post office only agitated him further. I had discreetly set up and was literally seconds away from cranking when they arrived upon the scene.

'C'mon Har,' he said in a crouch, ready to vault across the thoroughfare, 'now's our chance.'

The quarrel which had been brewing blew up between us when he regarded me, hand on the lever, eye focused on the viewer, about to use the last of my reel to record the Lancers' charge.

'Why, man alive!' he remonstrated, his eyes wide and manic, caught up in the reality of it all. 'Let that alone and come on!'

He gripped the stand as if to throw it to the ground. I was shocked that he would threaten my cinemachine in such a manner, especially after he had aided me on many an occasion when we used it to further the nationalist cause. I had painstakingly explained the delicate nature of the machine to him numerous times. Although the leather-covered wood body, the leather carrying strap, the brass winding handle, the folding Newton-type viewfinder, the spirit level and silver scale calibrated footage measurer may have looked sturdy, the internal mechanisms were delicate and incredibly prone to sudden, violent movements. A carefully constructed clockwork of components, the eighteen-tooth sprocket, the coaxial spool arrangement, the velvet-lined film gate, the round metal spool box, the sprung-steel drive belt, the shutter mechanism with shuttle claw arrangement and the flywheel shutter and gear-activated chain mechanism, not to mention the lens, were a fragile technological world of wonder and reverence that needed to be respected.

'Davy!' I bellowed, struggling with him. 'Don't be so damned foolish!'

A shot rang out. The air was charged with confusion. It seemed to jar Davy, and he released the stand and jolted back under the reassuring shade of the Imperial's awning. Our scuffle, thankfully, was ended. Davy went for his revolver. I began to crank. A Volunteer was down in the middle of the thoroughfare, and I was rolling.

Another shot rang out, and this time I caught it. A young chap, a straggler from the Volunteers, was felled on the road. A silence took possession of the street. The loud whip-crack of the gunshots hushed everything. Even the gawkers at the river stopped murmuring.

Davy was silent. My camera whirred smoothly. Our hearts palpitated when a rough voice, restrained and deep, unmistakably that of an English rally cry due to its casual-yet-threatening timbre, called out, 'Forward!' I panned, hands trembling, slowly to the right and into the clamour of hooves rising from a canter to a gallop. I tried to keep my rhythm steady.

'Why aren't we shooting?' hissed Davy.

The horses were magnificent in their irregular line, the men atop them dazzling and horrifying. We may have been on the street they were charging down, the noise growing into a spectacular din, but it was obvious, even behind the tiny lens of my Pathé Kok, where they were headed.

'Why aren't we firing on them?' Davy asked again, his shoulder set against the door frame, half hidden from the street. The thunder of the hooves on the cobbles and tram lines, like a rising score of an opera, increased in intensity, and just as my composition was seconds away from having the Lancers' charge with the GPO in the background, a deafening crack rent the air. I stopped cranking for a moment, unable to keep a steady rhythm with the terror of it all.

Davy's left arm was still supporting the revolver, having helped his right arm aim, when more fire rang out, this time from the windows of the GPO. These shots were tiny pops compared to the crack Davy had made. I began to crank once more, mechanically now, letting my right hand do as I had hoped it would in such situations, regardless of how my brain was operating. I had, by not cranking, saturated a few moments of the film. It was an amateur mistake I had hoped I would not succumb to under the pressures of war!

Lancers dropped from their horses, horses flopped, mid-gallop, skidding onto the cobbles. The rest of the charge retreated. Stray, riderless horses, trotted around lost before turning and following their saddled friends back behind Parnell's monument.

As I knew there were merely seconds of film left, I felt it superfluous to pull out the knob and end the scene. I decided to continue cranking until the magazine ran out, and so I panned the camera farther to my right and brought, first, Davy's extended arm with his smoking revolver into the shot, and then the profile of his face.

'Davy,' said I.

He turned, his hat having fallen off, his hair exposed and slick with sweat. A queer look was on him; a distant wistfulness washed over his eyes, colouring a slight smile. Very calm and defiant he was, with a stance of pride, his chin raised ever so slightly for the camera. For a moment – moments – he peered into the lens, as if to say, 'There. I did it.' He was changed then, charged with an aura of confidence that endowed him with this calm detached countenance. Our silence was interrupted by the metallic *click-click* of the hand crank ending the magazine and the sprocket wheel whirring around without any film to oil its progress.

Once he realised the film was over, he blinked back to reality and patted my shoulder, sucking his gums again, shaking his head ruefully, not bothering to pick up his hat.

'It's started,' he said. 'There's no turning back now.'

'No,' said I. 'There'll be no turning back now.'

We were about to take off for the GPO, seeing the locked doors open and men come out to take up the youngster sprawled in the middle of the boulevard, when a tall man with frightfully large nostrils and tendrils protruding from them like something from the Viceroy's wife's hat, accosted us.

'They've gone and done it now boys,' said the old chap in a haughty provincial accent. 'There'll be trouble tonight, and I won't get any blasted sleep I'm sure.'

Davy turned to him, the revolver still in hand but hidden from view.

'Who's they?' asked Davy.

'Them buckos there,' said the fellow, nodding across to the Volunteers at the barricades and out on the cobbles. 'They've gone and done it and they'll get their comeuppance tonight. Mark my words. They'll get their comeuppance, and they'll deserve every bit of it. Ruffians. Up for the Easter and I'm to be like a sheep caught in a ditch in this mess. They'll get their comeuppance and they'll stop playing soldiers then.'

Davy's reaction, the speed and ferocity of it, rather than the violent intent – or rather, before I countenanced the violent intent – was shocking. He lunged for the unfortunate man, the barrel of his .32 Mauser, a dull flash of light, pointing up towards the now flaring nostrils.

'I'm one of them,' said Davy through his teeth, his eyes wide, his revolver no longer hidden. 'Does this look like playing to you?'

The man dropped a few inches, his legs doubtlessly giving way with the sudden terror of having a pistol pushed into his face.

'Steady on,' I whispered, sliding up close to Davy so as not to alarm him or bring undue attention upon us. We were, after all, fighting for the people of Ireland, and this poor unfortunate, although his attitude had been found wanting, was only an innocent bystander. Davy tugged at the man's collar, the gun still set hard to his face.

'No Har. I won't have it. We're fighting for the likes of him. We're fighting for you,' he said.

'Come on,' said I, 'this isn't our fight. Come on. Let's get across to the men.'

His grip loosened as, once again, my words brought him back from somewhere I had never seen him go before. The revolver, it must be said, had the most peculiar effect. Heretofore he had never been so quick to take to violence. True, he had a short temper, but the fuse, when lit, would only ever explode with strong words and colourful language. This sudden compulsion for violence seemed out of character. But, I suppose, when one considers the setting, maybe I was the one who was being peculiar in not accepting that violence was what we were standing for by coming out. My motivations were being teased out. Differences of culture and constitution were becoming apparent in the early stages of war, and would do so later as well.

Our predicament was cut short by a tardy group of Volunteers converging on, and being greeted outside, the GPO. Davy saw how they were welcomed, let the poor man slide away with a grateful whimper and, without even a by your leave, charged across the road.

'You made it men,' declared Davy, as if he was the leader and controller of the thoroughfare. I had barely even heaved up my stand and camera before he had clasped hands and shaken shoulders and ingratiated himself with the new arrivals, as if they had been friends for life.

A great heat had settled into the day, causing my shirt, by the time I had made it into the GPO, to become damp with sweat under the weight of my apparatus. On arriving in the GPO, Davy had surrounded himself with men. I could only catch snippets of the tale of how he had fired the first shot at the Lancers from across the road. Knots of men had formed inside the building, those around Davy, those at the barricades, those around a table which had the look of a war council and those at stretchers where two men were groaning and cursing their luck.

With men snapping boots off the glistening tiles and wood still splintering and large benches toppling and scraping as they were pushed into position, it was only those at the barricades who heard the glass shatter out on the boulevard. I stood on my tippy-toes behind them, trying to catch sight of the commotion on the street. I could hear the smashing of windows and the shrieks of pleasure from the bowsies doing the smashing. The men at the barricades, having only been informed of what to do should the enemy appear, called back over their shoulders for instructions.

Eager to capture all elements of the drama and how the fight would play out on all aspects of Dublin life, I was at first anxious to get back out into the sun and see how the citizens were reacting to our call. Yet I was also frustrated at not having husbanded an extra magazine on my person, as I had been taught to do by my dear friend Ridley, back in London.

Davy had somehow detached himself from his knot of followers and joined me at the windows to ascertain from whence the sound of the shattering glass and chatter was coming.

'The bastards,' he hissed. 'Scroungers and football fans the lot of them.'

He called back to an officer, menace painting his face like a mask, and took out his revolver.

'We'll put an end to this farce,' he said and tugged at my arm. 'C'mon Har. I've to take a posse with me. We'll not have looters ruin our name.'

I was perplexed by his reaction to the looting. He was a staunch supporter of the 'downtrodden' classes, as he phrased it, and had, on many an occasion, argued with me about the need for a social revolution to accompany a political one. He was, or at least, had led me to believe he was, on the side of those out front breaking into the shops.

'We'll teach these corner boys a trick or two about respecting our revolution,' he said.

'Hold on Davy,' said I, 'my OC is over there talking to Connolly. I should really let him know I'm here.'

'I know yer here. Now come on and give me a hand with these ruffians.'

If requisitioned I had meant to fight. I would have fought. However, the thought of playing at being the DMP without the uniform didn't appeal. Yes, I was able to see what was driving Davy crazy: the thought of our actions being sullied by the actions of a few looters. Nevertheless, I also had an unshakeable confidence in the power of my Pathé Kok and the film I would take. It was to be the definitive source and account of our efforts. Davy thought so too – or so I had thought.

'Forget about that, Har. You're to come with me.'

I found myself, once again, in a pickle. I was all too aware of the used magazine in my camera and the three lying idle under my bed. I would have had no problem in joining Davy if I could have acquired some footage. Alas, my lack of sufficient planning sullied any urge to get involved in another battle. Not accepting my response, and once again trying to separate the stand and camera from my person, Davy was a moment from violence when Leo Houlihan, brother of my captain, Frank, called to me.

'Harry,' said he, confusion creasing his brow, 'what are you doing here? The rest of F Company are outside.'

'Outside?' said I, surprised they had come in, still hugging my camera and stand, feeling embarrassed and relieved all at once.

You see, I had set out on my bicycle for eleven o'clock Mass that morning (Monday) and had come across the brothers McGinley on Jones' Road. They asked me had I not got word and I innocently said, 'No.' They had tutted at this and, leaning in close, dipping their voices to a weighty whisper, told me to mobilise immediately at Father Matthew Park. Needless to say, I turned my bicycle around and made my way back without delay to Clonliffe Avenue for my pistol and camera and stand.

I would have gone to Father Matthew Park too, had it not been for the fact I had met a Miss Lowe coming from her house as I dismounted my bicycle and opened my gate. She was a neighbour of mine who worked at Volunteer headquarters at 2 Dawson Street and was secretary to Eoin McNeill. She informed me, in no uncertain terms that we, the Volunteers, were not going out, despite the fact that she had seen Davy in his finest storming down to the GPO, and that it was only the Citizen Army that were out.

The thought of missing the action, even if it was only to be the Citizen Army in action, was horrifying, particularly when I thought of Davy and his incessant ribbing should I not capture him in his moment of glory. I left the three revolvers belonging to F Company under my bed, along with three spare magazines of film. A new magazine quickly loaded and fed through the spool, stand under my arm, the Pathé Kok strapped to the front carrier of my bicycle, I skipped by Father Matthew Park and headed straight for the opening scene on Sackville Street.

'Casey!' shouted the brothers McGinley, when they saw me peeping over the barricade at the Company lining up for inspection under the shadow of the columns. They were with Citizen Army men and a convoy of three or four carts laden with cabbage and other vegetables.

'Where've ye been, man?' asked one of them. 'We thought you were lifted.'

The other one called over to my OC, Frank Houlihan, who had come to the end of his conference with Connolly at the rear of the building.

'We found him, sir,' he said.

Frank strode over with great purpose. He made to shake my hand, but stopped short when he set eyes on my camera and stand.

'We thought you were a goner, Harry. Did you bring the revolvers?'

'Revolvers?'

'The three revolvers we left with you. The company needs them. The McGinley brothers told me they informed you to mobilise earlier.'

'A misunderstanding, sir,' said I.

He pursed his lips and began to cogitate on my cumbersome apparatus.

'Never mind,' he said after a time. 'Join us out front. Connolly is about to inspect the company.'

I started to move off, and he put his hand on the stand and asked, 'You do mean to fight, don't you, Harry?'

'Of course, sir,' said I.

'Well then,' he whispered, coming close, so as not to be overheard by passing men, 'get rid of the circus you're carrying. This is war. Not the theatre. We're moving out again, so we'll need to carry ammunition, not toys like this.'

He knocked on the camera and laughed, and I laughed too, since I didn't want to upset him at such an early stage of the fight.

'But, sir,' said I, 'where can I leave them?'

I had carried the apparatus from London to Dublin under threat of imprisonment if caught doing so, and then laboured with it around the city, capturing moments of great importance leading up to the week in question. I was never going to let the camera down, but nor was I, on the first day, going to appear uncommitted to the cause and the men of the company.

'Leave them over yonder,' said Frank, with an impatient nod of his head to a vague space over my shoulder. 'This is war, man. Sacrifices are being made. Maybe the greatest of them all. Your camera is the least of your worries.'

He regarded me with a stern eye, almost appraising my reaction to his words.

'Right you are, sir. Apologies. I'll just leave them over here and be out to you in a jiffy,' said I.

I waited until he darkened the door before I turned and searched for a suitable hiding place for my new burden.

A Family Dinner

'OK, let's get down to business,' Eoin says, seizing his opportunity while his older brother Jim deals with a bout of coughing. 'We all know why we're here. A consensus is needed on what's to be done with Ma.'

Neil's grandad brought him to a hurling game in Croke Park when he was about seventeen. An all-Ireland final. Cork versus Kilkenny. The accents around them were rough and hilarious. The passion ridiculous. How people work themselves up into red-faced embarrassments to themselves, their families and their counties, was beyond him. But the intensity and brutality of the game made an impression. He's reminded of it every time there's a family meeting: Uncle Jim, Uncle Eoin, Aunt Maura. And Neil – taking his deceased mother's seat at the table.

'It's a simple choice,' Jim says, composed now and using his place at the top of the table and his height to speak over Eoin. 'Two options. Persevering as we have all been doing in the current climate.' Eoin, mouth open, pushes his glasses up the bridge of his nose, grunts, but lets him speak.

Eoin 0-1, Jim 0-1, Maura, 0-0.

'Or,' Jim pauses for effect, breathes through his nose, 'uprooting her. Taking her out of her home of sixty years and bringing her to a place she has, for sometime now, let be known, she has no intention or impulse to ever go to. An old folks' home.'

'It's as simple as that guys,' Eoin finishes.

Eoin 0-2, Jim 0-3, Maura, 0-0.

Maura, Gran's closest ally in the boardroom, shifts back on her seat.

'Well, it's not really that simple. She can – could move in with one of us.' Maura has a three-bedroom terraced house in Killester, with four kids. Two girls and two boys.

'That's impracticable,' Eoin winces. 'For you especially, Maura.'

The indirect referencing of all the financial rungs they find themselves separated by is a high-pressure game they destroy each other with. What makes this particular situation all the more competitive is the nature of the siblings' jobs: they are all civil servants. Some have moved higher up than others, depending on their circumstance and departments. Not because of intellect or talent, the ones left behind insist. There is an edge to all gatherings because of such insistences. Neil never wants to be like them. Ever.

Eoin 2-3, Jim 1-3, Maura 1-0. His aunt Rita comes in with more tea. She doesn't ask if Neil wants another beer.

'If we sold the house now, or last year, like we'd discussed, it would pay for the nursing home for months, years,' Maura says, trying hard, but not succeeding, in hiding her desperation. It's no secret that her hopes of climbing back up the social ladder have faded. Her husband's pending redundancy is a mitigating factor. 'Or, there's always the Fair Deal. I've read up on it.'

Eoin 2-3, Jim 0-3, Maura 2-0.

Eoin shakes his jowls, snorts to gather attention and takes off his glasses. 'Maura, Maura,' he goes, 'you know what number twenty-six went for last month.' Maura keeps her lips pressed tight. She knows she has given up her position. Eoin looks to Jim, Neil, his chest rising with the silence. 'Three-fifty,' he says. 'That's what? Two, two-fifty less than what we could have got if we'd sold three years ago like I said.'

'Two-fifty,' Jim affirms, a rueful smile on his lips.

Eoin 2-3, Jim 0-4, Maura 2-0.

'She didn't want to go then,' Neil says, surprising himself with the sound of his voice. A brief cameo to clatter a few shins, knock a few heads. All eyes on him. 'She didn't want to go three years ago. Pappy didn't want to go three years ago.'

'Pappy is gone. Things have changed, Neil. Circumstances must be taken into account. We've all been burnt by not taking the initiative and deciding, for once and for all, what's best,' Eoin says.

'What's best for who?' Neil says, and there's a stunned silence. 'She didn't want to go three years ago and you listened to her. Listen to her now. Why isn't she here?'

'Look,' Eoin booms, cutting Neil short, exasperation painting his words, 'we're wasting time talking about the past. If we had sold the house three years ago, and put them in a home, we would have got a net outlay of two hundred K each.'

Divided three ways. Neil isn't stupid. Why's he even here? The façade of familial democracy.

'As it stands,' Eoin continues, 'if we put the property on the market tomorrow, we will get less, less than one hundred K each if you take into account the fees for a nursing home and whatnot. Now, correct me if I'm wrong, Maura, but I too have read up on the "Fair Deal". Fair Deal my eye. They want a percentage of the estate. Really? Are we going to let the government take a percentage of our rightful inheritance when, to all intents and purposes, Ma is perfectly fine where she is now? Now, now, Jim, back me up on this.'

'Realistically we have two options,' Jim says. 'Sell now and put Mother in a nursing home, or let her continue as is and sell when things out there have settled. Olga tells me Ma was only saying yesterday how content she is at home.'

'But she's having doubts,' Neil says, clearing his throat. All faces turn in the semi-darkness, as if they can't quite see him. It's rough out there.

Jim smiles and taps the table as if he's reassuring him. 'It's only natural after Pappy's passing. We're only a month out from it. It's still raw. She's confused. She's said for years she always wanted to stay in the house. Years, Neil.'

Eoin 3-3, Jim 2-4, Maura sent to the stands.

'We owe her that much,' Eoin says. 'We are in no hurry. Well, sorry, I'm in no hurry. I can't speak for the rest of you.'

He lets the silence – Rita clinking glasses out of sight in the kitchen – accuse everyone, insinuate monetary desperation. The need for money, financial desperation displayed, from what Neil learned as a youngster from his mother, was thought of in this family as unbecoming. A sign of weakness.

Eoin 4-3, Jim 2-4, Maura sent to the stands.

Neil doesn't want to play this game. But he can take the hits.

'I get what you're saying,' he goes, brave because it's dark, 'but c'mon. She can barely get out of her chair. She had another bad nosebleed last Friday. What if I wasn't there?'

They dwell on his words for a few seconds. He looks at the deep oak table and rolls his empty bottle.

'If it's the money,' Eoin says, 'if you're pushing to have her moved now because you want to take your share in the house for your trip to Canada,' he stops and looks around the room, dwelling on Maura just that bit longer, 'we could buy you out now if you want. A few grand for your share.'

Yellow card Eoin.

'My inheritance?'

'Our inheritance. There are nine grandchildren. You'll all get a share. I can give you yours now.'

'No thank you.'

Neil's disgust goes beyond Eoin, to the other two for not backing him, or at least pulling Eoin up on his ludicrous suggestion.

'I think,' Eoin says, pushing his glasses up his nose again, 'what we're all agreed on is forgetting about moving Ma – and selling the house – at the current market value. Agreed?'

Eoin 5-3, Jim 3-4, Maura sent to the stands.

Pursed lips, solemn nods. Maura takes a deep breath as if she's about to say something.

'It's not about the money,' Neil says, but they're too preoccupied with their own troubles to pay him any attention.

'A year, two years max, and the market should improve. Cards on the table, I'm happy with that,' Jim says. Eoin raises his finger, 'Second that.'

'It's not about the money,' Neil repeats.

'What's your angle?' Eoin accuses, trying in vain to hold his temper. 'What?'

'There's something wrong with you. Get it off your chest.'

'I just don't think she's able for it.'

'If it's about the cash,' Jim offers.

'It's not about the cash. Jesus,' Neil says, losing what little patience he had in reserve. 'It's not about the cash.'

Eoin's elbows hit the table, 'If she wasn't able for it Neil, the home help, Olga or Isabella, would tell us. I think they'd be able to tell. You're there once a week. You're not qualified to give an opinion.'

Red card Eoin.

Neil launches his chair back, his head shaking.

'C'mon Neil,' Eoin says, 'don't be so childish. Sit down. We're here to have a mature discussion. A mature family discussion.'

'And there's me thinking it was a board meeting.'

Match abandoned.

Something to Keep
Him Occupied

The gap between breaths is so long that Neil doesn't sit or breathe himself until he sees her chest rise and hears her snore. It's a long time coming. He gasps quietly, like he's been kept under water. If there was no snore, no expansion in the inhale, and he was left looking on her as she was for the last time, what would he do? Would he kiss her like he'd kissed his mother, on the forehead, and forever have that cold reminder that she was no more?

Neil sits and waits. Olga puts her head around the door, all smiles. 'If you want, I say you call.'

'It's OK,' he whispers. 'I'll wait.'

She nods and says, 'OK. I go to bed. Will you put the alarm?'

He gives her the thumbs up, and when he returns to Gran, a slight lift in the lips blooms and lights her face. Her eyelids flicker and she looks to the picture of the old pope hanging at the end of the bed. The goalkeeper. She dwells on the picture for a moment before turning to him.

'Hello dear,' she whispers.

He puts his elbows on his knees and takes her hand.

'Hi Gran,' he smiles, relieved she's awake, happy in her company.

'I knew you would call,' she says, with a weak, dry cough.

'Did you now.'

She nods slightly, pleased with herself.

'I'm not great today dear,' she says, a shrug of sorts lifting her shoulders.

'No?'

'No. Olga was very good, though.'

Neil rubs her hand, the soft, thin skin shifting loosely with his movement.

'I miss Tommy so. I'm glad you're here.'

'I'm glad to be here.' Because he is. In the last throes before he leaves, he feels it is his duty to embrace the woman and her ways, her voice and her presence. Make an extra effort to remember these moments. She is all that is left of what he calls family. And she holds the key to what he has been promised. He's starting to wonder if the story of her father, his great-grandfather, will prove to be of worth to him too. Kathy thinks so.

'I often think about my father of late,' she whispers, her eyes closed in concentration, dwelling on the message, not the receiver. 'I never knew him, you see. I could only imagine him. His words were all I ever had. Of course, my mother only gave them to me when I was of an age to understand them. But it's only now, since Tommy's gone, that I feel they have become what he hoped they would become. Tommy said they would. He was always right. He said he'd never leave me, though. I really didn't think he would ever leave me. Go so soon. Apart from the fall, he had never been sick. Or once, a year or two after we were married he got phlebitis. He hid it from me, just like he hid everything from me this time.' She pauses and opens her eyes on the empty side of the bed. 'He was sick for a long time, but he never told anyone. The men drag on. There were a dozen things wrong with him when he passed, they said. The men just don't ever say what is wrong. They keep it to themselves. I wish he hadn't, so I could have comforted him.'

Is this why he's here? He feels a gag of guilt at hearing such things when he didn't come for this. Why did he come? He really doesn't know. He's confused, looking for an answer to a question he doesn't even know how to ask. Should I leave? Why shouldn't I leave? Cowardice can be camouflaged. A word will do.

She comes out of her dip and blinks with an almost confused look at Neil.

'What is it you asked me about dear?'

Neil doesn't know how to respond.

'I hope you don't mind,' she says, frowning now, as if he has answered her. 'I'm not feeling too well. I'm a little tired actually.'

'Oh' he says, disappointed. If she talked, he knows he could have manoeuvred the conversation around to his grandfather's promise. He can't force it though. She's not stupid. And impressions, at this stage, will be last impressions. Lasting impressions. He wants to only make good ones.

'OK, Gran. I'll leave you to it.'

The Treadmill

A lean muscular physique is what he wants. Consistency. Not some top-heavy, skinny-legged inverted triangle. He has to apply the same attention to detail to all areas of the body for the complete, supped-up, high-end look. The treadmill needs to be conquered. He needs to be fit, as well as ripped. Look like an athlete without the athletics.

He starts off fast. A short, intense stride. He has researched the ways to maximise his efforts on the track. There are five – in this order – that he needs to be aware of: shoulders and arms. Stride. Foot position. Head position. Breathing. He got the techniques from Google. He got the email addresses for people who deal with archival material from Google too. The words 'archive' and 'history' got him what he wanted. Google has an answer to every question. Even ones you haven't asked yet.

Shoulders and arms: try to hold your elbows at a ninety-degree angle and allow your arms to go back and forth aggressively, to keep your stride and balance. So far so good. He feels good. He sent away a few emails. One to Trinity, one to the IFI, one to UCD, one to NUIG. Everything was kept vague, but eager. Only one person responded within twenty-four hours. And when Neil replied, the other guy replied within twenty minutes. Which was a good sign. Nerds are all the same. They agreed to meet up at his lab on the Trinity campus. Two women in tight Lycra bottoms smile as they pass him.

Stride: if you are practising sprinting – he's not, but it sounds like a good tip anyway – then you will need to lift your knees much higher to achieve maximum leg power. The lab Neil visited was just off his apartment on Pearse Street. In the Developmental Sciences building on Westland Row. He skipped in behind a backpacked student, and after a few questions and false turns, found his way across the cobbles, behind the museum, down a slip of path beyond the cricket pitch and then finally into the Developmental Sciences building, with its frosted glass walls, dimmed late-night hallways, slab stairwells and cold, clear lines, and then into the circular-window loneliness of a sparsely lit room, where he found a depressing, cold, sterilised white glow from a computer screen.

Foot position: ensure that your toes are pointed in the direction in which you are running. The pace is beginning to strain. Sweat is forming on his brow. It's getting harder to keep up the cool, untroubled façade. The room was empty and dark. A bit strange. They had agreed to meet at nine – at night – which made Neil wary. The door opened behind him, and in stepped the six-foot-two frame of Enda, his head raised in immediate appraisal of the figure he saw invading his space. Although imposing, Neil was put at ease by his apparent age. The lad, Enda, seemed only a year or two older than him.

'You must be Neil,' he said in a hybrid accent. A cross between Dutch and American. A weird, computerised lilt, drained of emotion. He lumbered forward, as if he was all too aware of his massive frame, his shock of hair lit by the glow from the screen.

'I'm Enda. Apologies for my tardiness. My movements aren't as regular as they once were.' Neil's offer of a handshake wasn't met.

'Let's not,' Enda continued, his hands raised. 'I got caught short and had to go to the first-floor toilet. Even though I washed, the old hand dryer probably increases bacteria by about two-hundred percent. So, in reality, I should have taken my chances and not bothered.'

The lad was obviously a freak. Neil had an urge to leave. But Kathy had insisted he check if the diary had any value. This, unfortunately, seemed his best way to find out.

'I couldn't bring the actual stuff. But I brought a few pictures on my phone. My Gran owns them. I only read them to her. Give them back afterwards.'

'On your phone?'

'On my phone.'

And Enda's face was lit up white.

Head position: always look straight ahead, in the direction in which you are running. Looking in another direction can hinder your balance and can also put you off your stride. Another girl waltzes by and Neil tries to meet her stare without moving his head and manages to return her discreet laugh. Enda took the phone and puzzled over the pictures.

'These are sheets of paper. You said archive material. I presumed, as I am in the archive department for film, that you would have brought film. You might as well have brought me fossils.'

Neil snapped the phone back from him and said, 'What?' Confused, his patience spent.

But Enda had forgotten Neil already. 'I should have used the toilet roll. You can dry ninety percent of your hands within ten seconds. It's the simplest answers that stare us in the face.'

'The what?'

'I never considered using the toilet roll.'

Neil hadn't made the effort for nothing. 'Would you know if they're worth anything? The diary is nearly one hundred years old.'

Enda hummed and hawed and took a long, lazy blink. 'I'm an electrical and electronic engineer,' he patronised, speaking slowly, as if to a child. 'I specialise in film. Authentic, sought-after archive film. Of high value.' He motioned to the dimly lit room, the shelves silhouetted by books and canisters, the white space from his screen showing a strange black contraption on his desk. 'You obviously have the wrong man.'

'But you said . . . '

'I know what I said. I said I could help you when your email asked if I could shed some light on the value of some, and I will quote you here, "archive material from 1916". I presumed if you read correctly, researched me fully, you would be aware my area of expertise was not paper.' And he scoffed. Neil gripped his phone and thought of the shitty hands that had sullied it. He tried to hold his temper.

Breathing: while running, breathe through your mouth and allow your diaphragm to lift and retract – this is referred to as 'belly breathing'. It will help increase your endurance. He's out of puff already. His face, he feels, is turning beetroot, his posture, the ninety degrees, the toes, the knees, everything is starting to fall apart. He should have started with the breathing. He continues on. No pain, no gain. Just before he left, Enda did offer one piece of advice.

'From what I have seen before, and in this field, let me preface, I am no expert. But, I'd imagine you would have some value attached to the pages if they were to go to auction.'

'Auction?'

'Yes. Auction. You know, where people from different backgrounds place a bid on . . . '

'I know what it is.'

'Good. Well, then, you could get a good sum at an auction for such archive material. On first glance they do look like authentic memorabilia, especially the handwritten sheet.'

Neil said his thanks and was making for the door when Enda called after him.

'I'm almost finished here. I've been on my own all day. As is usual. Would you like to go for a coffee? You look like you work out. What do you bench?'

Neil didn't respond.

'I could help you improve your proportions. You're much too top-heavy.'

'Nah, you're all right,' Neil said, 'you're the last person I'd want to take advice from.'

Politics Is an Analogue Show on an HD Screen

Despite having had only a few hours' sleep, Neil's still wired. Everything has that heightened, urgent, vital glow about it. That still-high intense detachment. He sees their warped reflections in the dull black TV screen and imagines they're in their own depressing version of *Fair City*.

The scene opens with Gran sitting at the table, an archetypal old dear, a prop swamped in props, her fork hanging loose from her fingers, clinking delicately on the lip of the plate. Beside her hand, the pill box is open on 'Sun'. The old teapot smokes discreetly on the cork coaster. Blackened toast – just as Gran likes it – is soaking up the butter, and her boiled egg, the top already sliced off, is in its cup, waiting to have some soldiers dunked in. Milk is in the jug, sugar in the stainless-steel holder. A pale glass of water taunts Neil. Only a glass of water.

'I didn't expect to see you today, dear. It's very early too isn't it?' she says, her throat dry, her voice grating.

'Well, Gran,' he responds, clearing his own throat, keeping his eyes on her hands, trying to hide the truth of his escape from the sweaty mess of bodies after a three-day session back in the apartment, the need for silence, sleep, refuge in his gran's spare room – even if it was only for a few hours. 'It's not that early, and sure sometimes a surprise is a good thing.'

She puts her napkin on her lap, and shuffles her free hand over to his and clasps it. She's squinting into the clock above the table.

'Besides,' he says, 'you forgot to give me the next chapter on Friday night.' She nods and grins as if he has given her the most satisfying of compliments. She edges her chair back. It's a plausible excuse he feels terrible for using. But in fairness, it's not a complete lie. An interest is growing.

'Not now Gran,' he says, impressed by her energy. 'Relax. Enjoy your breakfast.'

'OK dear,' she whispers, and settles back in to the table. He puts on the talk show the home help Sky-plussed for her last night.

Television offers nothing. Irish television, especially, leaves him joyless. If he watches it, it inflicts him with vague embarrassment, bordering on annoyance. Especially after he got stung with the TV licence for the apartment. He had the misfortune to be nearest the door when the knock came. The well-rehearsed, easy-going demeanour of the inspector and the line, 'Sorry for disturbing you, but is your name William Murphy?' And Neil falling for the informal tone and saying, 'No, it's . . . ' and offering up his name without any explanation. 'That's great. Your name is now on the TV licence for this address.'

Irish television does not represent his life, reflect his struggles. It is a vehicle continually reminding him that he doesn't exist in this country. He doesn't belong. There is an accent on Irish television he never hears: his. Or ones like it. There is a type of person he never sees on Irish television: him, or people like him. Desperate, disillusioned, angry, annoyed. Everything is bland, veneered with paper-thin glamour that would blow over if anyone huffed. No one does on Irish TV. No show displays this better than the one he is about to watch with his gran. And that's why his channel is YouTube. No content restrictions, limits, accent prejudices or borders.

The presenter, some square-headed, tunnel-browed Corkonian, reads stiff jokes from a cue card and patronises with the line, 'We're a great little country, aren't we, ladies and gentlemen?' Once his studio audience have expelled the last of their canned laughter, he sits behind his mahogany desk and begins: 'Our first guest hails from a long line of distinguished Irish heroes and political patriots. Schooled in the family academy of winning Irish hearts and minds, not content with guiding our economy into the brightest days of the nation as Minister for Finance, and having the nous to be bold enough to look for help when, as Taoiseach, the world economy collapsed around us, Alby Ashe, ladies and gentlemen, is here to tell us about his next adventure.'

Gran's toast doesn't reach her mouth. It hangs inches from her lips as they twist and curl. The old politician comes out in the uniform of the new Irish patriots: cream suit jacket, dark slacks, open collar – casual – expensive shirt. He stops at the top of the steps and waves to the crowd. They cheer as if they've been addressed by a monarch. He smiles his wide, bleached-white denture smile and, manicured hand across his stomach, kind of jogs towards the presenter. They embrace as if they're best friends and then whisper pleasantries. The politician blows out a breath for the audience, as if he's tired, and after he opens the button on his suit-jacket and shifts his trousers on his knees, he sits on his throne, happy, content, remote.

Politicians turn Neil's stomach. Put him on edge. Bring out the cynic in him. He refuses to believe they have the intelligence to really appreciate the enormity of their undertaking. Most of them are teachers – primary-school teachers trained to talk down to children. '*Na bi ag caint*', and '*sui suieas*'. He doesn't vote anymore. He did once. When he bought the bullshit lie that every vote counts. The young fool with his voting card filling every box with a number from top to bottom, earnest and eager to contribute. Being generous with his transfers. Proportional representation is a lie. No proportion has ever represented him. He has given up on the idea that his vote will determine any alternative course for the nation. It's led by cash, not compassion. He reckons he'll have more of an impact on the country by not paying back his motor loan. That's his vote. His protest. That's their philosophy used against them.

The politician goes through what he's been doing since he retired from politics.

'Very little, in fact, nothing really.'

He smiles, and the complicit audience erupt into hysterics, looking to the monitors above their heads the moment the camera alights on them. The self-conscious generation unused to the high-definition reality of a screen. Bad teeth beyond the too-bright lipstick and bald patches lurking underneath the purple rinses. The interviewer forgets to mention the six-figure lectures around the world, or the massive ministerial pension enabling him to holiday in the south of France. Neil reads the online news. The headlines.

'Can you turn it up dear?' Gran asks, sliding her plate away, lost now in the theatre of it all. Unaware that she too is projecting for the cameras.

Neil turns it up just in time for Gran to hear the presenter say, 'So, really, tell us, why are you here tonight?'

With all the timing of a screen legend, conscious of his own myth-making, Alby pouts like he can't believe he's been asked such a question, and, with a shake of the head, pretends he's struggling with whether to disclose or not. All politicians are cut-and-pasted Word documents of rehearsed lines, second-hand buzzwords and cute-hoor evasiveness. The performance sickens Neil. Finally, Alby exhales and announces: 'I'm going to run for president.'

The audience explodes with joy at the unexpected news. Camera to audience. Audience to the screens overhead. Gran, in a show of distaste Neil hasn't seen from her since he was a teenager, forms an angry grimace and moans and turns to him. There's a dip in her brow and she fidgets with her napkin. Great TV. An IFTA is coming. *RTÉ Guide* and *VIP* spreads.

Alby talks about his father helping to establish the republic, bringing dignity and inclusiveness to a submerged people. He speaks about the pride he has in his father's career as a civil servant in the early years of the Department of Home Affairs, and then as secretary general for the Department of Justice, 'helping to shape the fledgling nation'. He says he feels a sense of duty to the past, to people like his father who gave their lives, their life's work, to make the country a better place for all the citizens of the nation. 'It's my duty,' Alby says solemnly, 'to don the green jersey and continue on with what the early idealists of the nation wanted. It is my duty to help this country by sailing it out of the troubled waters we find ourselves in today.' No interrogation as to how he initially sailed into the rocks, or why he jumped overboard. Just a platform to spout any old shite.

'I cannot abide the man. I cannot abide such nonsense,' Gran says, turning the TV off.

Gran has never been political. Never with a bad word to say about anybody. So Neil's intrigued to hear her views, get a peek behind the normally dignified, calm exterior. Draw out some more lines for the license-fee payers. Delve deeper into her character. What kind of character would he be in *Fair City*? Neilo, for sure. A Northside bad boy with an eye for the ladies. But with a Gaeity School of Acting Southside version of his Northside accent.

'Oh,' she says, in response to his questions, a new, normal smile restoring the warmth of her face. 'Don't pay any attention to me, dear. I'm old. Like your grandfather, I have old views.'

He's disappointed the show won't get a climax. He is wired.

But something propels her on. 'The views of an old republican's daughter are views, dear, I'm afraid, which have been tainted by the reality of the country and men like him.' She nods to the blank television. He thinks a flash of jealousy shades her words. Her father, by what Neil can tell, has been written out of history. The reels, if they existed, surely would change that.

Her chair slides over the carpet and, as usual, he helps her up. She applies more weight than he's used to.

'Wait there, dear. I'll get your next instalment.' She whispers the words, 'next instalment', and, just as she's out the door, says, 'and you can make your own mind up about such things'.

His mind is already made up. The never-ending sentences and rambling reminiscences of his great-grandfather's chapters are so foreign to him it's like they're reporting on a different country – in a different language. The words, the voice are nothing like Neil's. Neil's have morphed into something more global after the last one hundred years of MTV, YouTube, cinema and football commentary. Harry's voice is Irish. Old Irish. Too parochial, too open. Not one Neil can really embrace, hear himself in. Neil is more than Irish. He's a citizen of the world now. Like with Irish television, he doesn't see himself represented in his great-grandfather's pages. He feels nothing for the reports, other than whether or not they're what his grandfather promised him. And how much they could be worth. And how many chapters are left until he can get his hands on them. Or even if the reels themselves are to be found.

He watches her slip behind the old door into the hall before he works up to the scene's climax: 'Are there many left, Gran?'

She's shuffling away to the stairlift.

'A few.'

'How many?'

'You'll find out in good time.' She has read the script. Leave them wanting more.

As the stairlift begins to whirr, Neil sets up the cliffhanger.

'Have you got the actual reels?'

'No one has, dear. They were destroyed in a fire.'

And the drums kick in and the fiddle plays and the credits roll down over Neil's wired face, his wistful stare reflecting back through the dark TV screen, a flashback of that black-and-white fire flickering as Neil's reaching in, like the hero he isn't, and rescuing the reels from obscurity.

Harry Casey - F Company, 2nd Battalion #3

Negative thoughts begin to muster – The first casualty of the rising – A haphazard march – Davy shows his true colours.

Under orders from Captain Houlihan, and having been inspected and offered strong, reassuring words of encouragement by Connolly, we proceeded back to Fairview. I was light of hand, heavy of heart. In the basement of the GPO, among the cabbage and first-aid equipment, I had hidden it. A piece of cloth and the shadows were its camouflage. One could see there were ammunition boxes also in the shadows, about 12" x 6" x 9" in size. Some had been emptied already. I was able to convince my OC to let me bring back with us to Fairview one box (extra ammunition is always sought-after), along with my bicycle. One may deplore the shamefacedness of my actions, but my mind was set, there was nothing else for it. The stand, once detached, made my cargo, and of course, motivations, less conspicuous.

Davy, unfortunately, was not there to see me off. He had managed to gather up his new republican peelers, and had led them, marching, their new guns heavy in their hands, beyond the road. A spirit of unruliness swept over the area like the mad gas we had heard about in Ypres: the rumbling of the lorries and the crates crashing down on the cobbles outside headquarters, the windows of many a business being decimated by urchins, and donkey carts being backed up and parked outside haberdashers, shoe shops and sweet shops to be filled. It seemed the very people we were out for, the ones hiding beyond the pretty façades of Sackville Street, were intent on having the gorge of their lives.

As we strode away from the chaos, I smiled. If this was our new republic, at least everyone, including those not out to fight on Sackville Street, was commandeering their own piece of it.

If a spirit of unruliness and bonhomie was what we left behind on Sackville Street, from my outpost duty on Fairview Corner some hours later, I could not help but note how this spirit was conspicuously absent in the revellers returning from the seaside. It was rather pitiful to see the number of parents with young children trying to find their ways home without any conveyances. The trams had all stopped running, and every face I bade good evening to, appeared, despite the good weather, tired, footsore and, in some cases, bewildered.

The next few hours were spent holding up all cars to make sure they contained no British military, and inspecting pedestrians. As the day faded away over the rooftops and darkness descended, a queer feeling came upon me. The day itself had been incredible, most favourable for my ends, the box nestled beside the wall behind me being proof. But, the pained faces of the men and women returning from the beach, the bemused looks they gave me as I waved them on, as if they were thinking, 'Who died and made you king?' troubled me. Not to mention the scuffles I'd glimpsed while wheeling my bicycle away from Sackville Street. Davy was in the thick of things, clawing and scuffing ruffians, claiming peace amidst the violence. How ironic that we should be the instigators of peace amidst the violence! In my heart, on that first night, doubts began to arise and tug at me like a child at the hem of her mother's skirt. They were new, and disquieting.

The late Paddy Mac Tuile, who was librarian in Charleville Mall Library and a well-known Gaelic Leaguer, brought me out some beef tea and sandwiches about midnight from his home in Cadogan. I was warmed by his generosity, and more than happy of the company when he began to talk of the day's events.

'It's a grand thing yis are doing, God bless yis,' said Paddy, blowing coolly on his cup.

'Is it?' said I, in the midst of my interior monologue of revolutionary doubt, wrestling with the idea of the republic being tarnished by the unfolding reality.

''Tis. It sure is. I'd be out here with yis myself, only me poor mother is inside in bed. Destroyed she is. I've a duty to her as much as to the people of this poor country.'

'You're right,' I said, becoming tired as the warmth of the tea took hold. 'I'm sure your mother is thankful for your intervention on her behalf. But us, me, Paddy. Did you ever see the likes of the looks of scorn on the faces of those that walked by here only a few hours ago?'

'Indeed and I did,' he said solemnly.

'Not them on Sackville Street jeering us, Pearse, as he read out their declaration, ye didn't. What I mean to say, Paddy.' I stopped and took a bite of the stale bread he'd brought out, the good Limerick bacon of Shaws hidden between it.

'Go on,' he said.

'Ah,' I moaned, 'I'm tired Paddy, is all. I've been standing here too long looking at the faces we've gone out for. And ye know what? They don't seem to be none too appreciative. The republic is for them, for all of us, for my mother, my sister, our families, their families. But tonight, I don't know, there's just a great stir of thoughts going on in my heart. Maybe we should've asked them if they wanted this republic. If they really wanted this to happen. It's for them, for everyone, after all.'

Paddy clasped my shoulder. 'A present such as is sometimes given, can never be known to bring joy until it is unwrapped. I believe in the goodness of what you're doing. And any man that worries the likes you are doing now Harry, is a man I believe will do this country proud.'

His earnest words soothed me briefly, however my doubts were yet to be fully appeased. And so I informed him of my undertaking with my cinemachine, and my hopes of documenting our proud rebirth as a nation. I told him of the hope I had for the images I was to capture. How they might be used as a beacon for our nation to shine proudly around the world, but how they seemed to be developing into a spotlight uncovering our deficiencies. My unease with such revelations was weighing heavily on my mind.

Hardly had I finished my lamentations when he said, 'My mother is an avid reader, and she has a book I browsed through only a few days ago. It was about a head. A severed head found in a bog in 1912. Preserved. For centuries, they think. Out near Easky in Sligo. And the head, oh the head, such a fuss was made about it you'd never guess. Why? Because it was preserved. The skin may have gone dull and waxy brown, but haven't historians and archaeologists fallen into a reverie over it. Why? Well, it was simply able to tell the story of the past by dwelling, untouched, until its present faded and it could speak without fear, to the future. Now, isn't that something?'

His short tale left me dumbfounded until he appended it with his concluding remark: 'I can offer you such a gift. Distance and time for your treasure to develop into something of worth, like the head. If you so wish. I have such a place.'

At first, I paid no heed to his offer, seeing no need for such precaution, but then, as events unfolded over the coming days, a remembrance of his plan roused my interest. Paddy, I was not to know that night, with his talk of bogs and heads, planted an idea that would bloom and become the saviour of the reels. A marsh, however, at 2 PM, was to be our intended preservation capsule, not a bog.

We shook on his promise, and his reassurances of help should I need it, and he bade me good night in order to return to his mother. The warmth of the tea faded, and the night drew on: slow, dark, cold. I was relieved about 3 AM and slept, my bicycle outside on the pavement, my box of 'ammunition' under my arm, in the corner of the Dublin Manure Company offices, on a bed of coats. About six o'clock Tuesday morning, after only three hours of rest, myself and the two brothers McGinley were directed to blow up the railway line beyond the sloblands. None of us knew anything about gelignite, but it mattered little. OC Poole got down on his hunkers in the grey morning light and demonstrated exactly how it should be done. (Why he didn't do it himself was beyond me).

We were told it was a three-minute fuse, so after we had placed the gelignite in a small hole under the tracks, we didn't think there was any need to run. We were only about twenty bloody yards away when the thing knocked us off our feet and sent me down an embankment, where I muffed some blasted barbed wire and tore my thigh badly. I squinted through the pain and the now softly falling drizzle and observed that the tracks were still intact. I was not.

Blood had already darkened my trousers when I hobbled through the door of the Manure Company offices. I asked OC Poole if I could go home and get another pair of trousers and attend the cut in my leg. Out to the devil with him, he raised his chin to an angle and he closed his eyes and refused. I held my tongue, nodded to him, and simply took my ammunition box from the corner of the room, placed it in the basket of my bicycle and wheeled down the road to see my company OC, Frank Houlihan, who was holding a house over Gilbey's at the corner of Fairview Strand. I had made up my mind that I was going to get treatment (and empty my Pathé and get the three magazines under my bed) at home; it was only three-hundred-odd yards distant!

Frank, fair play to him, saw that there was nothing else for it but for me to go home. Since I was going to Clonliffe Avenue by Clonliffe Road and by Richmond Road, Frank requested that I collect arms and equipment on my way back, from men who had failed to turn out. He offered me a bag to carry the load, whereupon I held up my ammunition box and said, 'This will do the trick, thanks, Frank.'

'What do you have in it, anyhow? It looks quite heavy already,' said he. He screwed up his face as he thrust his eyes into mine in a most unfavourable manner. 'I thought it was ammunition you were taking from Sackville Street.'

A hot flush invaded my forehead. For a moment, I was stood silent, my tongue glued to the top of my mouth in search of an appropriate response.

'My mother,' said I, fixing him with a steady eye. 'I was in getting her messages when I came across the commotion in Sackville Street. I feel silly about it sir, but I'd rather not lose them since I'm so close to home.'

When I got home, the fan light above the door was casting a homely, golden hue in a long rectangle over the worn tiles in the hall. At the instant the door closed behind me, her voice called from the pantry. Mother. She called for Eimer, thinking me away and fighting for Ireland.

Her voice made my heart palpitate for a moment. I think I longed to hear it, dwell near it and be home, think of nothing, only being home. However much I wanted to believe it was a normal Tuesday, I could not ignore the errancy of my thoughts. The decision was mine. We were at war.

I called back that it was me, and that I had only returned for a moment. I didn't wish her to see the state of my leg, nor the blood-covered trousers, and saw there was nothing else for it but to leave her be and go on up with my ammunition box to my room.

The room, through the lace curtain over my bed, was suffused with dusky, tawny light. My nostrils sucked in the familiar smell of dusty cretonne. I thought of the Imperial and the *clippidy-clop* of the Lancers' horses and the whip-crack of Davy's gun. The smell there was so foreign, strange and unexpected. It smelled of death. And the cretonne, the dust, the slight damp in my room smelled of home, and life.

Once in the room, I applied myself to taking out the used magazine with the pictures of Pearse and the GPO and the Lancers and Davy. With a thick bed sheet over me like an Arctic explorer sheltering from a storm, I bent myself to my Pathé and used the dim light to do the change and load one of the three empty magazines I had stashed under my bed. I covenanted with myself to endure the adventure and only return to the house when all three magazines were full to the brim with pictures to share with the world! The used magazine, safely ensconced in its silver container, was hid neatly in a drawer, and the other two magazines, still in their silver arks, I taped together and put back into my wooden ammunition crate, alongside my re-loaded Pathé Kok.

Only once I had finished reloading my Pathé did I become acquainted again with the searing pain in my leg. I rose to my feet with spit whistling through my clenched teeth, and rooted for new trousers and some ointment to administer to the wound. A little hand mirror used to hang above the washstand, and it was there, for a brief moment, that I caught sight of a scared, shivering wreck of a boy. Such a sight put the wind up me and drained me of all my fighting-talk bravado.

The stairs creaked only two steps from the bottom.

'Harry dear,' mother called, and I made a dash for the front door.

Perhaps it was the fear of seeing her while in the middle of fighting, or her seeing something in me that betrayed my resolution to take part in the fight, but I didn't wish for our eyes to meet. They are a window to the soul some say, and if anyone could read them, my mother could. I was afeard of what she would see. I was only a man, a young man after all, and what with the doubts about motives, the faces of the passers-by still leering at me, the cut in my leg stinging me, Davy's face after his shot still haunting me, I was a maelstrom of conflicting emotions. The only one I could hold tight to was the determination to capture on my cinemachine whatever was to unravel over the coming days. And it was with this determination that I held fast to my wooden box, turned the latch in the door and refused to turn to wish my mother well.

On returning to Captain Houlihan with my new load and his abandoned arms, we received orders to fall in. We took with us all of our spare ammunition, equipment and food. We were paraded outside Gilbey's on Fairview Strand, at which point Frank, on regarding me from a distance, took it upon himself to inspect me more closely. He strode over and shook his head.

'What's with the bicycle, Casey?' said he.

'It's for my load sir.'

I displayed to him as best I could how I had fastened my box holding the Pathé cinemachine and two spare magazines to the front carrier of the bicycle.

'You can't wheel your equipment down Sackville Street,' said Frank, with a distasteful grimace.

There were titters of disbelief from the others.

'But my leg, sir,' I said, playing the fool and the wounded hero, 'is badly gashed. I cannot put much weight on it. It's my crutch. Just for the walk, if you please.'

He tutted with great displeasure, and puckered his lips. I needed the bicycle to take the weight of the Pathé and the extra magazines. Not to mention my pistol and ammunition for the fight, should it come.

'I'm afraid you'll have to do without. This is a war. Bicycles must be left behind.'

'That is most unfortunate, sir. If that is to be the case I have no choice, but to stay behind also. As you said to me earlier, I am the first casualty of the war. Well then, so be it. I will be your first casualty.'

His face, fleshy and pallid, touched with a warmth in the eyes, turned dark. He opened his mouth to admonish me, before I said, 'I'll bring it as far as the Pillar. Further than this it won't be possible to go. No one need see, sir. I could very well be a scout.'

'As far as the Pillar,' said Frank quickly, still not convinced. 'I'll be damned if I'm the captain seen wheeling a bloody bicycle into war!'

A look of perplexity creased his brow. Those within earshot shook with mirth at my strange request, and a weak ripple of laughter broke out amongst the group. But it mattered not. I had secured my luggage for the trip.

The first twenty-four hours had been a discordant hodgepodge of commands, counter-commands and off-the-cuff actions. This march was no different. The men under Poole from the Manure Company's offices joined in with us at the corner of Poplar Row and Ballybough Road. Their addition to the ranks must have increased the competition, as before we got half way along Ballybough Road, the pace had become terrific. Competitive. Our unit, and Poole's by extension, did not present a very soldierly appearance as we were greatly loaded, and we commenced to struggle. I, of course, ambled along gleefully, always watching, spying a chance, if it should come, to split from the group and capture a moment of war.

We were becoming increasingly anxious with the unfavourable rumours of troops closing in on us from the Howth Road, when we halted to facilitate Frank Houlihan's blathering with a woman on the footpath. Our ragged group took on a somewhat foolish appearance with this abrupt stop. Men began to grumble impatiently and gather into knots. Nevertheless, the woman proceeded to address Frank and, in good time, he saluted her and came back with new information pertaining to Lancers taking up positions in North Great George's Street, on the very route which he had planned for us. Only for getting the information from the woman we would certainly have been caught in an exposed position and undoubtedly would have suffered some casualties!

Her remarks changed our route, whereupon Frank gave us 'Quick march', and proceeded down Parnell Street, thence up Cumberland Street, again into Marlboro Street, along Marlboro Street and up Sackville Place where, at the cusp of the road, there stood an improvised barricade at the junction to Sackville Street.

Frank Houlihan raised his arms and called my name.

'Casey,' said he, searching for me at the back of the group, 'say cheerio to the bicycle. You can hobble across the street now.'

'Right you are, sir,' said I, a nod and a wink to reassure him I was satisfied.

Had he not given me the heads up, I would have separated with the bicycle regardless. I was eager to capture the ordinary folk of Dublin amongst my pictures, and up ahead, at the barricade and beyond, at the shopfronts and stores, was a great gathering of my fellow Dubliners, eager, again it seemed, for their gorge!

A great commotion was beginning to blow on Sackville Street as a cacophony of whizzing, cracking and popping charged the skies.

Again, the sound of windows smashing and the cheers of the mob filled the streets. I became excited almost, hastily extracting my Pathé from the wooden case and looking furtively, so as not to warrant any undue attention, for a spot to lean and begin cranking.

Heretofore I had not considered the weather. In the morning, drizzle had beat pitilessly on us at the sloblands, and on my return from my house too. I was pleased to see, once a suitable pitch was found to capture the crowds on Sackville Place and at the barricades, that I did not have to worry about rain immediately. The skies in the distance, however, were grey and fat with a stormy promise.

In their haste to join the men at the GPO, no one had taken any notice of my brief desertion. It would be brief. I was particularly strong on that point! A few cranks, some yards of pictures, and I would be standing beside them once more. They marched through a gap in the barricade in single file, and then disappeared into the background of my lens. For it was through my viewfinder that I regarded their movements, as I had set myself up, devoid of my stand, on a somewhat slippy, yet sturdy errant wooden barrel.

My settings, once adjusted to take into account the change in light since the last time of shooting, were suitable for cranking. It's like riding a bicycle. For a moment only I monitored the speed of my turn, just to be certain I was correct. Then I concentrated on the composition before me.

A thrill of excitement shook me once more. Although I could not hear it amidst the noise of the mob, with their unashamed looting of the buildings, I could still feel the magazine whirring beautifully through the lever. I dwelt on shopfronts, urchins and shawlies entering premises unburdened by material goods, and emerging with broad smiles and even broader loads. This, not just Pearse and his proclamation, the men at the window of the GPO, the Lancers charging, this was our insurrection. Their revolution. Our new republic!

A familiar voice appeared from out of shot.

'Let out and go away. Let out at once,' it called. I wished to see if it was who I thought it was, yet I wanted not to shake the picture with a quick turn, so I panned slowly from the shopfronts on my right, back to my left, to the barricade.

Being a good fifteen yards from the barricade, I was perfectly situated to capture the subject of the disorder: a dishevelled man stooped and gripping the shafts of a cart lodged near the centre of the barricade. He was perfectly in place, taking up nearly the height of the frame. A figure came from stage left and entered into my view, a yards, two yards at most from the man gripping the cart. The man with the cart had the butt of a cigarette wedged into the corner of his mouth. He lifted his chin, and, still holding the cart, stood erect and moved closer to the new arrival. Since they were standing still, I was able, once I had stopped panning, to look closely on the aggressor. Indeed, it was Davy.

Davy gesticulated wildly, giving orders again about letting out and going away. The man with the cigarette did not attend to them, and instead began to draw the cart out of the barricade once more. The din of the mob subsided, everything was perfectly silent while my steady up-and-down grinding purred peacefully before me.

'He's the owner of that there lorry, mister,' called a voice from out of shot.

This street performance had brought the shenanigans around us to a standstill. The man, chin still lifted defiantly, stared hard at Davy, and, all the while not moving his eyes off of him, slowly drew his cart away from the barricade, towards the path.

'We, the Volunteers of the new Irish Republic, have commandeered your cart. It is a vital part in the barricade which will help us repel the English advance, and thus, reclaim our sovereignty.'

Davy's words halted the man before he exited the shot and saved me having to pan. Davy, almost as if prompted by a director, stepped into the centre of the screen. The barricade, brown and dull as the street it rested on, was the backdrop. On I whirred. I edged a smidgen right.

'You'll quit this now,' continued Davy, 'or you are a dead man.'

A whisper warmed my ears with, 'He has some nerve.' But it mattered not, as I was concentrating on the players, not their lines.

'Go before I count to four.'

I held my nerve and remained focused. The man stood still as a lamp, the butt of the cigarette clinging to his lip, his head defiantly erect.

'One.'

A seagull squawked.

'Two.'

A window smashed some distance away.

'Three.'

Two revolutions of the lever made up each of Davy's seconds.

'Four.'

The man moved to the right, away from the barricade, his grip on the cart not slackening a jot.

Accustomed as I had become to the sound of gunfire, especially since Davy had opened up on the Lancers, I was nevertheless shocked and repulsed when his hand rose to the poor man's temple, and two further strokes of the lever later, his revolver fired with a deafening, ferocious devil's whip-crack. I did not flinch. Nor did I halt or lessen my turning. Steady as you like.

The force of the shot propelled the poor man's head to the most unnatural of angles, and with a pitiful last half step, his hands still gripped to his cart, he fell in atop it, and then slumped and sagged like a sack of spuds out of it to the ground. Being fifteen yards away, his whole body, even on the ground, remained in shot, and Davy, perhaps shocked at his own violent act, stood over him peering down at the deed done. Perhaps he thought himself wronged somehow, perhaps he thought our fight had been lessened; whatever his thoughts, he kept them to himself, leaving me perplexed. When he looked up from the lump, his eyes large with an unknown menace, he did not address a word to us, the witnesses. He merely scanned the vista before him. No one dared speak, dared breathe, yet on I whirred. Devoid of thoughts, conscience, condonation. Simply a painter surveying a scene.

'Let that be a warning,' he said finally. 'Don't trifle with us.'

His voice was all I recognised.

It was only as the last word left his lips that he spotted me amidst the crowd, crouched and hidden behind the black-leather camouflage of the Pathé. Strange to relate, I don't think he knew what to say, for he opened his mouth as if to greet me, but instead appeared momentarily shocked, eyes wide, worried by his portentous revelation of what I was after capturing on film. Then he scowled, lifted his revolver, took aim in my direction and began to stride towards me. A new mask turned him into a fiend I had never before known.

'I'll be needing that there film, Har,' he said, on arriving at the barrel where I was standing. Manners deserted him, and he grabbed at it without asking. On I whirred. He was, despite his gun's nasty black hole eyeballing me and insisting otherwise, still my friend.

'I'll be having the footage, Har,' he said again, this time talking through gritted teeth. 'Let's not make a scene.'

I quit my grinding and turned the knob. I thought it only right to stand up to him, chest to chest, and reason.

'Davy, for God's sake man, put the gun down.'

'I'll not tell you again, Har.'

'What'll ye do?' whispered I, moving in close, so as not to let the bystanders hear. 'You thinking of shooting your best friend?'

His face, the tightened jaw, the lifted chin, the wide-eyed, glazed-over stare, spoke volumes, and made me go a little weak at the knees. He didn't need to say anything. Nor was he given the chance, for Captain Houlihan sidled up beside us and barked, 'What in the name of blazes are you two eejits playing at? Get through that barricade and into headquarters at once.'

Davy didn't stir.

Frank edged between us, his back to me, his forehead touching Davy's.

'You heard me. Move.'

Still Davy stared. The crowd began to whisper. Gossip.

'Last chance, now. Quit this, I'm telling you, or you're going home.'

Davy finally relented. Though he may have relaxed his stance and, on Frank's prompting, turned away from me, his eyes lingered, their message still echoing. Frank walked closely behind Davy, expecting me to follow. I did. Just not directly.

I used a few more feet of film to capture that terrible composition: the cart Davy had killed for, at a severe angle by the side of the road, a dark pool gathered beside the poor unfortunate lying lifeless by the wheel. The scene was over. My greatest friend Davy's latest cameo in our brave fight for freedom had taken up about 150 feet of film.

The Permanent Ink of Google

A Celtic design, lines between lines, like a maze, with his grandad's name, Tomás, in decorative Celtic writing chiselled into it. His first was his mother's. At sixteen, not quite nervous, but not totally sure, on edge, he had entered into a tattoo parlour in Temple Bar and had her name, Fiona (the utterance seemed already unfamiliar), etched in ink on his left bicep. A dark, Gaelic font reminding him of her. Even then, he was capable of realising that the pain was fading. But the ink of her name would be permanent.

This is his third tattoo. He is in the zone. A daze of thoughts blocking out the staccato prickling, the intense drilling of the skin, the lift of the needle, a brief pause, the wiping away of ink, clearing of the canvas. The seeping in of the ink, reverse-drilling for oil. Extraction, that's the word. Insertion. All skin sheds, but this remains. The stamping of his grandfather's name into his very being. The Celtic design, the name, *as Gaeilge*, how he would be best represented. He had a soft spot for such things.

Neil thinks of the queue in the college for the *Book of Kells*. The American tourists, the drizzle starting just as they got inside the building. Into the ark. Dimly lit reverence. Being underwhelmed, but aware of the object's importance. The glass case opened on a softly washed early page, what looked like the viaduct from his home town, drawn in weak but stubborn ink. Seven arches and a large top like he'd seen earlier at the building his grandad had brought him to. A character from Ireland's history, in bronze, draped over a rock in the window. His grandad had taken Neil's teenage hand and placed it on a column. A cold, rough slab of grey.

'History is the proof of action. Action translated into story. It can be as tall and proud as this here building, or it can be as minute and hidden as the bullet holes up high there. The main thing is, son, you open your eyes for it, and appreciate those who have left their stories for you to find.'

Every tattoo is a story. There's a reason for the ink. The best stories have life pouring from every letter, every stroke, shade, angle of design. Word. Words. Neil's not mad on conversation. Symbols and pictures communicate who we are now, what we have experienced. A shorthand display of identity. Thumbs up. Like. Star. Favourite. Heart. The tattoo artist before him has a lot to say. He's inked in sleeves from each hand to each shoulder. Swirling designs, images of eagles rising from flames, hearts, a child's face, a script in a foreign language. A story.

'Cool tats,' Neil says, in a break from the drilling. 'What does that say?' and he motions with his head to the inside of the artist's forearm. The artist glances down and smiles.

'*Qui tacet consentire videtur.*'

'That Italian or something?'

'Latin, man,' he smiles. 'The language of languages. It's eternal. If you're gonna get something put on your body in words, I always recommend the language that's pan-European.' He nods to Neil's inky mess in progress. 'Unless, of course, it's in Irish.'

Neil is impressed. He winces involuntarily as the buzz starts again. The slow dig. Quick wipe. Latin. The eternal language. He asks the artist if he can speak it.

'A bit. Had to, man. I went to St Columba's. It's beaten into ye there. My dad spoke it too.' He nods to his forearm again. 'It was his thing. Whoever is silent, gives consent.'

Neil's thoughts wander away from the pain, the etching of his grandad's memory. Latin. He has seen it somewhere recently. With his spare hand, he fetches his phone, opens the pictures and zooms in on the end of his great-grandfather's handwritten letter home. He holds it out to the artist.

'What does this line mean?'

The buzzing halts and the artist rolls his lips and sits back in his seat. After a beat, he sits forward again and creases his eyes at the screen. It must appear from some hidden vault of memory as he raises his latex-gloved left hand, finger to the ceiling and goes, 'Eh, something like, "Mind what you say," or, like, "Beware when you talk or who you talk to."' He laughs to himself. 'Good man, Father Carroll, ye aul prick,' he says, and ducks again into the ink.

A strange line to finish the letter. Neil reads over the lines above it. Begins to think of what he just read in chapter three. Ink is smeared off his upper arm, and the digging starts again. Insertion. A slow seeping of language. The same name appears in both: Paddy Mac Tuile. In the letter home after the rising, 'He has agreed to aid me in a matter.' And later in chapter three, when there's talk of a marsh. A marsh. At 2 PM. The line stuck out because it was so ridiculous. A time. Why mention a time? He never asked his gran about it. It just didn't seem important.

Things slow down. Time draws out. Neil tries to recall his great-grandfather's lines from chapter three. The name. He remembers it because of the half-African Gaelic player of the same name. The place. The time. The needle continues to buzz as the tip of it slips in and out like a lizard's tongue, translating into the skin. Slower and slower, the reverse drilling. Neil's digging deep. Paddy Mac Tuile, marsh, 2 PM. Saviour of the reels. But they were destroyed?

Phone still in hand, Neil flicks onto Google, taps in the name, the place, the time. Just to see. And there, down at the bottom of the page, in thick, bold ink, etched into eternity thanks to Google, under the headline 'TCD STAFF DIRECTORY FLOOD – Search family announcements – All notices – Staff . . . Results 1 - 10 of 31', is the name, and the place.

FLOOD – Death Notice, 23 May 1919

FLOOD (Dr Beatrice) (Marsh's Library, Dublin and late of Trinity College Library) Survived by her son, Padraig Mac Tuile . . .

The slow-motion beat of the needle, the distant drone as it punctures the skin, the blue, red, orange, blue, green and red tattoo banner, the keywords, the blue headline, the bold blue proof. The name and the place, rescued together, forever in the twenty-first-century permanent ink of Google.

Marsh's Library, 2 PM

He doesn't hate libraries. That's too strong a word. He is indifferent to them. They're the establishment. A pillar of a society he's no longer part of. He never feels comfortable in them. He is detached from them. Their purpose, make-up is a foreign landscape.

Each mammoth bookcase in this library is about ten, twelve feet high, with a ladder attached – and about two, three feet wide. Pictures or paintings decorate the sides of most of the bookcases facing out into the corridor. Glass cases, displaying various ancient memorabilia block off the right-hand bays. A dying culture. Fading customs. The first corridor, lined on each side with a leather-bound load, looks fairly drab. Libraries are museums in the digital age. Quaint, obsolete spaces. The silence in them, like churches, like the buildings themselves, he sees as unnecessary. The space leads to thoughts. Thoughts, invariably always lead to questions, and questions, invariably, always lead to an interrogation of his life, its direction, his happiness with it.

He prefers the white noise of modern distraction. The neat, tidy space of a touchscreen. The democratic access to information, indiscriminate in its availability. Wi-Fi is the new Carnegie.

A red rope separates the beige-carpeted corridor from each book-walled chamber on the left. Above the pictures on the side of each case, in an ornate kind of green woodcarving with sculpted white curtains, are the numbers and letters of the bays. '1 A.B', '1 D.E', '4 G.E' and so on.

'All the dark-oak cases here, they're here since seventeen hundred and one. All Irish oak. Fabulous. Fabulous, aren't they?'

Neil diverts his puzzled gaze from the numbers and letters to the old librarian standing beside him. The cliché: glasses around his neck, thick woolly jumper, vague, grey face.

'Really?' Neil says, feigning interest – distracted by his new discovery and its possibilities.

'Never been moved, not a one of them. All intact and accounted for since seventeen-o-one.' His voice is proud. 'Joyce mentions in *Ulysses* the "stagnant bays of Marsh's Library". He chuckles, 'There's none more stagnant than them there bays.'

Neil's bored. 'What's 2 PM?'

'Lunchtime,' the man replies, delighted with his prompt, mocking response. 'So, if I was you, I'd hurry along.'

A friend of a friend who worked for HMV was given two days notice. Neil never asked why. Does it matter? The day of his sacking – just for the hell of it – he got a one-terabyte hard drive and downloaded the store's whole catalogue of music from its main computer. It took twelve hours to grab everything. Five hundred and fifty gigabytes. Album upon album upon album. Every 'Now That's What I call Music'. Number one to whatever. Madness. About one hundred Beatles albums, sixty Dubliners albums, twenty Thin Lizzy. All in one phone-sized hard drive. This friend of a friend then gave it to his friend, who copied it, and gave it to his friend, who copied it, and copied it, and copied it. And somewhere down the line, Neil got a copy of a copy of a copy, and, for the hell of it, downloaded all 550 gigabytes. He shared it too. That's what people do now: share things of worth until they become worthless.

Neil will never listen to *Now That's What I Call Music 1*. Or *2*, or *3*. He will probably never listen to fifty-eight of the sixty Dubliners albums. Scratch that. He won't listen to any of them. But he knows they are there, in his own private library of music, in a tiny digital box, stashed under his bed. Beyond restrictions. Worth thousands, thousands in actual physical CDs. Neil looks forward to the day books go the same way. The borders open. So lads like this tool, with his patronising, pseudo-intellectual bullshit, become obsolete.

'There's not much to hurry for.'

'Oh, but there's more.' The librarian points ahead to the end of the library. 'This is – this part here is only the half of it. Through the old reading room up ahead is the other half. You have "M", "N", "O", "P", the whole alphabet – minus "J" of course – up there, so ye do.'

To get to the second area, Neil walks through the old reading room. The whole building is like a capital "L": the short bottom right is the horizontal entrance, where Neil has come from. The angle is the old reading room. Ahead of him, somewhere in the vertical is, he hopes, a clue. Anything. Because this is the first time he's ever done anything like this. He'd love it to be worth the effort.

It's noticeably colder. 2 F.G. The red rope still goes from bay to bay, bookcase to bookcase. Still the blinds are drawn on all the windows between the cases. 2 H.I. Pictures of people in ridiculous eighteenth- and nineteenth-century dress decorate the panels at the end of each bookcase. 3 K.M. Old dark-oak seats, like pews in a church, are in the middle of each book bay in this corridor. This is the only major difference he can see from the other room. 3 L.M.

'The Baptiste Atlas of 1599 is stored here.'

The librarian is standing behind him. 'Although, I'm afraid you won't find it up there.'

Neil returns from his discreet search for 2 PM, exasperated at being followed.

'It's there.' Neil doesn't follow where the man points.

'Really? Wow.'

'Mmhh. We have some massive, massive books here. Some, invaluable. Not even on display. Of course, we keep many of them downstairs in the old living quarters, where the deputy keeper once lived.'

'Really?'

Neil remains semi-interested, vague, but preoccupied. His mind's racing. The librarian waffles on. Neil wants to shut him up.

'Of course you wouldn't be able to see that today, what with us closing now at two for lunch.' He laughs and points at his watch before nodding to the bay number hidden behind an exit sign.

It's the small bay beside the window, back from where he came. Red barrier rope cuts it off from them. A metal ladder is at an angle in the bay. The wooden pew is empty. Neil strolls over, undecided. He peers into the bay, all too aware of how ridiculous this is. He thinks of *Indiana Jones, Jason Bourne*, and almost cringes. This is lame. But something makes him check. Why not? '2 P.M.' at the top of the outside panel between bays is an ornate shaped design. But it's too open. There's nothing behind it. No space up there.

'How often do you take the books off the shelves?' Neil asks.

'Not very.'

'So, like, never?'

'Oh no. We would. Maintenance.'

'And what about this 2 PM? How come it's out of sequence?'

The man smiles, pleased with Neil's interest. 'Very good spot. An idiosyncrasy we think, from 1882, when . . . '

The books, behind the books, the bookshelves aren't an option then. At his feet there's a square panel between the shelves on each side. Must be about two, three feet wide. The shelves only start about three feet above the floor, as there's a space for your legs if you're sitting on the pew and facing into the bookshelf. But if he stands back, at an angle, he can see that the wood where you put your feet, between the bays, is wide. There's space for something in there. A space large enough to hold 400-foot film reels. He has Googled their size. They're chunky things not easily stashed.

'I can see you're interested,' the man says. 'Alas, another day perhaps?'

A Quick Detour Home

They sit opposite one another on the couch beside the old Welmar upright piano with the dead keys. Formal and stiff. They're not in the breakfast room, since the home help is in there. Neil's not due until Friday. The television, their usual point of reference, is missing, and there's a strained, self-conscious silence because of it. The wallpaper in the room is a weird two-tone silver paisley design, the carpet a trippy Jackson Pollock splash of grey and black.

Neil picks up the slack from his last question. 'That's the way things are now, Gran. I don't read much anymore, myself. Anything I want's on Google, and I just read it there or on Wikipedia.'

'What are they?'

'Eh, things, portals I suppose, to get you quickly to what you want to know.'

'But is the fun not in the journey?'

'Journeys are hard work. Information is easy. There are no journeys anymore with the Internet. You pick a word, an idea, and you put it in and there it is, fully explained.'

'Sounds terrible.'

'But it saves so much time.'

'For what?'

'FIFA.'

She doesn't bother asking. She knows he is teasing her.

'But you liked to read, though, gran, didn't you, when you were younger?'

'I did.'

'And grandad did, too, didn't he?'

'He did.' She smiles warmly at the thought.

'Did you or grandad ever visit libraries?'

The question puzzles her, makes her look into space.

'What's that, dear?'

'Libraries. Did you or grandad ever go to them?'

She dwells on the sentence, her hands massaging her lap. She smiles, embarrassed.

'I did of course. He would have too. But not together. I don't think we did. But your grandfather loved to read. Loved to read.' Her head dips into a memory of the man for a moment before she whispers, 'Loved to read.'

Neil lets the silence settle again. He is not in a rush, or wired or hung-over. For once there is no paranoia. He is actually ready to talk, chat. Ask questions. Listen to answers.

'I never liked libraries myself.'

'Oh, you should be ashamed of yourself,' she chides, smiling as she does, easing back into the couch. 'You should enjoy libraries for what they are, dear.'

'And what's that?'

'A bastion of ideas.' Her sentence elicits a sense of pride in its utterance. 'A place for words and contemplation. For silence. I really thought you liked to read.'

He wonders if she really knows him. If she ever could. He has known the woman before him all his life. Lived with her – and Pappy – for four years. For four years, he spent every day in their company, her company, after his mother's death. And yet, he still doesn't understand her. Love. He undoubtedly loves her, it's just that the distance in years makes any real, meaningful relationship, any understanding of world views impossible. And he knows she must feel the same too. As much as she thinks she does, she doesn't know him. She's not naïve. She must realise this. It must be a strange sensation for her also. Can she trust him? Rely on him? Depend on him? She can't know the answers, when he doesn't even know them himself.

'You do like to read my father's chapters, though, don't you?'

'I like reading them for you.'

'Oh.'

His honesty makes her retreat into herself. He has to bring her out again.

'Did you or Grandad, did you ever think the reels might still be around? Like, hidden somewhere? Did you ever check?'

He thinks she smiles as if she's about to break some bad news. 'There was nowhere to check, dear. They were destroyed.'

'But did you not read the Latin in his letter? Did Grandad not read it?'

'He did, dear. And it relates to his friend. You'll see later.'

'Why? What happens?' Neil wants to know, because for once, Google has no answers – not about Harry Casey. Nothing. It's like the twenty-first century refuses to acknowledge him.

'If I tell you now, you won't call anymore for the other chapters.'

The couch creaks as she shifts. A car whooshes by outside. There's a lot Neil could say, maybe should say. There'll be other times, other opportunities. He'll keep his thoughts to himself, for now.

Guilt

Neil and Kathy discovered the Iveagh Gardens on a fresh, sunny March afternoon two and a half years ago. The closeness of their embrace covered them like a cape. They were the only people on earth, and they were explorers in a new corner of the city, a new world.

They had gone for breakfast on Dame Street in an old, run-down café, were you could buy two-day-old lasagne and dried pasta, burnt sausages and undercooked bacon. They ate with the air of children discovering the wonders of such food for the first time. A joyful, pleasant, new time. One of their first mornings together. Each found everything the other did – every smile, comment, slurp of tea, habit of eating – a revelation. Something new to discover. Afterwards, satisfied and bloated, they strolled to the Iveagh Gardens. Everything was bright and glowing and anything was possible.

The wood pigeons' hollow call was their soundtrack. He wonders, hopes, Kathy remembers the time they sat there and she asked about his mother. Not for the content of the conversation or the reminder of his debt of gratitude to his grandparents, but for the feeling he had, and he hoped Kathy had, of a closeness blooming in its aftermath.

He told her his mother was dead. How she was only sick one minute, and the next, she was home from work when he came in from school. At first his mother idled impatiently around the house, cleaning up after him but then she was in bed calling down to the hall when he came in. He told Kathy how his gran and granddad started staying with them when things deteriorated, and then his mother was in a hospice, and then she was gone, and the house was so empty, so quiet, so lonely.

Kathy's warmth when he told her his tale, her hands on his neck, soothed him. He rarely, if ever, spoke about his mother. He lived in the present, always looking forward.

'That is so sad. I'm so sorry,' she whispered.

'It's OK,' he said, because it was. He had learned to remember the time as if someone else had lived through it.

'So did you go live with your dad?'

Her interest in his past was both disconcerting and comforting. To have someone ask about his history, make him vocalise it, create it, was a new experience.

'No I didn't,' he laughed, 'didn't even know him. Still don't. The house was rented so I was out after two weeks. Gone. Pack up, get out. My gran and grandad took me – all the way out to Raheny. I stayed in my old school, though. Travelled in and out on the train every day. Stayed with them for four years 'til I was nineteen. They were cool. Let me be. I didn't go too mad, I suppose. But, I dunno, I was hungover, in bits one day, I just let rip, said something stupid like, "You're not my ma, ye can't do anything about it." They were crushed by it. My gran especially. Straight away like, I regretted it. I felt so guilty. Still do. After all they'd done. And they were old then. Like, really just trying their best. They shouldn't have had to put up with a waster like me. They deserved better. So I moved out. It was best for everyone. Coly and Dee were friends from home and that was that.'

Water trickled down the statue with the raised hands beside them. Kathy leaned in and kissed him with a tenderness he had never felt before. Their foreheads touched lightly when they stopped. Wood pigeons cooed in the trees. A silence embraced him and he knew love was the feeling growing around them. And this was somewhere he wanted to stay.

The Weight of the Past

2 P.M. was still red-roped off, the old ladder still at an angle between the pew and the top shelf. Before ducking in, he looked over his shoulder, at the winding, screw-like stairs with the 'Staff Only' sign over it, listened carefully for steps – heard none, opened his gym bag, took out a Philips screwdriver and then went for it.

Old, dusty cardboard boxes with long-forgotten pamphlets. He shoulders them out from under the table. Once the boxes are moved, they become cover for anyone climbing up from the basement. He has managed to avoid prying eyes so far. The trick was entering with a group. Three round-bellied Americans labouring up the steps were his perfect disguise. He was just a palm holding €2.50 and then he disappeared.

Footsteps, high heels sound on the metal stairs. They get louder. Closer. Neil goes rigid. Takes up a foetal position in the space for legs – if you are sitting in the bay – under the bookshelf. The footsteps clatter on the metal and then pound on the carpet. The stair-climber takes a few carpeted steps away from the stairs – towards him – and stops.

The darkness is heavy with dust. Neil's nose twitches.

A sigh breaks the drone in Neil's ears. A tut, and the footsteps *tack-tack* away, down the corridor to the old reading room.

Neil scratches his nose, eases back a few inches from the panels, lets some of the cream light filter in from the pulled blinds over the window in the middle of the bay.

No movement from the panel when pushed. He knocks it. Sounds hollow. He feels around the edges, checks for any ledge, chance of a ledge. He can't see a thing. Speckled darkness. What is he doing? Mining. For what? Gold.

A bell rings. The old reading room's door opens.

Neil grips a sliver, a centimetre at most, of wood whispering out from where it was eased in. He keeps a finger on it so it's not lost, before going rigid again as two sets of steps, one marked by the *clickety-click* of heels – accompanied by trousers swishing and mumbles – move through the corridor. They stop outside his bay.

'There, you see.'

Air through a nose.

'I'll shift them when I get a chance.' The old man from the other day.

A long, fed-up breath.

'Make sure you do, Ciaran. This isn't the first time I've asked.'

Feet pound off the thin carpet in one direction, heels arrive at the metal steps and grow fainter as they corkscrew down. The old reading room's bell rings, the door closes and everything's quiet again.

With his finger still on the tiny ledge, he grips the screwdriver. A blind shove with the screwdriver splinters wood. He drives the screwdriver in deeper. More wood creaks. The violence of the noise excites him. He feels the panel come loose at the corner. He pulls the screwdriver away and, shifting onto his back, with one good tug, releases the corner of the panel further, and manages to pull the whole thing loose from under the bottom of the shelf.

A heavy silence. He slides back out from under the table – lets some light in – and there, glinting slightly, under a thin cover of dust, are three circular film holders, stacked flat on top of each other like a pile of massive two-euro coins.

He's on his side, propped up on his elbow, only a matter of feet away from them. His fingers reach out for the containers. Not to lift, but to touch, as if touching them where they have stayed for so long will transmute their worth, give him a clue to what his great-grandfather saw in them that made them so special.

He's hidden, between the shelves, wedged under a table, behind dusty cardboard boxes, but it only becomes real – what he's doing, why he's doing it – when he feels the canisters, stacked there secretly, waiting all this time to be disturbed, resuscitated. And it's him, of all people, who has been given the responsibility of ownership.

They're heavier than he expected. Thick, cold, mute things. More visceral than the empty images he captures on his phone for Kathy. They shift easily. Only a small film of dust is disturbed when he lifts them out. He places them into his gym bag, stretches himself straight and makes for the exit.

Our National Sport

Neil crests the steps with Enda and arrives into the blinding sunshine of the Hill just as the crescendo of 'Amhrán Na bhFiann' roars from the stands. The noise of the crowd hits him like a punch. He's preoccupied by that word. 'Punch'. Probably because Neil's expecting one soon. If not a punch, some sort of retribution. At least a wisecrack or threat of aggression for being seen with Enda, the six-foot-two lumbering mess oblivious to the stares he's been getting in his hand-me-down 1980s yellower-than-green Donegal jersey.

The only reason Neil accepted Enda's offer of a ticket – apart from the obvious – was because he presumed Enda was a Dub. He claimed he was. 'I had no other sporting attire to wear.' Enda's rag is a taunting 'fuck you' to the supposed sanctity of the Hill. Neil knows the Hill. Violence is only a stray look or careless word away from the surface. Aggression is the energy that heaves the terraces.

'Come. On. You. Boys in blue, come on you boys in blue, come on you boys, come on you boys in blue . . . '

Blue, navy. Blue, navy. Flags and hats meshing into a two-tone patchwork of Dublin identity. Stewards are insisting the steps be kept clear. No one else seems to be listening – other than Enda. But somehow they find a space a few steps down from the entrance, manage to squeeze in and it begins – the abuse.

'Ye fat fuck – get outta the way.'

'What the fuck? Gerrup to the Hogan with ye, ye culchie cunt.'

If anything kicks off, it'll be Neil's duty to protect Enda.

The murmur of the Hill, the complaints and the moans, don't sit easy with Neil. He's trying to catch each call, on alert to pre-empt any that might be about Enda's jersey. Before they met on the North Circular Road, Neil was in full GAA sentimentality mode. This is the stuff I'll miss. The sun shining, all-Ireland semi-final day. The banter. The buzz. Soak it up. Breathe it in. There's nothing like it.

Dublin score a point at the far end. An eternity away. Light travels faster than sound and the celebrations whip around the stadium in a delayed Mexican wave of noise and land in the Hill late. Neil grabs Enda's shoulder, shakes it and shouts, 'Yeeow!' Getting into the swing of things, trying to work up some excitement. There's a heave from behind and Enda drops a step and knocks a straw cowboy hat off a head in front, the cramped anonymity of the crowd suddenly broken. The aul lad's hands go to his head too late to catch the hat, and Neil sees the Indian ink of a scrawled 'Mum. Dad.' on his knuckles, punctuated by dark, irregular full stops.

'Me fuckin' hat!' the man shouts, dipping momentarily into the forest of legs. He rises empty-handed and turns to Enda. The yellow and green confuse him and his mouth, a gaping hole of rotten teeth and swollen gums surrounded by scabby white stubble, drops into an expletive, and there's extra menace in seeing that an impostor has cost him his hat. 'Yer after knockin' me hat off me head, ye scaldy prick.' And he looks to the bare blue sky and winces at the sun beating down on his uncovered crown. 'Get me me hat!' he shouts.

'Excuse me?' Enda asks, unfazed. The lull after the point doesn't last for long, with Dublin on the attack again. The crowd are already growing frustrated with Donegal's blanket defence.

'Find me hat.'

'I'm sorry,' Enda says, calm, 'but it was an accident.'

'I'll give ye an accident, ye impudent prick.'

Enda's shrug of indifference only seems to anger Indian Ink further. Neil steps in and puts a hand across Enda's chest and says, 'Leave it out and just watch the game, yeah?' Again, the explosion of noise and Indian Ink turns back to the match. Enda leans in to Neil and shouts, just as the noise deflates, 'If they bombed the Hill, Ireland's dole epidemic would be solved in a stroke.'

'Come. On. You. Boys in blue, come on you boys in blue, come on you boys, come on you boys in blue . . . '

And, again, Enda leans in. 'Can no one remember the lyrics for another song?' And Neil bites his tongue and perseveres.

Alan Brogan goes through, one on one with the keeper, and slices his shot wide. In the expectation of a goal, the Hill lurches forward. Neil's able to counter the push, hold his ground, but Enda, being Enda and devoid of grace or balance, lumbers forward and only prevents a fall by grabbing the hatless Dub in front. The hatless Dub then stumbles forward himself. He turns savagely to Enda, and, his tongue wedged tightly between his teeth, his face creased with anger, shoves Enda in the chest.

'Ye stupid prick!' he roars, his face reddening.

'Come. On. You. Boys in blue, come on you boys in blue, come on you boys, come on you boys in blue . . . '

Enda's relaxed shrug at Indian Ink further enrages him, and he shouts, 'D'ye want yer go? D'ye want yer go?' Scarves and jerseys on the periphery turn from the game. A chance trembles through the silence and the Cusack stand roars. Donegal must've gone close. Enda's trying to reason. 'Take it easy. It was an accident. Enjoy the game.' And the extra eyes on Indian Ink compound the pressure of action, and again a heave of sorts from the back and Enda stumbles chest to chest into Indian Ink, and a dig is thrown.

'Come. On. You . . . '

An 'Ooohh!' bounces around the stadium, and Enda bats the dig away, but trips on the step and falls. Neil has to jump in to stop Indian Ink from swinging a kick. A dull thump lands on the back of Neil's neck, but Neil can't turn because Indian Ink is trying to get a hold of Enda, who is sprawled out on the steps. And the tongue is between the teeth again, and 'Mum. Dad.' is like a Cluxton free kick, sailing towards him from distance.

These reels better be worth it. And it's a beautiful day, and it's great to be Irish. Breathe it in. If only our national sport was cricket. Bowls. Curling. Anything cordial and slow. Not manic and passionate, violent and aggressive. All-Ireland semi-final day. Nothing like it. All crowds mirror the sport they gather to see, or is it the sport mirroring the crowd that gathers to watch?

Insurance

Gran's alone, but secure, in her private room. Neil watches her sleeping with the usual trepidation during each slow, drawn-out, shallow breath. He turns Radio 1 on. He's glad he brought the portable radio. It means she'll be connected, tenuously, with the world outside her double-glazed hospital window. It's company of sorts – he hopes – that will fill the gap for the long stretches of time she'll find herself alone. The voices, addressing the nation, smooth and constant with their gravitas, will give her, even in sleep, the comfort of conversation. Company.

The politician is on – again – the ex-Minister for Finance, Taoiseach. Only he's not giving a political sermon or trying to persuade the listeners he'd make a great president. He's just chatting, amiably, smugly, about his life. It's an arts show, a daily magazine Neil has heard his gran listen to. They're discussing the politician's family business. The politician, Alby, laughs away the presenter's claim that he'd be too busy with business matters to take up residence in the Áras. Neil feels a dull contempt for such words, talk. Politics. Politicians. Shove it up your Áras.

'Not at all, Miriam. Not at all. In fact, eh, recently now, I've passed full control of the reins, if you will, over to my son.'

'And you, of course, followed your own father.'

'We are what our history makes us.'

They share a laugh.

'Your father did establish Ashe and Sons, did he not?'

'Guilty as charged. He did, he did. But in a different guise to what we operate today. It was a hobby hound of his from an early age.'

'Auctioneering?' The presenter laughs. A breath through her nose.

'No, no. Antiquities. Objects from the past. An appreciation for them. Auctioneering was later.'

'And how, then, did he develop a love for . . . '

Gran rubs her nose, the drip, the white dressing, the purple bruise where they broke the skin. A little snore. Neil pulls up a stiff leather seat beside her. It's been three days since her turn. He had gone to the house on Friday as usual and found the lights off, the porch door locked. Jim and Eoin both replied to him on Saturday morning, by which point Neil was too wired to go into the hospital to see her. So, tired and feeling the post-weekend blues, stiff and sore from his visit to Croke Park, he's made it to the hospital on Monday.

Neil stretches for the radio, to move the dial up to Lyric for her. There's a knock on the door. A nurse pops her head in, pleasant smile, turn in her eyebrows at Neil's discoloured eye, and then looks at Gran and whispers, 'Everything OK?'

He nods to reassure her and she leaves.

' . . . but after the War of Independence, Civil War, it seems he finally got to do what he'd always wished to do, and that was to buy them, and enjoy them in the comfort of his home. So, in a way, yes, it was his hobby too.'

The mention of the War of Independence, Civil War, stops Neil's hand above the dial. Up until recently, history has meant nothing.

Apart from being a series of events that have brought him to where he is, it has no real significance. It is so distant from his life he doesn't even recognise the echoes of its origins. The noise of the past has been swamped by the avalanche of the present, by media, images, chatter. He has no depth of knowledge for any of the things he reads, sees. At least he's self-aware enough to realise this much.

He has no true feelings for the things he passes judgment on: films, TV shows, sports, unemployment problems, the dole queue. The noise of the twenty-first century: global headlines, global problems, the riot of magazine-stand images skimmed from three-minute expert opinion on everything, everywhere, leaves him with a command of nothing, a sense of belonging nowhere. He is a cheap dweller in the shallow momentary anecdotes that scandalise the world, line by line by line. The ever-revolving present doesn't offer space for the future, never mind the past.

But Harry's images are of the past. A past that until now, never existed on a screen. That's where the world exists now. On a screen. Waiting to be judged. And these images will be original, new. In the present. And for once, Neil will know their circumstances, their origins, their worth. Neil is excited. Neil wants to know more.

'And the auctioneers then?'

'Well, Miriam, as sure as the leaves fall off the trees in winter, my father wished to maintain his interest in the field. He had a keen eye and ear for history. And, in turn, I learned to appreciate the past. As I feel we all should. Grasp our heritage, our legacy, embrace it and let it inform who we are now. I've branched the business out, moved into the twenty-first century if you will, but we remain, and my son has been given strict orders to ensure we remain, an auctioneering house, and the country's foremost one also.'

'Which brings us neatly, to your recent patronage of the . . . '

She just lifts her lips when Neil notices she's awake. A smile, of sorts. She swallows hard and blinks a few times. Neil turns the radio down, leans in to kiss her forehead. Her hand finds his and squeezes it. A connection. Love.

'It's always nice to see you again, dear.' Her voice is a silk whisper.

Fingers warm, delicate, fine. Neil keeps his bruised side to the door.

'You can't keep me away. I was tuning in the radio for you.'

'You're very good to bring it, dear. But I'd rather not listen to his nonsense.'

She moves her eyes to the voices hiding under their whispers.

The muted radio lets in the noises outside her door: a trolley rattling by, a phone ringing, the swish of someone walking. Neil looks around at the get-well-soon cards, the sweets, 7 Up, grapes. Feels the heat, sees the numerous church spires through the window.

'Were you able to bring my case?'

Neil takes the old leather briefcase from his gym bag. Gran's request was sent in a text by a nurse. He lays it on the end of her bed. Gran lifts her chin, cranes her neck and grins. Neil hands it to her and helps her undo the two straps. But he knows it won't open. He has tried. There's a rusted, robust lock in the middle.

'My purse, dear.'

He gets her purse. She takes out a short key.

'You don't need to do this every time you want to give me a chapter, Gran. I'll bring them in one by one and read them to you. It's dangerous to keep them here, don't ye think?'

There are three reels. He is only aware of the first reel's contents. If he could read all of the chapters at once, he'd have a good idea of the reels' potential worth. Rendering the reels will take time, according to Enda. There is no hope of an analogue projection. It's too risky. It will have to be a digital copy. The easiest way to determine the value of the reels for now will be to determine their content, Enda has said.

The chapters, pages, whatever, hold the key to the cash. An idea of a price. A price to tell Kathy, a figure, would make things smoother, easier.

Neil's gran shrugs slightly. 'But I like your visits. And something tells me you might be too busy to call if I don't give you a reason. My eyes are not what they were. You read so well.'

'I'll still read to you, Gran. I'll bring a new one each time. Promise.'

'I'd rather I held onto them. I appreciate the offer. But I like your visits. They are exciting, don't you think? The papers, his journey – our reading of them?'

Neil doesn't argue. She's set in her ways. She has her reasons, has her fears. She opens the satchel and roots through all the chapters he has returned, and the chapters yet to be read.

Harry Casey – F Company, 2nd Battalion #4

A brief history of my formative years – Losing my father, from which I recover with the aid of Aunt Bridey and Joe – My friend Davy – A first adventure in images described.

Some perspective at this stage of my report is required, I feel. Background, as it were, to show you how I came to be a Volunteer and how myself and Davy came to be such close chums.

Not wanting to diminish the influence of those closest to me in my formative years, I feel duty-bound to spare some moments in discussion of these very years (if not for myself, then at least for you), before I move on to Davy. My home life, my childhood, my mother, my late inspirational father, my dear father's friend, my aunt, all have a role in bringing me to this point.

But, as it shall become clear, this was all prologue. And as much as I wish it were not, the events of Easter week and thereafter will be judged to be grander in influence than the preceding twenty-six years in providing the reason for this story and the necessity to type upon this very piece of paper.

As far back as memory will permit me, the ideal of the Fenian faith was planted deeply in my soul. It was poured into my ear as a baby by my father and subsequently fostered at our fireside through tales of landlords and their methods, hanging gales and rack rents.

In a most unfortunate and unusual move, my grandfather, on dying, disinherited my father over a matter never sufficiently explained, and left his house in Clonliffe Avenue and quite a tidy sum to my Aunt Bridey. Of course, Aunt Bridey, being a spinster Catholic schoolteacher in London, was not in need of the large sum. Yet she kept it all the same.

The bitterness of being overlooked, excluded, forgotten, twisted my father's face, soured him somewhat. He would never mention it to me, for I was too young to be burdened with such family politics, but some nights, while we sat at the fire and he told us tales of the past, he would stop, as if the stories of betrayal by foreign names stirred his memory, and I could have sworn he would mouth the word 'father' as one would a curse, before shaking his head in disgust and continuing on with his tale. He bore the loss of his inheritance badly, and as a result, spent the rest of his days as a bookbinder, with a quiet, defeated dignity.

'Betrayal,' said he to me once, near the end of his life, the flames in the hearth licking the side of his face, drawing out his cheeks so that they had the appearance of being shallow, empty things. He stared deep into my eyes, with an almost pleading desperation, his hand gripping my knee, his face imploring me to take heed. 'Betrayal is the one thing the Gael is plagued by. It comes with a smiling face, son. It leaves with a smiling face. For betrayal is a friend, and that is how you will know when he strikes. His smile will linger while yours fades.' The fire crackled between us. I gave him the silence his confession deserved. 'I am not long for this world, son, and I fear the stories I have brought you up on will lead you astray. Betray you.'

Days after this warning, he lapsed into a state of depression, and he died thereafter. He had seen such corruption and degradation after the Fenian defeat of 1867 – the founding of the Invincibles, their collapse, the Parnell split and the death of the Chief – that he had become embittered. He had lost hope. Hope for the success of the fight for Irish freedom through physical force. Hope for a better life for his family. I think, God love him, he had been defeated by life a long time before his heart finally gave out. His stories were what kept him going, were all he bequeathed to me. And by going out to fight for Ireland, in some irregular way, I did what he had asked me not to, and yet, oxymoronically, I hope that with my Pathé, I would have made him proud.

In an ironic twist of fate, my Aunt Bridey, on hearing of my father's untimely passing, found it in her heart to leave London and help look after my sisters and myself – and my mother, who was struggling to keep the home together. We left our residence in North Richmond Street and took our goods with us to Clonliffe Avenue.

A number of months after we settled into Clonliffe Avenue, a friend of my father's came passing. I remember well the first time he called, for the smell of tobacco smoke drifted up the stairwell to my bedroom, alerting me to a rare masculine presence in the house. Mother called me down and there, at the foot of the staircase, bathed in the early morning sunshine of a Saturday in summer, she introduced Joe Deasy, my father's friend and sometime collaborator, premier photographer of the city!

I stood atop the stairs, silent.

'How ye son,' said Joe through the side of his mouth, his clay pipe gripped firmly between his teeth, setting his jaw ajar. He took off his cap gently and smiled up to me. 'Your father had me heart broke talking all about you. We worked together many's a time. He said you're good with yer hands, and I need a pair in my studio if you're willing to pass the time.'

I was idle, if truth be told. My mother knew it too. Ten, eleven years of age I was, fatherless, with a mother, younger sisters and now an aunt fussing over me. It was no accident that Joe came calling. He was a short yet stout man. His moustache was lighter than my father's and his chin was more pronounced. I recall being struck by the size of his ears: enormous bulbous, cauliflower things. I never grew tired of inspecting them. After some moments of wringing my hands and contemplating his peculiar ears, I nodded and agreed to his offer.

One of my keenest recollections of this day is the smile that graced my mother's face, and how a peal of laughter burst from her upon my acceptance of Joe's offer. 'Wonderful,' she said giddily, 'wonderful.'

Between himself and my Aunt Bridey, I was simply spoiled. My father had, despite his later warnings, enkindled in my young heart a strong affinity for Irish cultural matters and a desire to strike a blow for the freedom of Ireland some day. Joe and Aunt Bridey, when I opened up and gave them the chance, stoked these dual desires until they bore steam like the trains that passed over Amiens Street station. I was a voracious reader. I took in books and spat them out as if I were a linotype machine. Aunt Bridey and Joe had a job to keep up. Lamb's Shakespearean tales gave me an appetite for the theatrical and the dramatic. My young mind worked through a combination of English classics and sentimental historical Irish novels and ballads. Joe, when we were together and I wasn't fetching him his bits and bobs for his studio on Upper Sackville Street, told me of the importance of perspective within which to view our struggle. Perspective, both historical and literal, was key to seeing things for what they really were. I will always be grateful to Aunt Bridey for the books she put my way, but it was Joe, on so many levels, with his tremendous passion for the liberal arts and their power in forming the march of a nation, who had the greater influence.

Notwithstanding all that he gave me in those important years directly after my father's departure, it was his equipping me with a particular present that was to change my life the most. It was my twelfth birthday.

I had called up to his third-floor studio after school to show him a book my mother had given me. Moments after I entered, whilst I was informing him of my gift, his final customers for the day swanned in, their nostrils searching out whether or not they had come to the right place. They flapped and flicked at their bonnets, their astrakhan jackets, the feathers in their hats, the frills in their stiffly starched shirts. They took the tips of their waistcoats with thumbs and forefingers and stretched them out over their protruding guts, fixed their cuffs and the bows of their ties and then stood, stiff as old Nelson himself, while Joe slipped in a plate holder.

Of course, they blinked uncontrollably once his flash exploded upon them. They were unaccustomed, as were most people in the city, to photography undertaken with flash-powder lighting. The dense, acrid fumes and smoke soured their faces. (I, on the other hand, took a deep, familiar, relaxed breath.) No matter how he warned them to fight the urge, Joe's clients insisted on closing their eyes, thus ensuring that he would have to do it all over again. Any number of negatives could be used for the one pose – plate holder after plate holder. Always, one client would squint, or shrink from the bang and flash.

When the customers finally left, Joe very much surprised me with his singular gift. I unwrapped the parcel with haste, and let my mouth open to an angle it had never before known. The gaping angle unfortunately did not signify unbridled joy, unspeakable elation or uncontrollable happiness. For I was young and foolish, and familiar only with cameras much larger in size. The little black box he presented to me seemed like an affront to my new found maturity, not to mention my ambition. At twelve, I thought myself no longer a boy, but a man who wished to take serious photographs. Surely, thought I, a midget camera with no stand was some sort of cruel joke. I was a man. If I was to have a camera, surely one with a tripod, at the very least, would be essential.

'What's up with ye?' said Joe on noticing the tremble in my lip.

'Nothing. Thanks,' I said, almost begrudgingly.

'Get out of that. Now, what's wrong with ye really?'

He took out his pipe and began to fill it with tobacco. My state, the size of my camera, surely demanded more attention than he was affording. I blew like a stick of dynamite.

'This, Joe!' said I, holding out the Kodak Brownie like it was a foul-smelling rat. 'You don't expect me go out and take photographs with this?'

'Why, you ungrateful little bollix. And why wouldn't ye?'

'Look at it!' I was crying now, for he had never spoken to me like that before. 'It's a toddler's jack-in-the-box. I thought some day I'd get something like that.' My extended finger, wet with snot freshly wiped from my nose, pointed to his eight-by-ten on the tripod. He laughed to himself, lit the pipe and took two grinning puffs.

'When I told ye to think big Harry, I didn't mean that big. Besides, this little beauty is all ye'll ever need.'

'You're just sayin' that.'

'Would I lie to you? You're young, I'm old. I won't be runnin' around the city like you in years to come. And that's why I'll be using these old things. But you. Don't let the size of the camera dampen the ardour of your photographic dreams. It's perfect for you.'

'Really?' I sniffled, inspecting the box anew.

'Really,' insisted Joe, his hands on my shoulders now. 'This little man here, when I teach you how to master the exposure adjustments, will be as good – no, I tell a lie – it'll be better than those lads over there. You'll have the advantage of using a small hand camera to get in close to the subject for intimate views. Make your shot, then get out. You'll cover a subject, have your negatives, have them developed and be home in bed before I can get my large plate camera on its cumbersome tripod and say "How's yer uncle?"'

'Really?'

'Really.'

While not wanting to dwell on sentiments already expressed in the preceding pages, I still find it necessary to explain the transformative effect such a simple gift had on me. In my definition of heroes, because of his initial support and, thence, never-ending encouragement, Joe Deasy, his gigantic ears lifted high with a smile, became the epitome of one when he handed over my Kodak. The warping viewfinder of the Brownie became the prism through which I was to find my place in the world. I not only found myself there, but found my country and all which encompassed it.

Joe was also kind enough to bring myself and my new school friend Davy to Sandymount Strand the next day to make a start on convincing me of the Kodak's powers. Davy had, as if by magic, arrived beside me in school by way of the south side of the city, and before that, as he never ceased to remind me, by way of Wexford, 'Where the grandest of heroic deeds took place in 1798.' Our common interest began in the playground. While the other boys, who had always ignored me, talked of cowboys and Indians and secretly read the *Halfpenny Marvel* and other literature of the Wild West, we would look at them with disdain; we preferred stories of Ireland's heroes of yesteryear. Up until this point, though, we had only ever spoken of seeking out adventures together – we had never actually done so. That trip to the beach was our first opportunity.

Davy laughed at the Kodak when I showed it to him, and tried trump me with his catapult. 'I brought this to have some gas with the birds,' he said. I shook my head at his toy. I was intent on capturing important moments on my camera, not injuring birds. Joe, all the time puffing on his pipe, escorted us to the beach, whereupon Davy set out to decapitate as many birds as possible. If Joe disapproved of Davy's actions, he did not show it. I was very grateful for his reticence, as I wished to make an impression on my new friend.

A steamer came by and, with Joe's help, I set about capturing it as it lumbered into port. A motorcar, parked by the footpath, gleamed a thousand suns on its incredible metallic exterior. Crouching so as to come level with the beast, Joe guided my settings and let me snap away. My new friend Davy, having grown tired of merely scattering the birds, scuffed the ground with the toe of his shoe and moaned every time I set myself up for a photograph.

'I'm bored,' said he. 'This is not the adventure you promised. I want excitement! Death! Destruction!'

After a number of hours (though not enough), Joe brought us for dinner to an eating house. We had corned beef and cabbage and washed it down with some ginger ale, before retiring to Sydney Parade station, as it was handy for our means.

Hardly had the train travelled a few yards when the carriage stuttered, and we came to an abrupt stop. Through the hissing of the steam outside could be heard deranged screams of ladies on the platform.

'Come on Har,' said Joe, nodding to my Brownie sitting proudly atop the table.

'What now?' moaned Davy, his eyes finding something suddenly interesting on the ceiling.

All three of us alighted from the now stationary train, and Joe beckoned me towards the engine, through the increasingly dense steam.

'Set yourself for a photograph Har,' whispered Joe.

I fumbled with the Brownie, thinking quickly about what he had told me of light sources and exposure.

'What are we looking for, Joe?' said I, becoming nervous at what we might find beyond the steam.

'A story,' Joe hissed, grabbing my shoulder, 'a taste of adventure. Chronicling the life of your city.'

'This is ridiculous carry-on,' Davy interjected.

The steam dissipated to reveal a body, head hidden from view under the monstrous wheels of the engine. A railway porter stood beside the body, hand gripped tightly to his mouth, colour drained from his terror-stricken face. A passer-by was doubled over and retching, an arm on his waist to quell the pain of forced regurgitation. The driver of the train brushed by me and jumped from the platform onto the track. What he saw beyond the buffer of the engine stopped him dead. He tore his cap from his head and covered his mouth with it.

'Quickly does it,' whispered Joe, through the dissipating steam, as he nodded to the scene before me. 'Compose yourself, boy. Look at the characters. The incident. The emotion. And take your photograph. Don't let the moment overwhelm you.'

'But, but it's too dark,' I protested, wanting nothing more than to return to the carriage.

"Tis not.' He nodded to the tracks. 'Look at the beam of light tearing through where the platform ends. It's perfect.'

The actual physical action of setting my camera gave me palpitations. However, I was able to compose myself somewhat.

'I have it now Joe. I'm ready.' My voice had an accent of forced bravery.

'Good boy. Now take it.'

After an interruption in the steam and the cries, the retching and the doors opening behind, I took my picture. I breathed easy and looked proudly to Joe. When one was done, I took another. I took a few steps to the lip of the platform and took another. Behind me, Davy heaved and moaned as his beef and cabbage spilled out all over the platform. A shrill whistle sounded and a peeler arrived. I stopped what I was doing and took the Brownie under my arm. The images were to become my first published work.

Some time later, after Davy's face had lost its green pallor, as we rocked gently home on the top deck of the tram, he found it in him to speak. He hadn't said a word since we had left Sydney Parade on foot.

'Why did we have to get out? Why did we have to see that, that disgusting . . . mess?'

I shrugged.

'Because, boys,' said Joe, looking out upon the city passing below us, drawing on his pipe, a soft glow smoking gently in the wind, 'facing that which we have not faced before, is a test of our character. And any test of your character you can call an adventure.' His eyes lit up at the word 'adventure'. He whispered it, gave it reverence, as if it was in some way spiritual. 'And boys, whether you realise it or not, today was an adventure. How you reacted will tell you a lot about your appetite for it in future.'

'That's claptrap,' retorted Davy, his face darkening, his eyes glistening. 'That was not an adventure. That was nothing like I've read about in my books.'

'OK, OK,' Joe answered, looking into the embers of his pipe. 'You're right, Davy. I'm sorry.'

The bell rang below and the tram slowed with a faint screech.

'It was the ginger ale,' Davy whispered belatedly. 'That made me sick. The ginger ale.'

I didn't respond. Instead, I thought of my first, strange adventure, and how, in the madness of it all, Joe had encouraged me to capture it for eternity.

The Wheel

She looks different. The image on the screen has transformed her. Something is more refined, sharper, sexier, edgier. He doesn't know if it's the make-up – rouge to draw out her cheekbones – or eyeliner. Mascara? A new fringe?

If he asks, she'll wonder why he doesn't know, which will inevitably lead her to think the long-distance thing is having another negative effect, which will only lead her to get restless and demand to know when he's leaving. He still doesn't know.

'So,' she says, a slight glitch catching her eyelids closed, like in a bad photograph, 'when do you think they'll be ready?'

'Hard to tell. It's not that easy, like. Straightforward. He's to do loads of stuff. And that's in between his normal stuff.'

Enda had been short with Neil when Neil had declined his offer of a coffee after the match.

'You have to allow for cleaning, inspection, film scanning, grade restoration and playout,' Enda had said, shrugging, kind of sulking. 'So, yeah, I'll have it when I'll have it.'

'But you said they hadn't been touched,' Kathy says.

'They haven't. Things happen over time. Deteriorate.'

'*Really?*'

Her tone, the word, carries a whiff of irony, a double meaning that catches him off guard. Pulls him back from the screen for perspective.

He's reminded of the time they went on the big wheel at the Point Village. His vertigo had been a slow-dawning terror once they scraped the bottom and started the climb upwards. The recurring fear of revolution.

She skips over the line and goes, 'Did he give you any indication of their worth or even, like, a rough indication of when he'll know?'

'Not really. He's a weirdo. He said it's too early. But he did say it's extremely rare – his words – that ninety-year-old footage is discovered.'

'Well that's something. It's a good start, I suppose.'

It was on her say-so that he had sent out the emails, so it's only natural she should take an interest. She is, he supposes, indirectly responsible for Enda's involvement. She studies the screen, moves her fringe out of her eyes. Neil's glad of her support. He isn't entirely sure what he's doing, and since he hasn't told anyone – including his gran – about what he's up to, he needs to hear words of encouragement.

'But ye know,' she says and squirms a little on the bed, 'some sort of idea for when they might like, be ready or even a price range, a general value would be great to get. Just so you know, like, you're not wasting your time. He's had them over a week.'

The screen flashes black. He remembers how the cab stalled at the top for a few minutes and Kathy shook it when she leaned over him to get a picture of the Liffey. He had gripped the handle and felt helpless in the seat of such swaying fear, wishing Kathy would just sit still. Neil is walking a very fine line. Kathy, ever so slightly, is letting him know this.

'I don't want to be hassling him all the time. Calling into his lab.

Like, he keeps on asking me to go places with him and do things with him. I agreed to the Dublin game just to get him started on the reels, and then I end up getting in a fight because of him.'

'What?' she asks, smiling, laughing almost.

'Look.' Neil leans in to the screen and points to the bruise under his right eye. 'This lad, Kat, he's a lunatic. He's like, he has no cop-on whatsoever. I think he's spent his whole life in books or at a screen. He is the stupidest intelligent person I've ever met.'

Kathy giggles and shakes her head. 'He's probably lonely.'

'Of course he's lonely. You'd have to be mad to hang out with him. The lad that gave him the tickets didn't even want to go with him.'

She giggles some more, and Neil laughs at the insanity of it all and shrugs his shoulders in defeat. The relief once the wheel jolted and they started moving down again.

'Why don't you go to a professional then?'

'They cost a fortune. I've checked. And they're not very secretive. Someone would hear about it. And this Enda, ah, he seems reliable in fairness to him. Like, he's really into the whole Irish history thing. He's genuine enough.'

'But mental.'

They laugh together again.

'Yes, but mental.'

'You could ask your uncles for help.'

'No way. Then they'd want a slice. Sure, they don't even know about it. I dunno why, but my gran hasn't told them about the diary.'

'Weird.'

'I think she's afraid they'll only argue over it.'

She puts her hands to her face in contemplation. Luminous yellow nail polish – she only ever puts the clear stuff on – draws his attention to her slim fingers as they drag down her face. The mood changes.

'We're in limbo then.'

'Don't say that. No, not at all. Enda's a good guy really. Look, to hell with it. I'll be his buddy. If it speeds things up, I'll be his buddy.'

She smiles into the screen, but Neil can tell she's somewhere else. It's the eyes. Her eyes have changed. She's looking at him differently. Canada is changing her. The memory of the stall at the top of the wheel remains. Kathy's unnecessary, impatient rocking. His secret wish she'd sit still.

'This place is a bit mental,' she says, finished with the reels. She has never – other than their year away in Australia – lived away from home. 'Yeah, the views of downtown and the mountains are amazing. Commercial Drive is cool and all, and yeah, Trout Lake is beautiful, I suppose. But the house, Neil, ye know, there's like, all sorts living here. You think you've got it hard with that lad Enda. Two lads living here are documentary makers, OK. And like, for research, they spend their days in the Downtown Eastside with the crack addicts. Like, I'm not talking sitting in a coffee shop and chatting over a latte. I'm talking, proper Aboriginal drug den – manky drug-scene stuff.

'They go missing for days and then smell the place up when they come back and freak us all out with their stories. It's not what I thought it would be. Kenny said, like, he said they were all arty types. But I need to work, you know? I'm in a room with two other girls – they're nice and all, the girls – one of them's a hairdresser, which is cool, 'cause at least she gets up in the morning too. But I'd rather be, ye know, I wanna be with you. It's not what I thought it would be. I want to be on our own. Wait a sec.'

She stops, looks left, out of shot, to what must be the door to her room. Neil hears a deep voice. She gets up from her crossed-leg position. Her T-shirt is short, and it lifts, exposing her lower back as she moves away. There's a dark patch there he hasn't seen before. After he spends several seconds staring at bunk beds and a single bed beside them, Kathy returns, legs first, then stomach, then face. The memory of the zenith still scares him. The inevitability of the rise and the peak. That feeling of helplessness. Just you and the wind and a rusted chain, rocking idly, loosely. A false sense of security.

'Sorry,' she says, flicking a vague hand to the door. 'Kenny says they're all off for drinks.'

'You going?'

She scrunches up her nose. 'Not really bothered. I can follow them down later.'

'Did you—' he says, but stops. Maybe he was seeing things, because he knows she wouldn't. Or, if she did, at least she would've told him. He has to say it.

'Did you get a tattoo? Is that a tattoo on your lower back?'

Her eyes go wide, like she's shocked he knows.

'You're not to go mad. But me and Jade and Kenny went last week and, yeah,' she giggles. 'I know I've always said I wouldn't. But, look. A new country, a new me. You didn't even notice my hair, but you somehow see a tattoo on my back.'

So it was the hair.

'What is it?'

'Two swallows.'

'Swallows?'

'Ne-al. Don't you remember anything I tell you? My philosophy – my saying. One swallow doesn't make a summer . . . '

Neil digs deep for it. He really does. Tries to hurry with the digging.

She sighs and shakes her head, says 'It's always summer,' and begins to explain the weak reasoning behind getting a tramp stamp, despite hating the fact Neil had one when they first met. She had nagged him to get it removed, but he never gave in. Until she got one, he'd told her, she wouldn't understand. He presumes she does now.

An EGM

Jim looks over his shoulder, out of their irregular team huddle at the bottom of Gran's hospital bed, makes sure she's still asleep and pours his stare over the hushed gathering. Neil, of course, shouldn't be there. He wasn't invited. The meeting was obviously planned in advance – despite their protests to the contrary – and was just underway when Neil popped in, expecting to see Gran and get another chapter.

After some hesitation, Jim sighed and said Gran's immediate accommodation – once discharged from hospital next week – had to be discussed. An all-out family meeting would have taken too long to arrange, he said, so he'd decided that an impromptu meeting would do. Once Neil heard what they were up to, he decided to stay, regardless of their hushed insistence that he leave.

'St Mary's,' Jim says, nostrils flaring, 'is a sensible, rational plan that is proportionate . . . ' Jim's voice reaches too low, goes into a deep murmur. Eoin glances over Neil's shoulder, back to the bed.

'And equitable,' Eoin adds.

'And equitable,' Jim continues, 'in these difficult circumstances in which we find ourselves. It is an extended-care ward. It is everything, everything, Neil, she currently needs. Pappy is gone. She cannot, would not be able for losing, or even contemplating losing her home too.'

Eoin adds, 'You pretend you're motivated by what's best for her, but really, Neil, we know it's for your own gain.'

'That's total bullsh—'

They're brought out of the confrontation by a moan. They turn to see Gran's pained face stir, eyes still closed.

'If this scenario doesn't work out,' Jim whispers, bringing them back in, hurrying along before she wakes, 'then yes, Neil, we will revisit your idea of a nursing home. But, for now, going forward,' he looks to each face, 'the house remains as is. And we take up the extended-care ward for, two, three weeks?'

Eoin shrugs with indifferent compliance.

'And after that period, we will return to the table and reassess the pros and cons and the burden-sharing agreement we have all undertaken since Pappy's passing.'

'Burden-sharing?' Neil interrupts, finding their hollow words need repeating to be sure they actually hold anything at all. Their language disgusts him, lays bare their motives. Neil despises them. Their poisonous words. He will never be like them.

The collective huddle at the end of the room, with Jim's six-two frame, and Eoin beside him, is a dark space despite the blue skies beyond the window. Sweat glistens on Jim's pulsing temple, Eoin's brow. Their shirt-and-woolly-jumper combos are rookie mistakes they wouldn't have made if they'd have visited the overheated room before.

'The house,' Eoin says, pushing his glasses up the bridge of his nose, 'needs to be looked in on. There was a robbery two down only a few nights ago.'

'I can do that for you,' Neil says without hesitation.

'And how,' Jim hushes, 'do you mind me asking, if you're in Canada, do you propose to do that?'

'I've been held up. Canada can wait. Gran needs me.'

Eoin studies Neil's face for a moment. Unconvinced.

'When are you going, as a matter of fact?' Jim whispers.

'Soon.'

'How soon?' Eoin asks, sceptical.

'I dunno. Soon.'

'What are you up to? What's your angle?' Eoin says.

Neil shrugs, laughs it off, gets ready to say something, when Gran's voice, thin and sandpaper-rough, floats into their circle.

'What are you whispering about, at all?'

The huddle suddenly disperses. The darkness bleaches and the blue sky blinds.

'Nothing,' Jim says, smiling. With two strides in his sandals, he is by her side, kissing her forehead asking, 'What's this dusty thing doing here, mother?'

'Oh, that,' she says, Eoin looming over her, shadowing her face, grimacing at the old leather bag. 'It's nothing really. Now, how are you?'

Their eyes dwell on Neil, an accusation in the look, threatened by the secret. They don't answer Gran's question, just stay on Neil, waiting for him to crack and give an explanation for the bag. It's strange that she hasn't told them about Harry's chapters. But he's not bothered by it. Couldn't care less. It would be a nightmare if the family were involved.

They start to talk about their kids, schools, neighbours, and Neil slips out, just offering Gran a soft wave. He has other things he could be doing other than listening to them remind her of grandchildren she never sees – because they never visit – and how they love her so.

An Irish Love Story

Before Kathy, every weekend had been an unending plethora of possibilities. Buckled, bleary-eyed, staggering, leering, mumbling, cursing, complaining, puking, moaning, laughing. He was all of them together and apart. Falling into women, spilling his Jägerbombs on their dresses, spraying them with stray spit when he leaned in close to talk shite in their ears. Before Kathy, every girl he came to know – and then, no longer know – was for a week, two weeks, three weeks – a step into a life about to happen.

Until, for some reason, after Kathy listened to him waffle in the smoking area about what was wrong with the country, her confused face softened into semi-interest – maybe intrigue – and she laughed. She made him laugh too. The next morning she had requested him on Facebook, and he pulled himself off – still drunk, he thinks – to her profile. It just felt right. He realised afterwards he had inadvertently "liked" her picture. There was no turning back.

Maybe it was because she didn't give herself up to him immediately that sent him wild for her. Piece by piece, week by week, they'd stumble into a bed, fumble on a couch, and he'd get a glimpse of her flesh – an unfulfilled glimpse – and he'd pass out or get sick, and he'd have to wait for another opportunity. Women before her, porn, television, the Internet, all offered up their bodies so easily he never knew what it was to truly worship a figure, need to feel the pleasure of it. He ached for her. Began to see, painfully, how value could be added to a thing simply by allowing time take its course.

Even when they made love for the first time – a half-drunk, almost asleep semi-dream – it didn't feel real until she got out of bed afterwards, naked, and walked to the bathroom. It was in Ha'penny Bridge House. His box room was nearest the toilet. She stretched out, side on, her breasts flattening out while her hands went to the top of her head and she took her hair and brushed down through it. He fell instantly in love with the image – her. She turned away from him, totally free of self-consciousness, her back half shadowed, and crept out. When she returned they made love again. This time he was clearer, awake, and her body was vivid and real. They had been together for two months. He was young, naïve, still high, and he told her in that perfection of early morning light that he loved her. She smiled and nestled her head into his neck.

His flatmates had become his family when he'd moved out of his gran and grandad's house. She understood how important they were, so moving in together after Australia never really became an issue. He liked the freedom, the evenings playing FIFA, GTA, getting stoned and being a waster. When she came over, he bucked up and went out with her, did something. He had the best of both worlds. Besides, he reckoned she liked the comfort and financial security of living with her parents. His room was her home from home in the city anyway, and at least she had an escape route if things went south.

After Australia, a year raced by in this easy routine. Neil in the mortgage centre on Stephen's Green, Kathy in the architect's office on Pearse Street. The mad weekends, her silent retreats to her parents' on Sunday afternoons – a taxi no less, because he'd be in no state to drive – was their comfort zone. How they worked. Never too much time together to become an annoyance, never so little that they'd exist separately.

He saw it coming, but chose to ignore the signs. After her architect's firm – where she worked as a 3-D modeller – moved offices in order to renovate their original building, Neil was moved to the 'Diary' in his place. He was the head-office point of contact for all of the branches around the country with queries about the progress of mortgage applications, personal loans, motor loans. If not by phone, they got him through the intranet. His job was to update the status of all loans.

It was meant to be busy. Yes, he was putting his name to reference numbers and pushing through millions worth of loans a week, stopping loans because the cheq req was needed, or the HOPP wasn't signed, or the names on the life insurance didn't match the names given on the mortgage application. But he wasn't flat out. Not that it mattered, because they were happy. Cinema, dinner, parties, gigs. They were insulated from the problems of the world because they were young.

She rang him one day in work, out of breath, upset. Her whole office had been called into a meeting. In two months' time, they'd been told, certain projects were coming to a close, and there were none to replace them. They were letting people go. He thought she was one of them.

'No,' she sniffled, 'I'm OK. But Joanne isn't.'

He told her that Joanne would get another job, and quietly thanked God it wasn't Kathy. He liked their life the way it was. It made him jumpy, and he stood up and looked past his cubicle, at the rest of the mortgage centre. Phones rang, printers printed, people called across the floor. Calls from branches continued to come in, and the intranet continued to pulse, roll over green on black with messages from Offaly and Letterkenny.

But, slowly, now and then, almost as if the computer system had started to glitch, half an hour would go by and the screen would remain blank. Just a slow, green pulsing pixel on the top left, like a beacon on the runway waiting for an enquiry to land. The skies were growing quiet. He'd refresh the page – because things like this had happened before – and if, still, nothing scrolled down on his feed, he'd take the headset off and go for a coffee. By the time he was back, there'd be new messages, and his phone would be flashing with voicemails and he would throw himself into the work as if he hadn't been away.

Kathy's next work-related call had no tears or double intakes of breath. Just a calm, almost detached matter-of-factness to it.

'We're not going back to the old office,' she said.

'That's ridiculous. They've spent millions refurbishing it. Why not?'

'It's too big.'

'Too big?'

'For us. The staff. They're gonna rent it to an accountancy firm and we're gonna stay out here.'

'Why renovate a perfectly good, functioning office only to turn around six months later and not use it?'

She giggled at the insanity of it. 'I know. I don't know.'

His green pixel dot flashed coolly at the top of the screen, almost tapping its foot, patiently waiting for loan queries to roll down.

He missed her third work-related phone call. He was down in the canteen taking a longer-than-usual morning break. When he came back up, the flashing on his phone gave him hope, until he saw the number and realised it was her. The voicemail was short. She was crying, sniffling, whispering, sobbing about redundancies when his manager appeared at his cubicle and lifted her lips to attempt a smile. She motioned for him to join her in her office. A perfect storm.

'What if something comes through on the diary?'

'It won't,' is all she said. He hung up without another word.

They met in the Swan, just off Aungier Street, to have a quiet drink and weigh up their options. The Angelus was knelling in the corner of the room, and the newscaster's voice talked of things Neil had never heard talked about – or noticed being talked about – on the news before. Language was changing. Everything was suddenly abstract. He was lost.

After some minutes of sighing and weak, forced words of encouragement, sips of their drinks, folding of beer mats, Kathy scraping the sticker off her bottle, she shrugged, as if she'd just heard something in a hidden earpiece.

'Well,' she said, 'there's only one thing for it.'

'Yeah?' He knew what was coming next.

'Emigrate.'

Like a sucker punch, it went deep. Took the wind out of his chest, tightened his gut. He held still. Emotionless.

'Yeah?'

'Yep. We'll have to go. Australia. Dubai. Canada. New Zealand. I've friends, family, in most of the places.'

Her decisiveness, coldness, scared him.

'We'll get something else, give it some time,' he said, nodding to the busy street outside, the city and all the recruitment agencies, downplaying their predicament.

'Don't you get it, Neil? Listen to her. Look at the news. This country has failed. It's sinking. I didn't spend four years in college to work in McDonald's while the whole place goes up in smoke. There's more out there. We don't owe this place anything. It owes us. And ye know what? It's not going to pay up anytime soon. I'm not . . . I'm not going into any of those queues,' she said, nodding to the file picture of the mandatory dole line on the news, the voice discussing unemployment and the rate of its increase. 'I'm worth more than that.'

'I know.'

'I don't think you do. We're worth more than that. There's a whole world out there that'll be only too happy to recruit us. Us, Neil. Me and you.'

He persuaded her to stick it out for a few weeks. But it was inevitable. Just like her desire straight out of college to go see the world, and her determination to do it alone if she had to, she would go. He would follow. He knew she wouldn't be willing to drop a few steps on the ladder even for the short term. As he found out later, she certainly wasn't able for the bottom of the ladder, the shit under the shit that was the outdoor dole queue they joined every week.

One morning in particular, while they shuffled their feet and shivered into their collars, she seemed more agitated than normal.

'Look,' she said, flapping her *Metro* in disgust at the people in front and behind, her breath smoking up, oblivious to the stares, 'look at the state of us. This. It's a sham. I feel like shit, Neil. I feel like shit. Don't you get it? They want you to feel this way. The queue outside, the rain, the shame. They're telling you, they're telling all of us, we're not wanted. Don't you get it? Can't you hear it?'

And she looked around desperately again, and then left the queue. Neil remained in line. Even after giving up the car, the parking spot, insurance, tax and petrol, he was still struggling for cash. He had spent the last three days chipping away at a solitary €20. Noodles, cheap bread, hot dogs and beans. He needed money for dinner. The lads needed money for ESB and NTL.

At first he didn't hear it. But then he felt it, like a whisper. More an unsettling, a murmur, a tremble. Like the DART coasting into Pearse Street unannounced. Quiet. But becoming slowly audible:

"You don't belong here. This is not for you. This is no city for you. This is no country for you." The ice-cold realisation that this place, now, wasn't for him. Would never be. He realised then he was a man in the world. The deep green oceans and white beaches in far-flung destinations were for him. The high mountains sticking up through wispy clouds were for him. The cities of neon splendour and anonymity were for him. He deserved them as much as the next person. He would leave Ireland. And join the world.

Market Value

'Nitrocellulose is a good indicator of authentic film stock,' Enda says, and Neil reverts his gaze to the goggles on Enda's head, the weak ceiling light flashing off them as he moves.

'What?'

'The odour. Smell,' Enda answers. 'Can you not get it? Your three metal containers reek of the stuff. The positive print was clean of any glue splices. Satisfactory once again. And the film. Only one brand, which is impressive.'

Neil smiles to himself, proud in some way. As much as he tells himself he doesn't care what Enda thinks, he does. Enda, with his head firmly up his hole and lost to the world outside books or screens, impresses him. He's as happy as a pig in shit in his lab. Neil wishes he had such a place. He had once. His grandparents'.

The hunched shoulders and stiff neck of Enda's monster frame start to contract, as if the conversation is mellowing him. 'Pathé.' He smiles, satisfied. '28mm, 1916 nitrate stock. Explosive stuff.'

Neil looks for a place to sit, take the weight off, get comfortable. Enda's lab is in disarray. Thick textbooks are stacked and discarded everywhere. Neil went to college. DIT. For two years. A higher certificate in Business Studies. A vague cop out. He is unnerved by this display of academia, because he was never able for it. Business? He doesn't know what he learnt. It was an excuse to sit around the apartment and be financed by a grant and a part-time job. He couldn't face the slog. Day by day. Frame by frame. The boring, mundane, predictability of it all. Submitting to the future.

'Is this good?'

Enda hears the question, but frowns as if Neil's query doesn't deserve an answer.

'I've looked at a bit more, even though I'm so busy, you know? The people from the IFI are hounding me for their reels. But,' he coughs, adjusts the glasses on his crew-cut, pushes his sleeves up, 'they didn't take time out to go to Croke Park for a game, did they?'

'No, they didn't. Exactly, Enda. Exactly,' Neil answers. 'And they didn't get a few digs in the head for you and your jersey for good measure either.'

Enda scoffs. 'Neil, they didn't like you. I was fine.'

There's no point in arguing. He's getting sidetracked, so he asks for more information on the reels. Enda looks disappointed for a second, and then says, 'The reels, OK. One shows slight melting of the emulsion in the section proximate to the core, for which, it is possible to foresee, that at least some footage will be lost.'

'Gone? So it's worthless?'

Enda can't hide his impatience.

'My God,' he says and sighs, 'you really don't have a clue. OK, so, I'll explain to you, again, that film, of itself, yes, is worthless. You get that? To appreciate a piece of film fully, to understand footage from the past – in your case, vintage, high-end material – you must understand the context in which it was made. So, if you were listening to me before, you would know that what is in the reels will determine the true value.'

The shootings, the killings, the running here and there with the camera, the actual physical content, has left Neil cold. The actions described can't add value to the reels because there's nothing new in them. It's *Call of Duty* or *Grand Theft Auto* on silent, in black and white. And everyone has seen *Call of Duty* and *Grand Theft Auto*. In colour, with sound.

'I know about the content, I know this. That's why I've been trying to get the diary chapters, so I can find out.'

'Good,' Enda patronises, smiling briefly, 'well done. But at the rate you're going I'll be finished restoring the reels before you've read about them.'

'I don't get you.'

'While you've been running around partying, I've put it through an ultrasonic cleaner and given it a wet-gate transfer.'

'So?'

'So? I've finished reel one.'

Shadows flicker by the frosted-glass in the door. Neil is speechless. It's suddenly becoming real. It's actually happening.

'Finished? So, like, what, I can start looking to sell now? Is there even a market?'

Enda sits down at his desk and clears some books off his keyboard in a bored, inconvenienced way.

'Yes, reel one is definitely of value. Your context – truth be told – is impressive. How he filmed it in such circumstances, for one. The constraints. And still such powerful shots, two. The skill to get the shots, three. To have the shots, the film survive, four and five. Yes, you've got something of value.'

'How much? Is there a market?'

'Also, six. The context. Here is an important element,' and he massages his fingers over the plastic keys, distracted, head lost in the computer screen, his goggles flashing again. He presses his lips together, giving a sense of anticipation to the moment – grandeur, importance, gravitas. Neil starts to record Enda secretly on his phone.

'The content of the next two reels will be very important. If they are not ruined, this could be a big find.' He takes off the goggles.

'How big?'

He rubs the glass, lost in thought. Distant. Distracted.

'How big, Enda?'

Enda returns to Neil with a shake of his head, as if he forgot he was there.

'Oh, sorry. Big. Really big. But, like I said, it depends. Pearse reading the proclamation: serious images. Kids smiling for the camera: nothing. Horses being shot and maimed: sure, that's new. Good work. But, if reels two and three have new content, like, I don't know – unseen before – then you're in the "A" league. I mean, a serious find.'

Enda smiles. Neil hasn't seen him like this before. As much as Enda has tried to play it cool, be casual, Neil can tell he's excited by the prospect.

'Unseen before? Like what?'

'My God, Neil. If it is unseen before, how am I to know? Check your diaries.'

Neil thinks of the other reports from Gran. What he has read. What he hasn't read yet. What they might contain. The words have a force about them now. That much he knows. A tidal wave of hope pours off the pages. A belief in the country that he finds so remarkable only because it's so ridiculous. An idea that doesn't ring true in any way. He has given up on the idea of the country, it being a place he can be proud of. And he has given up on ever really finding something worth believing in.

That's what is mad about what he has read so far. The pure, wholehearted idealism of his great-grandfather. The ill-judged, misdirected idealism of everyone in the reports – apart from Davy. Davy impresses

Neil, because Davy is ahead of his time. Davy is modern. A twenty-first-century hero, struggling – no matter what the cost – for self-advancement.

'And,' Enda says, his head leaning in to the computer, casual, almost reluctant, 'I've eh, made a few enquiries for you.'

'Enquiries? I don't get you.'

Enda sighs again and looks to the ceiling.

'Of course you don't. Enquiries. I have asked around like you requested. Made contact. There's a market. There's a buyer.'

'Already? But, like, I haven't even seen them. Neither have you.'

'No need to thank me. And no, not yet we haven't. But we will. He's keen. It's a lucrative market if you have the goods. He's intrigued. But the content will determine the price.'

Prices and content and markets and values. This is something he has to actually deal with now. Take responsibility for. It's like an exam is looming and he hasn't bothered to study, hasn't bothered to attend a lecture, get the notes. He hated college. He felt depressingly inferior there, in the lectures, the tutorials. Words, phrases, sayings, theories. He crammed them into his short-term memory.

'This is great. How quick can you get the other two ready?'

Enda shakes his head. 'I'll do them when I can, but restoration involves digitally scanning each and every frame. Then I must convert it into a high-definition image before I can put it through an algorithm.'

The jargon frustrates Neil. Those that use it annoy him. He doesn't want a lecture, just straightforward answers. Results.

'So, when? Can I at least see the footage from reel one?' Neil stands up and eases his phone into position.

'OK, you're taking an interest. It is a big decision after all. You don't have to . . . '

'Have to what? The decision's made.'

'Perhaps we can discuss it later?'

'Discuss?'

'Yes, like, go to the gym or maybe a glass of wine or coffee.'

And before Neil can reply, Enda's hand is raised to Neil's iPhone.

'Hold on, you can't record it. That's insane. It devalues the footage immediately.'

'But, I just thought, ye know,' Neil protests, holding the phone out so it takes the computer screen in. 'I wanna show my girlfriend in Canada. Only her.'

Enda taps a password into a file and then stands up, towering over Neil.

'Put the phone away. If we're doing this, we're doing it right. How can it be exclusive if there's copies?'

It's a plausible argument. A pass business certificate has taught him some basics of economics, market demand.

'I have it on my computer. Four minutes and forty seconds. It's really cool.'

'You said no copies.'

'Yes, no copies. This is a digital version. The original digital version of the original. How else do you think we would watch it?'

Neil stops recording and leans in to the computer to see the opening seconds of Harry's footage flicker black and white before the GPO bursts into shot and the dark figures of the assembling crowd jump intermittently on the snowy, jittery screen.

Conversion Rates

Gran's asleep. He has an urge to pull the curtains around the bed. Cut himself and his gran off from the cruel sunshine draining life from the ward, blinding off tiles and the numerous metal abstractions surrounding each and every bed.

The three beds on her side, moving away from her towards the window, are occupied. Not filled out. Not closed off, unfortunately, to troubled glances. The bodies are twisted and pale. They create harsh angles under the sheets. Now and then the slow lift, shift of a leg hitches up bed clothes, exposing a thin thigh, all bone, no meat, or a saggy arse, or the dark, unspeakable hoped for never seen.

Neil shudders. This is where we all end up, if we're lucky: in a run-down, overheated, religious-relic-lined nursing home purgatory. He really wants to pull the curtains around the bed. Block out other people's decrepit declines. His love for his gran blinds him to hers.

An old lady, buttons awkwardly opened on her nighty, pads into the ward barefoot. Smiling, toothless, she turns to Neil and stretches her hand out like she wants to touch his shoulder, feel his face. Neil stays still, repulsed by the terror of her watery red gums, lost eyes. Her stink moves on by and takes the handle to Gran's bedside locker. Neil is frozen by confusion, but another hand – Gran's, bruised and skeletal – grips the crazy woman's.

Gran croaks, 'No, no. Go away.'

Neil is startled by Gran's voice, the indignity of witnessing her having to take action, fight off the intruder. He gets to his feet and gently, with the slightest of touches, ushers the mad lady away from the locker.

'She too —' Gran coughs a surface cough, nothing near her chest, clears her throat without moving her face, and starts again. 'She took a watch from the gentleman next door. The other day. They returned it to him. Sometime later. She had hidden it, they said. She had taken numerous bits and pieces from the wards. In her bag. Under her bed. Imagine.'

Her hands, fingers waltz together slowly, hurdle over one another on her lap. Neil takes her hand, feels the loose skin. The warmth he has missed.

'My memories, dear. They're merging. It's difficult to sort them from dreams. People, I'm afraid, are beginning to disappear. Their lives feel like a dream now. When someone dies, a whole world disappears. The only proof I have of their existence is their physical things. How else am I to know I didn't dream them?'

What do you say to such things? How do you respond to such questions?

'They might as well have been a dream, really,' she continues, her whisper scratching the white noise around them. 'I dream of him a lot. I miss him. I miss him so. I wish I had a picture of him with me. To remind me he existed. I don't want to forget his face.'

'You won't forget him, Gran. Sure, yis were married for fifty years.'

'Sixty, dear.'

'I can . . . I can bring you a picture, no problem.'

They forego a greeting.

'Yes,' she smiles, 'you could, I suppose. But. I don't know when you would be back.' She taps his hand, rubs his fingers. 'You're busy. I know that.' Her voice is thin. Strained by the shortest of sentences. Giving way as if each sentence has a hill to climb before it can be finished. She's out of breath.

'I'm not that busy, Gran.'

She nods to the door. 'She tried to steal my father's case too, you know.'

'You stop her?'

'The nurse did, thank God.'

'When?'

'Oh, days ago. I had it out. I thought you might . . . '

'I was busy. You already had visitors.'

'You see.' Her cheeky smile. Sharp when she needs to be.

'No,' Neil protests. 'I can make it tomorrow with Pappy's photo. I'm not busy now.'

'I can't remember him very deeply anymore. I'm so ashamed. We never spent a night apart.'

The life drains suddenly from their conversation, and she peers into a space at the end of the bed. Her eyes are darkening. 'And your mother. No matter how hard I try to think on her. My own daughter. I fail to see her face. I'm so sorry.' She squeezes Neil's hand. 'But she's not there anymore.'

'I can get you a photo. I can bring one with Pappy's tomorrow.'

'They're not here anymore. But you are, dear. And I'm so glad you are. I'm glad. I really am. It's so quiet. Isn't it? Up here.'

'It's busy now.'

'It's quiet. Lonely.'

On that accusing word, she settles back into the pillow, spent, vacant. Her hand retreats from Neil's, and rests on her lap. A nurse walks by and stretches her lips at Neil. The extreme heat of the ward has curdled Gran's plastic glass of milk.

'Pappy spoke to me, Gran. A few days before he passed.'

'That's nice.' Her eyes are closed, her head against the pillow.

'He said,' Neil bites his lip, reaches out for her again, 'he said he was going to, I dunno, he said he had something that would change my life. I thought at first, ye know, it might, I thought it would've been cash. Money. Something practical. Necessary. Something like that. 'Cause ye know, he knew I was going to Canada to start a new life. I'm still going.'

She simply nods, eyes closed, telling him she's listening.

'I was meant to go weeks ago. But, I stayed here cause. I thought you might . . . '

Her eyes open and rest on Neil. 'I might have it to give to you?'

'No, no,' Neil retreats. The honesty of her response, the opening up of his motives brings a new intensity, pressure to the situation, the words he's speaking.

'No. I thought. Yeah, in a way. 'Cause, you know, Kathy's waiting for me. But, I'm more than happy to be here to look after you.' His own words make him cringe.

A defeated smile betrays her.

'There will be no one left if you all go.'

'Of course there will. Jim, Eoin, Maura. They're still here.'

'Young people. You. You're leaving. Your grandfather thought it was our failure if you did. It used to be his own children he worried over. Your uncles and aunt, your mother.'

'But there's nothing here.'

'Your country is, dear. Your family. I am. My father thought he started something. Your grandfather fought to keep his children here: "Where you going?" "London." "Why you going to London?" "Work." "Can you not get work here?" "What do you think?" "Leave it with me." He always managed to find his children something. Help them stay. To keep them here. He wanted the same for you.'

She breaks off, lifts her shaking hand and moves it over towards the bedside locker. Neil reaches ahead of her, takes the water jug, pours it into the plastic glass and puts it into her hands. It spills as she moves it to her lips. Small drops stain her yellow nighty. Neil winces for putting too much in. She sips – a tiny sip – and, as before, the container shakes and spills while she trembles with it back to the bedside locker.

'He told you he had something, because he knew. You had told him a few months ago you were going.'

'Everyone leaves. It was never a failure on his behalf. This is the twenty-first century. Ireland, England, America, Canada. There are no borders, if you're educated. They're just lines on a map, Gran. They mean nothing now. Wealth is what defines you, not your passport or where you're from. Nothing else matters.'

'I don't understand you. Your great-grandfather's story, his history surely does.'

Neil wants to capitalise on history, not understand it.

The high-pitched metal *hush* of curtains being pulled draws their eyes across the ward. A whimper starts up. An old, tired moan. Two more nurses disappear behind the swaying blue divider, and then the curtains jolt and rustle. Mumbles silence the ward, mute the television. The moan turns to a pathetic, undignified cry. Neil feels like he shouldn't be there. No one should. Her hand grips Neil's. This place is worse than a graveyard. Headstones are simply another page of words, a closing chapter on life. Here, death is live, in HD, with surround sound. A fully subscribed HBO miniseries.

'Stay with me a while, dear. Please. The chapters are yours. There is no money. They are what he wanted you to have. He wanted you to understand your past. Value it.'

'Value it?'

'Stay with me a while,' she continues, as if she didn't hear. She reaches out again for the bedside locker. Points vaguely to its door. He opens it and takes out her father's leather satchel.

'Read me some more, would you mind? You are sure to find their worth there.'

She struggles with the lock, then the clasp. After some sifting of sheets under the flap, she lifts a sheaf of yellowed paper, a rusted paper-clip staining the top left corner. She lays it on her blanketed lap. 'Not everything of value has monetary worth, dear.'

Harry Casey - F Company, 2nd Battalion #5

Despite protests, I leave the GPO – A new hero of the republic enters – Davy further abandons the cause.

There was much talk of our German friends' imminent arrival, and of how the whole country, irrespective of the rumours in the press, had risen in our support and, therefore, under reasonably sanguine conditions, we could make a fight of it. Sackville Street may have been at the mercy of pockets of ramshackle looters, but outside headquarters, the mood amongst the newly arrived Volunteers was light; there was gaiety in the air.

I merged into the crowd of Volunteers, kept my head down, my eyes on nervous handshakes and ill-fitting belts and bandoliers of ammunition. I did not make eye contact with anyone, as I did not wish to engage in conversation. (On account of the still-lingering shock of seeing Davy kill the cart owner.) I was afraid to meet the glare of my OC, Frank, who, I presumed, had he not been so busy with more pressing matters, would have bawled at me until my eyes bled. Nor, of course, did I wish to see my chum Davy.

In the midst of all the noise and calls to line up for an address from Pearse, James Duggan, a talented organist in Gabriel's Church, and close companion of Pearse's, asked if I still had my camera. I meekly told him that I did, and he requested that I, on behalf of Pearse, move to the bottom of the group, beside the last line of men, and record Pearse whilst he spoke. Pearse, said Duggan, had given him leave to find me and ensure that I recorded, for posterity, some of his orations.

'He had a mind to say it to you after he read the proclamation, but emotion swept him away, and he went back in without commending you on your foresight in bringing the camera to, as he put it, "The greatest show Dublin will ever see."'

Everyone was lined up, and Pearse, his sword and hat differentiating him from those around him, poured his passionate words into our ears as if he was speaking to each and every one of us directly.

'By getting out, you have performed a great deed,' said he, with all the timing, aplomb and gravitas of any actor one might behold upon the stage. I only cranked for a few feet, mind. I had to husband my reel for action, principally because speeches and the like did not make for interesting viewing on a silent screen, and I had not much film stock left. 'You have lifted the stain that has rested upon Dublin's fair name since Emmet's execution was carried out without protest from Dublin citizens.'

Connolly took over from Pearse and ordered the last twelve files (myself included) to proceed across the road to the Imperial Hotel. The Imperial Hotel! How was I to chronicle the events from across the thoroughfare? How was I to record the main stage of the rising from across the thoroughfare?

I delayed for a few moments whilst the files moved off and then, discreetly and politely, accosted Connolly and explained how I was only about ten or fifteen minutes in the GPO. 'If it were not for Pearse asking me to take some footage from the vantage point at the bottom file, I would have surely stayed where I was, which was right there.' I pointed to a space some feet away.

There, in that space, was Davy. At that instant, the moment our eyes met, I knew something had gone askew with him. Davy's eyes, cold and steady, savage as the point of the bayonet he carried, sent a shiver down my spine.

'Do ye hear me, son?' Connolly yelled, returning me to his thick bristling moustache. 'Such impertinence, shamefacedness. Whoever you are, you have too much talk . . . '

I didn't give him a chance to finish, merely apologised, backed away and cast a quick glance once more in Davy's direction. I increased my pace – foot-weary already from lumbering around with the Pathé, and hobbled on account of the gash in my leg – as I moved out from under the portico's dark shadow, clear of Davy's glare, sans stand.

In the Imperial Hotel, I was under the command of Liam Thornton, who, it didn't surprise me in the least, was none too appreciative of my leather apparatus, either. I held up my pistol with my other hand and remarked, 'I'm here, aren't I? Don't doubt my ability with this,' whereupon he simply nodded at the raised pistol and directed me to break glass and barricade the windows with the furniture available.

Sometime later, I was called to a meal and met some Citizen Army men. During the meal, they gave me a rather good account of the fight at the City Hall and the Evening Mail office prior to their retiring to the Imperial.

Seeing that nothing was stirring, my commanding officer advised me to get some rest. Exhausted by the events of the day, my leg having grown somewhat numb, my arms aching from carrying the weight of the Pathé, the extra reels and my ammunition, I duly obliged and took a neat space under the sill of a window I had barricaded on the first floor, in the shadow of the grand balcony. Through a gap in the barricade, with my arms behind my head, I spied the splendour of the Dublin sky and, drifting off into the twinkling embers reaching me from far-off stars, once again let negative thoughts crowd in on me.

What had I got myself into? Would future generations see the very same sky and look on it as I did, and would they have the very same thoughts and motivations as I did at that moment? Would they understand my actions? Our actions? A clearer picture of the motives that had brought me to that point began to develop in light of such thoughts, and a mountebank began to emerge; they were not the truest of motives.

I was honest with myself then, perhaps because I felt myself lacking amongst men who were there to fight and die for a new republic: my motives were artistic before they were political. I wished to capture the revolution for all to see on film, for the future. Others wished to bring about a revolution for the sake of a new republic. A pang of guilt stirred my stomach because of this.

Davy, I had hoped, would have been the reels' symbol, a hero with whom to witness the whole insurrection play out. He was my everyman – not an Achilles, but an Odysseus. A hero to guide us through the dark underworld of war. However, his actions over the previous two days – in particular, most troublingly, only a few hours earlier – made me reassess what it was that men like him, men I had considered pure of heart, really wanted from this revolution.

I had lain awake and matured my thoughts on Davy's and my own motivations for some time, when I finally started to drift off to sleep. I was roused by a soft chorus of men, beginning in a hushed whisper, and then with the bravado of a collective, striking out into a full-throated rendition of 'The Soldier's Song'.

The rousing melody floated atop the air, emanating, so far as I could tell, from the GPO, where my friend Davy was no doubt resting. Davy, armed and willing to sacrifice himself for our new republic. Davy, willing to murder an Irish citizen in cold blood. A citizen merely looking to liberate his cart from a barricade. A cart, no doubt, which was his livelihood. There was something frightful, portentous even, in that action.

The next morning, Wednesday, the sun was shining brilliantly over the city and through the shattered window under which I had slept. A thick beam of light, given depth and life by the sparkling dust particles raised by the barricading, bombing and general vibrations of the city, swept across the window's frontier. Seeing as I had only a few feet left of my reel, and since no call had come from my commanding officer to report downstairs, I took a few paces backwards with my Pathé, stood at the threshold of the large entertaining quarters, and after adjusting the view to its largest opening, I began to crank, somewhat more slowly due to my being indoors, but peacefully, nonetheless.

Whilst I may have been in a beautiful room of the hotel, I fixed my camera only upon the barricade at the window, the spider's-web-like cracks that jutted out from glass unbroken at the bottom of the window itself, and the beautiful thick beams of light shining through. Only a few cranks in, Gogan, a young Citizen Army fellow whom I had met at dinner the night previous, a small, quiet fellow, my junior by a number of years, stumbled to a confused halt by my shoulder and reported that I was required downstairs. He had a furtive hunch that gave off the air of someone always expecting to be assaulted, yet this characteristic, when matched with his large, trusting eyes, endeared him to me almost immediately.

'Don't rush off,' said I, still cranking. 'Hold your rifle up and walk slowly to the window. When you get there, aim the rifle and scan the thoroughfare below.'

At first, Gogan smiled patiently, only to frown doubtfully. However, before I could say anything to persuade him, a lift in his eyes indicated that he must have remembered what I had whispered to him the night before at dinner about my camera, and my calling.

'OK, so,' he said, 'where shall I go?'

Not ceasing my circular motion, all the time watching the window, I said, 'Simply walk to the window, and when there, aim your rifle.'

With one final look in my direction, he nodded dutifully, went stern of face, and marched, with all the affectations of an actor entering a stage for the first time to a full house, towards the window. He disturbed the beams of dust beautifully, gliding through them like a dancer. He came to a halt at the window, his hunched figure, his cap and drawn collar, remaining still for a moment of photographic perfection. It was majestic!

'What do you want from this rebellion, Gogan?' I said, to get a better sense of the fellow. He remained crouched and aiming his rifle.

'To better the circumstances for me and my wife, and have my son grow up in a country free of an imperialist's yoke,' was his passionate (dare I say rehearsed?) reply. It was just what I needed to hear.

Although indoors, having had time to adjust to the conditions of light before I had begun to film, the shot was spectacular. The morning of war! The lookout! Gunshots rang out like a church bell pealing for morning Mass, bombs boomed intermittently like the response from a congregation, the dust rose like incense spreading between pews. I had found my new Odysseus through whom to view the journey of war.

After some moments at the window, he promptly raised his rifle and extended it through a hole.

'Done,' I called, exuberant to have such a scene with which to finish my second reel of the rebellion.

'Is that me in there now, for good?' Gogan whispered, on turning to face me. 'I mean to say, will I be able, or my mother for that matter, my son even, will my mother and father be able to see that there film?'

'When all of this is said and done, no matter what happens, how we fare, this will be seen, Gogan. Your part will have been recorded for all of time.'

His lips puckered, and he shook his head in silent astonishment. Thereupon he moved towards the Pathé and reached out to touch it, almost as if it was a religious relic.

'It's something, isn't it?' he said, awestruck by the power of the thing. 'I mean, to be part of this, our push for freedom, but to have been lucky enough to be honoured by your pictures. I've been in picture houses, with my da, I have. And some day, mind you, I'll bring my son. I've seen shows, in the music halls and just round the corner from here too. Never now, did I think I'd be on that there screen, moving around, not in the crowd like, but actually part of the story.'

'But you are,' said I.

'What?'

'Part of the story. This is your story. All of it. Every action you take, bullet you use, is a part of a bigger story. Without you, us, men like you, there'd be no effort, no rebellion.'

My words struck him silent for a moment while the distant crackle of bullets charged the morning air. I should think he might have stood there, motionless, letting my words project onto his own screen for some time were it not for the shout that came from the foyer.

Gogan came to and said, 'Oh, that's right. I'm to grab you. There's a Mrs Redmond downstairs offering to take messages from us to our home.'

'Is that so?'

I didn't ask how she planned to do it, nor what she was willing to take. Promptly I grabbed my bag with the two spare reels, found a room with no window, more than likely a maid's closet, and set about unloading the Pathé in as near to total darkness as possible. I sealed the canister with the exposed negative using twine, and thereupon sealed it once more in some spare cuttings from a flour sack.

It goes without saying she was none too pleased with this rather cumbersome package, but on account of my knowing her husband, Mr Paddy Redmond of F Company, a caretaker of Father Matthew Park, where my company had drilled over the past months, she saw it in her heart, with some additional earnest persuasion, to relent.

'It's simply a memento for my dear mother of this great day,' I called as she trundled away. How she succeeded in getting there under fire or getting back is something I don't understand, as we believed that there was now a complete cordon around us.

After giving us a short sketch of the reports and events from around the city, our OC chaperoned us, two at a time, down to a men's outfitters' shop adjacent to Clerys. Myself and Gogan went forth after the first two runs. My newly loaded Pathé, gripped tightly by the leather strap, was ever-present and ready should any action present itself, as was the pistol in my left hand.

We slid out from under the awning of the Imperial and blinked into the sun as if we had been in a darkroom all day. No real damage had occurred to the street, although smoke, thick and black, rose ominously from behind some buildings' facades. An odd pop or two of gunfire hurried us on our way and prevented any undue scanning of the vista. Davy, thought I, might have been one of the shapes ducking along under the parapet of the GPO. We moved sideways along the shopfront, our backs to the wall, like criminals trying to break out of gaol – except of course, we were breaking in!

Inside the outfitters' porchway, away from the sound of gunfire and the light of the sun, we walked onto the impressive shop floor. It had two levels, a lofty roof and old mahogany tables and presses lined and littered with upturned clothes, shoes, boots and hats. Our OC ordered us to provision ourselves with overcoats and boots, for a probable march to the country districts. He had no answer to my question of when such a march was to take place.

Our OC must have recognised Gogan's slack-jawed, wide-eyed wonder, for, before he bade us goodbye to fetch the next two, he remarked: 'Don't forget to make out formal bills, detailing each and every item you take, which you must then sign and produce for me to countersign. You hear?'

'Yes, sir,' I remarked.

'You hear, Gogan?'

Pulling his gaze away from the many expensive, yet seemingly discarded garments, my companion returned a distracted, 'Yes, sir. I hear you.'

A great stir of excitement came upon him with the departure of our OC.

'In the name of Jaysus. Look at this. It's an Aladdin's cave of clothes.'

He lingered no longer, discarded his rifle on an upturned locker and swiftly threw himself into his task. Caps and overcoats were swept up, odd boots tossed about with derisory curses.

'Haven't the Hooer's ghosts gone and mixed up all the good boots!'

'Be quick about it, like a good fellow,' I called across the store to him. 'He'll be back in no time.'

'If this is to be my first outfit in the free republic,' Gogan answered, doffing a ridiculous purple suede hat in my direction, 'I'm going to make damn sure I dress the part. Start as ye mean to go on, Harry, start as you mean to go on.'

Caught up in his merriment of it all, for a brief moment I became a consumer, not a chronicler of war, and I too, like the looters outside, like Gogan inside, and I should think, like the others before us, became giddy at the prospect of having free rein over one of Dublin's most expensive outfitters.

Oh, indeed, and didn't I get into the spirit of things! So much so that I donned any number of coats and hats and called across the store to Gogan each time, asking for his opinion on the foolish costumes. An assortment of overcoats were thrown over my shoulders and discarded without a second thought.

The most outlandish of them all, an extra-heavy, three-quarter-length drab moleskin cloth coat, with sheepskin lining and an almighty, peacock-feather-like collar cushioning my head, was barely on my shoulders, when, even before I had the opportunity to turn to Gogan for his opinion, I experienced the unmistakable feeling of the barrel of a gun being thrust into the small of my back.

Of course, I had good reason, in that moment of terror, to think that the English had captured me.

'Har, old pal. Where's the camera?'

Not the English enemy – Davy.

'It's back in the Imperial,' I replied, trying to turn. He wouldn't relent. He maintained our strange pose, both facing forward, him leaning over my shoulder, whispering into my ear, the accusing barrel of his gun jabbed violently into my back.

'Don't be moving now, or codding me. I know you carry it wherever you go. I want the reel, Har.'

'Why ye getting yourself in knots over such trifling things? We're fighting a war, Davy. *You're* fighting a war, for God's sake.'

'Don't talk to me about fighting a war. Do ye not think I know that's exactly what we're doing. A war. Not that you'd fancy it from looking at the pantomime coat you're wearing.'

Still with my back to him, the barrel of the gun between us, him whispering over my shoulder, I tried to distract him until Gogan noticed us, or my OC returned.

Against my better judgment, but out of some absurd sense of needing to face my attacker, ascertain if it was actually Davy, and not some imposter imitating his voice, I turned. He eased up and let me move, ever so slowly, to look him in the eye.

It was upward of twelve hours since I had last encountered him, and in that time, the fighting had produced a great change in his countenance. He looked jaded, lost, dark of eye and bitter of mouth. Fear flickered across his face, only to be replaced, when he became conscious of the fact that I could see it, with a defiant rapaciousness. He angled his head, tightened his jaw and tried to become that stranger I had seen him become when he felled the Lancer, or shot (murdered even) the poor unfortunate with the cart at the barricade. This stranger was becoming something of a regular acquaintance.

'What's wrong with the coat?' said I, trying to delay him.

'It's too queer a coat, even for the likes of you, Har. Swanking it around with that blasted camera and now, with a cock-of-the-walk coat. Dressed up like someone gone astray down the Monto. Mind how the enemy will spot you a mile off in such a thing.'

'Looks like you had no problem anyway.'

He raised his rifle to his shoulder, his jaw tensed, ready for action.

'I'm giving you fair warning, Har. I'll not be delayed any longer. I want the camera.'

'You don't really mean to shoot me, do you?'

His lips curled into a sneer.

'I'm afraid I do. I've been too long with you to be ignorant of the power of your camera. I mean to live. I won't be tying myself to any rock and becoming a martyr anytime soon. I aim to prosper once this is all over.'

The Pathé was safely stowed beneath one of the cast-off overcoats behind him. While he was talking, I shook like a branch in the wind, for I knew he had a formidable temper. I didn't doubt in the slightest that he would fire.

'Think this through, man,' said I. 'There's soldiers everywhere. My

OC will be back in a jiffy. There's a young Citizen Army fellow over yonder. You cannot shoot me. Not for a few pictures, surely.'

'You've gone to war to get those blasted pictures. I've listened to you, Har. I've heard your philosophising on the subject. You're very persuasive. You think they're more than mere pictures. And so do I, now. I'll be damned if they'll ruin me before I even get a shot at becoming someone in this new republic.'

'But you'll be caught, should you shoot me.'

'A ricochet, Har. I'll say it was a ricochet.'

My legs buckled. A loud boom shook the chandeliers above us, rattled the windows, and was followed by a storm of gunfire, fierce and rapid, from across the road. Dust charged the air.

'I'll not say it again, Har. I'll give you 'til the count of three.'

'But what about the legacy? I thought you agreed with me on the importance of the legacy.'

'I don't care a damn. I care about the future. And where I'll be standing when it comes around. Quit tryin' to thwart me now. One.'

'Or the importance of chronicling our times?'

'Blood in ounce, man! Our times will be defined by those who are still standing when all is said and done, Har. Don't be minding all that intellectual nonsense. I'll not be beholden, answerable for my actions because of your blasted camera. It's the gun at play now, and the gun that'll get me where I want to be. Two.'

'Where's that Davy?'

'Farther up than I was before this God-forsaken escapade began. I'm not fighting to have no down-at-heel idler, no ignorant yahoo servant of the empire tell me what to do once it's over. This is a once-in-a-lifetime opportunity. And I'll die for it. Or die trying. You know it just the same, and that's why you're here with the camera. Now hand it over. Three.'

A great boom shook the building again. So scared was I that the hair rose up in my head and nearly stretched through my cap. More revolver volleys followed it. The big pane of glass in the shopfront fractured into a hundred pieces. Obscured by fallen mannequins and displaced garments, I spied snippets of explosions erupt out on the thoroughfare. Being unaccustomed to such destruction, I was peculiarly awestruck, despite my predicament.

In the midst of it all, as I turned back to my friend's face, he threw himself upon me with violence, crashing the butt of his rifle into the side of my head, blinding me momentarily with the sting of pain, and thence, the gush of blood, whereupon I staggered into him and, being brushed off his shoulder, collapsed in a heap onto a mound of over-coats.

'For God's sake, Har,' he pleaded, before thrusting his body towards me for what I thought was an offer of help, but what I soon realised was his reach for the camera I had unwittingly uncovered by collapsing on the coats and moving them aside.

With madness and menace clouding his eyes, Davy raised his rifle by the barrel, meaning to crash the butt of it square down on the Pathé.

'Please Davy,' I whimpered, desperation shaking my voice, my eye clogged with the blood, 'spare the camera. Let me take out the reel for you. Destroy the reel, not the camera. I beg you. You know what it means to me.'

Emitting a grunt of displeasure, a pang, no doubt, of guilt and conscience, he sprang for the camera and began shaking it vigorously, grappling with all the knobs for the means to prise it open and take out the reel.

'Let me, you'll destroy it,' I implored, and he held the camera at arm's length, impatiently.

'Be quick about it.'

After I struggled to my feet and opened the camera, he dug his hand into the belly of the box and, with one savage pull, ripped the film out like he was gutting a pig. The reel slithered heavily to the floor, spraying its dark emulsion everywhere.

'You know as well as I do, Davy, that's it ruined now.'

'Just to be sure,' said he and he slung his rifle over his shoulder and swept up the unravelled reel, as slippery as seaweed, and marched to the door, the bright sunshine whitening the porch beyond it.

Perhaps he had seen the whole affair unfold, perhaps he had been paralysed by fear, who knows, but it was only as Davy approached the door, had literally stepped upon the tiled threshold, that Gogan took it upon himself to enter the fray.

He had opened his mouth to question Davy, disbelief lining his brow at what he saw happening between us. The exact amount he had witnessed, I never got to ask, but he must have been privy to Davy mauling the camera and gutting the thing, for he put out his hand in protest at the door, like a ticket inspector on the tram; an affronted accusation rounded his lips. Davy had almost tramped beyond him when he heard Gogan's perplexed call: 'What do you want with that empty reel?'

Thereupon Davy halted, straightened, for he had been slouched as he made for the door, and looked to the source of the question with a savage intensity that demanded a response. I tried to stop Gogan. I should have forewarned him, yet how was I to know he fancied himself to be aiding me?

'Never mind him, Davy,' I called, the blood now flowing freely from my wound and into my mouth, causing me to retch. I was dizzy and unsteady on my feet.

But neither Gogan, nor Davy – obviously engulfed in the noise from outside – heard me. I staggered towards them, collapsing over a toppled hat stand. It was too late.

'What ye destroying the reel for? He didn't even get a chance to capture anything! He's doing no harm to anyone! Give it back!'

He thought he was doing me a turn, defending my artistic vision.

'He didn't capture anything?'

'We emptied the old one this morning.'

I yelled, 'Don't listen to him, Davy!' But to no avail.

Davy dropped the reel at his feet and made for his rifle.

I was still some distance from them when the most peculiar whizzing sound, a fizz, like someone whispering in my ear, rent the air.

Davy's rifle had only settled on his shoulder, his eye had only just got in line with the sighter, when the sound yielded, for a second or less, yet long enough to regard Davy, his left eye closed, his right eye taking aim on me.

Suddenly the room heaved, my ears were deafened, my eyes were blinded and I was thrown into the air and thence felled uncompromisingly, as mortar, glass and fabric exploded upon us.

Antivirus

'And then he got me a cab. Thank God. And he made sure I didn't choke on my puke.'

'How did he do that?'

'He stayed with me in my room.'

Neil's eyes stare back at him from the corner of the screen. Jealousy is stirring. He is freaked, frustrated. She's a world away, out of reach, being swayed by people who have no loyalty to him, no regard for the sanctity of a relationship. Their relationship. All is not as it was. Things aren't running as smoothly as they once had. It puts him on edge.

'Ah, Kathy,' he moans, looking away to the ruins of his life around the room. Cans of beer, ashtrays, DVDs, clothes.

'Neil,' she's calling. 'What? Come on, babe. Don't be like that. He's a friend. He slept on the floor.' She puts on the innocent-me-I'd-never-consider-a-male-female-friendship-in-any-way-open-to-sexual-tension-or-misreading voice.

'You know what,' he says. 'You know. C'mon, really? In the same room? He's not stupid. If he's not thinking it, then he should be. And if he says he isn't, he's lying. I know Kenny. Knew him. I know how he thinks. I know how men think. Don't be so naïve.'

'Naïve? You're just being weird. Cynical. And, frankly, I'm a little hurt you would even think I'd consider anything like that. He's a friend. Sure, Lydia was staying there too. Lydia was in the other bed. He was just making sure I was OK. Like, everyone doesn't have to have ulterior motives. He knows about you. He knows how much I miss you. He listens, you know, when I need to talk about you, say how much I miss you. I really, really miss you.'

There's no denying it. Kathy is beautiful. More beautiful the less he sees of her. More unique the less he knows about her. More sought after the less he has of her. She is an actress he can only dream of knowing, a porn star he can only wish to touch, an image on the screen he can only hope to know. She is just that though. Now. An image. The last weeks. An image. A screen goddess he dreams about holding, caressing, smelling, feeling, tasting. Her image is becoming his reality. He needs her warmth. Her reassurance after a shitty day, a hard weekend. A chemical comedown pick-me-up. Words aren't enough. This isn't enough.

'And I miss you. You know that, Kathy.'

Even Neil's getting tired of this rerun. The same lines, the same screen.

A pop-up window blocks his view. He minimises it. As soon as it disappears, another one pushes the Skype screen into the background and flashes 'SLUTTY FUN XXXX, SLUTTY FUN XXXX'. He closes the screen and looks again to Kathy.

'What's wrong? Why'd you make that face?' she says.

'There's a virus on the computer. It's Dee's computer. He's after ruining it with porn.'

'Ugh,' she whispers and frowns. 'I hope the keys aren't sticky.'

They laugh together.

'No. But I could fix that.'

'That's disgusting,' she protests. A guilty smile warms her face.

'I'm not joking. The lads are out. How about we make our own little transatlantic porno? There'll be no virus to stop us.'

An avalanche of pop-up screens, 'BIG TITTY GIRLS', 'ASIAN FUN FUN FUN', 'ANAL ADVENTURES', '18+ PUSSY', 'LESBIAN ACTION', mirrors within mirrors, one after the other after the other, scattering onto the screen. Options, endless options, destroying the computer. She squirms.

'I'm still hung-over, babe. Sorry. You know I'd normally love to get down and dirty with you, but I'm like, I'm still in bits. Sure, we can do it for real in a week, ten days right?'

Neil breathes though his nose. Struggles to clear the screen, close out the Internet temptations. He could do with a wank. Release this tension.

'You are, aren't you? You're here on the nineteenth.'

'I was gonna tell ye. I just didn't know how. I didn't want to disappoint you.'

'But you told me last week.'

'I know I did and I'm sorry to have to change on you.'

She just blinks quietly. Says nothing. Blank face. It unnerves Neil. He'd rather she shouted at him, roared something. Gave him an indication of what she's thinking. He needs to hear what she's thinking.

'I know it's been hard for you,' she says, composed, clear of emotion. 'Like, I know how much your grandfather meant to you. And your gran. And her being sick.' She shakes her head. 'And I know I told you to follow the reels and do what you could with them. And I know you said they look like they could be worth a lot. I know all this. And I support you, you know I do. It's just, you know, I'm lonely, OK?'

'The YouTube things you do for me, they're great and all, you know. The Screen and O'Connell Street and that. But they're only clips. I'm homesick and lonely for you. Your touch. A kiss. I'm here two months now. And it's hard. I'm meant to be here to start a career, but like, everyone in the house is just partying all the time doing mushrooms or fucking yoga, and I hate staying in on my own. This isn't meant to be a holiday. It's meant to be the start of our lives and you're not here.'

'I know I'm not there. You don't have to remind me. Jesus, you'd swear you're the only one who's lonely. It's always about you and how I'm wronging you.'

'Don't say that,' she answers, her brow wrinkling, 'Don't be like that. Don't make me feel bad for trying to tell you where I'm at. I need to express how I'm feeling. I need to talk to someone about it, and Kenny only listens so much.'

The name stuns him again.

When they argued before, he'd been able to draw on the silence. Sit it out. Let her temper subside, level out, and know that when it did, he'd be able to slide up beside her, only the bed or their clothes making any sound, put an arm around her, snuggle into her, whisper something warm, soft, stupid and reassuring. Just get close to her, as if touch could say more than words. The warmth of an embrace cured everything.

She mouths a hair clip, takes a piece of hair in her hand, removes the clip from her mouth, and secures the hair. A glitch. A screenshot. Blank screen. The antivirus software update swallows up the screen. 'SCAN COMPLETED'. He minimises it. Her face again, her hand moving to her hair. Neil's blank face alone at the bottom blinking dumbly into itself. And then the antivirus update page forces its way back onto the screen and announces that it needs to be renewed. Silence. The fan on the laptop hums into action.

'I just need some reassurance,' she whispers, deflated, shoulders slumped, head dipped. Eyes hidden. Lips drawn. 'I'm not feeling too great recently. I'm down. Kenny has been great, you know? The girls have boyfriends, or they're out seeing guys. Kenny listens.'

'Of course he does.'

'Please stop being like that, Neil.'

'Like what?'

She's about to talk but the screen goes blank. The Internet closes and a warning comes up. 'TROJAN HORSE DETECTED. ANTIVIRUS SOFTWARE HAS EXPIRED. RENEW TO RUN PROTECTION. GOOGLE CHROME HAS STOPPED RESPONDING.'

He tries to ring again. But the Internet won't work. The computer stalls and goes blank, as if the battery has gone, but it's plugged in.

He has booked for the tenth of next month. Just three and a bit weeks away. He'll be over. Gone. And, if all goes well, rich. They'll be together. They'll be free to be whoever they want to be, not some poor Paddys fresh off the boat, looking for a few dollars for board, telling their hard-luck stories from back home.

He's not leaving this country poor to arrive in another poorer. That's not emigration, it's exodus.

His Future Self

He turns and moves down the hall once they're all gone. A brief meeting called in Gran's house while she's still in the home in Phoenix Park. It has been decided: Gran will be back here by the end of next week. The home, centre, whatever, is costing too much. Pappy's prolonged illness was expensive. His accounts, dissected when he passed, were an eye-opener. The house is it. They're going to get maximum value. Scavenging after the remains of their parents' lives. Meat on the bone. No matter how they dress it up with their big words, dignified note taking, polite listening, excusing, they are vultures sucking the marrow. Is he one of them? No. He's taking what's his. He was promised the chapters, and he earned the reels. He's not hiding anything, pretending to be something he's not. He'll be upfront when the time comes.

A silhouetted figure seated by the radiator in the breakfast room shocks him before he realises it's Eoin, his legs crossed, all relaxed, in the darkness.

'You frightened me,' Neil says, managing a smile, turning the lights on before moving to the television.

Neil doesn't bother asking why Eoin's there. Without hesitation, Eoin slides a paper bag out from under his chair. Brown Thomas cream-and-black. The bag of affluence, reused time and time and time again by single-purchase customers.

'What's with this?' Eoin asks.

The television would be a suitable distraction, but Neil needs the remote to turn it on. Gran's old leather satchel comes out of the BT bag. Neil instantly forgets about the remote, supports himself on the back of his gran's medical chair.

'Dunno.'

Eoin narrows his eyes while he tries to read Neil's response. Silence. He lifts the satchel out of its glamour cover, uncrosses his legs, his white socks still on show, and holds it over his lap.

'Neither do I,' Eoin says. 'But it's been in her locker. At the hospital. You saw it. I know you did.' He shakes his head, flicks his glasses up the bridge of his nose. 'Then at the home. She was beside herself with worry when that lady took it. I spoke with the nurse. She said she even tried to get out of bed to find it.'

'Really?' Interested, surprised pitch of the voice, eyebrows arched.

'Don't "Really?" me,' Eoin snaps, rising now. He takes the one step needed to bring him square to Neil's face, the satchel still gripped at his stomach.

Neil once looked up to Eoin. A male role model. Eoin brought him to football games, Gaelic games. Neil was impressed with his passion for sports. His disregard for what people thought about the volleys of abuse he spat from the terraces. His willingness to send back a burger from Eddie Rocket's if it wasn't up to scratch. His lack of patience for barmen or waiters if the pint was muck. His appearances on the *Late Late Show* as an audience member three times, because he was friends with the floor manager. Having the Internet – the dial-up *eh, eh, eh* – before people even knew what it was. Giving Neil a lend of his camcorder for a week. A big chunky thing you slipped a VHS cassette inside to make your movies. The Porsche he picked Neil up from school in once, a lend from a friend who rented classic cars. His microwave, his massive TV, his DVD player, CD stereo. Eoin was to be admired. Copied.

'The nurse said she had it out the other day – a few hours before it was taken. She said the lock was open, bag opened, on the bed. Paper, old-looking, spread out on her lap – and a young man, "her grandson, possibly" on the edge of the bed, reading to her.'

Neil doesn't respond.

'Reading to her,' Eoin strains, as if he remains perplexed by the idea.

He shakes the bag. 'What's in it? And why did she ask you to read it?'

'Nothing.' Neil wishes he had the remote. He wishes the TV was on. The lights were off. The lamp was on, so he could hide in the shadows.

'It must be something, since you brought it into her.'

'No I didn't.'

Eoin's stare is intense but lacks conviction. He's unsure of what exactly he's doing, what he's accusing Neil of. 'The paper, Neil. The paper. You were seen reading it.'

'No I wasn't'

'Don't play games. You were. She was at the bed across from you. She saw it all. I'm onto you. The others may not be wise to it, with your "Let her stay where she's most comfortable," but I'm onto you. You want this house. You're after the will. I see you talking with her. I know you know she has to redo the will now Pappy's dead. You're making your move with this,' he shakes the satchel with a slight flutter, 'whatever it is. What is it?' He edges forward, growing more desperate, agitated.

'I didn't know about the will. I'm just visiting. That's all. She's lonely, so I'm visiting.'

Eoin throws his head back, releases a deep, mocking laugh. 'Don't give me that horseshit, Neil.'

Neil has to restrain himself from trying to gain control of the bag. The contents, surprisingly, have become real, as real as paper that represents currency, as real as the four-minute clip he has seen can represent a slow-forming sense of his past. A currency. His great-grandfather's words, his deeds, his actions, his thoughts, his story, everything becomes a commodity someday. They are a commodity today. A currency tomorrow.

Neil wants to own them. Exclusively. His reports, his diary, confession, whatever it is being flicked around in the cracking leather satchel, is of worth, importance to Neil, just as much as the reels. A commodity becoming a currency. Words becoming real. Because the reels, now that Neil has seen the first one, are taking on a new, disconcerting meaning.

He's used to finding meaning in a three-minute clip from a music video on YouTube. The lyrics and melody of his favourite songs have helped him to see the world in new ways. It's no surprise the four-minute clip of the first reel has had a similar effect. Even though they're black and white and splattered with brief white glows exploding temporarily on the screen and beset by small, white-noise inconveniences, his great-grandfather's images have finally come into the HD world, and against all odds, somehow, discreetly, but gradually, their power has affected him.

An appreciation? Possibly. Neil wants to know what happens next. What else there is to see. What else he can hear Harry say. He wants his voice to guide him. Help him. He wants to read. Now that the pages are threatened, he wants to read.

'I'm going to burn the bag, Neil. That's what I'll do. Tell mother the mad lady took them again and they're gone. I'll burn them out the back at the rose bush.'

His jogging runners and denim trousers, tucked-in chequered shirt, overhanging gut, thick bristling moustache, nose hairs creeping out, creased, scaly dark stains under his eyes behind the thick frames, comb marks still ploughed into his grey hair, the condescension and impatience with everyone, not just Neil. The greed in his voice, desperation in his eyes. To think Neil wanted to be like him when he grew up. He wants to be nothing like him. He doesn't want to be even near him, to be reminded he is related to him. They have nothing in common. Nothing. They have nothing to bind them. Nothing. They are completely different people, looking for different things, for different reasons. A different generation with different expectations and rules.

'They're letters,' Neil says, with a resigned sigh, making the disclosure all the more dramatic. 'Letters. Old letters that she wants me to read to her 'cause, I dunno, she's lonely and she wants to remember things. Make sense of things.'

A triumphant smile. Eoin leans into Neil and looks over the rims of his glasses, as if to prove his point.

'Letters? About what? Written by whom?'

Neil looks to the leather case and wonders if the value will hold once, or if, the letters are shared.

The Thin Red Line

Scumbags, scummers, wasters, dirt birds, scangers, junkies, smack heads, slappers, slags.

'NEXT STOP ABBEY STREET, SRÁID NA MAINIST-REACH.'

Enda takes out a pouch and withdraws from it an antibacterial wipe. He rubs it on the bar in the Luas, and then offers the used wipe to Neil.

'It's my last one.'

A fat lady with greasy hair and a kid biting into a plain roll, both sitting down, watch Neil and Enda. The Luas makes its *ding-ding* sound and jerks before moving off. Neil shakes his head and looks up to count the number of stops he will have to endure Enda. You can tell a lot about a city from its public transport. The Red Line is Dublin's shame. The SkyTrain is Vancouver's pride. Kathy loves it.

'The filth being exchanged on the handles would make you sick,' Enda is saying. 'Public transport is a hotspot for bacterial cross-contamination.' Enda doesn't care who listens in on their conversation. Neil pretends not to hear him, starts to scroll onto the SkyTrain website, lost again in the screen. The Luas is busy, but there are empty patches of purple. Neil looks up as they glide past the Irish Life building, the bus stop he gets for his gran's. The junkies milling around the methadone clinic.

'You'll love this place,' Enda says. 'So glad you could make it. I've been so busy. I really need a break. A bit of colour. The black and white can get a bit tiresome. Not that I'm complaining. The reels are amazing. You know that, don't you? It's not that I don't love them. I do. A bit of colour, you know, the real world will refresh me. Culture.'

To be polite, Neil smiles in his direction.

'Our culture. Irish culture. It's so, I don't know, grand. Dignified. Unique.'

Their carriage rocks and begins to slow as it comes to the next stop. 'NEXT STOP ABBEY STREET, SRÁID NA MAINIST-REACH.'

A young girl with a dirty buggy tries to get off, but the rush to get on means she has to push through. Shouts, and the beeping of the doors. Neil's at the top. He can see all the way down the tram, hear young lads mouthing off and cursing. There's tension in the air. A couple beside Enda, plastic bags bulging with cans, are moaning about losing something. Neil hates public transport. Especially the Luas. SkyTrain. Sounds like the future made real.

'NEXT STOP JERVIS, JERVIS.'

Three teenage girls in low-cut tops, wafting cheap perfume, block the aisle. One of them starts music on the thin, trebly speaker of her phone. A four-four beat distorted by a waspy synth and some exaggerated vocals. Headphones are a thing of the past. What was once private is now public.

The Luas stops at the junction to O'Connell Street. Waits for the lights. Enda looks over heads towards the GPO and says, 'It hasn't changed much since the reels, has it?'

Neil just sees a chaos of buses, cyclists, beggars and protestors with bloody foetuses in the shadow of the Spire.

A man in a suit talks into his phone. A woman in a long cardigan announces into an earpiece about how happy she is with the new arrangements. The couple with the beers continue to growl at one another. All those seated near Neil look on quietly. This is not the place for a history discussion. The Luas is not the place for any sort of discussion. The Luas is a place to hold your nose until you get off. The SkyTrain is old-school Concordé glamour, gliding across the city sky.

'NEXT STOP JERVIS, JERVIS.'

Again the lurch forward as the Luas glides to a stop. The grey depression of Jervis Street. Again the rush to get on, preventing an old woman with a shopping trolley from getting off. And again, Enda, his hand stuck to the spot on the handle he cleaned, refuses to budge. Neil eases back onto the far door to make space. The carriage is packed. He thumbs through the SkyTrain stops. Millennium Line. The future awaits.

'I feel as if the reels are lost on you.' They are separated by a number of people, but this doesn't bother Enda. It does Neil. He likes the anonymity of crowds.

'I mean, you don't realise what you have.'

A red-faced baby in a buggy starts to howl. Its mother tells it to shut the fuck up and throws a teddy in on it.

'How can you bargain for something if you're ignorant of its value?'

Neil shrugs. There's a time and a place. Lake City Way Station.

'NEXT STOP FOUR COURTS, NA CEITHRE CÚIRTEANNA.'

They sway as the speed increases. The noise, the chaos, hands up, holding the grips, buggies rocking, babies crying, the loud voices of the young lads, the dance music piercing, the screech of wheels on tracks, nasty faces breathing on him, swaying into him.

'I mean, these guys will be professionals. Your ignorance of its potential value could really hinder your judgment. They're not mine to sell, although, if you ask me . . . '

Everyone shifts forward as the Luas slows. Only one or two get off. A junkie, staggering, eyes closed, yellow face, lumbers on, a can of Devil's Bit slopping in his hand. He moves through the crowd and staggers into Enda when the Luas moves. *Ding-ding.*

NEXT STOP SMITHFIELD, MARGHAD NA FEIRME.

The junkie tries to shift Enda aside. Enda towers over him, his broad frame unmoved by the junkie's efforts to get a steady hand on the pole. Enda frowns at Neil. Neil shrugs.

The noise around them increases: the music, the phone conversations, the baby crying, the screech of the wheels. But still, the junkie's slur can be heard.

'For fuck sake, pal,' he moans in his long, lazy drawl. 'Just gissa bitta space, I'm not well.'

And, this time, he drops his shoulder into Enda. Neil smiles to himself. He's not getting involved. Enda, he knows, will not want to give up the disinfected spot.

The grinding of wheels and the faint push forward before the next stop sweeps into view. Two more squeeze on. Neil is tight against the far door. Buggies, shopping trolleys, shopping bags. The language of the masses and the voice of the skag head. The open air of 29th Avenue Station, Renfrew. The claustrophobic, constipated, contaminated, jaw-tightened moan of Dublin scum.

'Fuckin' move. I'll spill me drink.' The drawn jaw, open mouth, half-closed eyes.

NEXT STOP MUSEUM, ARD-MHÚSAEM.

Enda ignores the threat. The junkie pushes again, and this time his drink sprays over other passengers. There's an exclamation in French from a couple near Enda.

'I'm after spillin' me fuckin' drink ye poxbottle,' the junkie moans. 'I'm after spillin' me fuckin' drink.'

NEXT STOP MUSEUM, ARD-MHÚSAEM.

A half-arsed dig is thrown, and Enda easily palms it away, but looks to Neil for support. Main Street Science World. DNA and what we're all made of.

'Fine, take it,' Enda says, and eases through the crowd to Neil, shaking his head in disgust.

'Ye fuckin' scumbag,' the junkie shouts after him. Science World. Euthanasia?

The carriage eases to a halt, and Neil and Enda have to pass the junkie to get out. As they pass him, they see he's pissing through his trousers onto the floor. Neil gags and the people around him, the man on the phone, the French tourists, the lady on the earpiece, the mother with the baby crying, all notice what he's doing, and there's a crush to clear his area.

'That's just fuckin' disgusting,' Neil's saying, as they step off the Luas and onto the track.

'It's a symptom of all that is wrong with this city,' Enda says. 'Degenerates like him go unhindered as they sully this country's fair name. It sickens me.'

They take the steps up to the museum.

'The whole place is a kip,' Neil says.

'That's unfair. Places like this here,' and Enda nods at the entrance to the barracks, 'this here, places like this are what we have to be proud of. This is what makes Ireland great. You won't find men like him in here.'

'This is a museum, Enda,' Neil says laughing to himself, 'a historical museum. The only reason you won't find men like him in there is because everyone's dead.'

I Just Called to Say . . .

Each time he has called recently, he's done so with a vague fear she might actually answer. Skype flatlined after his housemate's computer overdosed on porn. Phone calls are the last resort. He has uploaded two new recordings since they last spoke on Skype, and she hasn't viewed either one. She has logged off. Disconnected. Signed out of their YouTube channel, their relationship, their collective experience. This is the longest they've gone without speaking since she left.

Neil has moved away from the noise of the city and escaped into Fitzwilliam Square to ring her. It's where they used to hop over the railings in summer evenings for a picnic and an outdoor ride.

When she answers, he forgets to speak, and instead lets the silence rest for a second between them. Lets her know he's not going to rush her. Startle her. Scare her off. But there's no small talk to ease them in.

'I see you didn't go onto YouTube.'

'Work's been really busy.' Her voice is drained of any warmth, colour. She sounds tired.

'Too busy for a phone call?'

A siren slices through the trees, pierces the shadows, sprays an indiscriminate blue towards Leeson Street.

'I was waiting for you to call, Neil. I thought you weren't talking to me.'

'Of course I was talking to you.'

'Oh.'

'It feels weird, though, the last few days. Like, I don't know. You're being distant with me, Kath. You've never not called before.'

'I'm just tired. Work's been mad. And I was out last night. It's hard. I have my good days and bad days. The last few days have been bad.'

'I'm sorry, babe. If I'd known, I would have called. But like I said . . . '

'I know, I know. You thought I'd call. For once I didn't put my life on hold and wait in my room like a good little girl to be rescued by my prince in shining armour.'

'Don't be like that.'

'You always said you were my prince. I'm not so sure anymore.'

The trees in Fitzwilliam Square are darker the higher up they go. Swaying gently, mutely, rocking as if they're at a wedding, a slow set when everyone – once the bride and groom are finished – has taken to the floor, and love-filled sweet nothings of 'I'll be your prince, if you'll be my princess', are whispered in her ear. Just swaying easily, freely, his face nestled into her neck, a stray hair tickling his nose, smelling her warm, soft smell, hands on her hips, her arms slung heavily over his shoulders, the ridiculous whisper, too real, too earnest, too exposed, too in love to know any better: 'I'll be your prince.'

'I'm sorry I'm not with you, Kathy. I am. I'm sorry my grandfather died and I had to cancel the flight. I'm sorry I didn't book straight away. I'm sorry. I'll come over tomorrow if that's what you want. I'll do it tomorrow. I have the money now. To hell with the reels. I don't even know for sure if they'll be worth anything anyway. And I'm not gonna lose you for them. Do you hear me? I'll forget about the reels. I'll get that credit union loan, and I'll be with you in twenty-four hours.'

'It's too late.'

'It's not too late. Don't say that.'

Her voice has a weird, detached, sleepy quality about it.

'It's too late. All of the running around since your grandad died is just an excuse. You're afraid to make the leap. More importantly, you're afraid to take the leap with me. You're not . . . '

'Where you getting this? I don't understand where this is coming from. I realise I've left you out there. I realise that. I'm sorry. It's over. I'm coming out tomorrow. I'll get the next flight.'

The lumbering whoosh of a bus straining through the gears. Its yellow upper deck flickers through to his feet. A car alarm, orange light pulsing through the gate. A packed, loaded silence.

'I don't want you to,' she whispers. The words ring out. Nearly take him off his feet. 'Not like this. If you were serious about me, about Canada, you would have come already.'

Someone has been in her ear. Kenny. That lecherous smile. He will not provide a crutch. Something to rest what she's trying to say on. He stays silent, his legs trembling, mouth gaping.

'Things have changed, Neil. Me and Kenny. I don't want to talk over the phone. It's not fair on you.'

A smooth, level cityscape hum. The compressed air hissing though the earpiece like a tyre deflating.

'Neil. Are you there?'

Love, he thought, was the certainty of belonging. Not the pain of separation.

'I'm sorry. He's here. He's been around. He's like . . . he's been a good friend. We talk, ye know, about stuff. Life. We talked a lot, and it, it just happened. He has vision.'

'Vision? His powers of sight made him attractive?'

'Vision, Neil. For his future. He knows what he wants to do in life. Direction. I need that.'

'Why are you saying this to me? I don't . . . I don't understand. I mean, you don't know him.'

'I thought I knew you.'

'Are you trying to hurt me or convince yourself?'

A deep breath.

'I'm sorry.'

The dead tone of a call concluded.

The trees, the city, the low hush of the square. The car alarm tweaks off, the silence leans on its extinction and becomes more apparent. He pinches the bridge of his nose and sees a flash of Kenny – his smirk – and Kathy. He grabs his head and grunts, breathes through the pain. Where to now? Canada. Now, more than ever, Canada. Break out. Strike out. His heart is breaking. Devastating him to a point where he cannot move. He has to move. He'll go to the meeting. Get the money. Then, Canada. There is no more time.

Kenny's face lingers. A flash of Kathy interrupts it, lying on a bed, naked, waiting. No longer for Neil, for him. The intimacy of her image. The perfection of it. The warmth of her embrace. The sound of her breathing in his ear, 'Don't come,' she says. 'Don't come.'

A Client

A fountain pen scribbles everything Neil says onto a yellow page. The writer's eyes divert from Neil's face at the beginning of each sentence, as they find the starting point on the margin of the refill pad.

The writer says the word 'client', and Neil turns his eyebrows. Neil moves back from the table, feels the cold, hard wood of the snug, and says, apologetically, 'Sorry, client?'

Neil is nervous. The enormity of this meeting isn't lost on him. As much as he wants to be strong, dominant, brave in the face of such obvious wealth, he is nervous. The delay needs to have been worth something, the reels have to be of value. The pen stops its scrape on the page.

'I beg your pardon?'

The inadequacies of college all over again. The writer sniffles, twitches his nose as if trying to adjust his glasses. Leers over the rims.

'Client,' Neil repeats, slowly, in case he pronounced it wrong.

The writer lets a brief grimace of bafflement undermine Neil, before he gains his composure and then looks to Enda at the end of the table for an explanation.

'Surely you were informed, prior to this meeting, as to my role in this potential transaction?'

'Your role? Are you not the buyer?'

Enda swallows and clears his throat.

'Em, no, sorry. I haven't had a chance to tell him. This gentleman here, Neil, is only representing the interests of the buyer.'

'Potential buyer,' the pinstripe with the pen adds, his face darkening. 'I presumed you would have had a consultation prior to this meeting.'

Pinstripe fetches a card from the inside pocket of his suit and displays it between his fingers.

'Smyth and Gallagher, Solicitors. I'm Gerard Smyth. Here on behalf of my *client* – who, as I was saying, would need proof of ownership, of some description, relating to the film reels.'

Neil plucks the card from him. Pretends to be interested in the text.

'You mean, we won't be finalising the deal now?'

The solicitor shifts his shoulders, hunches forward, then back – his jowls bulging and sagging as he does – lays down the pen and rubs his cheek. He musters a patient smile.

'At this meeting, no. This is purely a preliminary discussion. I thought you were aware of this. However, if you can provide sufficient proof of ownership, I cannot foresee any adverse circumstances arising. My client,' he slows down on the word 'client', 'will be more than happy to make an offer for the three reels, in their entirety, and exclusivity, once the proof of ownership issue is resolved to our satisfaction.' He turns to Enda and nods, 'And, of course, provide a facilitator's fee, also.'

'But it's just what I said,' Neil goes, sups from his pint, trying to remain calm. 'They were in my gran's attic 'til I found them – and she said I could have them. It's that straightforward.'

'And I appreciate your honesty with us, I really do. However, what your grandmother has told you is irrelevant. We need proof to ensure that there are no issues arising once we – if we – decide to purchase.'

'But we never discussed a price.'

The solicitor, packing up, stops and grins. His eyes flash to Enda. Enda hasn't opened his mouth. Backed Neil up on anything. Informed him of anything. Helped him in the slightest. He's almost sabotaged the sale. The solicitor's eyes close in contemplation. He lays the refill pad down, noticing a wet patch on the table as he does. He inspects his sleeve. He eases back in his seat. The one o'clock news gains volume above the bar outside their enclosure.

'The matter of an agreement on a purchase price and the facilitator's fee is dependent upon proof of ownership,' the solicitor says, calmly, slowly, at ease with the situation, a smile of collegiality tight on his face. 'As a matter of principal, my client – until said proof can be verified, as we have discussed – would rather not partake in the undignified spectacle of haggling. Needless to say, once you have furnished us with conclusive proof of ownership and exclusive first-refusal on the reels, I can assure you that my client will be willing to pay a handsome five-figure sum, which he thinks you will see, from other such sales, will be quite a substantial amount more than what such antiquities normally fetch.'

A number, zero, zero, zero, zero.

Neil makes to break in, but pinstripe is only too happy to continue. 'You have piqued our interest. We have now made an offer. We are willing to buy. On the terms now laid out, we will proceed. And one addendum, also. My client will need an answer by next week at the latest.'

'Next week?' Neil looks to Enda. As much as he wants the money for the reels, he wants to know what they hold. The pressure for a decision flusters Neil, confuses him, panics him, makes him question the solicitor's motivations. 'But the second reel isn't even completed yet. I haven't even seen it. Why the rush? Your *client* doesn't even know what's on it.'

'This is standard practice. Negotiations for such offers should not be protracted.' He taps his card with his pen. 'You have my contact details. I'll expect a call by Monday to arrange the formalities.'

He rises, holding his tie over his gut as he does, settles his suit jacket and eases the writing pad into his briefcase with a slight whistle, pleased with himself, jolly almost.

'If no call is forthcoming, we will presume your interest in the transaction has cooled, and our dealings have ended. My client is more than willing to complete the deal. The only question that remains is, are you?'

The Park

A clear green view dulled by his conscience. Silhouettes of spires and towers wink through trees. Not quite summer-warm – but not autumn-cold either. A request from her, and an acceptance from him, on the say-so of the nurse, for a stroll. He's glad too; the open spaces will take the pressure off of his appeal. His appeal, which was once an ambition for cash, has become a necessity for success. He has to go, he has to see Kathy, he has to succeed.

Pyjamas, bathrobe, slippers, cotton blanket, thick, chequered fleece blanket, wool beret. Blue skies and the soft *sshh* of trees. Deer, delicate and dainty, leafing through a meadow in the distance. Slowly, without stopping – for losing momentum means that the wheelchair is a dead weight – he pushes her along. An outdoor workout.

Far-off traffic pollutes the long lull between words. Her words – as ever – are carefully chosen to give maximum value, impact and worth. Neil's words, tripping over the one sentence he should say, are many and valueless. All his thoughts, the nonsense he's spouting about the weather, how dark the evenings are getting, everything is compromised, coloured by the gel of the sentence he can't bring himself to utter: 'I found your father's reels, and I can get a fortune for them if I can show proof of ownership,'

'What's this now, they sang over his grave?' she whispers, her head leaning back to try and see him.

Neil has to lean down to catch the sentence again.

'Sorry, Gran?'

'What was it they sang over his grave?'

'Whose grave?'

'Your grandfather's, dear. It was a beautiful rendition. I remember that. Beautiful air. For the life of me, though, I can't remember.'

'Eh . . .'

He scans hard to recall the lowered coffin, the gravel flaking in, the roses dropped by each of the grandchildren, a flash of colour in the oppressive brown, the crisp crunch of those who were not immediate family making their slow retreats, the sniffles and shoulder hugs of the uncles, aunts and grandchildren, the clearing of throats, the call of a blackbird, the low, deep baritone note of his uncle Jim, like a trombone, finding the key and unravelling into the beginning of the song. An air. A sombre, sober air coming from one, then two, and the family are gathered, arm in arm, united, singing his grandfather's party piece one last time over his grave. Only Neil didn't know the lyrics.

'Danny Boy,' he whispers.

The covered grave, the multicoloured flowers, the last drips of rain. His head down, afraid to meet the eyes of the others as they put deep mourning into every line.

'It was his perfect send-off,' she says. 'What he had always wanted. To be surrounded by his family. Have them there when he passed. In Ireland. Together.'

'And he did, Gran.'

'But you see. That dear, to keep everyone in Ireland, is what he always wanted for his children. What he gave up for them. To keep them close. Particularly hard in Ireland. To keep all of your family together. And, then . . . ' She sighs. 'You know, he felt responsible for your mother's death. He cried. Wept for her, and you. You became his son then. And it broke his heart, believe me, to think of you, the last one, leaving. He had battled, made a promise to keep you all here. And, right at the end,' she coughs lightly, 'he suffered very badly to think of you leaving.' Again, she trails off. He wants to reassure her that he's not leaving out of necessity like everyone else. He's leaving because he wants to.

'But times are different, Gran,' he says, the wheels still sluggish over the grass. 'Remember, I told you. Leaving your country doesn't mean that much anymore.'

'But what about what my father fought for? What your grandfather battled for? To keep his family close. He gave up a lot. A lot of people did, to have people stay here.'

'But here, Gran – Dublin, Ireland. They're nothing. There's nothing different anymore between Dublin and Liverpool, Sydney, New York. Whatever. Pubs, cinemas, sport – *jobs*.' Neil emphasises 'jobs' because, at the end of the day, they're what count.

'But an idea, dear. My father had an idea, God rest him, your grandfather too, and they thought it was worth the sacrifice.'

'And it was, Gran. Their idea made this place worth living in once. Made it great. Now, though, ideas of a country are for tourists, for slogans to put on T-shirts to say you've been there. It's as arbitrary as the climate.'

'That's terribly defeatist.' Her throat gets caught, phlegm sticking on the last consonant. 'I thought you would be interested. Tommy thought it too. That you would be inspired by what your great-grandfather spoke about.' The voice is losing weight.

'I'm interested in money, Gran. Having it. Holding it. Affording a life with it.' A deer pops its head up, flicks its gaze from one vacant spot to another. Alert and relaxed all at once. Innocent. Neil thinks about what he is saying. How it sounds. What it means. Is it really him? The smell of the brewery snakes over the meadow. Like hot Weetabix at his grandparents' breakfast table. Sentimentality pollutes the scene. He must keep a clear head: 'And, that's why I've something to ask.'

Neil stops pushing and comes around to face her. This is him facing up to it. Convincing himself he is nothing like his uncle. He hunches down at eye level with her, an A4 piece of paper in hand. Desperation scrapes at his throat.

'I need your signature on something.'

He thought about forgetting the request. Forging it. A scrawl: her first initial, squiggly line, last initial, squiggly line. Only, as easy as it seemed, felt – he had practised it – the actual act of forging of his gran's signature to sign over her inheritance, selling it without her knowledge, was a pang of guilt too far. Betrayal. He has read that it comes smiling.

She glances at the paper with silent caution. Doesn't say anything. A lift of her chin tells him to proceed.

'You said the diary belonged to me. So, like, I could find its worth and do what I wanted with it.'

'OK.'

'Well. I read some things in it, and, well, what would you say if I said I found the reels?'

Her eyes move from the paper to his face without emotion. The look is cold. As much as he has told himself that the reels are a commodity simply to be traded for cash in the open market, he knows, deep down, that they are worth far more than that.

'Which reels, dear?'

'Your father's. If they existed, what would you say?'

The question induces a grimace.

'I'm not sure, dear. I suppose, perhaps, I'd like to see them.'

'But if I was to find them, would they be mine?'

The words are simply said, but uneasily felt. Their meaning and the motivation behind them not lost on Neil. This is wrong. But necessary. This is the twenty-first century. No time, space for sentiment.

'I suppose, since we, your grandfather and I, did decide to give you the chapters . . . ' She coughs lightly, pulls at her blankets. Her face is pale. 'I don't see why they shouldn't be yours, if you found them.'

'And could you then . . . like, would you . . . I'm just thinking . . . if I was to find them, I'd need proof that they were mine. Would you sign this for me?' He holds up the sheet again. 'So I could prove it. Just your signature would do.'

'My signature?' No emotion. Reaction. She whispers, 'Why?' A note of confusion. Almost hurt.

'In case I needed to show someone I really owned them.'

Neil lays the paper on her lap.

'You see,' he points out what he has typed. 'I've written the reels are left to me – to do with as I wish – as a present.'

Her mouth moves as if to utter a word, her face becomes drawn and she gazes over his shoulder, at the green space behind.

'And what, dear, would you do with them?'

He holds the pen out to her, like an offering, a guide. His sudden relief at the lack of a third-party witness disturbs him. 'I dunno, Gran. I haven't thought about it. I'd like to just have the option in case someone wanted to buy them or something.'

'Option?' It's uttered as if she has never combined the two syllables before. The meaning of his response, its coldness, confuses her. The word disappears behind a clearing of the throat. A slight breeze creases the paper. Closes her eyes.

'The option to see what they'd sell for.'

Her lips purse like she's tasted something bitter. 'And who, dear, do you mind me asking, if anyone, would be interested in giving you this option?'

'Somebody would be. There's interest already.'

His excited announcement twists her face further. She grips the blanket and pulls it up her lap.

'Whatever they offer, it would never be enough. Whoever they are. Who are they?'

'I don't know. They sent a solicitor.'

'Well then, I wouldn't sign if they were found. Not unless I knew who had such an interest in them.'

Her stubborn resistance and her retreat behind the blanket are a surprise. She's normally a calm, serene projection. Afraid of conflict, always placid and compliant. Decent.

'But you said they would be mine. You – you said I'd learn the worth of the diary. Grandad said I'd learn the worth. I have.' He holds up the paper. 'The money is life-changing. It could change my life. Grandad said the diary would. He was right. The reels though, they're worth more than the diary ever could be.'

'I was mistaken. He was mistaken. He would never have signed.' Her voice is thin now, grating, tired. 'Especially without knowing who the buyer was. They weren't to be signed away. I won't sign them away.'

She closes her eyes with a slow purposefulness. Her body shifts in the chair, signalling the conversation is over. Neil lifts the typed page and pockets the pen, shaking with frustration. He turns the wheelchair away from the open meadow, towards the distant shadow of the home. He wants to run, burn up what he's containing.

It's a slow progression, pushing with arms outstretched, his back arched and strained, guiding her up the stubborn gradient.

'I'd like to read you another chapter, Gran, if you'd like.' A level of composure finds its pitch. He needs to hear what reel three has to offer. He was afraid to ask too much of her, but there's no point in holding back now.

'I'm not so sure, dear,' she says. 'Maybe it was a bad idea asking you to take responsibility for them, after all.'

'No Gran,' he protests, 'I'm the right person for them. I am interested. I love reading them. Honestly. I do.'

'I don't think you do.'

Neil keeps his head down, watching his feet disturb the long grass, feeling the strain on his neck, his shoulders. Feeling the hill, but not looking for the peak. If there's one thing he has learned from working out, it's to stick with it and the results will come.

Harry Casey - F Company, 2nd Battalion #6

A brief survey of my relationship with Davy – I bend myself to the Gaelic revival – A riot – Future plans become clear.

Being a Dublin lad, I had always held hurling and Gaelic football in contempt. The only buckos to play those games were the country lads. Of which, Davy (of course) was one. He would tease me terribly, prod and pull me, blow raspberries at the mere sight of a football.

'Give up that aul empire game and play with real Irishmen!'

'I am a real Irishman.'

'Not if yer running around with that there ball like a lackey of the empire.'

It seemed my regular attendance of the Gaelic League, the Irish language classes and such like, meant nothing to him when it came to establishing myself as a true Gael.

We would wrestle hard, scuffing our knees and hands on the ground, rolling and turning each other over and over, panting stubbornly, gasping about who was the most Irish. You see, being of a weak disposition, I had a great interest in soccer, as it brought out the best of health in me. Not like the Gaelic games, which were reported to cause a feverish brutality in all participants.

My football team was winning everything before us when, not long after the all-Ireland final between Kerry and Kildare, the news reached us of the ban on foreign 'garrison' games by the GAA. Young as I was – thirteen at the time – and dispirited by Davy's incessant ribbing at what he imagined was my capitulation to his teasing, I reluctantly turned my back on football, and, simply to quell his blathering about being a 'real Irishman', joined his hurling team of the Ard-Chraobh in 1903.

Seeing I was obviously inferior both in technique and talent, Davy being the good friend I knew him to be, would tutor me patiently on the finer details and skills needed to succeed.

Davy helped me out positionally, showed me how to handle a *camán* and flick up the *sliotar*. But, thereafter, when it came to a public game, he took leave of all responsibility. He let me alone in the wide open spaces of the field to fend for myself. Unfortunately, my nerve was found wanting whenever a challenge would come my way. Rather than meeting a chap head-on, I would, still playing the sport like a football player, try to disengage from the tackle, or better still, ride around it.

By the end of my first year of the sport, innumerable cracks on the shins, stung fingers, throbbing thumbs and numb hands had almost lain waste to me. Yet I persevered. Two years thereafter, still suffering the slings and arrows of being an uncommitted player, one game, a friendly, changed everything. Our opponents, St Laurence O'Toole Hurling Club, for some unknown reason, found themselves shorn of a fifteenth player. Our captain, despite Davy's protests, was eager and vocal in offering them, for the sake of a fair game, my services. Our team was oversubscribed, and I, it goes without saying, was the excess.

Our captain, a condescending bucko by the name of Farrell, fancied himself against me and, indeed, he passed by my flailing hurl unchallenged a multitude of times. Oh, but there comes a time in every young man's life, when the silent humiliation inflicted by an aggressor, be it on a sports pitch, or on the battleground of adolescent identity, becomes too much, and one, irrespective of the consequences, has to act. Is forced to act.

When I found the *sliotar* dropping equidistant between myself and my new nemesis, Farrell, only yards from the goal, I charged. With muscles tensed, I charged, in a bullish rage towards the ball. Farrell, being the quicker, got there first, yet I was not to be stopped, and I shouldered him with such formidable force that he bounced against my stiffened frame and lifted into the air before returning to the ground with a mighty crunch and crack, as his hurley, sandwiched between his head and the dry summer pitch, snapped in two.

It was almost like an electric current had been prevented from making its connection by the simplest of obstacles. All I needed was the one flick of a lever – confidence, belief! – and hurling suddenly made sense. I became electrified by the speed, precision, quick thinking and bravery required to excel at it.

Within a year, I was one of the foremost hurlers to draw on a ball in midfield. I had set my mind to understanding the game: the strength needed to succeed, the skill required to better the opposition. Davy and myself became the boiler room for Ard-Chraobh, each of us a piston powering the forward motion of our collective steam engine!

The months drove forth: school, our friendship, my jaunts around the city with Davy and my Kodak Brownie, the dark room, the Gaelic League, lectures and classes, the playing fields, muck and thunder. Fate charged ahead, Davy and myself seemingly in control and at the helm. Our friendship, now that sport had become our common ground, was formidable, unbreakable.

And yet, in January 1907, although still the closest of chums, an incident would occur that should have warned me of his subversive capabilities. Being young and foolish, trusting, I paid no heed to Davy's underhanded ways then. The referee had just called an end to the Dublin Championship semi-final when two men in flannels and blazers, flanked by Jack Hogan, our imposing and heroic team captain and defender extraordinaire, prevented me calling on Davy and my other teammates and celebrating our impending county final.

'Har, stall it there a moment.' Jack beckoned, and waited a few more strides before yielding his march.

'It's sure to be a fine final next week, wha?' he said before introducing his two finely dressed gentlemen.

'Surely,' said I.

Jack noticed my reticence to engage in small talk without an introduction to our two interlopers. He smiled, slapped the damp face of his hurl, and said, 'Where's me manners, at all. Don't be minding these two bowsies, Har. This is Sean and Gerard, fellows of the right kidney in my book.'

We shook hands in a manner ill-fitting for the middle of a sports pitch, and too sombre for the celebratory tone of the afternoon. Their seriousness and Jack's forced smile, nervousness almost, roused my suspicion. Behind them, his hurl over his shoulder like a redcoat's rifle, Davy was appraising our gathering from afar.

'That was a fine game, young man,' the flannel by the name of Sean said. He was a tall, rotund-bellied man, long out of the days when he may have known what it was to play fine in any active sport.

'Thank you,' I replied.

'Indeed,' answered Gerard, another rotund man, slightly squatter than Sean. He had sharp eyes behind thick frames that he continuously, with a pinch of thumb and forefinger, pushed up his nose.

The four of us stood in dumb silence in the January sunshine, the cheers and laughter and colour of the sashes at the side of the field filling our unnecessarily long pause.

'We've been watching you for some time now, Harry,' Sean began. I simply smiled in appreciation. 'And there is something frightful in the manner in which ye go up against lads twice the height of ye.'

Jack and Gerard nodded in agreement.

'Aye,' said Gerard, regarding Sean, tipping his hat back on his head. 'We admire fellows who are up for the fight. Ready to defend their team vigorously. Prepared to give their all for a cause.'

All went quiet again. After a time, Jack took up the slack.

'What we are meaning to say, Har, is, well, you're a grand fellow, young an all as ye are. But you've impressed, so ye have. Matured. Not only on the field here. And we,' Jack motioned, his palms raised, his hurley pointing at his comrades, 'we were thinking of seeing if you'd be interested in joining our organisation, on the quiet now, and learning some few things about what we do and what we foresee may be coming our way in the near future.'

'A new club?' said I, wishing they'd just spit it out.

Davy, a forlorn figure on account of the desertion of our players and supporters for refreshments, stood looking on from a distance at the edge of the field.

Sean puffed up his chest, straightened his tie, shifted his neck, leaned in. 'Of sorts, Harry, yes. We're the IRB, you see. So, we are, in so many ways, a club.'

'An exclusive club,' Jack appended.

'Very exclusive,' continued Sean. 'And we're offering you a way in.'

I was not surprised by who they claimed to represent, yet I was baffled by their choice of candidate. Indeed, my only wonder, besides their selection of myself, was why it had taken them so long to spit it out. I had heard that what usually happened was that any suitable person who proved himself well at hurling clubs was approached by a promoter of the IRB with a view to becoming a member.

If such an approach was to be made on our team, I had always presumed that Davy would have been the one to get the nod. He had spoken of it plenty enough. And, in so many ways, showed himself to be an exemplary club man. He was always blathering about how only an elite few were selected, normally on their strength of character and the ability they had shown on the field of play.

I had never given serious thought to joining the IRB, or any such organisation. Truth be told, I was more interested in my Kodak, and following my love of the image to London and learning more about the motion cameras I had read about – and seen in action on the big screens in Dublin. And, maybe, becoming a newsfilm cameraman.

Lest I should offend them by giving too prompt a response, I asked that they give me time to ponder the question. 'If you don't mind, I'll need time to square it with the pronouncement of the bishops.'

Their lips all turned white, being pressed so hard in maintaining their composure, and it was Sean, after an intolerably long silence, who said, 'No problem Harry. Sure, we'll be back to see you play in the final next week. You'll have an answer for us by then?'

'Indeed and I will,' said I, solemn, brow knitted in faux contemplation.

Davy was apoplectic when I joined him later and explained what had held me up.

'But you've no interest in such things.'

'I do,' said I. 'I surely do.'

'You do not. The shamefacedness of ye, saying you'll consider it. You're for England, you've been sayin' it these last months. Ye even have Joe writing letters to his friends over there to look out for a job for ye. You're about that blasted camera and your motion-picture houses!'

Davy knew me only too well. While maturing at hurling, I had remained steadfast in my ambition to become a master of photography. I became at first eager, then desperate, then reckless to announce myself on the photography scene in the city. You see, the scene in the city amongst the photographers, of which I knew a tidy few through Joe, was cut-throat and dismissive. In order to gain the respect of one's peers, one's fellow enthusiasts, one had to sell pictures and get photographs onto picture postcard covers. Joe brought me to many shoots, but he left me in no doubt that one had to be inventive and bold when the opportunity arose to get a unique composition. Such an opportunity presented itself the week before my county final.

One of my keenest regrets from my early days with my Kodak Brownie was that I had not managed to somehow sneak into a performance of Synge's *In the Shadow of the Glen* in 1904 and get a shot. It was said that the atmosphere in the theatre on the second night of the play was electric, the audience charged with rage. I could only guess what it was like, as, being late to the theatre and the story of condemnation, myself and Davy had to content ourselves with soaking up the mass hysteria outside with the peripheral revellers from the Finnegan's Wake and the Lanigan's Ball.

I resolved, therefore, after missing out on the first riot, that there would be nothing else for it but to go to the next Synge play, in the hope that some scandal would ignite the audience again, and I would be prepared, as all good cameramen are, to capture the moment. A saucy-sounding play by the name of 'The Playboy of the Western World' was to run for a week at the end of January. Saturday through to Saturday, skipping Sunday. It was current that if there was to be trouble at the theatre, more than likely the trouble would manifest itself on the opening night, when the material would hit the audiences raw. Unfortunately, the opening night was the night before my hurling final!

Word spread like typhoid of how the play by Synge was full of low, unsavoury thoughts, libelling the Irish race, and filled to the brim (in three short acts!) with indecency and blasphemy. A second riot was a sure thing.

Davy (who else!) was recruited to help me get set up for our operation in the theatre. It was great gas at the start, planning our ruse – for a quick enquiry with the theatre had given us short shrift at the mention of bringing a camera to the show.

So I had to improvise. Davy managed to get a ticket. I, after some while of nagging and persuading, managed to convince Joe to loan me his eight-by-ten-inch camera and tripod for the whole of Saturday. 'If anything should happen to it, Har, you'll be paying me back forever!' he warned.

The plan, like all best-laid plans, was straightforward. I would enter the theatre via the stage door early in the day, when all was quiet, with camera and tripod in hand, and, once down under the stage in a dark corner, I would stay until I heard some commotion, at which point Davy, being already seated in the theatre, would watch for my arrival and, once the picture had been taken, clear a path for my getaway. It was so simple it was ingenious.

I don't know how I passed the hours waiting for the stage door, indeed, any blasted door to open, but I was very glad when I spied – from my vantage point on the ridiculously conspicuous corner across the street – one of the stage hands opening up the theatre door. After some moments of tapping my foot aimlessly, I raced across the street, opened the stage door, peeped in, and charged ahead, my stand and camera weighing me down terribly.

I had never set foot behind the stage of the theatre, so, being slightly nervous, and anxious lest I should give away my ruse, I ghosted light of foot through the semi-darkness. Out front, behind the backdrop, I could hear a deep, haughty voice and another gentler voice in discussion. There were yesses and if-you-insists and I'm-terribly-sorry- but-I-must-insists being thrown around amidst the trampling and hammering.

Being acquainted, thanks to a friend of Joe, with the layout of the theatre, I was able to find the door to the space underneath the stage. Once there, I made myself one with the dusty furniture, and, dwelling surreptitiously in its shadows, waited, as all artists must do, for the muse to call.

I waited. And waited some more, in the complete darkness, until a weak light was cast in upon me, wherefore I curled up in a tight ball like the most unobtrusive hedgehog you ever did see. Some footsteps clattered about. Wood was dragged on the cold, damp ground, metal bars clattered, the carrier of said metal bars cursed his luck and hissed when a bar clanged off something. He sucked his teeth and then made a slobbering sucking noise and then spat and then sucked anew and cursed and spat once more.

When the door closed, I heard him call up to whoever it was he was working with about how he had gone and near chopped the top of his finger off searching for one of them bars below the stage when they had the very same ones up above the stage, and "If he so pleases, he can get his own bloody bars in future." He must not have pleased, for no one else came down to throw light into my secret corner thereafter.

I recall sitting in the dark, on a cushion from a broken old chair, listening to the footsteps and the lines above, dull and deep and repetitive, rhythmical, creating colours in my mind's eye. Holding fast to my camera and stand, I concentrated on what exactly I would do when the commotion kicked off, maturing my plan and playing it out in my head, like one of the motion picture shows I had seen in the theatre in Dublin, over and over again.

At first, I was troubled to say when the theatre performance might start, for the incessant rumble of seats and low murmurs and talking made it hard to tell exactly. Yet, the moment the curtain was raised, I swear, I could have heard a pin drop, or indeed, a mouse scurry across some of the discarded furniture keeping me company! It was fantastical to hear the performance unfold mere yards above my head!

After a moment of silence, when a hush had drawn its breath, footsteps sounded. They were loud and pronounced and moved towards the source of an earlier knock. Deep dialogue, the rhythm of words once again and more footsteps back into the centre of the stage. Fast at first, then slowing to a serious, onerous, heel to toe, heel to toe. The footsteps remained solemn above my head, while about them little flurries, heels, circled.

A female voice, high-pitched and lilting, played tenor to the baritone and many phrases, the likes of which I'm sorry I couldn't make out, were uttered between them, bringing titters of laughter, then joyful guffaws from the audience. Amongst them, I swear I heard Davy's wild cackle run loose too. I let the curtains of my cheeks be drawn and, as if I could see the stage above me, kept my neck arched and my face to their floor, my ceiling, and imagined I was looking upon a screen.

Becoming lost in the cadences above, I managed to get comfortable. An hour or so passed, with the colours of the language unfolding before me, when a line from a man – desperation straining the sentence – sparked off a flurry of lines from a woman, and there broke out a voice of discontent not from above me, but from afar. It came from near the back, maybe even above the stalls. The actress's voice stopped mid-sentence. Her words, normally full of music, were cut short as if her instrument had lost a string!

Nobody, no voice did gainsay the dissenter. Another voice, this time much closer to the stage, bellowed a short, abrasive word. There was a great stirring, feet shuffling, stage heels retreating. Rehearsed lines started, and stopped, like a scratched gramophone record. I stood up, felt the settings on the camera, made sure the stand was well attached, clicked the flash into position and listened. In the midst of the catcalls, I had to ensure it was not a false dawn. I would be able to take one shot, and one shot only. There was to be no dress rehearsal.

Right enough, a din of unruliness broke forth, and I charged over the stray furniture, towards the door. When I saw the strong yellow light emanating from the bottom of the door, I considered myself already out and stepped upon one of the blasted stray metal bars the stagehand had earlier cursed, lost my balance, flailed about for something to stop my fall, and, being as good as blind, found nothing of substance to grip and tumbled to the floor, where I was knocked unconscious.

In the dark of that underground den, I awoke, perfect silence ringing in my ears, my head heavy and dull, my eyes pulsing brightly. While I lay horror-stricken on the cold, damp floor, numb and sickly from the mossy touch of the uneven surface beneath me, I blinked back to life and called out, feebly at first, for help. No response was forthcoming, so, I went forth with another call. An empty, dark nothingness was my response. It would be my response for an intolerably long time. I had knocked myself out, and Davy, curse him, had not come to my rescue. I was incarcerated under the stage, unable to do a thing until the theatre reopened for the second performance, in a full day's time. My most pressing concern at this juncture was for my life! I was facing the possibility that I might perish there, and if I wasn't to perish, at least not be freed from my underground cell in sufficient time to make the county final!

A caretaker was to be my liberator. Nevertheless, I did not make the game. Indeed, I only reached the verge of the pitch not long after the final whistle had brought to a close – as I was to later learn – our team's defeat. On arriving to the field of play, I had to quicken my already hasty pace to join the conspiring group of Davy, Jack Hogan and the two other IRB men.

'Apologies, apologies, gentlemen,' I hailed, hand up in weak submission, admonishing myself for my tardiness. 'I'm sure Davy has you told about my unfortunate circumstances.'

Jack merely knitted his brow and shook his head. 'Davy has apologised for you, but like us, is none the wiser as to why you chose this day, of all days, to become an idler. But, no matter,' he said, shaking Davy by the arm, a grand, important embrace. 'We have got what we wanted, albeit, not as we expected. But nevertheless . . . '

'Oh, but surely you want to hear my explanation?'

'Your actions have spoken louder than any words,' said the IRB man with the spectacles. And, with that, the three men nodded in my direction, smiled in Davy's, and left me there panting. Davy, who was now wearing a ridiculous grin, nodded to me also.

'What was that all about, at all?' I asked.

'Now, that'd be telling, Har. I've been sworn to secrecy.'

'You can tell me, Davy. What were they sayin'? Never mind them, where were you when I needed ye?'

'What they wanted, Har, is of a strictly confidential nature. And where I was, is irrelevant. You let the team down, you let Jack down, you let the two lads there down. But, never fear. They've gone away satisfied anyhow.'

I didn't argue with him. I knew too well what he was like. To jostle him would be futile. Seeing his opportunity, Davy had stepped in and joined the IRB in my place. What stuck in my craw, apart from Davy being in such a hurry to take my place, was the fact that he had neglected to aid me in the morning. Knowing I had not come home, as he surely would have learned when he called to my house on the way to the game, he had let me alone under the blasted stage! I made my displeasure known in the fiercest of language.

'Let you down?' he guffawed. 'Man alive, Har. You knew the game was on today. You could've gone to tonight's show.'

'But, that would have been pointless. If there was to be a riot, which there was, as you bloody well saw, partook in for all I know, it was going to happen last night! I had to be there last night!'

'And I had to be here today. And, between the two of us now, we should both take responsibility for the repercussions of our actions, the good, and in your case, the bad.'

'But, we're friends, Davy. I thought. There was me thinking we shared in our joys and woes.'

'It seems, Har, I've had more woes than you. And for once, when a good thing comes my way, you have reason to question it and blame me for your woe.'

'Don't be like that, Davy,' said I, putting out my arm to soothe him.

'Ah, leave me be. I've things to be doing, Har. Real things, important things now. Not running around with you and your pictures.'

However much I may have jostled Davy about filching my place with the IRB, it mattered not, as I had elected in advance to decline their invitation for the simple reason of the Church having prohibited 'secret societies'. I could not reconcile the two viewpoints: the aim of the Brotherhood and the prohibition of the Church. At such a young age, I find it now commendable that such strong convictions steered me clear, for a time, of the IRB, wherefore I was able to travel to London to pursue my dream of becoming a motion-picture cameraman.

Yet, from a more mature vantage point, with the help of hindsight, I see now that I was also leaning on the crutch of religion, and all of its symbols and meaning, in order to extricate myself fully from the cause of Ireland and her request. At the time, you see, symbols of Christianity outnumbered and outweighed the symbols yet to mature in the name of our republic. I always knew I would be there for the fight against the empire; I just wasn't sure in what fashion. The prohibition of the bishops against secret societies was a convenient sidestepping (to use hurling parlance) around the argument. However, when the Volunteers openly asked the young men of

Ireland to unite, I had no way of circumventing the call. I joined, and I joined meaning to capture it on camera, and of course, to fight if so obliged.

Notwithstanding all that was said between us, Davy was soon back on side with myself and the camera. Nevertheless, after his actions and remarks that day, it always felt as if something had changed between us, I just chose to ignore such instincts – to my detriment.

When the Party's Over

A riot of noise. The floor vibrating. Loud calls. Eyes closed, faces raised to the lights, green lasers across the dry-ice haze. Aftershave, perfume, sweat. Drawn chins and tight, stiff pouts. The heat.

DUN, DUN, DUN, DUN, DUN, DUN, DUN, DUN.

'Is this enjoyable for you?' Enda shouts.

Neil looks to Enda, surprised to see him still there. 'What?'

'Is this enjoyable for you? Do you actually enjoy this?' Enda stays erect, unmoved by the music, his straw circling between the Coke and ice.

'Of course I do,' Neil shouts back, his shoulders loose, dipping and swaying to the beat. 'Of course I do. It's . . . I live for this. This is what keeps me going, man. Kept me going. Every weekend, I live for this.'

'When does it stop?'

'What?'

'This. All of it.'

DUN, DUN, DUN, DUN, DUN, DUN, DUN, DUN.

'It doesn't. This is the start of the weekend, man. Thursday night, maybe Friday morning. Friday night, Saturday morning. Saturday night, maybe Sunday morning, maybe Sunday night. Monday to Thursday, Monday to Friday is my weekend. Thursday to Sunday is my week. This is my life. This is what I'll miss about Ireland. This. The craic. My friends. You see them? Dancing? They're happy. I'm happy.'

Open and exposed, spouting shite and believing wholeheartedly in it, Neil is happy. Neil is off his head. He wants to join his mates dancing a few feet away, all together and apart, lost in the music. He wants to be with them, enjoying the few moments of forgetful bliss – not babysitting Enda.

DUN, DUN, DUN, DUN. DUN, DUN, DUN, DUN.

Enda surveys the heaving room, unimpressed. 'If this is the craic. No wonder you're leaving.'

Neil laughs away the dig, immune to negativity. 'Lighten up, man. Have a drink. Enjoy it. This is what it's all about.'

'But none of it's real.'

'Of course it's real.' Neil smiles, revelling in Enda's innocence. 'You don't get it do you? Of course it's real. What I'm feeling now is real, the music is real, the buzz in this club, man. Of course it's real.'

'And this is what you'll miss about Ireland?'

'This is the only thing I'll miss about Ireland.'

Enda frowns. 'That's ridiculous.'

Neil sees humour in Enda's naïvety.

'OK. OK. Not the only thing. One of a few things. I'll miss afternoon pints in beer gardens. Evening pints with the lads in Anseo. A spliff down the canal. Leo Burdock's sausage and batter, SuperValu chicken-fillet rolls with coleslaw, Tayto, *Love/Hate*, all-Ireland final day, Ireland matches in the pub, Robbie Keane's tumble, Eamon Dunphy and Johnny Giles, the *Late Late Toy Show*, Christmas with old friends. The bus journey out to my gran and grandad's, that feeling when I'm on the top deck and I look out and see the Pigeon

House towers across the bay and the bus takes the corner onto the Howth Road and I know that in a few minutes I'll be in the safest place I've ever known: my gran and grandad's house. The thick powdery smell of their house – you know, real old-people smell – their burnt rashers, Superquinn sausages and burnt toast. I'll miss my gran for sure. But that's it, Enda. My family. That's it. The place outside, the real Ireland you probably think I don't know anything about, I don't belong to that place. The place where you live. It's a poxy place. One big fuck-off illusion. A poxy illusion that is bleeding me dry. It has no soul. No soul. See this? There's more soul here than there is out in your Ireland.'

'This club is on drugs. What you're feeling is the chemicals.'

'And the place out there? What's that? Is that any more real?'

'Out there?' Enda smiles to himself. 'Really? OK. You want to do this? Out there is Ireland. The Republic of Ireland. The country I love. Ireland. It's Trinity College and Samuel Beckett, Oscar Wilde and James Joyce, W. B. Yeats and the Abbey Theatre, Lady Gregory and J. M. Synge, Paul Henry and John McCormack, Éamon de Valera and Michael Collins, the Dáil, the Seanad, Áras an Uachtaráin, the National Gallery, the Hugh Lane Gallery, the Natural History Museum, the Decorative Arts & History Museum, the Ring of Kerry, Malin Head and Hook Head, the Cliffs of Moher, the Aran Islands, the Blasket Islands, Skellig Michael, old country villages, turf, fishing trawlers, a thousand welcomes, Mass on a Sunday, the Gate Theatre, the Peacock Theatre, the IFI, Charlie Haughey and Jack Lynch, Mary Robinson and Mary Harney, the Dubliners, Ronny Drew, Enya, Sharon Shannon, the War of Independence and the Easter Rising, Daniel O'Connell, the 1798 Rebellion and Vinegar Hill, the ancient Celts and the Hill of Tara, the *Book of Kells*, the Shrine of the Cathach, the O'Kalem films, *The Quiet Man*, *My Left Foot*, *In the Name of the Father*, *Garage*, *Taffin*, *About Adam*, Irish dancing,

Riverdance, Daniel O'Donnell and Joe Dolan, the GAA, *RTÉ*, *TV3*, *TG4*, U2, the Republic of Ireland, the green, white and gold. That's Ireland. That's what is out there, Neil, if you must know. That's what Ireland really is.'

'A Bord Fáilte history lesson? Bullshit.'

'Bullshit? No, you're bullshit. You have a piece of Ireland and you don't even know it. Those reels are more Irish than all of this nonsense put together. But you're so off your head you don't realise that. Well, you better, because tomorrow morning, whoever you're meeting, they'll know what they are. And they won't be in a club talking nonsense like you tonight. They'll be ready for you and ready to take the one true piece of this country you might ever own from you. And the saddest thing is, you'll never know what they were really worth.'

A brief moment of clarity, lucidity, sobriety, sanity. The meeting is arranged. The sale to be made. The penny drops. Why is he babysitting Enda?

'Your head's so far up your arse hiding out from reality in your college lab, ye don't even know how shit your own life is, man. Never mind mine. I've no use for ye anymore. You've done your bit. You'll get yer kickback cash. Now, fuck off.'

Enda moves to say something, but shakes his head instead and leaves. Finally.

Smoke and Daggers

Neil can hear their voices, low but clear, during the dips in the horse racing on the TV opposite the bar. He has a pounding hangover-comedown headache. He recognises one of the two: the solicitor's. He was going to go straight into the snug, where their blurred shapes are shifting behind the rippled glass, but the second voice has unsettled him.

The commentator's breathless monotone reaches its peak of intensity as the race ends and the hooves' rhythmical rumble fades. He comes up for air, the cheers die down and a more relaxed, steady voice runs through the placings. Neil takes a light step over, head raised to try and catch the faintly familiar voice behind the glass: a heightened, impatient whisper.

The barman appears, and, seeing Neil idling, opens his mouth for an order. Neil puts his hand up to stop him and says 'Alright' before he launches himself into the snug as if he has just arrived. The voice becomes a face he knew he'd heard before. Neil is struck immediately by how pristine the owner of the voice looks – his hair, his skin, his suit. He is that manicured, Photoshopped façade of emptiness on the election posters for president. The living, breathing version of that charismatic cartoon of a man Neil saw on the TV in his gran's, the voice on the radio in the hospital. Alby Ashe. The establishment. Ireland in a suit.

Neil manages a reluctant, cautious smile. Alby stands and gives a nod and a strong, exaggerated handshake of friendship. 'You must be Neil. Pleasure to finally meet you,' he says, and settles back into his seat. Neil is aware of an extra turn in their brows – probably disgust – at his dishevelled appearance and his late arrival. He doesn't belong in their company.

'Apologies,' Neil says, shifting behind the table, his back now to the window facing onto Baggot Street, his head looking through the small square gap onto the empty, pre-lunch bar. 'I'm sure you're all very busy.' Alby's smile patronises, and Neil lies, 'I slept it in.' He never went to bed. Neil hopes they're too preoccupied with the business at hand to notice his unchanged clothes, unbrushed teeth, stale sweat from the heated chaos of the comedown party.

Alby drums his fingers on the polished oak table in a giddy show of energy, before turning the saucer under his empty cup. The solicitor opens his writing pad and unscrews his pen. Neil doesn't know if he's being paranoid or if their silence is a sign of repulsion. The solicitor breaks the silence with a playful clap of his hands, and goes, 'This is the buyer – just like you requested. I'm sure you're well aware of who he is.'

They chuckle.

Neil shrugs indifferently. 'No, should I?' Trying not to stare at the smooth, rich consistency of Alby's skin. Ireland in a suit, the smooth, rebranded Fáilte Ireland face.

The solicitor laughs through the turn in his brow. 'It's our president elect. Former Taoiseach, Mr Albert Ashe.'

Neil shrugs again. Broken capillaries slightly blemish Alby's cheeks.

'You're too kind. I wouldn't be counting the eggs yet.' There's a pristine, defined sheen to his wrinkles that make them look painted on. As if he's wearing make-up. It's a face that draws you in, makes you want to emulate, somehow wear. Steal. Be. It's a mask of wealth. An otherness that, even beside a solicitor, separates him – an aura almost – and makes him exude importance. Ireland in a suit. Fáilte Ireland smile. Face of a thousand welcomes. Ah, the blarney and the craic is only mighty.

'Mr Ashe,' the solicitor hurries on, 'is delighted to have the opportunity to indicate how serious he is about his offer and, to reassure you of his intentions. I presume this is why you requested his identity? And I assume you have brought your proof of ownership also?'

'Unfortunately, I wasn't able to get that.'

The solicitor draws a rigid, frustrated line across the page. 'Oh,' he says with a mock frown.

Alby's smile falters momentarily before he quickly resumes his composure. The saucer has stopped turning.

'But,' Neil offers, 'I'm sure we can come to some sort of agreement? Broker a deal as they say.'

No one laughs.

'I suppose,' he continues, 'ownership and all that wouldn't be an issue if you just had all three reels in your possession? Like, possession is nine-tenths of the law, yeah?'

No response.

'I can give you all three now – as in, like, today. I can go to Trinity. Done. Take all three. You own them.'

The saucer starts to spin again. Eyes consent in a two-way exchange.

'And, young man,' Alby says, his finger turning the slow, slow ceramic record, 'if I may be so bold as to ask what you will request of us?'

'Money.' The simplicity of Neil's response makes Alby exhale a nervous laugh. 'A sale. Now. Today. Done and dusted. I get the money, you get the reels. No strings attached. No receipt. Straight exchange.'

Alby wags his finger at Neil, a grin of devilment lifting his eyes. Ireland paying out, instead of Neil paying in. Unlikely.

'I like the cut of your cloth. You make it sound so very clear and easy. However, when you are in this business as long as I have been, young man, there's always a catch. You expect me to pay now for an incomplete set? I didn't come down in the last cloud, you know.'

'It's my offer. You either take all three – the last one not rendered – or I go elsewhere.'

It's a game of bluff. Neil wants to cash in.

Alby's eyebrows lift. 'Well,' he grins, 'you really do mean business don't you?' His lips falter momentarily. Alby is in a bind. His presumed superiority over Neil has been undercut.

Neil's legs shake discreetly under the table. His heart beats heavy at his chest. The headache is blinding. His mouth is parched. Neil has vague memories of television debates, news, a thirst for a villain, someone to blame for the mess. Alby blanking questions about his culpability, capability, competency, his grin glued across his pristine face. His stutter and his bland, tail-chasing sidestepping responses, political babble, evasive toreador-type red-flag-lifting distractionism. And here he is now, where a stoned and coming down, soon-to-be emigrant has him by the balls. Neil tries not to smile.

'Well now, it seems . . . ' Alby begins.

'What Mr Ashe is saying,' the solicitor interjects, 'plainly speaking, is that he is not used to such forceful negotiations. He's a man of a bygone era. And, really, well, we're a bit sceptical, to be honest with you. It comes down to trust. How can we trust you? Reel three hasn't even been seen. Reel two still isn't complete. How . . . how do . . . how does he know it has any worth?'

Alby and the solicitor share a quiet nod.

'But it has been seen,' Neil answers. 'The guy in the lab looked through them. Ask him. They're in good nick. Deal today. You put your trust in me. I put mine in you.'

The solicitor and Alby glance at one another.

'Mr Ashe will need some . . . '

'It's OK, Gerard,' Alby says with an apologetic wave to his friend. 'Take out the chequebook. I like this young fella. In fact, eh, he's got some neck, reminds me of myself way back when.' Ireland Inc is open for business.

The solicitor lays his briefcase on the table, lifts out a chequebook and hands it across to Alby. This game of poker becomes very real. Neil's head is pounding. The colour, he fears, is draining from his face. The room is spinning.

'OK,' Alby says, his words full of energy again, lifting an eyebrow like he has just hit upon a plan. He opens the chequebook in a deliberately dramatic manner, unscrews the pen with theatrical intensity, dwells on the process, draws it out. Another horse race begins to stir the commentator's drone over their heads. The syllables from the monotone voice start to slam into one another in a breathless crescendo.

'I'll tell you what.' Alby begins to write, each letter given careful consideration. 'I'll do out this cheque here.' He finishes the first flourish of pen work, and starts on a new line before continuing. 'For twenty thousand euro.' He draws a line under the word 'only'. He transcribes the figures. 'And you will bring the three reels to my solicitor's office by – what will we say? – two o'clock OK with you?'

Neil is delighted to be included in the finer details. He shrugs surprised compliance. Alby's signature dances across the cheque, and he rips it out, and, with his elbow on the table, dangles it between his finger and thumb.

'If you don't mind me asking, why all three?' Neil can't help himself. 'I mean, you're willing to pay for them all without even seeing anything of reel three.'

Neil is interested. He hasn't read the diary entry yet, so he doesn't know himself. He doubts they do either, but he just wants to know what it's like to annoy the establishment. Rattle them. Make them work for what they want. He'll never have a chance again.

'Simple really.' Alby responds without a beat. 'The Holy Trinity. Three acts. Three is the magic number. It simply makes up the complete collection. If it's as good as the other two, of which, as you know, I have been assured are in good condition, it will be a fine collection.'

It's not quite brown envelopes under the table, but it is Baggot Street. Strange, sinister, in some way illegitimate.

Alby returns his pen to the cheque and scribbles another few strokes.

'Do we have a deal?' he asks.

The cheque is held out again, and he reaches across the table and places it – without letting go – in Neil's palm: '20,000.00'; 'twenty thousand euro only————————'; two, zero, zero, zero, zero.

Neil forces a dry swallow. The scrawl of a signature. Just 'A', squiggle, 'A', squiggle. He thinks of the *Book of Kells* in that dark room, the ink and the slow curving letters, the aura of history, the hand of his grandad on his shoulder. The cheque ever so slightly vibrates until Neil lays his elbow on the table. He stares at the numbers. Eliminating everything else. All other thoughts. Zero, zero, zero, zero. Only.

'OK,' Neil says.

'Oh, apologies. There's one other thing,' Alby replies, and instantly pages are placed in front of him. 'We'll need your signature on a confidentiality and exclusivity agreement. A small formality.'

Neil shrugs and smiles through the desperation. He wishes he wasn't hung-over, coming down. His head was clear. They mean business. But so does he. 'Cool. OK. Make it twenty-five thousand and I'll sign.'

Decisions

Kathy's asleep in his bed when Neil comes in.

He stops at the door, unsure of what to do, what exactly he sees. A swell of emotion. A strange sensation of relief.

It's like the death of his grandfather and her departure are one and the same thing – a huge loss – and seeing her here now, back in the apartment, in Ireland, eyes closed, hair over her face, gently snoring, serene, it's like nothing has happened. The past two months were a dream. A reprieve. A second chance. A way back into the life they had planned before his grandfather passed away. Maybe before they decided to leave. It's too much to take.

She senses his presence, stirs, brushes her hair clear of her eyes, remains with her head on the pillow.

'Surprise,' she whispers, in a sing-song voice, as she stretches and props her head on her hand. 'The lads let me in before they went to the early house. I didn't know when you'd be back.'

It seems like moving towards her would be the most natural thing in the world. But he remains against the door. Away from her. Despite their history, there's an inescapable barrier between them: everything unsaid in Fitzwilliam Square. The devastation.

'You glad to see me?' She is reserved. Delicate. The light outside slips through the twisted blinds and draws an uneven – but illuminating – line down her face when she sits up.

He has missed her so much.

'I don't know what to say to you, Kathy.' He thinks of the justification for his delayed departure for Canada, folded into his wallet. The zeros. They have options now. Two. Five. Zero, zero, zero. Only. He keeps it hidden. He wants to meet her as they were.

'Say anything.'

There's too much to say, so the mundane comes out.

'When did you get back?'

'Last night. I haven't slept. I came straight here.'

'Are you back for good?'

She tries not to smile. 'No, no way. I'm going back Monday.'

'This Monday?'

'No,' she says again, this time with a slight laugh, 'Monday week. I'm back for nine days. I came back to get you.'

Only a metre lies between them. He could cross it easily and take her hand, her shoulders. Embrace her, smell her. Just feel her warmth.

'I know what I did was wrong, Neil. I regretted it immediately. I didn't want to lie to you. I was feeling down. That's why I'm here. I'm back for you. I had to see you. You don't understand. It's so different over there. I missed you.' She drags at her face. 'I mean – you have no idea, Neil. No idea how lonely I was. And you – you had the guys here. Your gran. I had no one. Kenny was . . . '

'Don't say his name.'

She frowns, winces. 'Sorry. It was a mistake. I mean it.'

He tries to compose himself, clear his head. The door is cold to touch, smooth. First things first.

'How many times?' he says.

'What?'

'How many times did you . . . were you together?'

Her fringe sways over her forehead. He grips the metal door handle.

'It's a straightforward question. How many times?'

'Once. Just the once.' Her eyes find his. Don't stray.

'And how did it happen?'

'Why you doing this?'

'How did it happen?' His tone has changed. Become glacial. Formal.

'I dunno. We were drunk. We'd been out.'

'Alone or with friends?' The lever gives way.

Every question brings a physical reaction, knocks her off guard, affronts her. She's not in a position, though, to argue. As much as she dislikes being dominated, if she is serious about coming back for him, she'll have to endure.

'Friends,' she says, her voice crumbling into a hushed acceptance that this is what needs to happen for Neil to move on, deal with the circumstances of their estrangement. And get over it.

'So your friends, who knew you had a boyfriend, saw this happen?'

She shakes her head, runs her hands through her hair.

'I told you. It's like . . . you're not . . . things . . . you don't understand. I was so removed from you. Here. Dublin. I didn't even know if you were coming out to me anymore. I was in limbo, Neil. I was wrong. It was wrong. I know that now. I knew it then too. That's why I told you. I told you, didn't I?'

'Lucky me.'

'No. No. I'm trying to convince you how, like, as soon as I did it – I realised how much I love you. Cause I do. I love you so much. I was lost, like, really, really lost. You rang at the wrong time. I was feeling so low. He was there at the time. He was really good to me. Kind.'

'Did he use a condom?'

The tone of the question unsettles her. Her mouth opens in disgust, her eyes crease. There's no response.

'Did he use a condom?'

'You're not really asking this.'

'I am. I want to know.'

The high ground is creaking. He'll test it further.

'I don't think. This, this is just, this is wron—'

'I want to know.'

She shakes her head and exhales.

'No. No he didn't. He didn't use a condom. Are you happy?' Her hands are spread wide in protest. Tired of having to play this game.

'I thought you were taking a break from the pill while I was gone.'

She throws her head back, exasperated. Whatever tolerance she had for his righteousness has reached its zenith. 'I was. I am. I'm off the pill. He pulled out, are you happy now?'

'And came all over you?'

'Yes. Yes, yes. He came over me.' She slumps back, defeated. Finished.

It disgusts Neil, sucker punches him, literally lays him low, makes him crumple up discreetly, shift against the wardrobe to withstand the pain. At least there is pain now. Not just a numb, far-off feeling of unreality.

As if her not being here, not looking him in the eye, not really accepting what she did and the fact that they were – even if it was unspoken – over, meant it was somehow a falsehood. Figment of his imagination. Her words bring her actions to life, forces them to become things in the world that really happened, really betrayed. Because, over a phone, through a computer screen was not reality, was not how people interact, live: sharing everything, gaining nothing.

This is real life. The details of the deed. And this is pain. He can almost see her, the act itself. Neil is in pain. Neil is still in love. And he feels a deep, deep sense of something he hasn't felt since his mother died. A longing to do anything to have her back.

'You have no idea how much you hurt me,' he says. 'I have nothing else in this world other than my belief in you and us. Our life. You devastated me.'

'I'm sorry,' she whispers, steady now, in control. 'Please believe me, Neil. Please. I am so . . . I am so sorry.' Her face creases in on itself and her hair drops down like a mask. 'I'm here now because I had to see you. I love you. I'm sorry. It's all I can say.'

A silence, like a stranger's voice, rises between them. Who is he fooling? As much as it hurts now, he knows it'll be remedied by being with her again. Close to her. He will fold. It's only a matter of time. He can't help himself. She is here now. He loves her now. This present will fade into the past, and they will be together in the future.

'We have our whole lives ahead. Canada, the future. Our future in Canada. I promise, I promise, it'll never happen again. I will never let you down again.'

Even if she hadn't done what she had done, returned so dramatically to him, he would have gone to her. Neil is not an image as before, a picture on the other side of a screen saying, 'Please don't cry,' holding out his arms to a pixelated representation, wishing he could hold her. Slowly, but with purpose, he closes the distance, eases onto the edge of the bed, casts a grateful arm over her shoulder, draws her in, feels her shudder and lets the relief wash over them.

'I'm sorry,' she sniffles – finally – and he places his chin on the top of her head, inhales her scent, hyperconscious of what it is to feel her move beneath him once more. Aware again of absence's long-echoing devastation.

'It's OK,' he whispers, 'I'm ready to go. No more messing around. We can start again.'

Backhanders

Enda's lab has that Sunday-evening, end-of-the-week feel about it. That depressing inevitability of Monday morning's onset once the credits of *Love/Hate* roll. An air of something ending. A goodbye, really. Enda remains seated, unimpressed, behind his computer. Shame, like a slow-burning reddener, is a self-conscious flush on Neil's face.

'I take it you heard.'

'They rang, yes.'

'I'm to bring them to the solicitor's by—'

'I know.'

Runners screech outside the door. A shadow passes by the frosted-glass window and calls down the corridor.

'Can I have them?'

Enda shrugs. 'Well, they're not mine. You made that very clear last night. So, I don't see why not.'

'I did. And you get your backhander, so don't sound so high and mighty about it.'

'I don't care about the cash. I don't need it.'

'Then why set it up? I don't get the attitude.'

'I didn't know at the time how valuable they'd be.'

'I got a good price.'

Enda shakes off a resigned laugh. 'You really don't have a clue. An appreciation. An interest even. To be so ignorant must be a wonderful thing.'

'I'm the one with the chapters. I'm far from ignorant. I can read about them. I don't need to see them.'

'Well, that makes two of you.'

'Huh?'

'He isn't bothered with seeing reel three, either.'

'How do you know . . . '

'His solicitor was in touch there. I offered to do reel three so he could have a complete set.' Enda shrugs, a smile mocking Neil. 'You know, I think, after the other two are done, it deserves to be seen. I want to see it. It should be seen.'

'And?'

Enda sprays his hands out in disgust. 'He's not interested. He wants them now, and that's the end of that.'

'You've reel two done though?'

A nod.

'Give me a look.'

Enda rises from his seat, his lips pressed, head shaking. 'No way. You made your decision. They're not yours to look on anymore.'

Neil moves towards him. 'You really gonna be like that?'

Enda remains silent.

'OK then,' Neil responds, giving Enda a sarcastic pat on the back, feeling a tinge of regret that this is how they'll depart. 'Be like that, pal. I've the chapters. I know what happens. At least I'll get to hear about reel three.'

The standoff continues. Enda's arms are folded, legs apart. Neil could take him. Should take him. Probably all muscles, no technique. Probably never threw a punch in his life.

'I can live with that,' Enda says, and turns and disappears into a darkroom before coming out with three silver canisters.

'There's your legacy. Sorry – what was your legacy.' He hands them to Neil and moves to the door and opens it. 'Enjoy your inheritance.'

Returning home

She's seated at the breakfast table, a shade lighter than when she last sat there. Fading. Like the pictures Neil has of his mother. Memories dissolving. Jim hangs around for half an hour. Doesn't go upstairs. Just reminds Gran to use the wheelchair – or the stick – at all times, and scrawls on the whiteboard the names of those minding her over the next week: Neil on Friday, Jim and Eoin the other nights. No home help.

Gran is quiet throughout.

'You'll be right as rain in no time, Mother, now that we're here with you for the week,' Jim says, and kisses her on the cheek. Before he goes he says, 'Oh, yes, I almost forgot,' and leaves the room.

Gran turns to Neil and finds his hand and pats it slowly. Jim returns with the leather satchel, holding it at arm's length, like the mystery it is.

'You nearly left this behind,' he says, as if he's chiding a child. 'They insisted I take it, even after I said they could throw it out.'

'It's a keepsake, dear,' Gran says, clearing her throat after the effort of the short sentence.

He seems shocked, bemused not to have been told before. 'I gather that, now, Mother. Eoin tells me they're letters from father to you when you were courting. Really. You can be so sentimental sometimes.'

Gran remains mute, despite her obvious confusion. 'I told Eoin,' Neil says, 'how you have asked me to read them for you.'

Jim tuts. 'Really mother.' He drops the satchel on the green velvet easy chair in the corner, and leaves with, 'I'll see you tomorrow. Eoin should be in in a few hours for you anyway.'

'He means well,' she whispers to Neil, once the front door closes, 'but he wouldn't understand. You were right to tell him otherwise. Pass it over, dear, if you wouldn't mind.'

Neil brings it to her, clears away the cup and saucer, biscuit tin and milk jug, and lays the bag on the cork table mat. Every move he makes feels surreal, as if he's recording it for posterity. He's hyperconscious of what he is doing, observing his surroundings, smelling the smells, feeling the heat, trying to soak up the calming nature of the house. Storing the feeling of belonging for more troubling, disorientating times.

'And my purse, dear.'

Neil goes out into the hall, to the table with the new roses he brought, and fetches her purse from her bag. She takes the key out, opens the satchel, eases the flap over, and, with what energy and precision she can muster, flicks through the returned chapters, the yet-to-be-read chapters, to find the remaining ones Neil now desperately wants to read. She draws out a thick collection by its rusty-paper-clipped corner.

'How many are left, Gran?'

'Not many, unfortunately,' she whispers, and offers a wry, sad smile.

'I'm just wondering, 'cause loads has been going on since I last saw you.'

'Yes?'

'Yeah. Kathy is back from Canada . . .'

'Are you staying?' Her head lifts momentarily from its defeated slump and a trace of light colours her eyes. 'I don't think so, Gran. She's just come back for me. I've met the – I found out who would be interested in the reels.' The sheets hover over his outstretched hand. 'Remember you asked me to find out who might be interested in the reels?' Neil looks to the sheaf. 'Is this reel three? I'd like to hear about reel three.'

He wants to take out the cheque. Include her. Convince her. It's been folded away neatly in his wallet since it left the politician's hands. He's afraid it'll rip, get creased. He can't bring himself to enjoy the thought of the cash, accept what it is, what he has done, until his gran sees it, gives her blessing.

'I want to show you something.'

She draws her chest up to respond, but the front door crashes open, and a voice booms through the hall. 'Mother, you up?'

Her head sinks back and the papers drop lightly into Neil's opened palm. Neil needs to tell her. Feels it's his duty. If every euro reminds him of how he has earned it, the money will be a heavy burden. He wants to unload the truth, open his wallet.

It's too late to try and move the bag, but, as the front door closes and Eoin's footsteps approach, Gran manages to close the flap of the satchel and, with Eoin bounding into the room, click the small lock shut. His smile retracts the moment he takes in the rushed silence, awkward stiffness, Neil's fake indifference, Gran's frozen pose, hand still on the lock.

'Have I disturbed something?' he says, staring at the satchel.

'We were just finishing our tea,' Neil says. 'You're early.'

Eoin ignores this response, moves over to Gran, kisses her on the cheek and lifts up the bag.

'This again,' he says. 'When will we have a read of the letters, Mum?'

'Soon,' she whispers.

The evasiveness of her answer riles Eoin further, stirs a jealousy he can't contain.

'I'll put them back upstairs for you, Gran,' Neil says, and moves to take the bag.

Eoin steps back. 'No hurry,' he says, keeping a tight grip. 'You can run along now, Neil. I'll look after everything.'

To show desperation for control of the bag would only give Eoin more cause to be suspicious. Instead, Neil simply nods and goes, 'OK. Cool.'

He kisses Gran's forehead and squeezes her hand, keeping the next chapter hidden under his jacket as he goes past Eoin without saying goodbye.

Harry Casey - F Company, 2nd Battalion #7

In which I meet my wife for the first time – Gogan and myself endeavour to reason out the madness – A new hero arrives – Something frightful occurs.

Whether it was the shock, or the fear of Davy with his rifle, I stirred myself, blinded by the thick dust, worse than any fog come in off the Liffey, and, on all fours, felt around for my Pathé. I was loath to lose it.

At last, after some blind fumbling on the cold tiles, hands stinging from broken glass, shifting through clothes and thick fabric, I rose, still dazed from the blast, but with the camera (miraculously) in hand! A table, having fallen at an angle in the vicinity, had protected it. Davy rose too, some distance away, his hands having been relieved of his rifle, his head bloody, his eyes closed to slits, seemingly bewildered in the thick dust.

With everything all askew, I managed somehow to stagger over to Gogan, who was lying flat on his face with his arms extended, and stir him. Davy, I was mindful, would not be incapacitated for long. I shook Gogan, and with what strength I could muster, heaved him to his feet, whereupon a chorus of voices broke through the mist, only to be followed by a set of new arms, strong and sturdy. They supported my own body, which had all of sudden started to give way with the shock, and pulled Gogan out of the smoking building with me. Where Davy went to, I had no idea, for, after I gave myself up to my rescuers, I passed out. And when I came to, later that afternoon in the Imperial, Davy was nowhere to be seen.

We were tended to, both Gogan and I, back on the first floor, where I had spent the night previous. I cannot describe the tumult of my mind when I awoke, nor how I tried to fathom in a quiet daze the events that had unfolded only hours earlier. Gogan had been put in a makeshift bed beside me, and, still unconscious, lay pale and quiet. I contended with a shrill, yet diminishing ringing in my ears, alongside a thumping headache owing to the butt of Davy's rifle.

I was deep in thought, patting my reloaded Pathé camera like one would a trusty dog, when one of the two Cumann na mBan girls present in the building, an Orlaith Murphy, of Leenaun, County Galway, arrived to change the bandage on my head. (You will no doubt have been acquainted with her!)

'You seem upset,' is all she said.

I was in no mood to talk. Nevertheless, I felt, the instant she spoke, that I could converse with her, unload that which had shaken my very belief in what I had come out for.

'I am, truth be told, very upset.'

She began to unravel the bloodied cloth, with so light a touch I almost could not feel it. Slowly, and with great care, leaning close to tend to my head, her warm breath caressed me to life.

'Sure, I'm a little shaken too, if we're in a truth-telling mood,' she whispered. 'The fighting has my nerves rattling like the window there with every explosion.'

'It's not the fighting that has given me a fright.' The emotion of the day, Davy's uncharacteristic, subversive actions, began to haunt me, and I think I let a tear slip.

'Are you thinking of a loved one, some children maybe?'

Her concern brought some comfort, and I shifted my gaze from the window to her face. She had a strong face, at first beautiful, but then kind in a way no beauty can ever know. When she spoke, her lips came together in the most endearing of pouts, which caused her to lisp in the slightest of ways. Her eyes. Oh! Her eyes, in that moment, through the salty tears which I regret to say stained my manliness, were orbs through which I immediately lost myself in, and would stay lost in forever.

'No,' said I, my smile suffusing my utterance. 'No loved one. No children. Though I am more alone now than I have ever been: I have just lost a dear, dear friend.'

Her hand abandoned the cloth and covered her mouth, too late to contain her gasp.

'Killed is he?'

'No,' said I, and her brow creased and those lips curled into a sweet, fulsome pucker. 'Yet, it feels that way. This has been the most lamentable day of my life. I've been betrayed badly. So badly I now fear for my life. My friend, a dear friend, has turned on me, now, of all times, and had meant to kill me were it not for the explosion.' I pointed a weak finger at my head. 'His handiwork.'

Her hand remained over the side of her mouth.

'It seems I came to war to find my true enemy: my lifelong chum. Would ye believe it?'

'I believe that whoever we were when we entered this war will be left behind when we leave it. Your friend, I think, being a case in point.'

I looked to her as if her words were a bell being struck true and clear on a cold, fresh autumn dawn.

'And if we leave this war,' said I, 'will the thoughts we had, the ideas that drove us, be left behind too, do you think?'

She dwelt on the question, giving it time to register, giving her response time to muster: 'It's hard to tell. But I believe, if our belief is honest, our ideas pure, then war should crystallise them. Ennoble them.'

A deep silence rose between us. I could not find the power to divert my eyes from hers. The bandage had long since been unwrapped, yet her warm, soft hand remained on my head. She held me like that while I spoke.

'My ideas are pure. So pure, so important to me, I'm here to see them come into being, or to die trying.'

Her lips parted. A small speck of her bottom lip, since the skin was dry, stuck to her top lip for a moment.

'Whatever idea has brought you here, to me, I believe in it too.'

My mouth opened in readiness to try and express what I hoped to achieve with the Pathé when, with a shallow cough and then a deep, distressed gathering of breath, Gogan awoke and diverted Orlaith's attention. Gogan, suffering from the devil's own throbbing headache, but nothing more, thank God, was all smiles on seeing me there beside him.

Gunfire broke out on the thoroughfare beyond the window, and I looked out to see a priest, a white handkerchief waving hopelessly from his hand, his back crouched and his legs bent, powering across the road towards us. His name was Father Headley, from Dominick Street Church, and although he was fired on heavily, he succeeded in making the Imperial without mishap.

Almost as if this charge by the priest was a wake-up call, the shots fired his way an alarm, I became aware again of the war. Things being quiet and still on our makeshift first-floor hospital, I took my Pathé and crawled a few feet away from Orlaith and Gogan.

'What on earth?' Orlaith said, visibly excited by the prospect of being on the camera, her fingers brushing through her hair and then finding blemishes on her skirt to iron out.

'This is what I do. This is why I'm here,' said I, and once I had my setting adjusted and in readiness, I began to crank.

'Smile for me,' I called to Orlaith, at which point she ducked her head into her shoulder in an embarrassed, bashful manner, but, on further coaxing, brought her face to bear in the middle of my shot and smiled self-consciously while I whirred away. I panned ever so slightly to her right and brought the still-horizontal Gogan into shot.

He flapped away the attention and said, 'Have I not been on that enough already?'

All three of us laughed. Orlaith, still in shot on account of being at Gogan's bedside, threw her head back and laughed freely. The spirit of the Gael, Kathleen Ni Houlihan herself, radiated from her.

'Could you not have waited until I had a chance to clean myself up?' added Gogan, and once more, smiles and laughter filled the screen.

Then Orlaith reached forward for the camera and put her hand on mine as I whirred. 'Go on, get out there. I've seen how you do it. I'll hold it steady,' she said.

I was hesitant to leave the camera, but her touch calmed me, and so I did. I slid over beside Gogan and smiled, a tense, uneasy smile. For, truth be told, I had never before been in front of the camera. Nor had I ever intended to be. However, it just felt right at that moment. After a time, I leaned over and pulled the lever and brought the first scene of the third reel to a close.

Our laughter had barely subsided when the priest's figure appeared at the top of the stairs. He heard our confessions, gave general absolution (which was a great relief, it must be said) and had to remain with us until darkness fell.

Only moments after the priest left the Imperial, Orlaith, a brief respite from the storm and stress of the day, was called away also. Myself and Gogan, yet to discuss what had gone on before the explosion rent our overcoat-incident asunder, were detailed (owing to the fact we had only superficial injuries) on guard duty at the entrance to the Imperial.

The streets were bare, of course, which felt unreal for such a time of the night. The electric carbon lamps, which were casting shallow pools of yellow light along the thoroughfare, were fitful. Our eyes strained to monitor the street under this weak electric glow while we leaned our shoulders against opposing door frames, our rifles (mine borrowed) slung across our backs.

'Who was that bucko, anyhow?' said Gogan, out of the blue, without an indication of whom he spoke. None was needed.

'That, Gogan,' said I, a rueful smile mocking my dejection, 'was my chum, Davy. A first lieutenant in the 2nd Battalion, G Company.'

'Well,' said Gogan, his voice reserved and smooth, 'he's a grand fellow, isn't he?'

I looked to my left, in his direction, to see if he was jeering me. He grinned and raised his eyebrows, and we both fell into one another with a hushed laugh.

'Thanks to your friend,' continued Gogan, 'I never got a chance to get meself a bloody overcoat! I'm freezing!'

We sniggered some more at this, finding the tragedy of it all, the farce of it all, hilarious.

After I had straightened myself and returned to a sober, upright stance against the door frame, I thought I saw a face looking out from the corner of Princes Street at the Metropole across the way. Davy immediately came to mind. The carbon lamp nearest the spot flickered intermittently, giving unfavourable conditions for determining whether I was seeing things or not. So rather than seem paranoid, and not of sound mind (and a source of danger to Gogan as I intended to stay close to him and maybe capture his movements on the reel!), I remained quiet.

'I wasn't quite sure what to expect, coming out,' said Gogan after we had settled. 'But I sure as hell wasn't expecting our own would be doing the likes of what your fellow was going to do to you.'

'War makes people strange, I suppose,' was all I could muster, feeling, despite his actions, a pang of loyalty for my friend.

'Surely he is the exception, don't ye think?'

'I do hope so.'

'You hope so?' He looked at me with a curious stare. 'He damn well better be. We are Irish men, fighting for a new Ireland. A republic, a fair and honest republic. He's not a part of it.'

'Is that what we are?' My mood was downbeat on account of the subject matter.

'Damn right it is,' said he. 'Damn right it is.'

Among the restless silence of the street, our breath became our rhythm, our shadows from the flickering lights, our dance. An easy lull grew between us until Gogan, obviously troubled still by what he had witnessed, continued.

'I mean, he was readying himself to plug you. Kill you!'

'That he was.'

'Over what? Your motion-picture camera?' He blew through his nose in disbelief. 'Over principals, a country, a right to an identity, yes. But, blood in ounce, a blasted camera! What in the name of God would drive a man to kill for a camera!?'

'My chum,' said I, my voice flat and tired, sorry to have to explain, 'has spent many's a day with me traipsing around this city with my camera. He has listened to me blather on about the power of the image. The mysterious qualities contained in a moving collection of images. He knows, and he has proved today he believes, that all I have said was not untrue. There is a truth held in the film. A witness to a truth he now wants destroyed.'

The lamp seemed to shine brighter than heretofore, and the head across the road became clearer in outline, yet woolly in detail.

Confusion clouded Gogan's eyes while he worked through my vague response.

'Surely the truth of this fight can't be destroyed.'

'This fight, no. But I fear there may be many fights,' I said, wishing to dwell on the subject no more. 'There'll be many fights, indeed, but only one truth. A terrifying truth for some. A liberating truth for others.'

'No. I'm sorry. I do not agree with you. There is one fight. And that is what I stand here for now.'

I thought I saw the shape of the head move. A glint of light.

'I stand for the republic Pearse spoke of,' continued Gogan. 'I was there when he read the proclamation. I was there and I heard it, and I believed in it. Believe in it now. My son will grow up in such a place if I have anything to do with it. My son will live in Ireland. A republic, not answering to anyone but an Irish head of state, not fearing the wishes of a foreign enemy. Not hoping to make a living under a foreign name, or having to travel to find a life of opportunity. I fight for the truth of our dreams, and the expectations of our new reality.'

There was something ominous in the flickering of the lamp. It dimmed again, as if giving cover to the watching man.

'Gogan,' said I, exhausted, yet preoccupied by the figure across the road. 'I believe that if men like you are looking out on this city tonight, rifle in hand, defending her from the English, this fight will be worth fighting. And maybe then this might be the only fight. I'm somewhat shaken though, and after today's unfortunate events, somewhat low in my estimation of our motives. My chum's motives, I thought were pure. For the good of this great nation. Alas, I have had to learn the hard way, they were not. They were – they are – selfish and cynical.' A lamentable breath streamed from my tired body. 'I just thought we would fight for the right reasons. Noble reasons.'

'Fear not,' said Gogan, reaching across the doorway and patting my shoulder. 'Fret not. You simply had your camera pointing at the wrong sort. We have hit it off well, no? Well then, trust me, and you'll see what the men of Ireland are really like. What the true soldiers of Éireann are made of!'

The lamp lighting the head across the road seemed to glow even brighter as Gogan's words rose up into the night sky. I suddenly realised that the once-shaded head was, in fact, an advertisement card in the doorway of Kapp & Peterson's tobacco shop, with a picture of the 'Thinking Man'. I laughed a dry laugh of relief.

'Do I seem like a joke to you?'

'No, no,' I insisted, suddenly aware that I had inadvertently laughed at the most inopportune moment.

'Well then, why would you mock me?'

'I wasn't,' said I, and to mollify him, continued. 'Listen, you're right. I believe you. I believe your motives. Sure, there's no reason why I should think any different after you tried to defend me and my camera at gunpoint today.'

'You're just blathering on now,' Gogan said, hurt.

'I'm not, man. Listen, tomorrow . . . I've got one reel left . . . tomorrow I will use your actions for my footage. How's that sound?'

His face frowned down on me. 'You're jeerin' me again.'

'I'm being perfectly earnest, Gogan. You will be my last reel. I trust you. I believe in you. There's nothing else for it, but for you to believe in me.'

No sooner had he looked across the doorway and smiled in acceptance, than we were joined by our OC, who gave us the low-down on the telescoping. After that, we were relieved of our duties and spoke no more of the camera.

The next morning (Thursday) I was washing myself when the first shells fell at eight o'clock. Gogan, who was using a rag to dry his face, stopped what he was doing and let the sun from the window finish the job.

'We'll be leaving soon,' said he, calmly, in such a matter-of-fact tone that I was full sure he didn't comprehend exactly what it was he was hearing. But, to be fair to the men of the Imperial, including Gogan and, I suppose, myself, the shelling did not cause great panic. As far as I could see amongst my companions, it did not have any effect whatsoever.

A couple of hours later, we were back at the first-floor window, watching fires starting in the GPO, when Liam Thornton asked Gogan to proceed through the holes made in the walls until he reached a premises leading into North Earl Street and, once there, in the still golden light of the April evening, create a suitable distraction with whatever means necessary, so as to draw fire from what intelligence had reported were machine guns stationed in Amiens Street Station's clock tower.

Whether they wanted Gogan to draw their fire in order to ascertain the exact guns they were using, should we make a dash across the street later under cover of dark, or whether they wanted to divert their fury while another mission took place further up or down the street, Thornton never stipulated, but he left us in no doubt: Gogan was to ensure that they fired heavily at the exit onto North Earl Street.

Taking pride in being singled out to undertake the order, Gogan sat silently, in deep contemplation, once Thornton departed.

'Well,' I said, excited somewhat by his elevated stature, 'you have the head for such lofty requests?'

He simply raised a finger to his temple to signify his thought process, and then closed his eyes ever so slowly. At last, able to bear his silence no longer, he lit upon an idea, smiled and nodded at the greatcoat I had unintentionally worn while being carried out of the outfitter's shop the day previous, which was lying on the floor.

'Hand me that monstrosity,' said Gogan, and I leaned over and took up the garish coat.

'You're not serious, Gogan?'

Standing up, he swung the coat over his shoulders and buried his hands in the fabric until they struggled through the bottoms of the sleeves like pink ferrets peeping out of holes.

'I am. I have an idea.'

'And it involves wearing that blasted coat? I was wearing it as a gas,' said I, taking my Pathé as I followed him out of the room.

'I'll be wearing it while we go through the holes, but once I get to North Earl Street . . . '

He paused at the ground floor. The assembled men shook their heads and smiled out the sides of their mouths at him.

Thornton beckoned him over, and they ducked into each other and began a serious, whispered discussion. After the delay, Gogan moved on, subdued almost. Only when out of Thornton's sight did he begin to quicken his pace anew.

'What is it you mean to do?' I asked, unclasping straps on the Pathé, winding the reel onto a new scene and twisting the dial for the light, as I walked behind him.

A blur of garish colours in the coat, Gogan went forth on his hands and knees, squeezing through a hole in the wall that brought us into the neighbouring building. Once through, he disappeared, and I had to hurry so as not to lose him.

'This here coat,' he called back to me hastily, wishing to execute his plan without a second's dawdling, 'can be seen for miles. I'll find some plank of sorts and hang it off it, dangle it from out the side of the building into North Earl Street. If I can't draw their fire with such an obscene garment, then they're not fit to be soldiers!'

'Hold up,' I called, preparing to start cranking, so as to capture him coming upon the door that opened out to North Earl Street. 'I'm about to get some footage.'

'Keep up, Har,' he called back over his shoulder, before ducking at breakneck speed into the final hole.

I was for stalling him, when I spotted beautiful intense, white light streaming through a huge window to the west of the final hole in the wall. It came to me in a flash. I would set myself up on the level bricks where the hole had been telescoped, and using the light, I would be able to see the building, and silhouette Gogan's movements when he opened the side door into North Earl Street. After kneeling at the hole in the wall, my body on the opposite side of the dishevelled divide to Gogan, I set myself to ensuring my vantage point was both level and steady.

Having everything in place and having started to crank, I looked into the viewfinder to locate Gogan, whence I saw a second tenebrous figure – larger because he had come up behind Gogan from off camera right – appear in my shot. Focused on establishing the shot, I remained entirely absorbed in the hypnotic whirling of the downward *swoosh*, the upward *click*. My eyes were fixed solely on the shape of Gogan ten yards away, and the second figure (purely because he was an obstacle) maybe five yards further back. I thought nothing of the second shape, only would it ruin the composition of Gogan's figure against the North Earl Street door frame in the background! My mind was focused solely on the scene, whence a flash of silver, a bayonet attached to a rifle, drew back over the second figure's shoulder, and I called in disbelief, 'Gogan!'

Gogan turned sharply, on completion of my exclamation, only to be instantly met by the silver heat of the blade. His face, a grin of devilment, excitement on expecting to be part of my scene, promptly diminished into a shocked, wide-eyed, open-mouthed voiceless question of incomprehension. His hands were raised to the figure's shoulders, and he slumped into him, instantly incapacitated.

The shape withdrew the bayonet as quickly as he had thrust it forward, and then turned to establish both the source of the cry and the vantage point the witness to the murder had availed of. While I knelt there horror-struck (my mouth must have been fit to drive a tram through), the face of the attacker regarded me. He had worked himself into such a passion his features were once again difficult to marry with the mien of my friend.

Nevertheless, even as he took me in, and as he let Gogan drop like a bag of mail to the floor, I continued to crank my Pathé. Murder left Davy's eyes for a moment, and thence spoke of a disappointment. A confusion. Neither of us could quite comprehend what we were regarding. Each other. What a shock! I found myself once more traumatised by a heinous act my old chum Davy had carried out.

Davy, I can only presume, from the look of confusion aimed in my direction, and then at the now-bloodied cream moleskin coat in which he had last seen me dressed, was just as bewildered. He had come upon Gogan in the coat, thinking it was me, and had meant to do me in! Still, I cranked.

Had he not made to run for me, I think I would have continued cranking. In times of shock, extreme crisis, we revert back to what we have repeatedly done, for sanity. The grinding of my camera was my link back to normality. And so I continued to grind, almost subconsciously.

I knew the game was up once he made to charge for me with his bayonet; it was dripping and bloody and being pointed sharply in my direction! Seeing that his pace was not slackening, and he was preparing to launch himself through the hole, I pulled out the knob, spun it rapidly so as not to saturate the footage, and made a hasty retreat into a thick, black smoke-filled labyrinth. It was, I hope you can see, not cowardice that prevented me from remaining still and confronting Davy, but a blind belief that despite all, the Pathé would always remain true to the moment (even if I divorced myself from it) and therefore be of more worth than any protestations I could offer.

Dense, putrid smoke had conspired to fill the room. Being in a panic now, and slightly disorientated by the lung-choking smoke, at first I was puzzled to say whence the hole I had last come through was located. I took some time to gather my bearings and hoped, behind me, somewhere hidden in the other side of the building, Davy too was lost in the sulphuric mist. Calls of 'Fire! Fire!' sounded through the smoke. I charted out my escape into the chaos, and set my course for it without delay.

An Illusion

An Italian-themed café on Westland Row, red-and-white chequered curtains, dark brown atmospheric interior, light operatic music, red-brick wallpaper behind black-and-white pictures of Rome and Venice. Her fork pings off her plate.

'I don't believe you,' she whispers, disgusted. 'Will you listen to yourself? Things are not picking up. This country will not get better. It's beyond better. Things are still shit and will remain shit. Whatever "they" say, take the opposite as truth. I don't think you realise, like, I'm gone, Neil. I've a grandmother too, ye know, and I've moved. I did a degree in architectural technology, and in case ye haven't noticed, there's fuck all architects at work here now. It's not an option for me anymore. I have a job. There's no maybe, or "Oh, what if the country turns around?" bullshit. It has failed me.'

She lifts her hands, looks away as if she'll find a counterpoint for her anger at another table. Her voice softens, as if she's realised how angry she sounds.

'You're still talking like you're not going, like you have a choice.

Like you haven't made up your mind. Do you know how uncertain this makes me feel?'

'In all fairness,' Neil says, leaning across the table in a whisper, 'before Saturday . . . '

'Don't, please.'

His initial feelings of trepidation, worry about the situation and how they would respond to it, have diminished the more he has been in her company. Walked with her. Felt her skin, the warmth of her touch. He thought what had come between them would hinder him, plague his thoughts, haunt him, but surprisingly, once he lost himself in her embrace – the doubts faded. A few shades at least. It's like it was before. Almost. It was a mistake. She has come over the Atlantic to convince him of the fact. Win him back. He is won. He is hers. He is won. He is hers. Repeat. Believe. Achieve.

'I had the cash ready, you know,' Neil says, taking her hand, dwelling on her nails, bright, pink-topped with a smooth white polish. 'I was ready to go. I have some savings left after the last few weeks. I have that credit union loan I'm never going to pay back, the dole. I was ready.'

'I know you were.'

'I was just waiting for the right moment. You had a job. I was jumping into the unknown. I had no security net. I find that hard.'

'I know, I know,' Kathy says, tilting her head sympathetically, comforting.

'And now I have this cash for the reels, ye can see why I was mad to wait and see what I could get for them.'

'I know,' she continues. 'I'm sorry, I was . . . I got impatient, that's all.'

'It's OK.' Neil pauses for maximum effect. 'You don't need to be impatient anymore. I'm flying out Monday too.'

'You are? You've booked?' Her face lights up.

'Yep. I'm booked. The sixteen-hundred-hour, Dublin-Chicago. Chicago-Vancouver.'

'We're flying out together? I don't believe it! I don't believe it!' she squeals, wringing her hands.

'We're going together. No messing this time.'

She consumes the space between them.

'Just think of all the things you can do over there with the money. You can start a business. Invest. Get involved in ventures. I always wanted to be my own boss. Start a café or deli. Branch out from there. This is so exciting.' She stretches over the table and kisses him. She sits back down, breathless, flustered. 'There's no space here for entrepreneurs. Ideas. Begrudgery holds anyone with ideas back. It's not like that over there. In Canada. You'll have opportunities, Neil.'

'Cool the jets,' he says, dropping his pizza slice onto the plate, no longer hungry, more sick and nervous, 'I mean, I haven't got the money yet.'

Her head twitches as if she missed the line.

'Sorry?'

'I haven't got the money yet.'

'Has it not come through?'

'I haven't cashed it.'

She suddenly stiffens, the politeness souring on the edge of her lips. 'What?'

'I haven't lodged it. I'm waiting. I dunno. I wanna prove to my gran. Show her, like . . . '

'Twenty. Five. Thousand. Euro.' Her glass clatters off her plate. 'Jesus Christ, Neil.' Conversations stop around them, killing dead the illusion of elegant Italy.

'Relax, I'm going to. It's just a matter of getting Gran at the right time. My uncles are there all week. It's awkward.'

She lets his words settle. Shifts on the chair and leans in close. He has never seen her like this. So intense, angry over something so silly. It's under control.

'The *right time*? We're going in six days, Neil. Six days. Why are you being so stupid? I don't get you. I mean, I really don't get you sometimes. But this, wow. Like, just cash the cheque for fuck's sake.'

Neil sips from his Coke, offers an indifferent shrug. She won't let it go. 'You even said yourself your gran is giving you some letters or something that describe the reels. So, she's as good as giving them away too.'

'It's not that easy . . . '

Again, Kathy's exasperated throw of the hands, a quick look around the tables, a prolonged stare to the side. She's facing away while she talks, slowly, with a drawn-out intensity.

'You have a cheque for twenty-five thousand euro. All you have to do is cash it. It's just some black-and-white film no one will ever see or ever care about. Literally, it is junk.'

'It's not junk.' Neil's surprised by his reaction to the accusation.

Her head snaps back to him.

'You said it yourself when you saw the first reel. You said it's junk.'

'It's not junk.'

'OK, it's not junk. Just rubbish then. Not even worth wasting your time watching.'

Again, a strange feeling of defiance flickers.

'That's a bit harsh.'

She stops messing with her napkin and looks deep into his eyes. 'You're taking the chance of a lifetime and blowing it as we speak, Neil. I mean, really, really, really blowing it.'

'I'm not blowing it. I need to . . . I want her to see it. The cheque. Justify it. He was my great-grandfather too.'

She laughs in disbelief.

'Have you any idea how pathetic you sound?'

'It's not pathetic. It's her history. Her legacy. My legacy.'

The words are out, and they both notice their strangeness immediately. Utterances, ideas never contemplated before. Arrived from somewhere deep. The head or the heart? He doesn't know. Until now, undiscovered. His confusion at their emergence is only matched by his surprise at the fact he has said such a thing.

'It's a bit late for that kind of talk,' she says.

Resourcefulness

Without warning, the woman from the dole office turns up at the apartment door. Strict glasses, tight bob haircut, disapproving thin lips, papers in hand. She doesn't even bother with his name. Simply asks to come in. In the shock and dumb surprise of having her – of all people – at the door, Neil simply steps back, suddenly conscious of his bare feet, and says, 'Yeah, of course.'

A scarcely contained displeasure pinches her face as she surveys the room. Cigarette papers and bus cards, train tickets with the corners ripped off, empty bottles of beer and Xbox controllers. She lowers herself awkwardly onto the couch and struggles to remain upright, and uptight, in the deep, low angled seat. A slow backhand clears a space on the coffee table big enough for her to lay out her paperwork.

'I've had a chance to review your file. And I've looked at your tax situation.' She peers for a response over her fashionable frames. Purple and severe. An eyebrow is arched waiting.

'OK,' is all Neil offers, taking a seat, hiding his feet.

'You worked while claiming Unemployment Benefit. This is fraud.'

We are resourceful, his grandad told him once. Resourcefulness was the one good thing to come out of the famine, he said. Those who stayed had to be resourceful to survive. We are direct descendants of those who stayed.

'But I rang,' Neil protests.

'If you rang we would have a record.'

'But I rang, I told someone there—'

'I'm sorry, no. No, I'm sorry,' she whispers, smiling across at him as if she hears such excuses on a daily basis, her head shaking as she goes, almost amused at his insistence. 'If you rang,' she says plainly, 'we would have dealt with it.'

'Maybe you were busy. There's always big queues.'

'We have no record. Therefore, you have defrauded the state of €2,256.' Her voice is sharp. Accustomed to cutting protests short. 'This is a statutory offence. This will be paid or you will be prosecuted.'

If his ancestors hadn't have been so psychologically impacted by the trauma of staying, not fleeing, not emigrating with the rest of them, the need to always find a safety net under the high-wire act of living in this country would never have been imposed on him. This is why he took the part-time job at Movie Mayhem and kept on the dole. The fear of the workhouses, the poverty line. Ireland now is less forgiving than England then.

'But I'm leaving the country.'

Distain turns to intrigue. She looks around the room, takes a moment.

'When?'

'What? Sorry?'

'Are you leaving? When?'

Neil shrugs, caught off guard by her abruptness. 'Next week.'

'For how long?'

'A year. Two. More maybe. For good.'

Her lips close to a narrow line. She sucks her teeth. 'For a year?'

Neil senses a softening. 'At least. I'm emigrating.'

'Emigrating?'

He nods.

'When, exactly, are you leaving? The date.'

Am I doing them a disservice by leaving now? They stayed when the country literally fell apart. He can stay in less trying circumstances. He can use the resourcefulness they have imprinted on his DNA to prevent his exile. His grandad was right. Neil is resourceful. Not in the way they were, though. The workhouses are gone. You survive Ireland by leaving.

Her pen hovers over her notes, waiting on his reply. There's a new indecisiveness to her actions that have her flustered. She reacts to the date with an aggressive. 'I want documentation. Your visa, ticket, passport. If I see documentary evidence by the start of next week, I'll let this go. Once you're off the register, gone, I'm happy, you're happy. We're all happy. If you don't furnish me with the documents, you will be prosecuted. No payoff. Prosecution. We clear?'

Neil nods, a serious, sombre, contrite nod of admonishment. Go and shite.

She tries to maintain her indignant anger but her compromise has given the game away. She is relieved at the outcome, just as Neil is. She wants him out of the country. Gone. 'If you return within a year,' she adds, as she's packing up her files, 'I will personally ensure you do not get a sniff of Unemployment Benefit or Unemployment Assistance, ever, and the fraud prosecution goes ahead.'

Stipulations effectively pushing Neil out the door and onto the plane, not to return again. It really pisses him off. This is not a whisper anymore. It's an order. Roared in his face by the messenger of the state: "We don't want you here. Go." Social protection is your social exclusion. He doesn't respond though. Just nods. Lets it fester, as all Irish problems do. Being resourceful, faithful to your ancestors, takes on many forms.

The Paper Trail

The room is busy with uncles and aunts. Wives and husband have been invited too. The atmosphere – considering Gran's state – is convivial, almost too casual, jolly. Forced smiles, nods and too-eager, overly interested requests to hear the next instalment of the riveting conversation, are too self-conscious. Neil's not stupid. There is no such thing as a friendly family match. Or a draw. Someone has to lose.

A family conference, out of the blue, with just a few hours' notice, and a veiled threat – 'It's of paramount importance that you attend' – down the phone from Jim, is not the norm. It is never of importance for Neil to attend anything relating to the family. These things are planned weeks in advance in order to facilitate everyone's schedule, apart from his. An official family meeting must include all siblings, must have all branches of the tree represented. To keep up this pretence of democratic decency, Neil must be there to represent his deceased mother. If ever he can't make it, he's reminded, 'Your mother would have made the effort.'

'Another beer?' his aunt Rita offers.

Neil doesn't let his appreciative smile fade while he registers that the others are ever-so-slightly trying to catch his response, and from it, gauge if he's suspicious. He is now. Insofar as he wasn't before she offered him another beer. She has never offered him a beer before, let alone a second. Something's brewing. The forced laughter is sickening.

'I'll be locked, but sure, I'll start the weekend early, why not.' There's light-hearted guffaws, and conspiring lifts of eyebrows.

Still no agenda for the meeting is offered up. As soon as Neil finishes his second beer, Jim calls for order. Ironic cheers at the usual faux-seriousness of the affair. The laughing stops the moment he leans down to fetch something from under the table. To Neil's horror, Jim pulls up Gran's leather satchel. Exposed, its buckles undone, the flap flaccid like an animal's gutted stomach. The satchel has betrayed him. Light from the lamp in the corner flashes off the buckles. The room dips into a deep lull. Eyes fall like dominoes to rest on Neil's stunned face. His reaction.

The element of silent surprise is the most vicious of all statements. Jim lets it establish its own tone. Menace.

'Well,' Jim says, the word given a grave intonation, letting the tension rise. 'Frankly, I'm shocked we haven't been privy to the contents of this bag before.'

'I have,' Eoin says. 'Neil here would have a better idea, however. He told me they're letters from Ma to Pappy and vice versa. Love letters.'

'Love letters?' Jim smirks as he lifts the flap and violates the bag. Jim tilts his head dramatically and looks down his nose at the sheets. 'They don't look like love letters to me. Do they, Neil?'

Neil has no chance to scan the table, check to see if everyone's literally on the same page and trying to tease out the truth through this charade. Neil feigns indifference.

'Where'd you get them?' he says.

'Mother's,' Jim replies, and begins to deal the paper-clipped chapters around the table as if they're playing cards. Neil tries not to strain to see if the final chapters are there. 'The bag was in her bedroom, under her bed. I came across it while doing the vacuum cleaning.'

'Vacuum cleaning?' Neil laughs, but no one follows suit, and he gets confirmation through their complicit silence that this is a set-up. The result has already been decided. Jim has never hoovered in the house. Never. The fact that no one else finds this strange means they're aware of the pretence too. They must have gone looking for them.

'It seems,' Jim says, studying his chapter, 'as you can see from your collection, that Harry fought in the Rising after all.'

Eyebrows dig deep into the delicate greaseproof paper to scour the uneven lines for words, phrases, clues. Neil wants to reach out and reclaim every page for himself, his Gran. The end of intimacy with Harry's words brings a sense of loss. Regret.

'What we have here,' Jim continues, revelling in the role of lecturer, 'are memoirs of a sort. I haven't had a chance to read through them. What I've told you is all I know. They're Harry's. And Mother had them.'

'And Neil has read them,' Eoin adds, 'or at least gone through some of them, haven't you, Neil?'

'How,' Maura says, 'how on earth would Neil have read them?'

'Memoirs?' Eoin's wife looks up from her pages. 'Surely that must mean they're worth something.'

'Hold on now,' Jim protests, hands out to gain control of the table. 'The contents surely will dictate the monetary value. And since I haven't had a chance – yet – to read through them after all I had to do yesterday, Neil, it seems, will be able to tell us.'

'Yes, Neil,' Eoin adds, taking pleasure in turning the screw. 'What's in them?'

'They're of some historical worth, that's for sure,' Maura's husband says, pointing to his sheet. 'This one for sure, listen to this.'

'Hold on, hold on,' Jim protests, reaching across the table for the chapter. 'I'm in charge of the collection. I'd like to read from it.'

Angered by his brother-in-law's intrusion, Maura's husband attempts to pull the sheets away. He's not quick enough, and Jim takes a grip of one end. They both dig in and pull, and a loud ripping shocks them apart. They're left with a bunched half each, speechless.

'Now, hold on a minute,' Maura calls. 'We all have a right to see them.' She gestures to the mess. 'If they're of value, we all have a right to read them – each of us – without interruption.'

'But, in fairness,' Jim shouts over the rising discontent, 'I found them. I feel someone, me, I should have control of them.'

Neil can't see the final chapter anywhere. The vultures are circling. Harry's about to get picked apart. Harry's actions, his story, when set against the undignified squabbling, become all the more impressive. The noise increases. Harry, his voice of comfort over the last few weeks, is almost gone. Each family member's eyes worry over the others' chapters. The reels will make someone in the family money. It might as well be Neil. He just regrets having to lose Harry in the process.

One View

The circular-window loneliness of a sparsely lit room, a depressing, dispassionate, sterilised white. Feelings of inadequacy – walking, trespassing even, after hours on university grounds – plague him.

Neil leaves the lights off. It's late. They'd only cause alarm. Steam ghosts from a coffee beside the keyboard, lit by the glowing screen. It's a Friday evening, and Enda's still working. Neil was hoping he'd be gone home. He should have known better. The seat is still warm. USB inserted, sixteen gigabytes free to load up the digital renderings of the reels. To have some secret, but deserved, exclusive ownership of the footage.

A password is needed to open the folder named 'NEIL'. The unnecessary precautions of the conspiracy paranoids. An obstacle Neil hadn't considered. The simple things. But then he remembers the clip he uploaded for Kathy that she never viewed. Enda at the keyboard, typing, about to show him reel one when he noticed Neil's phone.

Neil takes his phone and goes onto YouTube – their channel – and finds it. Before he presses play, he's stopped by a new number. His finger hovers over the screen while he considers what he's seeing: 'Views: 1'. One view. The implications. The first view on one of his clips for Kathy since Fitzwilliam Square's phone call.

His channel. Their channel. Maybe someone stumbled onto the clip? Possibly. But unlikely. No one ever has before. What's on the clip? What did he tell Kathy was on it? The password's on it, or at least Enda typing it is. That wasn't the selling point. A text message to Kathy: 'Check out new video. The lad talking about the reels!!' She never replied.

The password isn't too tricky. Just a matter of pausing it on the first letter and then the second. The third is easy to find. And so on. Once 'SCAN' is established, 'NAN' is obvious.

Enda's desktop is neatly organised. There are ten blue folders ordered two across, five down. 'NEIL' is one of them and it opens with a deft click. Insert the USB, open the file, move reel one and reel two across. Only 700 megabytes each. Enda's voice calls down the corridor. A vague response a distance away makes him laugh. The blue bar on the transfer reading slides along steadily. Not quickly enough.

Keep sketch over the screen to the door. The steam has died down on the coffee. Ping. One done. Enda's voice turns in to the door, still carrying the end of his laugh. His shape is dark on the frosted glass. Another distant call from down the corridor. Enda's silhouette lightens. Mumbles. Ping. Second one. Eject. Ease the USB out, log out, stand up and make for the door.

Enda fills the doorway. He puts his hands up to stop Neil from leaving. Gently forces him back into the room. He turns on the lights. Neil blinks into the flickering.

'What are you doing here?'

'I was looking for you.'

'And here I am.'

'No need to be a prick about it.'

Enda looks over Neil's shoulder at the computer, the swivelling seat. The truth dawns.

'I thought you didn't care about the reels?'

There is no point in lying. The USB is in his pocket. Enda wouldn't be able to stop him.

'I don't. Not in that way. I wanna see my great-grandfather. See his face. See what he's like.'

'You know you signed an exclusivity agreement?'

'I'm not going to share it.'

'You don't have to share it. Why take it in the first place? I don't get you.'

'Of course you don't, Enda. You never do. I want to see his work. See what he saw, what he captured.'

'You want to have your cake and eat it?'

'Don't be an arsehole all your life.'

'Watch them here then. On my computer.'

'I want to watch them myself, on the USB.'

Enda smiles at Neil like he's a child, 'You're starting to sound like you care.'

Neil doesn't respond. Doesn't need to respond. The USB is secure amongst the coins in his pocket.

Home Truths

Kathy's waiting for him outside the apartment when he returns from the college. He's in a rush to set up the USB, watch reel two and then get to his gran's for his last night with her before heading off on Monday. He could have done without Kathy's presence. The one view on YouTube will need to be addressed.

They move through the hall into his downstairs bedroom. A snippet of noise filters down from upstairs. His housemate's obviously got the computer fixed, but judging by the sounds coming from his room, he's back to his old habits. Viewing the reels will have to wait.

Neil closes the bedroom door behind him and tells Kathy about the USB. She sits down on the bed and yawns.

'Why'd you do that?' she says, casual.

'I dunno. I panicked a bit. Like I said, my uncles were going on about the memoirs. Ownership. Control. How much they might be worth as a book, not even knowing about the physical reels themselves. But they'll find out sooner or later. If I copped it, they will. And they'll cause problems. I just. I dunno. I think, I really want to see them now. Have a connection. It's important to me.'

Her face can't hide her astonishment. 'But you have the chapters.'

'I don't. My uncles do. And the last chapter's missing. Reading about it when you can see it is pointless anyway.'

She doesn't respond, only reaches out for the USB. He puts it in her hand and slides away from her, up the bed. He rests his back against the headboard and says.

'There's something else,' he says.

'Yeah?'

'Why did you come back?'

Her eyes betray her laugh.

'I'm serious,' he says. 'Why'd you come back?'

The question catches her off guard, and she turns to him, anger emphasising every syllable, 'What kind of question is that to ask? I've told you, already, I wanted to see you. Convince you I wanted to be with you. Be near you.'

The aggressive charge of her response shocks him.

'I don't think I believe you, though.'

Her eyes narrow.

'You watched the clip I made of Enda talking in the college about the reels.'

'So,' she says quickly, without thought, still smarting, surprised by the statement.

'You never told me. You never texted back. You heard him say how great they were and how much they could be worth, and you never told me. Why didn't you tell me you knew, instead of just playing all innocent, asking about the reels as if you didn't really care?'

'It makes no difference now. I came back to get you. To help you, 'cause I love you.'

'And you saw a chance of money. Admit it.'

'OK. Yeah, OK,' she shrugs. 'I'm not ashamed. So what? So what? I wanted to help you. Help you make up your mind. I know how you can be. How sentimental you get. How you always, always make the wrong decision, get easily sidetracked when it comes to your gran and grandad, and get tricked when it comes to money. I just wanted to help you. Push you in the right direction. But if you'd known I knew, if you'd thought I was interfering, what would you have done?'

'I dunno. I would've probably got thick, done the opposite.'

They share a light smile. 'Exactly,' she says. 'You see. It was for your own good.'

'It was money first, love second, though.'

'What?' she snaps. 'How can you say that? You know it was love first. It was you. It's always been you. And OK, yes, a life for us, a life with some financial security in a new country, yes, that's important, so money, yes, money is important. Don't pretend it's not. So if it comes to money first, well then, maybe yes. Yes. I want a life free of that dole queue. I can't do it. You may be able for it, Neil. Working with a stupid yellow T-shirt in a DVD store. That embarrassment every week, being a burden on the state at the dole office. Holding your hand out to those bitches behind the counter who wouldn't know a degree or experience if it bit them on the arse. But I'm not, Neil. I'm better than that. I deserve better. I think I deserve to be treated better. You need to realise that, and yeah, OK, that's why I'm back. I wanted to make sure you got what you deserved for the reels, because I know you. I've seen you get all sentimental. And we,' she shifts closer, and holds out her hands. 'And we, you and me – we deserve a good life, don't we? A good start in life with the help of this money. If it meant convincing you to offload the reels, get their true value, well then, yes, I came back to help. And, as it turns out, I didn't need to. You weren't sentimental after all. You sold them – like that – without my help. Like a true businessman.'

'I see,' is all he says.

Stunned, impressed by her honesty, shocked by his actions laid bare. Money first, love second. Her argument for both. The subtle manipulation to push him into the sale. Would he have done it anyway? Accept the deal? Any deal. Take the money. Sell his past. It was never his past to start with. And, after all the doubts, he did sell it. Move on. Move away.

'You never asked me about the reels, though. You never once asked me what was in the chapters, the letters I got from my gran. Never showed an interest.'

'And?'

'They might have meant something to me. His words. Actions, like. His life. My great-grandfather's life. It might have been important to me.'

'Regardless of what it meant to you, Neil, it's what it was worth to you that was important. Don't lose sight of that. Money is real. Memories, the past, you, of all people should realise, doesn't have to be your present. Not if you don't want it to be. Why do you think you never talk about your mother, or visit her grave? If you think about it, it upsets you, so you never think about it. You have control over the past in a way you never had over the future. This is your chance to have control over both. You know that. I know that. Forget about the USB. What's the point in having it? Make the break. Remember what will impact our lives, make them better.'

She speaks so articulately, passionately, he can't help but be swept up by her words. Her confidence in the ideas she's espousing. The sureness of her explanation. Philosophy. It has an inescapable logic that leaves no room for sentiment. There's a tinge though, of indignity, callousness, disregard for the words, ideas, life of his great-grandfather. A sour note. A strange note he has never heard before, or at least been conscious of.

A & E

Only after Jim leaves does Gran decide to get up from bed and go to the toilet. Jim's presence, the glaring silences not filled by the mention of the leather satchel, had an oppressive influence on the room, and Gran, hidden under her blankets, pale, but insistent – 'I'll be fine. I just need some rest' – was diminished in it.

'I've something for you, dear, when I return,' she whispers to Neil, shuffling in her dressing gown into the bright lights of the landing, towards the toilet. She has been in bed since the afternoon, after complaining of feeling light-headed.

Neil sits on the side of the bed, on edge, turning over Kathy's reassurances, Enda's warnings, the location of the last chapter, reel two, the cheque. Harry's words matter. His thoughts, his views on things. Guidance. Neil needs guidance.

He unzips his tracksuit top and prepares to tell her, somehow: I found the reels, I sold the reels, I have a cheque. Maybe ask her for the last chapter before he makes the announcement. He's interested in how Harry's story ends. What's on the last reel? Why did he hide the reels in the first place? Why were the reels hidden for so long?

Neil has the wallet out on the bed when a dull *thump* from the hall snaps him to his feet. The panic button – set to go off if Gran falls – activates the emergency number, and he's in the landing, crouched over Gran, who's face down on the carpet, as the voice on the phone's loudspeaker at the foot of the stairs goes, 'Hello, Mrs Downes, are you there? Are you OK?' And before Neil can turn Gran onto her back, he calls, 'Hello, an ambulance. Can you get an ambulance, please? My Gran's just collapsed. An ambulance.'

Because she's old, they bring her through the emergency waiting area on a stretcher – and, still on the stretcher, leave her behind the thin wall in A & E. A doctor takes her blood pressure, checks her pupils and asks a few questions. They want to know what tablets she is on, any existing conditions she has, and whether this has happened before. She answers them accurately, with the aid of an emergency information sheet all the family were told to bring to the hospital should anything happen while they were staying over. 'But, I only felt a little light-headed. I simply tripped. It is nothing too serious. Nothing to be concerned about. Some air was all I needed. Cooped up for too long in my bed.'

Her protests aren't heeded, and she's helped off the stretcher and given a seat – much the same as the one she has in her breakfast room – and told that a nurse will come by to check up on her every now and then until a doctor arrives to examine her fully. Neil fetches a plastic chair from the bedside of a sleeping patient on a stretcher. They're not out in the A & E proper, with its bright lights and sliding doors, coffee and vending machine, television in the corner and thick glass panels, but behind a security door in the slightly dimmer, somewhat more comfortable, definitely quieter, more cramped waiting area inside the waiting area of the emergency room.

After Neil pulls up his plastic chair next to her leather one, they face forward – as if on a bus – into the next stiff leather chair, just as the people behind them are doing. On Gran's left is the wall and sill of an administration office, and the black-and-white security screen of the A & E outside – the Friday-night crowd growing larger and rowdier. On their right, where Neil is, are stretchers: people pale, unshaven and in their pyjamas looking out at them, their feet, some exposed, others covered by blankets, only a yard or two from the chairs. At the top of the collection of seats is a random assortment of patients on trolleys too. It's chaos.

'I'm a little tired, dear,' she says and her head dips as if she's nodding off to sleep.

The lights in the makeshift ward go off, and the talking around them becomes hushed, broken intermittently by the rough calls of the drunk or drugged losers polluting the place.

'Don't worry,' Neil says, 'the nurse said the doctor will be here to see you soon.'

'I do hope so.'

Her head remains bowed, at an angle, as if she's praying silently. He fixes a stiff blanket over her shoulders, smoothes another one over her legs. She's still in her pyjamas, dressing gown and slippers.

'You know, dear, they took the case.'

He doesn't need to ask what case. He takes her soft hand on her lap, his fingers entwined in hers, his thumb on the top of her hand, gently rubbing.

'I heard.'

'Things will change now,' she whispers, a new hoarseness corroding the clarity of her voice. 'They will argue over him. His writings. Want to know about the reels. If they are anywhere to be found. How much they can sell for.'

'You think?'

She nods and brings her free hand to her mouth to cover a yawn.

'Tommy and I always knew this sort of thing would happen. It's why we kept the pages to ourselves. We thought about doing something with his words. His papers. In the early '60s, we had an offer, you see. Someone sought me out. Enquired, ever so nicely, about my father. His past. My knowledge of it.'

Another weak cough, an apology, and Neil hears how dry her throat is, how much of an effort each word takes.

'Relax, Gran,' he whispers, putting his arm around her shoulder, going close to her ear. 'Don't worry about anything. It's grand. You can tell me tomorrow.'

'No, dear. I'd rather. I'm feeling better. Just a little thirsty. I'd like to tell you now.'

She takes a number of delicate sips from the creased plastic glass of water.

'Your grandfather, God rest his soul, was a great man. Very smart. Astute. He loved his family dearly. Every one of you. He loved his country too. Loved it.'

'I know Gran,' Neil says, rubbing her back, feeling the trouble of her breathing.

'He thought the country needed its young. To grow. To become, as he put it, "A free-standing nation of the world." Youth and education was the key. And so, when they came looking for my father's memories, his reels, your grandfather didn't sell. He couldn't. We couldn't. "Money is a poor substitute for your legacy," he said. Instead, he came up with an alternative plan. A solution, if you will. A promise. He knew why the gentleman wanted the chapters. He knew what the reels meant to the gentleman's family. We knew they had been destroyed, but your grandfather, God bless him, said they hadn't been. In order to make a deal, you see. If the gentleman could guarantee all of our children – your uncles and aunt, your mother – work in Ireland, we would have a deal. Secure, lifetime jobs to ensure that they would never need to emigrate, and we would not release my father's memories, or, indeed, sell them, in our lifetimes.'

She coughs gently and slowly lifts the glass of water to her parched lips.

'But how,' Neil asks, because he has to ask, 'could he, the lad that wanted the reels. How could he get them all jobs?'

She smiles a wan smile. Lifts her head as if the answer is a cruel joke she shouldn't really laugh at.

'You see, dear, he was a very powerful man. He had been the secretary general for the Department of Justice.'

Neil has no idea what this means. But it sounds ominous. Important.

'What was the Department of Justice doing looking for Harry's reels?'

'Because, dear,' she says, finding mirth in the fact that Neil hasn't worked it out yet. 'The head of the Department of Justice was in them.'

'In them?'

Neil thinks of all the pages, the people Harry met during Easter week. Gogan. Dead. Frank Houlihan? Thornton? Paddy Mac Tuile?

'He was Davy, dear. Davy, my father's best friend, became very powerful after the Rising.'

'Davy? How? That's ridiculous. After all he did? The people he killed. How could he get into such a position of power?'

'His son did too.'

Neil is stunned. The madness of it all. The plain injustice. Ireland.

'His son?'

'Albert Ashe, dear. You have heard of him, surely?'

His heart gives way, bungee jumps into his gut and makes him lurch on the rebound.

'I'm tired, dear. Could you read me this, his last chapter?'

She pulls from under the blanket a thick, square wad of sheets. It's Harry's last chapter, hidden in her dressing-gown pocket. He can't believe it. He'd given up hope.

'I didn't know if you had it or not. Of course, Gran,' he says, delighted, pulling out his phone to light the pages in the waiting-room gloom.

'Thank you, dear. It's important. I haven't heard his words in some time. They reassure me.' And Neil clears his throat and whispers: 'Harry Casey, F Company, 2nd Battalion. Chapter 8.'

Harry Casey – F Company, 2nd Battalion #8

A hasty retreat – The tenements offer refuge – A charge like no other – After the storm – Why I write.

The smoke made an enemy of all shapes, each silhouette a frightful shadow of ominous intent. If it hadn't been for Liam Thornton recognising the Pathé, I dare say I might have tried to evade coming into contact with any of the figures running around the smoke-filled floor.

'Be damn, Casey,' he called, coughing through a filthy looking handkerchief, 'did your friend Gogan do as I asked?'

'I'm afraid, sir,' said I, all the while looking over my shoulder into the darkness whence I had come, 'he did not. His efforts were . . . '

Before I had opportunity to explain further, there was a wild scream, and then a bone-shaking shudder brought plaster and dust raining down upon us.

'Blast it anyway,' he called, ducking out of the way. 'Never mind. We'll have to take our chances. Follow the men ahead.'

With that, I evacuated, my Pathé still in hand, trailing the opaque shapes as they grunted, blustered and shouted obscenities to this new republic which had them scattering for their lives. I proceeded through a different set of holes than the ones I had only moments earlier gone through with Gogan – at times, we had to climb up ladders, through other floors – until we reached a premises leading into North Earl Street. This we crossed to another doorway and reached Cathedral Street.

From there, we marched, the flames from the Imperial and all of Sackville Street warming our backs and throwing shadows before us. The sky was bleached orange. We marched in double file down Thomas Lane, by the side of the Cathedral and out into Findlater Place. Each turn lured us into a new level of darkness, and each new descent into darkness seemed to silence us further (grunts and obscenities, all) and speak of our desperate sense that the lack of light was mirroring the lack of foresight afforded to manoeuvring us out of our predicament! We turned towards Marlboro Street, yet all the while, I was trying to peek over the crouched shoulders in front of and behind me, to see if I could spot Davy's soot-covered face. Without delay, we crossed Marboro Street and went up Gloucester Street.

Thornton raised a hoarse whisper from the front, and, turning to face us, his eyes large, the streaks of clear skin from the beads of sweat rolling down his blackened forehead giving him the look of a terrified savage, halted. It was obvious his desperation at our situation had outrun his common sense, even before he spoke. For what I had thought he was thinking of doing, he confirmed in his breathless orders: 'Our objective is to break out to Fairview.' Neither Thornton nor Brendan Whit, his second-in-command, were local men, and I let them know my thoughts on their plan.

'Oh, get out!' hissed Thornton his brow furrowed in menace. 'What do you propose we do? Set up your camera and record our last stand?'

'Things being as they are, sir, I'd rather not. But, for the men's sake, and all of our safety . . .'

I stopped to let the not-so-distant sound of an explosion die away. 'I propose we break into the Gresham and take it over, or, alternatively, let us crawl across Sackville Street in the shadow of the pillar to our comrades in the GPO.'

Fewer heads nodded to the latter suggestion than the former. It was quite dark, yet I could still make out Thornton's face as he came to the realisation that my suggestions – both of them – and my rationale, and description of Fairview and how it had been too dangerous to approach even on Tuesday afternoon (two days previous), were correct. But this put him in the awkward position of being usurped in a moment of crises by a mere cameraman.

'No,' hushed Thornton, 'this is not some ha'penny adventure for your motion-picture camera. This is war, and we are to retreat in order to fight another day. We proceed as originally set out: up Gloucester Street.'

And so I did, dispassionately. Unsurprisingly, we were only some distance up Gloucester Street when the most terrifying hail of searing noise that I had ever encountered suddenly opened up on us. We scattered like disturbed rats, the machine-gun fire sending us in assorted directions. Some of us strove to take refuge in houses, but found that most of the doors were locked. This was most unusual, as we knew that these were tenement houses, where the doors were always open.

One of our party, Flanagan, a tall glass of water with a dandyish face, removed a crowbar from his longcoat, and, in three long, muted pulls on the makeshift lever, splintered the wood on the door to one of the tenements and cracked it open like an egg. We all bundled forward into the dark-windowed house and fell atop one another into the hallway. There were, I reckoned, a half a dozen of us, and although we thought we were silent, we seemed to have alerted all and sundry in the house to our presence.

When the machine-gun fire lapsed, we could make out the reso-nant calls of a British voice: 'They've taken shelter in a building. Root them out and let them 'ave it!'

We were collectively holding our breath to gather from what direction and distance the English voice was resonating so volubly, when a timid, strained female voice broke through the tenement darkness and begged us to get up and be gone. 'You'll bring the whole British army down on every last one of us.'

In spite of her entreaties, no one stirred. We all remained perfect-ly still, cocking our ears to the now loose-hanging front door, trying to hear the proximity of the ominous clatter from the army boots coming upon us. Having begged us from the anonymity of the top of the first-floor landing to leave, the voice became a shape and then, from the faintest of strips of light between the door and the wall, was exposed as a strong-featured young girl, only partly dressed with a shawl over her shoulders.

'Please don't be bringing them in here, for crying out loud,' she whispered, catching my eye and, for some inexplicable reason, main-taining contact and looking on me with open hostility. 'My mother's unwell and there's families with little'uns and women with no hus-bands or nothing. Take yourself off to the streets and fight yer—'

'Whisha, shut up yer blatherin', Flanagan barked in a half-whis-per, his voice going dangerously close to a shout, but being kept low by the manic rasp in his throat. 'Get yourself back up them there stairs or I'll redden yer arse for ye.'

'Have some manners,' a north-of-Ireland accent strained, from the darkness down the hallway, 'and don't be talking like that to poor Mary and go along to hell out of this like she asked. It's not a war we were looking for when yis barged in here.'

The voice was a woman's, older than the young girl's, harsher, stronger.

No rebuttal was forthcoming from our group, for our attention was focused on the hammering, only some hundred yards or so down, on the corner house. Boots pattering off the damp cobbles quickly followed.

'Surrender!' the English voice barked into the night, directing the call indiscriminately to both sides of the street and all the dark tenement buildings. 'We will find you, and we will make an example of you guttersnipes, and the tenement you're being aided in will be blown to smash!'

A new voice entered the fray, a delicate, quivering male one, from a door frame behind us on the ground-floor hallway.

'For the love of God, men, listen to the girl. There's families residing in this here building. There's only a chiseler after being born in the back drawing room. Leave us in peace.'

'Shut up outta that,' Flanagan hissed once more, remonstrative, but desperately so, his reply now scraping the very breath he emitted in high-pitched exasperation. Our group began to whisper amongst themselves quickly.

'Here, mister,' the young girl called again, leaning down and tugging at my sleeve, 'I've no time to be standin' here gosterin' with the likes of you. Did yis not take heed of what Mr Costigan was saying? There's babies asleep inside.'

'Please,' I whispered to her, 'please. Go back upstairs and hide yourself.'

'I'll do no such thing. I didn't come to yis to raise no argument, but if you won't be moved, make a run for it, I'll have to alert them. Sure there's no other way out anyways. The back door's been bolted this last week.'

The others were too busy in their whispered panic to hear what she had said. I shushed her threat and slid over to her at the foot of the stairs, a new terror having been roused by her confirmation that we were most definitely trapped.

Another *rat-a-tat* from the butt of a gun, only this time closer than before, pounded heavily on a door down the street and set my heart racing still faster.

'OK,' said I, leaning up to her, the solitary light from the lamp coming through the gap in the door and exposing in her face something honest and agreeable. So desperate was I, I'd have seen whatever I needed to see to justify what I would request. 'I'll rouse them and lead them away from here if you do something for me.'

I cannot describe the tumult of my mind at that moment. Self-preservation? Maybe. The survival of my art, my truth? Definitely. She nodded her head solemnly in acquiescence to my request, and took herself at breakneck speed back up the stairs. Before I had a chance to reconsider, I stood up and announced to the men that I was making a dash for it, and if they so wished they could join me. They tried to jostle me fiercely. Nevertheless, able to bear it no longer, I made for the door, disregarding their remonstrances, and said, 'It's now or never. We'll not have more deaths of innocent citizens on our consciences if we go now!'

Once they saw me ease open the door to make ready for my escape, they got to their feet in a rapid motion and with that, I vaulted down the steps, took a sharp turn left and ran like a fox from a hound. I ran, the initial rush of breath giving way to the sound of my comrades' feet clearing the steps and clattering off the ground too. Amid my heart leaping near out of my chest, I heard a British voice cleave the air in a repetitious blaze of, 'Open fire! Open fire!'

Hardly had his words abated when high whistles of fury popped by as clean as tuppence, both machine guns and rifles opening up on us, the air close by my face charged by the near misses! The sudden realisation that the bullets were only inches, less, from my body, prodded me into a zigzag sally up the street. Flanagan was doing the same until the front of his forehead was blown clean off, the blood from his injury spraying fiercely onto my face. He dropped in a heap at my feet with a guttural grunt. I had no time to look back. He was dead for sure.

I came to the conclusion, while on that run, that I had a charmed life, as bullets seemed to be hopping like rain around me. No sooner had such a thought leapt into my head than I felt the devil's own shooting pain in my ankle. I had been shot! Terrified by this stinging pain, I quickened my pace, the spike of fear reaching a point I had never before known.

Suddenly, I saw a barricade about ten yards in front of me with British soldiers firing over it. I had no bayonet fixed to revenge myself for the ankle shot, yet I charged, with nothing else to do but charge. Without time to consider anything else, I gripped my pistol with all my might, as I had done on many occasions with my hurley, and ran into the face of war.

I charged, jumped on the barricade and lunged at the soldier on the other side. As I did I fell on the barricade's jagged edges, and found that I was not able to rise. I was wounded but did not know it until I had occasion to put effort into rising. It seems the barricaded soldier had also lunged, with his very own bayonet fixed, and got me in the thigh as I was falling. Suddenly aware of the injury and its seriousness, my whole body was overtaken by the pain and I began to moan.

After a few moments of this, I decided I was not going to let these British soldiers hear me give out, so I asserted myself and suppressed it. I was almost unconscious from the pain, flat out on the sketched implements of the barricade, when the soldier caught me by the back of the collar, pulled me up to the top of the barricade and, since the rest of my crew were still making sporadic attempts at escaping from the street, used my limp body as cover to rest his rifle on and fire at them.

Losing a lot of blood, and drained of hope and effort to challenge the predicament, I was unable to move. Some few moments later, the soldier again caught me by the back of the neck. He pulled me over to his side of the barricade and let me fall like a sack of mail, loose and uncontrolled, to the ground. My head stuck in the back of a chair which formed part of the barricade. My body, completely incapacitated after the initial collision, fell over. My final thought before losing consciousness was vivid, and strangely lucid: my neck was broken.

And therein ends my experience of the war, for the next I knew, I was having iodine poured from a bottle onto my chest in a dressing station in Gardiner Street. Strange as it may seem, I was unable to feel it, I was in such pain already. I had intermittent spells of consciousness. Words, half-phrases, snippets of conversations and judgments were passed down on what turned out to be me (at the time, I was unaware of who was talking about whom). 'I don't think he has a chance. At any rate, he deserves it for mixing up with that crew.' I somehow recall being searched by two Tommies, who found in my pockets two of our home-made bombs and a box of Peterson's matches.

The next thing I remember is being carried up some steps on a stretcher with lights blazing all around. I was informed it was the Castle hospital. I listened to the talk that was going on around, the whispers about how it had all ended, who was shot, escaped, surrendering. At one point, I tried to bid my tongue to speak, to shout down an English accent which was scandalising the rebels' motives, but I could not. I was too weak, my body having lost so much blood, my throat too dry. I could feel my legs, it must be said, yet I knew, without having to put pressure on them, they would not support my weight if I had wished to take leave of the hospital.

I lay in bed without moving for a fortnight, and I was a full month there before I was able to raise myself sufficiently to see the ward. I was left alone amongst the British Tommies for six weeks before I was transferred to my own colleagues. Needless to say, such a long, quiet period of time gave me plentiful moments to ponder what had occurred during my four days of reconnaissance. I had survived; many had not. I had seen a side of the Irish Republic many would not. I was deeply troubled by this. Things would be changed when I got out of hospital, and thence, out of jail. How much they would be changed, I was not completely cognisant of until some six years later, when, having kept my counsel for such a long time, I received an unexpected, violent call from Davy.

We had, you see, communicated very little since we last encountered one another amongst the ruins of Sackville Street. Of course, being both 'heroes', who had fought in Easter Week meant we had occasion to meet one another at events and gatherings, but always it was with an uncomfortable nod, lift of the cap, or reluctant smile. Our last meaningful conversation, or exchange of words before his most recent visit, occurred about the middle of July 1916.

I had been removed from the Castle hospital on a Saturday by lorry to Kilmainham. There I stayed until the following Monday. Word of our transfer to Kilmainham seemed to have got out very rapidly as, on Monday morning, hours before we were to leave, most of us had visits from relatives and, amongst others, some men who had just been released from Frongoch. Davy was one such man. He was my last visitor.

'I've just spoken with your dear mother,' he said, on sitting down before me. Not even a hello or enquiry after my health. 'And she was delighted to see me. I've been invited to tea whenever I find the time.'

My heart misgave me. I was all too aware of what he was up to. I kept my composure and, after an interval, smiled at him.

'Well, at least she'll have someone looking after her, so.'

'I'll be there, don't you worry, Har. Every day if need be 'til I find what I'm looking for.'

An English voice interrupted the whispers with, 'Let's be 'aving ye. Two minutes.'

Still Davy watched me earnestly, waiting for me to crack and blurt out answers to what he had not yet asked. I was loath to make a clean breast of it, give in and offer up my story, not after all that had happened between us, and to young Gogan. And still he sat silent while others around us offered one another handshakes of camaraderie, spoke of good luck and offered encouragement. The words of support falling around us made me all too aware of how our very own relationship was now beyond repair.

Amid the whispered farewells, screeching of chairs and final call of, 'All right, that's it. Out!' Davy finally broke.

'I want them. I'm not codding.'

'They're destroyed.'

'Lies.'

'They are.'

'Not all of them.'

'All of them.'

'I'm inclined to disbelieve you, Har. You're resourceful. I know you only too well.'

'They are. Burnt. All of them. In the Imperial. First floor. I had a witness to it only you—'

In a rapid motion, he was on his feet with his fists clenched, teeth biting his top lip.

'Don't you dare go there, me boy!' he hissed volubly, before catching himself and easing down to a whisper once more. 'Don't you dare. And I saw you, remember, before the fire in the Imperial, with your 'cinemachine,' whirring away. So, mind your blathering and tell me where they are.'

Perturbed eyes turned to us. A khaki uniform made its way over.

'They're all burnt. You saw the fires for heaven's sake. They're destroyed.'

'I'll keep a close eye on your mother for you, Har, regardless,' he whispered menacingly. 'All alone in that house. Fires can happen so easily at home. Especially with chemical film reels inside.'

My hands thrust well forward onto his. I took a firm hold of them with what strength I had on account of my injuries, and I warned him, 'Don't you dare talk of such dastardly things, Davy. You're not that far gone to the devil yet, surely.'

He shrugged off my limp grip and leaned in as if to embrace me, but, instead whispered, 'You said you'd give your life for your reels. I'd be only too happy to oblige, but since you're going now, I'll have to use your family for insurance. I swear to you Har, I mean to prosper now we've begun the reshaping of this land, and nothing will get in my way. If any footage, a single frame of your film, comes out, I will ensure that you wished you never let it see the light of day. Do you hear?' It was now his turn to grip me, only he took my shoulder and poured his hateful words in my ear. 'For your sake, you should hope you're not being too bloody cute, because I'm in earnest, to the top of this here land. You and your family, Har, will be a footnote to my ascent. Be wise, and make sure they really are burnt.'

And so they were. Burnt. Erased. After Paddy Mac Tuile's passing in 1920, there is no one to say otherwise. Until only last week (the beginning of August 1922), when without warning, Davy came knocking on my door. In the intervening days, I have bent myself to a typewriter and resolved to let you hear my words – for I know you will never see my images.

I hope my words do not recount so strange a time you will be unable to understand my motivations. I hope you find in them something, a legacy of sorts, which will, I hope, inform the progress of your life. I have read recently of an Abyssinian saying that goes, 'You see the present, you hear the past'. It is, I think, an apt adage for my future, your past.

I can only hope that you never see the likes of what I captured on my reels in your present, but I hope my words, somehow, will be heard by you in the future, and thus, you will come to an understanding of your past, and me.

Love, your father,

Harry Casey

The End of an Era

Her eyes are closed when Neil looks up from the last page. Closed in such a way that it seems she's facing into the sun on the beach, relaxed, lost in the intoxication of the moment. Satisfied. Happy. Content.

Neil dwells in the echo of the moment. Lets the words and their meaning, the voice of his great-grandfather, settle into him, whisper in his ear, enter his bloodstream. Communicate through the decades. 'Love, your father.'

History's demand on the present is not something he has felt before. Is imagination the key to history? An imagined, empathetic response to circumstances so far removed, it's almost impossible to believe they once occurred in the physical space he now occupies.

The black-and-white security screen in the admin office shows the unmistakable figures of Jim and Eoin storming into the waiting area and approaching the counters. It's 3:07 AM.

'That's something, huh, Gran?' Neil says, to bring her back. Eyes closed, she nods ever so slightly, smiles softly, finds his hand and squeezes it.

'Now, do you see, dear, why they shouldn't be sold? They are worth more than any offer could ever hope to match.'

Her eyes open on him, distant, tired. Her smile catches the light and fills her cheeks.

'It's something all right, really something,' Neil says. 'They're like, well . . . everything's just . . . I dunno. I'm speechless, really. I can't. I dunno.'

'He gave everything for them. His whole being. His life.' She brings her hand to her forehead, sighs.

She goes quiet again. Neil tries to rouse her. 'His story really is amazing, Gran, isn't it?'

'Pardon, dear?' she says, distracted, massaging her forehead, eyes closed.

'It's amazing, Gran. Your dad's story. Inspiring. But, ye know. . . ' He has nothing of worth to say. His words sound so cheap now. Lacking.

He needs to tell her, though. He has to tell her. She grimaces. He leans in to her, his hand on his wallet, ready.

'You OK?'

'I'm just a little . . . feeling a little light-headed.'

The ward is empty of staff. Neil scans the chairs, trolleys. No one has been to see her in hours. A drunk staggers off a trolley and collapses to the floor with a grunt and gurgle. A puddle of puke blooms under him.

'I'll go to get someone for you . . . '

'No dear, stay. Please stay.' Her grip is strong. 'The time wasn't right for his story you see. You see, now, don't you? You . . . you're . . . it's right now. We always thought you would be the right person.'

'But . . . Gran, would it not be better if I could make a new life because of them? Do what Pappy promised I could do. Start anew. He told me. Said it to me. Told me it would change my life. There's only one way your life can be changed these days, Gran, and that's with cash. Ideas, film reels, images of things, ideas about countries your dad had, they're amazing and all, but of no value anymore.'

She looks at him through her fingers, still massaging her forehead, her eyes dark.

'I'm tired, dear. I'm sorry, but I don't understand.'

Now is not the time. But no time ever is. Will ever be. He's leaving Monday. He has to explain himself. Help her understand his motives.

'Money is the glue for everything. Ideas are not for the sake of ideas anymore. But opportunities to make money. A country is not for the sake of a country, or its people. But jobs. Profits. Figures. Yields. These reels, Gran. I found them. They weren't destroyed. I need you to see that they're not a thing in themselves anymore. They're real. And, like, they're my one big opportunity for a new life.'

Two fingers and her thumb push the skin on her forehead back. Her eyes close and she grimaces. Her lips are dry and they move to say something, emit a shallow cough and open again. 'I was cold,' she whispers.

'Will I get you another blanket?'

Her hand waves away the offer. 'When I went to the stand, Croke Park. No, not Croke Park. Another place. For the Gaelic. How was I to know we would go there? Poor Tommy, he didn't notice for the first half, he was so nervous. Shivering there in the stand. And for the first quarter I was thinking, "What kind of a thing is this?" But I didn't pass any comment. Only stood there shivering. He was embarrassed, God love him, when he noticed. I didn't give out. He gave me his coat as soon as he realised.'

She smiles, her eyes closed. 'It was so warm. So warm. You know the type. A long, bulky overcoat. It covered me from head to toe.' She giggles lightly. 'I will never forget the warmth of the coat after being so cold. Nor poor Tommy's shame. He promised me after that day, our first outing, that he would always think of me first. Look after me. Never let me be cold again. Never. He had a sense of duty. That was love, wasn't it, dear?'

Everything is still. He doesn't know how to respond. 'Your mother loved you, Neil. Your grandfather loved you. Really loved you. He thought the world of you. As do I. But, I'm sorry, I just don't understand you.' Her hand pats his, the fingers weak and silk soft, and then her head dips, her hand relieves his and flumps onto her lap, and, almost as if it was being held up by a piece of string and the string has snapped, her head drops heavily, her chin tucking into her neck. Her body lurches forward.

Neil takes her shoulders to stop her from slumping off the chair. He pins her back and stands, his hands holding her in place, and calls for a nurse. One appears from behind a corner and jogs over, but Neil knows when she gets to them – even in the morning darkness of the ward – there'll have been no point in hurrying.

Copy and Paste

Devastated. Numb. Thinking of nothing only concentrating on the walk, Neil leaves the hospital and goes to the Malahide Road.

Of course, Jim and Eoin were furious that he hadn't notified them earlier, let them in to see their mother before she died. Their anger – aimed at him – outweighed their sadness at her loss. After sitting around for a while, answering the nurse's questions, the doctor's questions, listening to Jim's whining at how he – not Neil – should have been by his gran's side in her final moments, Neil got up to leave. 'What did she say?' was pressed upon him time and time again, as if her final words held some reassuring key for them to live the rest of their lives by. She had nothing of the sort to say. Nothing Neil was hoping to hear anyway.

With what little battery Neil has left, he finds the map of Fairview on his phone and goes to Fairview Strand, where Harry stayed for the first night of the Rising, before departing to the GPO. Neil takes the bridge Harry crossed on the Tuesday and then walks, in the silent, orange-street-lamp darkness, down Summerhill, thinking – or at least trying to picture what fears might have filled

Harry's thoughts as he marched into war with his truth apparatus under his arm.

On Neil goes, Summerhill bleaching into Parnell Street, the empty and closed Chinese restaurants, the off-licences, the odd stranger coming from a club, head high, swaying, drunk. Still he thinks of what propelled Harry down this route. What it must have felt like to have his intensity of feeling, love, ideas, passion. A spur to enter such a situation where his life would be risked. The bravery. The Pathé. The belief in his vision, or at least, the power of the truth in creating a vision, not for himself, but for the place he thought would come into being. His vision. Ireland? He could never have imagined this.

Can Neil imagine an alternative? A left before the towering Parnell monument, onto Cumberland Street. Two junkies down a lane, sparking their faces by a dumpster, deep black holes where their eyes should be. High heels and their irregular *tack-tack*, bare arms, goosebumps, linking each other, giggling, shivering, stumbling, short skirts, faded fake tan, coming from a house party. Wrecks. The dangerous shadows of the pillars on Marlborough Street, the nerves perhaps, buzz of adrenaline, really living, questioning motives, necessity. Time to turn back? There will be others to chronicle the events. There will always be others to give a representation of this nation's birth. Others who will take responsibility for bringing us the revolution. Hold those who succeed accountable. Ensure that the foundations laid are ones of integrity, bravery, loyalty, honesty, democracy, justice, equality. Neil never uses these words. Why would he?

A lonely taxi waits at the top of Sackville Place. The yellow whimper of desperation for one more fare. The red tail lights highlighting the exhaust fumes. A black man. A cautious, hopeful smile. A nod. Sorry, no. And Neil stops and leans against the wall of Clerys and peers up into the pillars and frieze, the high windows and cool, pale historical reality. Looks over his shoulder and sees the sketched barricade, Harry some feet away from it, cranking, and Davy, Davy, father of the new republic, holding a gun to the head of the working man. A tax. A levy. Put on the green jersey. The crack of the gun, the thump of the body as it falls into that which he died for. And Harry, his great-grandfather, brave Harry keeps on cranking, keeps a steady hand, holds his nerve in the face of brute force and does what is natural to him. Doesn't flinch from recording, revealing the truth of this nation.

Still they stagger by, McDonald's drinks tinkling, grease-patched brown bags, drifting off the pavement and back on. A fight, two girls pulling at each other's hair under the spire, across from the GPO, screams of agony, helpers wading in, blue lights, a siren, the swoosh of a taxi. Someone pissing gleefully on the statue with the cane. It's 6 AM. Things are dying down. He tries to concentrate on the GPO. Find in its shape, the shadows, its memory. Block out the unravelled chaos around, passing it, and attempt to look on it as Harry might have. If he can, feel something of the passion, the idealism Harry felt for this shit hole.

He walks over to the GPO and puts his hand to the pillar. It's still cold and indifferent, but something's changed since he last felt it. His grandad beside him, whispering about how history always asks questions of us – those of us who are willing to listen.

A large window frames the bronze statue of that martyr, slumped over a rock like a junkie on the quays. Stuck to the bottom corner of the window is a notice of trading. A bank name beside the An Post logo points to new Saturday opening hours. 8:30 to 12:30. Neil feels the cheap imitation leather of his wallet, looks at his phone and decides to have a few pints in an early house – there's one on Townsend Street – before coming back, and finally lodging the cheque. There's nothing to stop him now.

Out of Left Field

It's her eagerness to leave that arouses Neil's suspicion, even in his tired, grieving state. But he lets it play out. Too tired to do anything else. Upset, confused, and angry at the ambush at the post office, he doesn't want more hassle. He looks through his faint memory of the morning when he got back – a lifetime ago, hours ago – and tries to bring to mind what he might have said, or done, to offend her, make her want to leave.

Only short whispers as he pulled the blankets over, mumbled nearly drunk half-sentences, took her in his arms, warmed his body against her naked body, whispered where he had come from: 'The hospital.' What had happened: 'My gran passed away.' Her turn in to him, her breasts, her leg lifting onto his, the shushed, 'I'm so sorry, Neil, I'm so sorry,' and the connection of their bodies, hers, every muscle, area of skin reaching out and surrounding him, comforting him, soft kisses of condolence on his cheek, his neck. His arms on her back, the tiredness, otherness, numbness, his manoeuvring for solitude, seclusion, forgetfulness, her responsiveness and warm, opening up, sideways, her leg hitching up, inviting him in, her lips on his neck, his chest, the shallow delicate intake of breath and the distraction from the world through love.

'Why you going so early? Stay. I could really do with you here, now.'

'I gotta go. I've loads, I've stuff to do for Monday.'

'But it's early. I feel like shit. I could really do with you, Kat. It's what,' he checks her phone on the bedside locker, 'only half one. Stay.'

'I'm really sorry, babe, I'll be back by five.'

He lays the phone back on the locker and notices the absence.

'Where's it gone?'

'Huh?' she answers, distracted by the effort of putting on her coat.

'The USB? I left it on the locker last night before I left. There. It was right beside the lamp.'

'Did it fall over?' she attempts a brief glance behind the locker. He shifts over, pulls the locker back. Nothing.

'It's not there. Did one of the lads come in here?'

'No,' she answers, dismissing his question with a flap of the hand.

'Well, then, where is it?' He jumps up and pulls the sheets off the bed, scatters things away from the locker, reefs it away from the wall. The stale pints lurch in his gut.

Kathy stands back against the bedroom door. Away from the violence. Fully clothed. Ready to go. She whispers something. Neil can't hear her through the noise of rooting.

'Sorry?'

She whispers the short line again. He sits up straight. Catches the ghost of it.

'You what?'

'It's gone. I broke it.'

'Why would you?' He shakes his head. The reasons baffle. 'Why would you do that?'

She looks to the carpet. To the locker on its side. To the window. Anywhere but at him.

'What would you have done with it? It was a distraction. I was doing you a favour.'

'What the fuck, Kat? You have no idea. No idea.'

Neil moves towards her. Is this why she was leaving? Is this why she called last night? He's aware of his nakedness. Suddenly self-conscious.

'You're tired, your gran has just passed away. You're emotional. I didn't plan it like this. It was foolish for you to take them in the first place. It could ruin everything. You're not thinking straight. What about the exclusivity agreement? I'm trying to help you.'

Neil starts to struggle with his clothes.

'Can't you see? I was guaranteeing your money. No more what-ifs and wondering, worrying.'

'But what if I wanted to . . . the reels . . . see my great-grandfather's work? See what he really saw, what really happened?'

'You don't care about those kinds of things. I know you, Neil.'

'What if you don't – not anymore? People can change. What if I want to see them now? If I'm interested in these things now?'

He wants to say more, but to win the argument would be to expose himself. A waster of the highest order.

'You'd give up twenty-five grand for this new interest?' She laughs nervously. 'Don't be so ridiculous. You're not fooling anyone. That USB was just your ego trying to get one over on the politician. They can't be touched – like, ever. Not in Ireland. It was never going to happen. People like you and me, we live in a different country to them, Neil. Money like this is a once in a lifetime opportunity for people like us. A new start. Take it while you can. It's just your conscience trying to fool you into thinking you hadn't really betrayed your gran. But you did. You made your decision. You sold out. You got the cash. Move on.'

He knows if he tells her what happened at the post office his anger will be justified. Her shame complete.

She steps towards him, puts her hands on his chest. 'Remember why you sold them: our new life. Who cares what's on them? What he saw? They won't change anything now. This place is doomed. It's rotten to the core. Let's leave while we can, with what we can.'

Neil looks once more to the window, then back to Kathy, her new calm demeanour, sincere tone. She believes wholeheartedly in what she is saying, and what she has done.

Temptation is a confusion in accepting her argument.

'I knew you'd be like this. You're so indecisive. I made the decision – once and for all – for you. For us.'

'But it was my decision to make.'

'Look at you, Neil. You're twenty-six and broke. Unemployed. Emigrating. The decisions you've made so far in life have brought you here. The one I've made for you will make you rich. You know I'm right.'

He can't help it. There's no point in prolonging the inevitable.

'The cheque, though.' He can't say it.

'What?'

'I don't know why, but he . . . I never checked. I just never copped. I was blinded by the numbers. All I saw was the cash. I mean, who looks at the date? I never thought.'

'What?' She's grimacing now.

'It can't be cashed for another six months, Kat. You happy now? I went to cash it this morning. Lodge it. Not 'til next year, they said. He's screwed me, Kat. He has screwed me. And now you've screwed me too.'

Inheritance

Neil's only feet from the grave, the small sparks of rain pecking at his umbrella, the muck squelching underfoot, when a presence begins to walk beside him. Neil ducks under the rim of his umbrella to see who it is. Jim nods down, stern-faced, and whispers, 'We're missing the final chapter.'

Neil keeps walking. He is hung-over and sick. Nervous. On edge about the flight in a matter of hours, about the loss of the reels, about Harry's last chapter. Everything. Everything's a mess. 'What chapter?'

'Don't be disingenuous. You know very well what I'm talking about. You have it. We know you do. You have more than a passing interest in his words, and the reels.'

The mourners bottleneck up ahead, in a mass of black at the narrow, gated exit. He spies Kathy, under a blue umbrella, amongst them. She hasn't been in touch since Saturday. Not a word.

Jim takes one long stride and turns and comes to a halt before Neil. The rain patters down. Crows rustle the trees, disturb the hush with their calls.

'Mind you, the others think you know something. They say you're motivated by monetary gain. You were after something. Eoin says you would never have visited her so often otherwise. He thinks the letters have something to do with it. Maura thinks there's much more to this than the letters. There's a growing consensus on that. Eoin says he's going to dig deeper.'

He sighs and dwells on Neil's face, waiting for a reaction. 'I'm undecided. But, I'm willing to give you the benefit of the doubt.'

He reaches into his pocket and pulls out a brown A4 envelope.

'I'm not even sure if this will be any use to you. Even if you have his last chapter, it may still be worthless. Unfortunately, I haven't seen it, nor read it, so I cannot say. Your grandmother had her reasons for picking you. I suppose it is only right you read this too.'

Rain splatters the envelope as it passes between them. Dark specks stain it.

'We found it. Cleaning her room out for the estate agent.'

DUBLIN FIRE

The jury at an inquest at the Coroner's Court on Harry Casey, photographer, aged thirty-two, who was burned to death in a fire at his residence on Wednesday, returned a verdict of accidental death.

Mr Casey was asleep in his house with his wife when the fire started. The jury heard on Saturday how he had aided his wife, who is with child, in exiting a second-storey window into a tarpaulin held to receive them in the street below.

It would appear Mr Casey retreated into a bedroom to retrieve items of value when a large explosion occurred. His remains were found in the second-storey landing; they were terribly charred and the house was completely gutted.

It is supposed that through some accident, the house became ignited and, having spread to the upstairs bedrooms where Mr Casey kept photographic materials, the fire engulfed the house in its entirety.

The civic guard turned out, and were joined by the urban council's fire engine, and they succeeded in subduing the flames.

DEAD GENERAL'S LAST JOURNEY

The First Stage
Body Removed to Pro-Cathedral
Immense Crowds in the Streets

The body of General Collins was removed last night from the City Hall, Dublin, where it had been lying in state since Thursday night, to the pro-cathedral, the procession being again witnessed by many thousands of spectators, who lined the streets through which it passed.

Shortly before six o'clock, the City Hall was closed to the public, and only the relatives of the late general, his brother, officers, and a few intimate friends were allowed to remain while the coffin was being sealed.

It was a touching sight that those who were privileged to be present witnessed in the central hall, where the remains lay. A large part of the floor space was covered with nearly 200 wreaths.

Three

Enda texted. Neil thought it would be Kathy. If not apologising, then at least checking if he was still going to be on the flight. Neil had to get back to the apartment after the funeral, get his suitcases and get out to the airport. Rain causes all traffic in the city to crawl, so, with about an hour to spare, he agreed to meet Enda in The Lombard on Pearse Street. As much as he didn't want to see Enda, his text was a life ring cast into the turbulent waters of his last hours.

His gran's death had plunged him into another storm of loss. His mother, his grandfather, and now her. He was drowning in doubt, swamped in questions about whether what he was doing was the right thing, if had done the right thing. At least Enda would eat up the empty minutes before he had to get the taxi. Neil would rather be in a pub with a pint than at home in his room peering into the cheque again for an answer to his oversight. It wasn't his fault. Who writes cheques anymore anyway? When was the last time he had actually held one, seen one?

'I'm really sorry to hear that, Neil. I didn't know. I just presumed you were out partying all night again.'

'It's OK,' Neil says, his hand raised in forgiveness. 'I don't blame you, I do look like shit. And yeah, I was out.'

Enda is silent.

'How old was she?'

Neil laughs at Enda's new consideration.

'Eh, I dunno. Eighty-six, eighty-seven, maybe eighty-eight.'

'A good innings.'

Just a shrug and sup of the pint.

Office workers shake off their umbrellas inside the door. Trumpets sound for the one o'clock news. A crowd gathers outside the window, waiting on the lights. Neil takes another sup from his pint. Waits on Enda to speak. He was the one who texted after all.

'You all set?'

Neil smiles at Enda's effort. 'It's all right, Enda. Ye don't have to be nice to me just cause my gran's dead. It's cool. Whatever ye texted me for, whatever ye wanna say, just say it. I'm not in the mood.'

A door opens and the traffic's hum increases.

'I'm sorry about the way I was the other night in the lab. You were quite aggressive.'

'And you were an arsehole.'

Enda sways away from the table as if to sidestep the words. Neil sees his alarm.

'What? You were.'

The waiter brings Enda's coffee. Enda reaches for the milk, and says, 'Well, did you enjoy them?'

Neil doesn't understand.

'Reels one and two. Did you enjoy them?'

Neil laughs to himself. 'Ah, so that's it. I was wondering why you'd text. If you'd found out. Kathy was on to you. Still freaked, is she?'

The milk misses the cup. Enda's face holds a disturbed, uneasy smile. 'I have no idea what you're referring to. I was only asking if you watched the reels.'

'Bullshit. No – are you happy? – I haven't, and yes, the cheque's a fraud. I'm sure Kathy told you that too.'

Enda breathes heavily through his nose, looks bored with Neil's rant. 'I know nothing about Kathy. Nor do I wish to know anything about the cheque. I was working all night, through the weekend if you must know. You surprised me at the lab. Made me think.'

'So you said.'

'No, you surprised me by your motivations, not your actions. The reason I asked you if you were on an all-nighter was because I was.' A goofy laugh escapes.

Neil will finish the pint and go.

'I planned to only keep it for my own personal perusal. A selfish artefact. If they ever realised, I planned to play dumb and simply exchange it for the real one.' He giggles at his pun.

'I have no idea what you're talking about.'

'I have something for you.' He places a USB on a beer mat.

'So it was Kathy who got in touch.'

Enda can't hide his annoyance. 'No,' he dismisses, 'you never listen. I was working all night. I have not heard from your girlfriend. This is for you. Do whatever you want with it. If you're interested in two, you should be interested in all three.'

Neil pushes back from the table, almost giddy at the thought. A smile betrays his mood. He can't help it. He tries to contain the suggestion. Dampen the expectations.

'What's on this?'

'The reels.' Enda reciprocates the grin.

'All of them?'

'All of them.'

Neil puts his hand out to take the USB. 'How?'

'I got angry when you came to bring them to the solicitors. You riled me. Mocked me. So I swapped an old canister for reel three and started it. For my own personal use.'

Neil holds the USB to the light like he's looking for a watermark on a note. He's speechless.

'And then you came looking for the other two. It surprised me. You surprised me. I completed it this morning after spending days getting it ready. Just don't share them and you'll be OK with your money.'

'I don't know what to say.' Neil weighs the USB, cupping it in his hands like coins. 'This is unbelievable. Thank you. I really don't know what to say.'

Enda reaches his hand across the table. 'I'm delighted you appreciate them. That's enough.'

Neil looks to Enda's offer, 'You sure you don't want a disinfectant wipe?'

'No,' Enda smiles, 'I'm up to my neck in shit now, too.'

Digital Reality

Even though he knows it's a silent clip, he uses his earphones to insulate himself from the outside world. The USB, the silence and anonymity of Pearse Street Library, only yards from the Lombard, the clunky box of a public computer. Worn concrete steps that he has never climbed before. A building he had no use for, offering him answers he thought he'd never get.

Reel two flickers to life. Brief, bright flashes of white warp the YouTube-sized viewer, and a bustling street, bare feet, discoloured dresses, hats – so many hats, darkening every head – scurry in and out of shops. Broken windows, empty doorways, faces wide with wonder at the bundles they are struggling under. When they see Harry – the camera – they come to a slow, bemused, almost drugged standstill and gaze into him, a smile of acknowledgment for the immortality being bestowed upon them. A line flickers down the screen, the people disappear, the screen goes blank, flaps. Specks of white rain down like a blizzard on the black blankness, and the screen jitters.

A man has his hands on a cart at a barricade and another man, gun in hand – Davy, no doubt – is gesticulating. Every action, gesture is carried out in a slightly-faster-than-normal, cartoon-like motion. Even though the argument is growing more intense, the onlookers turn their heads like zombies and gaze dumbly at the camera. The shot. A shock. Neil becomes interested. Disturbed. This is real life. He pauses the piece, skips back a few seconds, and watches it again. The drama forgets the silence. The action forgets the local. Becomes something greater, bigger. The gunshot smoke and the violent shudder of the man with his hand on the cart. Faint spray of blood.

Neil is reminded of the stuttering, hazy film of JFK. He pauses it on the shot again. Thinks of the man falling like an arrow from the twin towers. A Vietnamese child running, naked, crying, to the camera. A lotus-seated burning monk. A priest with a white tissue, crouched, leading two men with a body. An explosion shaking the camera on a Northern Irish street. Davy with his gun to the head of the working man. For Ireland. Witnessed. Neil feels a stirring. A reaction. An opening up into the library of atrocity images he has stored subconsciously. This is a new one. That says so much. That deserves to be seen. That has to be shared. This is history. Ireland then, the world now.

Davy staring into the camera from his compromised position above the corpse. And an empty scene, the man dead at the foot of his cart. An intolerably long scene. The looting continues around him. The people look at the camera confused, as if it will have some answer for the madness that's tearing though their lives. A jump, and someone's talking outside the GPO. Again, the soldiers turn to the camera like it calls them, wants their faces to colour its canvas. A room. Dark and atmospheric. A bright window, a terrace outside. Smoke drifting across the picture. A haze of white specks. A warping of black spots. Hairs sizzle in black and white. Blank. Then a figure walks to the window, hat on head, gun over shoulder. A crouch, and he points.

Neil is growing bored. Three minutes, twenty seconds. No sound.

No colour. Scenes that are too long. Only one piece of real action. A lot of bemused, doleful spectators. A man at a window. The screen flashes to black and it is over. Reel two. Neil presumes that if you knew Davy Ashe, you would recognise him at the barricade. His face is clear.

If the twenty-first century is the digital century, he has just brought the 1916 Rising and his great-grandfather's story into being. But the images might as well be dead unless they move or open out into more images. The screen is his twenty-first-century mirror. Every image he sees in this mirror is the unthinking consciousness of his time. What he sees strikes a note of confusion. An image in a world saturated by images, in itself, shouldn't shock. This has. An authentic response? All responses are based on previously seen images. This is never seen. Neil feels something. Something disconcerting. Something new.

Reel three speeds onto the screen, and there's a man and a woman smiling self-consciously, stiff and unsure of how to act before the camera. Gogan, Neil presumes is the man, his great-grandmother, the woman. Then the screen washes out in a blaze of white and darkens again, and there, staring back, head straight, chin tucked in, with a still smile and raised eyebrows of embarrassment, is Neil – Harry, of course, but Neil. A black-and-white replica copied, but only just pasted.

Neil pauses the piece and slumps back on the chair and breathes out to compose himself. He blinks into the paused face, stares hard, and wonders if he's really seeing a similarity or only wishing it. To put himself into history. Actually contribute to the life of the country. But, no matter how he looks at it, Harry has Neil's features. The thick eyebrows, elongated chin, creased-eyes smile, definite, angular jaw. His nose. He looks like Harry. He smiles, a sense of pride washing gently, sublimely over him. He plays on.

Harry's laughter lights up the screen, and he suddenly becomes real for Neil. Gogan, laughing with him, might as well be one of the lads Neil has recorded at a party for Kathy. A white haze and more black speckles distort the picture. The screen wobbles, and suddenly a figure is silhouetted against a large hole in a wall. Gogan. A blurred shape arrives from the right of the screen. Creeps up on Gogan. A flash of silver – the pace of the shot never relenting, speeding up or washing out – and Harry keeps the images running. Gogan falls to the floor, and Davy, his face lit from a light source to the left, is easily discerned. He charges towards the camera. His eyes are wide, deranged, and the picture is enveloped in black-and-white noise. Darkness fills the jumping screen, flashes of white stain the picture, and it ends.

Neil is spent. He checks the time. He doesn't rewind the stabbing. It's not as visceral as the shooting. But his new discovery – of his likeness on the screen, behind the screen – has brought a whole new meaning to the reels. He has made the imaginative leap. Empathy is where he lands. And, once there, he wants to know Harry better. Read his words again. Listen to his voice. Understand him. Understand the images.

Departures

The airport is a confusion of notes, bells, calls, voices. About two hours after leaving the cemetery, Neil puts his bag through at the check-in desk. The woman at the counter, lipstick staining her smile, says she has a daughter in Canada these last two years. She asks to weigh the bag; there's nothing of worth in there, just jeans, jumpers, T-shirts, boxers, socks, runners. She asks then to weigh his carry-on bag too. It's over weight by about a kilo. Her pink-stained teeth flash again, and she says, 'You've enough to be worrying about, I'll let ye away with it.'

In one hand, as he walks away, he has his wallet, the cheque neatly folded back inside. In the other, the USB. He is nervous. This is his barricade.

The bank at the end of the terminal is open. A teller is at the window. Just a dark shape. He is thirsty. There's a vending machine for overpriced Coke inside the sliding entrance doors, next to the Internet booths. He has plenty of change. The departures board flickers. There's half an hour to spare. He hasn't seen Kathy yet. Or her family. If he's to see her, he'd rather it was after security, at the gate even, away from prying eyes. Undue influences. He twirls the USB between his fingers. Thinks of the reels. The power of his images. And how they'll never be seen. The words of his Gran. The faith his grandfather had in him to do the right thing. His great-grandfather's work. His life. His death. And the value of their past. The value of his future.

Excited couples breeze by, families returning home with their bags piled high on trolleys, the front wheels spinning in tight circles. The queues at the check-in desks crawl. The shuffle for the security at departures is lengthening. Boarding card, passport, all change out of pockets, belt off, shoes off, phone in the plastic container, no rings, no pins, no liquids, no drugs. The red light, green light, quick pat down, no turning back once through. The only way back is up and away.

The belief of his gran. Love of a woman. A woman of a different era. An era long gone. Ideals long forgotten. When he touched her hand, felt the warmth of her embrace, he was touching an Ireland of nearly a hundred years ago. Their connection somehow spanning the republic's past (her father), the republic's present (her), and the republic's future (him). She's dead. He has never been more alive. The reels lay in wait for him for a reason. Never seen. Never to be seen. Twenty-five grand will change his life, change a life. Never to be seen again. What's on the flickering, hazy footage is authentic. Real. History. His history. A history never acknowledged. A state without foundation. Rotten to the core. Destroyed from within. A failed enterprise. A failed experiment. A corrupted idea. An ill-formed theory.

The slow, green-mile walk of the ones leaving – not the ones returning home after their cold, dull Irish holiday; the ones who are the collateral damage from this republic's implosion – are slump-shouldered and defeated. They move with a slow, brave inevitability as they face the queue to leave, after leaving the queue to survive.

Neil owes this place nothing. It has used him and has discarded

him. Wants rid of him. Wants his statistic to prop up its bullshit figures for the 'live' register. He is alive. Living. Living in the future, in
that space beyond the date the cheque can be cashed. Despite them.

It's a while away yet. He doesn't know how he's going to get
through the next six months. Every day will be tolerated until he can
return and cash the cheque. There's a doubt, though. It's been lurking
since the GPO. Is the cheque legitimate? Is the cheque a fraud? Is the
date a diversion?

He sits on a silver bench, takes out the cheque to look at the figures once more. He doesn't have to wait. He could know for definite
if he went to the bank counter and asked. He won't. He's afraid of the
numb truth. He'd rather push the possible out for as long as he can.
Live with the hope instead of the crushing certainty. He wants at least
to dream of what the cheque could hold. A year's work. Maybe more.
That's what it holds. A year off. He was that shallow. Gullible. Easily
manoeuvred. He closes his fist on the cheque just as Kathy arrives.
She doesn't say hello, mention the morning funeral, only asks sympathetically, 'Is that the cheque?'

The sandbags and sketched barricades loom.

He nods.

'What are you doing with it out like that?'

'I dunno. Thinking about it. He's made a show of me. I doubt it's
even real.'

'Go and ask then.'

'I'd rather not.'

She tuts with an aggressive impatience and snaps it from his distracted palm.

'There's only one way to find out.'

She's turned and is gone before he can get up and stop her. He hasn't
got the energy. He is drained. Confused. Maybe happy she has taken
the responsibility out of his hands. A convenient cop-out.

The seconds before certainty weigh down on him. He eases the USB out of his pocket and heads for the Internet booths. She is no longer his guardian, confidant, lover. As far as he is concerned, they are over. Maybe not now, but soon. If the cheque's a fraud, it will be over for her too.

When he gets to the computers, he will log in to YouTube, and there he will upload the digital version of each reel, and then he will mail every friend he has online, spam every acquaintance he has ever favourited, retweeted, liked, shared, hearted. He will reply to every mail he has been cc'ed in, every one that has been forwarded to him. He will do this because his great-grandfather's reels are now priceless. And images, even the most worthless of images, only exist in the world if they are on the Internet.

The reels' images are a testament to the beginning. A call, unheard for decades, to warn against what they have built this chaos upon. The crumbling, decrepit, never-really-interrogated, teased-out, thought-through idea of a nation. A black-and-white witness to the truth of a beginning, a document of undisputed authenticity, beside which all other documents will be seen as obsolete. A game-changing, life-affirming, legacy-destroying, empire-tumbling roll of clips that will derail the anointed political dynasty of this country and scupper a presidential push.

A never-before-viewed YouTube account will amass hundreds of thousands of views – millions even – and be spoken about in lecture theatres, pubs, classrooms, clubhouses, buses, trains, post offices, shops and waiting areas. Will be spoken about in French, Spanish, German, Italian and Chinese, on television chat shows, current-affairs programmes and news bulletins, replayed and copied – copied and copied and copied and copied and copied – into an unending line of undiminished copies that will jump and shake their black-and-white images across screens around the world and whisper and shout a truth about this republic, because the image, the moving image, is the undisputed medium through which we come upon universal truth in the twenty-first century, and an old, broken set of images will start for this republic a retelling of the story of a nation that hasn't heard the truth in a long, long time. Because he is a citizen of this republic, and he can make a difference.

Kathy has turned back from the bank in the distance. The cheque is in her hand. He has logged onto his account, has the USB inserted. His hands are shaking. The bayonet fixed. The enemy in sight. Her face is hard to read. He thinks he sees a smile. A tight, puckered, stiff smile, rueful maybe. Her head, he thinks, shaking in astonishment – or frustration. He can't be sure.

Acknowledgements

Thanks to Seán O'Keeffe and everyone at Liberties Press, especially Sam Tranum for his sharp editing and patience and Ailish White for her enthusiasm and support; to my early readers Gerry Stembridge, Rob Doyle, Graham Nolan and Stephen White for your observations and suggestions; to Manus McManus at the Irish Film Institute for the expertise and know-how; to Sebastien and Fleur for the smiles; Una and Robert Laird for your time; Harry Colley for his idealism, bravery and detailed account of his adventures; Una and John for your guidance; and Helena for your unwavering encouragement.

I also wish to gratefully acknowledge the support of the Arts Council of Ireland and Fingal County Council's Artists' Support Scheme, particularly Sarah O'Neill.